Flames Of Rebellion

Also by Aaron S. Jones

A Long Way from Home (A collection of short stories from the world of The Broken Gods)

Flames
Of
Rebellion

The Broken Gods:
Book One

Aaron S. Jones

This is a work of fiction. Names, characters, places, and incidents either are the product of the author's imagination or are used fictitiously. Any resemblance to actual persons, living or dead, events, or locales is entirely coincidental.

First edition 2020

Book cover by Mars Dorian

ISBN 9798679954014 (paperback)

Imprint: Independently published

If you enjoyed this book, please leave a review on Amazon and Goodreads.

Visit www.aaronsjones.com for more information. You can sign up to the mailing list to be the first to find out about author events, interviews, and will always be the first to hear of new books from the author.

For Dad,

Thanks for introducing me to worlds of wizards, magic, swords, and dragons. I doubt I will ever leave...

THE SIGNAL

It wasn't the first corpse Arden had ever seen, but a sight like that isn't one you get used to. He fought the urge to vomit as he glanced at the man's leg. Half of it was missing. Dark red blood stained the snowy ground around it; a couple more patches circled the mass of curly hair on his head and the ground next to his shoulder. The snow continued its slow descent, but it had not yet blanketed the unmoving body. A good sign. The bastards must be close.

Footprints in the snow trailed away from the body, heading further into the tall, thin trees. Following probably wasn't a good idea. Not on his own anyway. He had no plans to end up like this unfortunate guy on the ground, just waiting to become nothing more than bones. He'd wait for the others, safety in numbers and all that. More importantly, his body shook, heart racing and teeth chattering at an alarming rate. Some might claim the infamous cold of the Borderlands caused it, but Arden had to be honest with himself. Fear gripped him today, winning out over the cold. Out here in the wild, if the cold didn't get you, then the wolves would. Whoever killed this sad bastard had to still be out there, and they wouldn't be alone. No one ever was, not here.

'You're shaking more than the land has been of late!' A booming voice rumbled through the trees. 'Anymore and the bastards will hear you! Then we'll all be dead.'

Arden whipped around at the voice, instinctively raising his trusty, worn, bone bow in defence. His left foot went from beneath him on the sodden ground and dragged his tired body downwards, ending up curled by the newcomer's feet, defenceless and at his mercy. Idiot.

'You'll need to do better than that, kid. If I was an enemy, you'd be nothing but bones in a moment or two. Try to be a bit more aware of your surroundings.' He could do nothing more than look up at the laughing, broad shouldered, red-haired man and take the scarred hand offered to him. 'And try to make less noise. Your best advantage is the element of surprise. The less your enemy knows about you, the better. Especially with your choice of weapon,' he said, poking a foot at the bow lying solitary in the powdery snow.

'Did you feel the land shake again? I thought the world was ending. That was the biggest one yet,' Arden brushed snow off his legs before looking up at muscular warrior.

'Aye. That was a mighty rumble. Could hear you over it though!'

The red-haired man pulled Arden up with a low chuckle, barely breaking a sweat as he accepted the weight of his whole body. Arden brushed himself down as the man peered past the trees; a warrior of a thousand battles, completely at ease with these situations. Messy red hair fell to his shoulders; his raven-black fur coat covered his upper body from the extremities of the Borderland winds – large, thick and soft.

'I'll make sure I shit myself in silence from now on then,' Arden replied, biting at his lip.

'Make sure that you do. Fear is normal before a battle; helps you focus on staying alive. Which I've found is always an important quality in winning a fight. Just do it quietly, eh?' He clapped his meaty hand on Arden's back, nearly undoing his work and knocking him back to the ground, 'No worries. Anyway, with a bit of luck, Socket will have half of them taken down by the time they realise they're in a fight. Always good to have an expert archer on the team!'

He winked at Arden before stepping carefully ahead of him, getting closer to the mangled corpse. He peered at the body, scratching his fiery, red beard speckled with bits of white and humming a low tune to himself as though surveying a new helmet on display, not viewing a possible battleground. So casual.

'So, what you reckon did this then, kid?'

Arden watched him roll the corpse over with one snow topped boot before turning his icy blue eyes towards him.

'Part of his leg is missing. Wolves I reckon, from the

bite marks. They didn't kill him though. Two stab wounds in the chest and a slash across the throat. A messy kill. He probably put up a struggle but not much of one.'

'What makes you say that?'

'No trail of blood leading away from the body, only footprints in the snow.'

The warrior clapped him on the back. 'You're learning. I agree. Now, let's find these fuckers and have a few words with them.'

All in the Borderlands knew the name of Raven Redbeard. Arden doubted there would be many words involved when they caught up with the culprits. Raven's preferred language could only be spoken with the long, sharp blade that hung loosely at his hip.

'Shall we wait for the others?' Arden asked, voice trembling. He'd been with the group for a few weeks – scouting, tracking, mostly the boring stuff. Like any young lad, he'd been eager for the heat of battle, the chance to prove himself. Now he stood on the edge of such an event, his knees weak, the bravado of youth seemingly eluding him. The corpse at his feet almost mocked him, a promise of what would happen next.

'No need. They'll catch up. They always do. Sly has never been one to stay away from the fight. You'll see.' Raven trudged through the snow and further into the trees, following the footprints to his destination. Arden sighed and followed.

What else could he do?

Arden crept through the woods, finishing his patrol of the perimeter of the camp, his eyes focused on the gaps in the motionless trees before him, glimpsing the distant men sitting together at the bottom of the hill. Silence was his ally. That's what Raven had told him before skulking off into the shadows, flanking the enemy to ensure that there were no others lurking nearby. He turned his head to one side, and then the other, looking out for any signs of danger.

Blood pumped through his head and his chest rose and fell steadily as he peered down at the men, shaking slightly as he got his best look at them yet, feeding on whatever creature they had caught that morning. The campfire flickered and danced as the six of them sat huddled around it, thankful for its warmth. For most of his life, Arden had run in fear at even the slightest hint of a fight, and yet here he stood.

He crouched low to the snow-covered ground, attempting to stay as hidden as possible. Not that it mattered. Those animals only had one thing on their mind and it sure as hell wasn't him. They tore at the meat like starving beasts, barely pausing to breathe.

A piece of meat sat alone, lying in the firelight on a small piece of cloth to protect it from the snow. Arden envisioned the cogs turning the heads of the two biggest and most ferocious looking of the group. The biggest one, a towering, mountain-like figure, slowly rose to his feet, pulling out a small dagger. Arden had seen Barbarians of the Far North before, but this man was a giant even compared to them. He could hear the man's growling voice echoing through the trees.

'That there meat is mine,' he said to the others, daring them to contest his words. 'I did the killing. I get the spoils.'

The looks across the firelight were a mixture of nerves and excitement. The next biggest man just held his icy stare on the beast of a man standing in front of him. The others knew their place. They couldn't challenge. This group had a structure and they were in no position to change that.

The challenger stood to his feet and pressed a finger against a nostril, blowing a huge stream of snot out of the other. Brave man. Or stupid. In Arden's experience, the two were often opposite sides of the same coin.

'I'm still hungry. I reckon the meat is mine.'

The challenger's fist caught the leader's mouth square on, the crack from the blow echoing across to Arden. His eyes widened as they stared intently at the leader just standing there, smiling as he licked the blood dripping beneath his dark, blue lips.

'That was your one shot. Sit down Son of Arog, now is not your time.'

The Son of Arog glanced nervously at his fellow warriors. All of them now facing away, finding useful distractions, anything other than meeting his gaze. The huge warrior nodded shamefully to his leader before turning back and taking his place on a log next to the fire. He hung his head like a child chastised by his parents. The leader gave a booming laugh and strolled over to the meat, his spoils of war. He tore at it with yellow teeth, gaze fixed on the disgraced warrior on the log.

Arden had seen enough for now. Picking up his faithful bow from the ground beside him, he raised his body slowly, turning his back on the Barbarians. He winced slightly as he felt his right leg cramp. Idiot. He'd stayed in the same spot for too long. Too tense. Breathe in. Breathe out. The ache will pass. It always did.

He turned back to check on the men, trembling at the thought that they had heard his muffled cry and may, at any second, set upon him, breaking his bones and cutting his throat, as they had done with that poor traveller, and countless others before him, most likely.

Sweat glistened on his brow but he had to make certain that they were not aware of his presence before he decided to bring his right forearm up to wipe it away. No risks. Not here. Not now.

'Off so soon?' a voice whispered.

Luckily, Arden caught himself before the scream forced its way out from his throat; instead a strange gargling sound escaped from his mouth.

Raven chuckled. At least someone was having fun.

'You almost gave me a heart attack!' Arden said, placing a hand against his chest to calm himself down.

'Almost. That's good enough.'

Arden breathed slowly in through his nose and out through his mouth, feeling the adrenaline easing from his body. 'What's the plan?'

Raven narrowed his eyes and gave him a grim look. 'Sly found three more bodies. One man, one woman, and a child. They were defenceless.'

Arden grabbed some arrows in preparation, stabbing them into the ground before grasping his bow tightly in his right hand, 'We doing this now?' he asked, unable to keep the fear from his voice. His first real test. Don't fuck it up.

'Better time than any I reckon.'

Raven unsheathed his sword and gave it a couple of practice swings, slicing through the air with a content look upon his warrior features. In that moment, the sheer magnitude of the situation dawned upon Arden.

Here he stood, barely a man, and yet standing next to the famed Raven Redbeard, one of the greatest warriors the Borderland tribes had ever known – son of Reaver Redbeard, the warrior who had brought the great tribes together for the first time in its history. A man at ease with his surroundings, his vast experience the opposite of Arden's. A veteran of numerous bloody battles for over two decades, keeping the people of the

Borderlands safe from harm; his own tribe and the others owed him a great deal. The full extent of Arden's battle experience could be attributed to hunting wolves who had strayed too close to whatever village he happened to be staying in. He'd done well enough.

Raven turned to face him, cracking his neck to the side while offering a warm, friendly smile to his young ally. 'All we do now is wait for the signal. Then we're good to go!'

After all the battles and scrapes the great man had been in, Arden marvelled at how Raven still seemed as excited as a young boy getting his first sword. He wondered how the great warrior managed to remain so calm, so sure of himself in a situation that could cause his death. Experience. Every battle he had ever been a part of had ended with him being alive. Why should this be any different?

He paused in the silence, going through Raven's last words. He felt the blood slowly drain from his face.

'What signal? I don't remember any signal?' Panic set in as he ran through the last few weeks' worth of conversation with his new allies, scanning every memory for details that he had missed, any talk of a signal before battle.

'Stay calm,' Raven said with a slight chuckle. 'You'll know the signal. Everyone knows the signal.'

Arden grunted, only slightly reassured. He attempted a few slow, deep breaths – just like Socket had told him to do. He didn't have the experience of the others: the fighting, the company, the pressure. He looked back towards the Barbarians. They had always been fond of battles and fighting; arms wide and welcoming for any opportunity to test their strength. The evidence of late pointed to the fact that they were travelling farther south, following a primal urge to locate more blood, more battles.

Arden was familiar with their methods. Growing up near the Great Lake meant being worryingly close to the barbarians. Raids were common. Men, women, children. Young, old. All would fall victim to the bloodlust of the Barbarians.

'Get ready, kid. Looks like the others are,' Raven informed him, pointing to the left of the Barbarians' camp site.

Arden's eyes followed Raven's hand but at first, he could see nothing. Just more snow. More trees.

Then his eyes found them.

Socket crouched low with one knee on the ground, bow

and arrow in hand, staring intently at his intended victims with his one good eye. Socket had lost the eye so long ago, the stories of the event were now more varied and stranger than any other told in the light of a campfire.

A vicious battle with a four-armed warlock.

A punishment from a drunken father.

A hungry wolf.

One toothless man from Arden's favourite village – with the aid of many jugs of ale – had claimed that Socket himself had taken it out with his dagger, 'Helps him with his killing, see? No need to close an eye when he's taking a shot at whatever poor fucker he's aiming for.'

In a world filled with warriors proficient with the way of the blade, Arden felt inspired by the tales of an expert one-eyed archer. The man who had helped Reaver Redbeard, Raven's father, bring the great tribes of the Borderlands together, who had killed three-hundred men in The Battle of the Wolf and the Bear.

The old archer waited, perfectly still. His long, snow-white hair swaying softly in the wind as he focused on the Barbarians. To his left sat the most famous woman in the Borderlands, Kiras. She was leaning against a particularly thick tree, scratching her closely shaved head and gripping a small, curved dagger with her other hand. Every now and then she would absently throw it into the air, catching it before it hit the ground without paying any real attention. Men dominated the Borderlands but she had carved a name out for herself, not content to fade into the background.

'Where are the other three?' Arden asked, unable to find his remaining companions.

'Three? Dakkar is waiting in the shadows at the back of the camp. He does his best to stay out of the battle. It's only Sly we're waiting for, and he's always late. Loves a dramatic entrance,' Raven explained, rolling his eyes.

'Where's Baldor? I can see the other pair. Socket's readying his first shot and Kiras is by the tree, but I can't see Baldor. He's usually difficult to miss.' Arden looked out once more for the freakishly large warrior.

'Kiras is by a tree? Take another look. That's no tree!'

Arden stifled a shocked laugh as he looked again, realising that Kiras had been leaning against her best friend, his huge Warhammer lying next to her in the snow.

Assured of his temporary safety, Arden took the time to

take a few deep breaths, preparing for the fight. He picked his target. The easy mark. He followed the man at the back, watching closely as he opened his mouth wide in a long yawn.

Suddenly, all six of the Barbarians stood as one, hearing a disturbance in the trees. They reached for their weapons, axes and swords lay within their reach as they prepared for a fight. Their eyes widened but not in fear – the thrill of the battle; a chance to prove themselves. Arden felt a large hand on his back. 'The signal.'

'Aaarrgghhhh!' came a cry from the trees. 'Come and taste my axe!'

Arden shook his head in disbelief as he saw a familiar warrior running straight for the beasts; his long, messy, dark hair flowing in the wind and his beard streaming past one shoulder, a crazed look burned on his face that would strike fear into the hearts of even the mightiest warriors. The Barbarians didn't know fear though. Unfortunately for them, neither did Sly.

'I take it that's the signal?' he asked with a smirk.

'If you ever see a topless, hairy maniac running towards your enemies, always take it as a signal. *The* signal,' Raven answered before roaring his own battle cry and taking great strides toward the beasts. Arden notched his arrow and pulled back, eyeing his intended target.

Sly raised one of his infamous axes and slashed as hard and as fast as he could across the neck of his opponent. The Son of Arog dropped his sword and clasped at his neck with both hands in a futile attempt to stop the flow of dark blood from pouring out of him. He dropped to the floor, legs twitching as a pool of blood stained the pure white snow.

An arrow flew straight into the head of the enemy Arden had aimed for – unfortunately, not one of his. Socket. Deadly as always. The unfortunate warrior stumbled around before dropping to his knees, hand grasping uselessly at the arrow sticking out of his head.

Kiras flung herself into the battle, a look of crazed delight on her bloodthirsty face. Her twin daggers gleamed in the light of the campfire, tips curved slightly and pointed toward the frozen ground. She blocked one swipe of a sword before circling her opponent.

He gave her a gummy grin that displayed his lack of teeth. He stepped forward again but Kiras danced gracefully around his blade. In one fleeting moment, she raised her weapons and spun towards her target, severing both his arms, causing a high-pitched wail to echo throughout the forest.

Baldor's turn now. The giant warrior thundered down the hill with all the grace of a rampaging bull. He picked his target, intense concentration on his brutish features and pulled back his mammoth Warhammer, a weapon bigger than Arden himself. *How can he even hold that thing, let alone swing it with any accuracy?*

The hammer flashed towards its target, whipping through the cold air. A sudden look of disbelief crossed the Barbarian's face as he dropped to the ground, blood flowing from multiple wounds. 'Gonna have to be quicker than that if you want to steal my kills, big man!' Kiras cried with a laugh, blood dripping from her daggers.

Baldor grabbed the nearest Barbarian by the throat with one great hand and threw him to the floor. The man gasped for breath but the hammer fell onto his chest with all the rage the big man could muster, destroying the torso of the Barbarian with one momentous swing. 'I'd like to see you try that, little girl,' Baldor challenged Kiras with a lop-sided grin. Thank The Four he was on their side.

Two of the Barbarians, the only ones breathing, glanced nervously at each other, aware of their predicament. The first one panicked, rushing towards Sly with a roar. The butt of Sly's axe slammed directly into the fool's temple. He staggered back; a confused look etched on his face as he grasped at something hidden on his back. Dakkar crept forward into the light and grinned, tongue sticking out the corner of his mouth as he pulled his dagger out of the Barbarian's back.

'I'd like this back, thank you. It's a favourite of mine.' Dakkar said, before using the blade to cut the man's throat. The Barbarian fell to the floor with a thud.

The leader stood tall, chest puffed out and shoulders back – confident and arrogant all the way to the end; defiant until death.

Raven stepped forward and pointed his sword towards his opponent.

'You killed defenceless men, women and children in a land that is not your own. You brought this death on yourself. Take solace in the fact that today you will meet your ancestors, courtesy of Raven Redbeard.'

The lone Barbarian spat, staring down at Raven. 'You

judge us? You kill just the same, Redbeard. My kind are just more honest about how we do it.'

Raven shrugged. 'You will die, all the same.'

'The quakes are destroying our lands; we are forced to head south!'

'Then you will walk to your doom.'

The two warriors circled each other, each weighing up their opponent. The others just stood and watched, not wanting to interfere.

Suddenly, Arden felt a blow to the back of his head. He fell to the ground, hands instinctively hitting the snow to soften his fall. He spun onto his back, staring up into the eyes of his attacker. They were manic. The Barbarian spat through his gritted teeth as he pushed his filthy hands against Arden's throat.

'You fucker! I will watch you die here, little man. Alone and afraid,' the bastard spat, saliva dripping onto Arden's face as his eyes bulged wide. 'Golden pupils? A fucking mage!' the Barbarian cried in horror.

Arden did the only thing he could think of as he felt the grip around his neck loosen. A good kick to the balls. Never fails. With a muffled grunt, the Barbarian tumbled off him. He breathed hard but his body didn't seem to be working. The Barbarian rolled down the hill before getting to his feet. Arden's eyes widened in panic as he saw the man reach down for a forgotten, crude dagger on the ground. He lurched towards the others, all distracted as swords clashed together in a fight to the death.

His voice failed him, ruined from the attack, only allowing a couple of short, hoarse coughs to escape. He had to do something. Anything. A hand fumbled around for his white bone bow. Fingers curled around the bow as he located it amongst the snow.

He took aim, drew in another deep breath, pulled back the string... and fired.

'Who the fuck are you aiming at, you little shit?' Sly cried as he whipped around, the mad gleam in his eyes focused now on where Arden was sitting, crouched and trying his best to not piss himself. Sly's dark eyes stretched wide as he finally spotted the intruder. 'Shit!'

The world seemed to slow down, each movement lasting a lifetime.

Dakkar continued to watch Raven's battle, blissfully ignorant to the danger.

The dagger made a soft squelching sound as the Barbarian thrust into Dakkar's back in quick succession. Six thrusts.

Raven roared and swung his famous sword, slicing off the head of the leader in one fell swoop.

Sly rushed towards the final Barbarian, face red with rage, spit flying through his yellowed teeth, hair flying wildly in the wind.

An arrow beat him to it. Dakkar and the Barbarian fell as one, landing in the snow together like lovers.

Arden's face grew hot as the whole group turned, looking for the arrow's source. He pushed himself forward and stumbled down the hill. The group surrounded Dakkar as his body twitched in the snow. He coughed up a load of blood, specks spraying onto Sly's legs.

Raven decided to put him out of his misery. One swing of the sword. Worked for friend or foe alike.

Arden winced, unable to keep his eyes open as the blow met its target. As quick as a flash, more filthy hands were on him, pushing him hard against a tree. His breath left him once more as pain shot through his spine. He managed to open his eyes to stare at the mad, blood-stained face of Sly.

'You were meant to check the fucking perimeter! He's dead because of you! I should cut you open right here, kid. I like doing my killing up close and personal, not like you and your cowardly bow. Don't feel right if I'm not covered in blood,' Sly warned, his yellow teeth speckled with the blood of his last victim.

'Get off him, Sly. Dakkar knew the risks. We all know the risks. This is what we do,' Kiras said, voice dripping with disgust.

Sly growled menacingly, his hand gripped his axe tightly. Baldor raised an eyebrow and took a step towards Sly, blocking his path to his friend.

'What? You wanna go big man?' Sly asked, not ready for the fight to stop.

'Less of the "who has the biggest cock bullshit",' Raven snapped, ending any potential dispute instantly. 'Anyway, we all know Kiras always wins,' he finished with a smirk.

'Glad to hear it,' Kiras winked, sheathing her daggers.

Sly dropped his hands from Arden but his eyes didn't

leave him. 'Last chance, kid. Make sure this is what you want. None of us are gonna die for you.' He stepped back slowly, muttering to himself.

'Nice shooting, boy. You might wanna get cleaned up somewhere though,' Raven grinned at him, making him feel uneasy.

He looked down at his chest to see that vomit covered his torso. He felt his face heating up as he flushed. Perfect. Didn't even realise he'd been sick.

'That's nothing. First battle I fought. I walked away covered in piss!' came Baldor's thundering voice, chuckling as he scratched his head, 'My own piss. It was warm at first, then very cold.' A small look of distress crossed his face at the memory before Kiras gave him a tough punch on his arm.

'You were nine. Stop beating yourself up about it.'

'Nothing scary about battle; I'm more likely to get blood flowing towards that region then piss.' Sly grabbed at his crotch and spat on the floor before turning his back on the group. 'I'll go see what's keeping old Socket away from this wonderful and heart-warming conversation, shall I?' He trudged off into the shadows of the trees as the rest of the group smiled at each other.

'He'll never change,' remarked Raven. 'You'll learn to listen to the few odd useful things he comes out with and ignore the rest. He's a great warrior, just a little underdeveloped when it comes to social skills.'

Raven patted Arden on the back in assurance, almost knocking him to the ground.

The wind howled around them, and it seemed as though darkness had suddenly descended during their discussion; with it came a drop in the already low temperature.

'What we gonna do with this one boss?' Kiras asked, casually turning the body over on the ground with a filthy boot. 'Shit. He's still breathing. Out cold though. Must have hit his head when he fell.' Arden saw a red mark on the Barbarian's forehead as he walked towards his victim.

'Get the rope. Tie him up,' Raven growled. 'He's coming with us.'

'Aye, aye boss.' Kiras saluted as Baldor threw her some rope.

'We'll give Dakkar a send-off with the words and then we can head back.' They all mumbled in agreement, staring down at the still body on the ground.

Arden stomped through the snow to grab his gear. The adrenaline in his body kept his heart pumping fast and although the cold threatened to attack his body, sweat drenched his entire frame from his efforts. He placed his right foot forward, slipping on a wet rock sticking out of the snow. Falling back, he banged his head on the ground, his feet flying into the air above him.

Clumsy fool.

His eyes stared straight up through the crooked branches of the trees and into the clear, starry night sky. The stars flickered, a small inconsistency with the rest of the night as though wind swarmed around a flame. It was a ship; a strange ship floating through the sky. As fast as it had appeared, it was gone. He shook his head.

'You okay kid?' Kiras leaned over him, struggling to hold back a laugh. Maybe his face would stay red forever – his embarrassment clear for all to see.

'I think so,' he managed. She lifted him off the ground and brushed some of the snow off his clothes.

'You look confused. How hard did you hit your head?' she asked, with a hint of concern.

'I saw... something,' Arden began. A ship, floating in the sky. That's believable. Right? 'It's nothing though, maybe I did hit my head too hard.'

'We'll get it looked at when we're back at the village. It won't be the last time you hit your head, trust me.'

The snow went on forever. It was the Northern Borderlands. It was home. Sly ambled through the trees, making his way towards the old archer, Socket. A cold wind blew across his naked torso, reminding him to put his remaining clothes back on. He could hear a nearby stream and for a moment contemplated a quick wash for the first time in a while. *Nah. What's the point? Only gonna get messy again soon.*

Men, women and children; all of them knew his bloodied face and torso. Appearances meant a lot in a fight, more than most folk gave credit. Sly knew how to use it to his advantage. A man covered in his victim's blood leaves a strong impression. Everyone knew the hairy, blood-soaked warrior, and everyone knew not to fuck with him. To those who didn't, Sly was always happy to give them a lesson or two.

Others might piss themselves and vomit at the thought

of entering a life or death scenario but not Sly. He craved the blood, loved the sound of battle and the honour and glory that came with ending the life of a man or creature intent on ending his own. This was the Borderlands and that meant a man must become fearless to survive the cold, harsh world of the tundra. Toughening up was not negotiable. Of course, it wasn't necessary to enjoy the way an axe feels as it cracks open a skull; the look in the eyes of a man as he knows you are about to bring an end to his sorry life, but a man needs to get his enjoyment from somewhere and what's wrong with that?

'What's taking so long old man?' Sly called out to the hunched figure in front of him.

Old, grey and the best damn archer this side of the Lapret River, Socket was a legend of the Borderlands and every man, woman and child knew of his exploits along with his late friend Reaver Redbeard.

Socket stood up slowly, the ends of his great, black cloak covered in snow, and turned to face Sly, his one good eye fixed upon the blood-soaked warrior. A smile broke out on his wrinkled and scarred face.

'Quick and easy. You're all mad fuckers, especially you, you filthy bastard – but you all get the job done quick and easy.'

'Filthy bastard? You're too kind. You should hear what they call me in some of the more depraved villages of our kind,' Sly retorted, taking the curse in his stride.

'I've heard all right. If all the stories about you are true, then you deserve for my eye to be kept on you at all times, boy. We need trust in this group though, especially now. Something is amiss, I can feel it in these old bones of mine and it's not often I'm wrong.'

'I hear you, old-timer. Sleep with one eye open, eh?' Sly winked.

'Funny little shit,' Socket's body shook with a chuckle, 'Now shut up for a few seconds and tell me what you think of what's on the ground here.'

He walked through the deep snow and stood next to the old man, who pointed at the ground. Footprints could be seen pressed into the snow, heading in the opposite direction to the battle ground.

Socket took a breath in through his nose and exhaled with a long blow from his red cheeks, 'I've taken a quick look around and these tracks certainly haven't been made by the ones we just attacked. They're coming south.'

Sly didn't like the sound of that. Fighting these bastards was entertaining when they came out at you in small groups, stupid and reckless, but if they were working in larger groups and heading towards the more populated areas of the Borderlands, then it would mean war.

The old man ain't lost it yet. He hasn't thought of the best option yet though. Take the fight to ' em. Head to the Far North and destroy these bastards once and for all.

'Best go tell the rest of them. It'll definitely make the young one sleep well tonight. That's if he manages to keep his food down this time,' he added with an evil grin.

'I remember the last time I was sick on a battlefield. I was ten. Ate hell knows what the morning of the fight and ended up throwing up on an arrow as I launched it. Quite funny actually...'

'I feel sorry for the poor fucker that got hit with that cursed arrow.'

Socket's mouth twisted into a wicked grin, 'His name was Reaver Redbeard. It was how we met. One of my favourite ways to meet someone. You only truly know a man once you've shot him. Of course, he was only a boy at the time. Worked out well for the both of us though.'

Sly shook his head and cracked his neck to the side, easing his tense muscles.

People call me crazy.

PART OF THE TRIBE

Arden sat as near to the fire as possible, watching closely as the flames flickered, trying his hardest to keep his mind from wandering to dark thoughts involving stories of night ambushes he had heard over the years.

The rest of the group seemed at ease, all things considered. They'd given Dakkar's body to the flames, as was the custom in the Borderlands. The rising smoke would speed his journey to his ancestors. Kiras lay on the ground, leaning against a sleeping Baldor with her bare feet facing the fire. Her large friend had his mouth wide open, saliva dripping, his low, booming snores so loud it seemed as though they could shake the snow-capped mountains behind them. Sly flicked some meat from out between his teeth with a sharp, curved dagger; every now and then he would cast a dark look into the distance, towards where Raven and Socket had disappeared an hour ago.

Arden stared at the sleeping body of the tied-up Barbarian next to him. In the light of the dancing fire, he didn't seem as intimidating as he had before. 'In the Borderlands, we grow up with stories of the barbarians being savages, a people who just love to rape, kill and destroy,' Arden said. 'He doesn't look so evil when he's sleeping.'

Sly chewed on his nails, then spat a huge load of brown saliva next to the fire. His dancing eyes darted in Arden's direction. 'Evil? You think they're evil because they kill?'

'Well, yeah. That's what we're told.'

Sly threw his head back and laughed, sounding like a barking dog as the firelight cast an orange glow on his wild beard. 'You're sitting with three of the deadliest killers in the

Borderlands. Think we're evil?'

Arden didn't know how to answer. Sure, Sly could be a complete dick at times but the others had been kind to him. But he was right, they were all killers. 'I'm not sure.'

'The Barbarians aren't evil. They just get in our fucking way. Too many mouths striving to gnaw at too few bones. That's what your evil is. There isn't a difference between the sleeping fool at your feet and the gigantic snoring bastard over there,' Sly said, jabbing a thumb towards Baldor. 'You just gotta pick a side and stick to it. Kill them before they kill you.'

'Doesn't seem fair,' Arden said.

'Fair? Drop any thoughts of that if you want to survive, kid. This world ain't fair. That's for sure. You should know that – glowing golden eyes but not an ounce of magic in you. That's the Gods playing a cruel fucking joke on you. Being shunned by villagers who fear you, but you can't even use your gift to scratch them. Hell, I'd have killed them or myself by now if I was you.'

Arden didn't know how to reply. The truth hurt. Being born with the golden pupils of a mage had been a curse. Most people feared the unknown and the rarity of magi certainly placed them in that category. Making it worse was not being able to perform a speck of magic, no matter how hard he tried. All he had was a pair of dumb, golden pupils. A souvenir of his ailment.

'Look who's up,' Sly said, licking his lips as Kiras stretched her arms into the air and yawned. 'Still having those dreams about me?'

'Yep. Every time I slice your head off, I wake up happier than a pig in shit,' Kiras replied with a wink towards Arden that made him blush. He'd still not become used to having a woman speak to him. Other than his mother, he couldn't remember the last female to pay him any attention. 'Raven not back from his patrol with Socket?'

'Not yet,' Arden answered before gesturing towards the sleeping Barbarian, 'and this one's still out. What do you think they're talking about?'

Kiras shrugged. 'As tribe leader, he's got two options. He can choose to follow the tracks and we kill whatever we find at the end. Or, we head back to Torvield and call a meeting with Saul and the tribes. The problem with the first one is that we've already lost Dakkar and there's a chance we'll be outnumbered. The problem with the second one is that it gives them time to reinforce and prepare for an attack.' She twisted her body to face

Arden, understanding that he was fairly new to the world of Borderlands politics. 'Raven would love to follow the tracks. The only problem with that is Saul. He's wary of Raven. He's always seen the son of Redbeard as a threat to his rule, always keeping one eye open for a challenge. Raven wants to be careful with his movements, he doesn't want any unrest in the Borderlands, not any more at least.'

'What do you think would happen if Raven acted without telling Saul?' Arden asked.

Kiras shrugged, her lips vibrating with a long sigh. 'Who knows? The man has a temper shorter than the length of my little finger. How much do you know about Saul?'

'He is the Leader of the Borderlands, of course. His tribal sign is that of the wolf and he is a fierce warrior. It is only what I've been told by a village bard. I've only seen him once before.'

'He is a decent enough leader, a great warrior,' Kiras admitted, 'but he's insecure. Saul is still cautious of having Raven around, the son of the great Reaver Redbeard. He's jealous. He fears that one day Raven will want to follow in his father's footsteps and to do that he would need Saul's head. It makes him edgy, and when Saul is edgy, he makes some bad decisions.'

'Would Raven ever want to take over?' Arden asked, staring into the dancing flames.

'Nah. It's not his thing. Reaver died with a knife in his back because he wanted more for our people; Raven doesn't want the same thing happening to him. He's happy enough doing what he's doing.'

'As long as Saul doesn't do anything stupid,' Baldor growled, adding his own thoughts to the conversation as he rubbed his sleep-filled eyes.

'If it was me, Saul would be waking up with a slit throat,' Sly said. Strange shadows danced across his scarred face as he bared his crooked, yellow teeth.

'Difficult to wake up when your throat's been cut,' Kiras laughed.

'It's a skill. I'd do it so he could. I'd want him to look at me and make sure he knew who had bested him,' Sly spat, continuing with his gruesome grooming.

Another hour passed before the two men returned, their shadows flickering in the light of the solitary fire. Sly stood, axe already in hand. 'You done talking yet?'

Raven sniffed and pinched at his red nose before pulling his hood up to combat the harsh cold. 'We head home. Time to get the tribes together. Kill anything you deem as an enemy on the way. The Barbarians are growing in confidence. If we head any further north, then we don't know how many we will come against. I'm all for a fight but being unsure of their numbers means we need to be cautious. We need to speak with all the leaders and decide. This doesn't just concern us. We'll see what this one has to say when he wakes up, Raven gave the Barbarian on the ground a small kick but, to Arden's shock, he didn't wake. Must have hit his head hard.

Sly's leer chilled Arden to the bone. 'Sounds like a plan to me. We can always come back and kill them all. I'm sure Saul will be happy with you calling him for a meeting.'

'I don't give a fuck if he's happy or not. He won't have a choice,' Raven growled. 'Let's move out.'

* * *

'The Borderlands really have gone to shit if the son of Redbeard is enlisting fucking mages,' the barbarian spat on the straw at his feet, body shifting forward before he jarred against the restraints attached to the wooden beam. Arden stepped to the side and peered behind the filthy warrior, checking to make sure the rope was still tightly pulling his hands behind his back, preventing any possible escape. Better safe than sorry, that's what his mother always said.

'I'm not a mage. Birth defect,' Arden said for what felt like the millionth time in his life, pointing at his golden pupils. 'No magic.'

'Just a fucking freak then!'

'Yeah, I guess I am.' Arden shrugged. He'd been called worse, often by his own people.

The prisoner shifted his shoulders about, obviously uncomfortable. He raised his knees and pulled his bare, dirty feet towards him, bloodshot eyes not leaving Arden. 'Have to admit, almost shit myself when I saw those golden orbs looking up at me. Thought I'd burst into flames.'

'Must have been your lucky day.'

'Maybe,' he replied, pushing his tongue through a gap in his teeth. 'Today could be better for me.' The spark in his sullen eyes made Arden take a step back. He knew that look: the look a man had when he wanted something that you had, and he'd do anything to get it.

'Doubt it. Once Raven's asked his questions, that's it for you. Sly will have his way.' Arden didn't like the thought of the defenceless prisoner being killed, but that was the way of it in the Borderlands. What else could they do?

'Sly? Sly Stormson. I've heard of him.' A dark shadow of fear crossed the man's face. His eyes darted around the room and he pulled harder at his restraints, starting to fully comprehend his situation. 'What's your name, kid?'

'Arden. My name is Arden Leifhand.'

'Well, Arden Leifhand. I am Ovar, Son of Erik. I have a family. The shaking of Takaara destroyed many of our villages, it even took down some of our main towns. Who knows what happened with the last shake? I want to go back to my family and hold them and make sure they are safe. I won't cause you any harm. What good will come of killing me? How about you let poor little Ovar go free? No one needs to know it was you!' His voice strained at the end as he pulled harder against the beam. It was as thick as the man's back and his restraints had been applied by Kiras. She didn't make mistakes. He wasn't going anywhere soon.

'Why would I do that? You tried to kill me.'

'Of course I did. We were in a battle. Nothin' wrong with that. This... *this* is pure murder. Taking me back to the Great Hall in Torvield is as good as murdering me. No honour in it. None at all. And I know you Borderlanders love your honour.'

Ovar was right. Honour was important to all warriors. Common sense more so.

'Good try, but it isn't working. If I let you go, it'd be my head on the block.'

Ovar's messy hair shook as he forced his whole body forward, pulling as hard as he could against that thick beam. Arden appreciated the effort. The Barbarian's eyes darkened, anger seeping through his every nerve. No support. No way out.

A roar from the back of his throat rose as he pulled again, staring into Arden's eyes. The whole stable shook with the effort.

A well of fear bubbled deep inside Arden for a moment. Surely the Barbarian couldn't escape? A second earlier he had been certain of his own safety. Now, the certainty had cracked, threatening to break altogether.

'You ever killed a man, Arden?' Ovar asked, leaning his head back against the beam with a thud, his breathing heavy and slow. Arden shook his head. 'I mean properly. Looked into his eyes and watched the light fade. It stays with you. Doesn't go away, no matter how often you do it or how good you get. I promise you, if you don't release me, you will feel the guilt of my death for as long as you live.'

Arden bit his lip and looked over his shoulder at the door that had been left ajar. A patch of snow had managed to sneak in as the wind continued to howl. 'I won't be the one killing you.'

'But you will. If you leave me here, you are marking me for death.'

'I'm sorry,' Arden muttered, unable to meet the prisoner's eyes, guilt swallowing his every thought.

'Please…' Ovar begged. 'I have a family.' His voice soft and low, pleading with Arden through tear-filled eyes, no longer the savage trying to take Arden's life. Now just a defeated man begging for his own.

'I'm sorry. I can't help you.' Arden turned on his heel and left the stable, heart thumping in his chest. Ovar didn't cry out. He didn't roar or curse. He knew his fate; the only outcome possible for his situation. There would be no help.

A cold, biting wind blew across the village as snow fell fast from the grey sky, landing on anyone unfortunate enough to be caught outdoors. The sun began its ascent behind the gloom and Arden decided that he would rather be outside in the storm than inside with the others.

He waited outside of the Great Hall, the home of the greatest tribal warriors and the one place in the Borderlands big enough to house the Four Great Tribes. The room felt fit to burst as raucous, angry men and women drank and gambled together: tension building, old rivalries resurfacing as they waited for the last tribe and the leader of the Borderlands.

Less wars had broken out between the tribes since Reaver's work, but some still harboured a great dislike for others – old grievances carried through bloodlines struggled to fade away, often rearing their ugly heads on days like this. Best to keep out of the way.

Yep, he would much rather be out here in the storm

than inside with the drunken, angry warriors, hoping for a chance to prove their warrior status. He could see only one issue with being outside – the company.

'Do you think he'll be much longer?' Arden asked, keen to end the uncomfortable silence.

'How the fuck should I know?' Sly answered, snapping the first words he had spoken for over an hour. He was not really the talkative type.

Arden tried to concentrate on keeping warm, rubbing his arms and jumping up and down on the spot.

'Kid, this is annoying enough without you prancing about. If Raven doesn't want me in there that's fine, I can wait out here until Saul arrives, but don't push me. I have my limits.'

'Just trying to keep warm. My toes feel as though they're about to fall off.'

Sly lifted a boot from the ground and stared down at it as though observing a lost lover. 'Lost two myself a few years ago. Harsh winter that one. Not so bad today. You'll be fine.'

Arden had jumped at the opportunity when Raven had asked if anyone would scout for him, acting as a lookout for the arrival of Saul and his tribe. Any job that didn't involve standing amongst the testosterone-filled meatheads in the Great Hall or keeping an eye on Ovar were fine with him. In the night he had tossed and turned, struggling to sleep, guilt filling his thoughts. Sly hadn't been as happy when Raven had told him to watch out for Saul, arguing that being cooped up with the members of the other tribes in the Great Hall meant there would be blood.

Arden looked at the fearsome warrior and swallowed. *Perhaps I can learn from him. It must be better than waiting in silence all the time.*

'So, any, erm... any tips for when we're in battle? Anything you can suggest that might help me?' he asked tentatively.

Sly cast him a sidelong glance, lowered his brow and bared his yellow teeth. 'Don't get killed. I've found that's the most important bit in a battle.'

Silence it is then.

So, they stood in silence and waited. Every now and then Arden would brave a look at his companion, standing like a statue and only moving to spit on the rising snow at his feet. And they waited some more.

The snow began to die down, improving visibility but

apparently not Sly's mood. The sullen warrior stood glum and silent; his disdain for the situation could almost be felt as a physical force.

They waited long enough for Arden to contemplate an attempt at another thrilling conversation, when a song could be heard from the distance, carried by the cold wind.

'About fucking time,' Sly said, spitting on the floor one last time, 'let's go tell the others. I need a drink. Still got all your damn toes?' His dog-like bark of a laugh cut through the wind's howl.

Relieved, Arden headed towards the Great Hall. A tight grip on his shoulder stopped him. 'Live every fucking battle like it's the last. Chances are, it could be,' Sly muttered.

With that, he stalked off into the snow.

Arden paused, savouring the moment. Then he followed.

There's nothing like a good drink. Especially after waiting next to some snot-nosed kid constantly bothering you. Snow covered Sly but he shook it off like a dog and moved towards the nearest roaring fire, drink finally in hand. Living a violent life meant appreciating small things, like the opportunity to have a good, quality drink. It made all the boring bits that much more bearable.

His eyes flashed around the firelit room and he spotted a few of his companions sitting together on one of the many long, wooden benches, deep in conversation.

'... it depends on whether he's mellowed down, I suppose,' Kiras said.

'Ha! Mellowed down. That man is like an old bear; his mood will only worsen with age I am afraid. Let us just hope he will listen to Raven,' Socket replied.

Sly took a seat, not really caring for the talk, his back to the corner of the room, able to look out for any potential enemies, another essential part of the bloody tapestry of his life. Too many warriors in this part of the world had died with a knife in the back and a good drink in hand; Sly would make sure that would never be him, at least the knife part. No coward would ever get the chance to stab him from behind, he would face his death head on, eyes wide open when it came with its cold embrace.

'Good of you to join us! Where's the kid?' Kiras asked,

taking a large gulp from her jug of ale.

'What am I? His keeper?' Sly snapped, already on edge with the threat of a fight surrounding him. The frowns the pair of them gave him only annoyed him further, 'He's grabbing a drink. Just like I fucking told him.'

Why do they care where he is? I give the kid six months. At best. Better warriors than him have lasted less. Lucky for him he has the best warriors around him, protecting his sorry ass. Still, six months.

'Where's the big guy?' Sly asked, noting the absence of Baldor with one quick scan of the packed hall; hard to miss.

'With Raven. He thought it would be best to take him to his meeting with Saul. Apparently, it makes Saul uncomfortable when he's around anyone bigger than him,' Kiras answered, flashing a mischievous grin.

Sly grunted and continued to drink his ale. The thought of Saul squirming next to the ferocious giant warmed him to the soul. He had always hated the man. Thought himself better than everyone else. Fucking bastard didn't deserve to lead his own tribe, let alone all the Borderlands. The sooner he had a knife in his back the better it would be for everyone. And Sly would gladly do the honours. That was the way of the Borderlands.

The conversation turned to their recent battle, the two of them analysing the fight and discussing points where they could have improved. Sly just kept an eye out for trouble and listened to them speak. Focusing on the past meant slipping in the present. As far as he was concerned, he had one plan in mind. Get his axe into as many enemies as possible, as fast as possible and get back to drinking. Fights were simple. He'd leave the thinking to the rest of them.

Kiras had her twin daggers out now, running through a technique she had used against the barbarians. Socket listened intently, offering his own advice where he could, and explaining to her what he had seen from his own standpoint in the battle.

Sly turned his gaze for a moment to the animated woman. A fierce woman, no doubt about that; deadlier than all the women in the Borderlands, and most of the men too. Not that they would admit it.

The door crept open and he spotted the young lad walk carefully into the room, a large jug held tightly in both hands, golden eyes focused on the drink to ensure that he didn't drop the heavy tankard. His slow pace barely hid a small limp.

'Hurt your leg?' Kiras said, her eyes following the same route as Sly's.

'Just a dead leg. Who would have thought the Borderlands would be so slippery?' Arden said with a nervous chuckle, still concentrating on his drink as he reached the table.

'Get some rest and you should be fine in a few days or so. You'll get much worse than that running with the big boys,' Kiras warned.

'You'll learn to appreciate the parts of your body that aren't aching, bruised or scarred, trust me.' Socket piped in with a wink – or just blinking? Sly never knew. Hard to tell.

The boy grimaced and winced before lifting his drink and taking a long, deep gulp of the brown liquid. He coughed and some of the drink went flying out of his mouth before he covered it with a fist and coughed some more.

'Something else you need to get used to?' Socket said with a laugh, 'Puts hairs on your chest, just ask Kiras!'

She punched the one-eyed warrior softly on the arm and joined in with the laughter.

'Just take it slowly at first. You don't want to get sick again and this is strong shit. Even Sly can only handle one or two.'

'One or two dozen maybe,' he suggested before taking a gulp of his own, 'only man that drinks more than me without puking up his guts is Baldor. That freak has it by the barrel – ain't natural. Though it is impressive.'

'If you're lucky, then after the first dozen, Sly might show you some of his best card tricks. Baldor can never seem to get the hang of them, no matter how much he loves play,' Kiras said to the youngster.

'Go get me another drink and then maybe I'll show you a card trick. It'd be interesting to see if you're any better than Baldor. If not, then I suggest you quit and head back to wherever you came from.' Sly felt gas rise from his stomach before forcing out a long, loud belch. Felt good. He waved his now empty glass and stared at Arden. 'Don't keep me waiting kid.'

He studied the youngster slowly rising from his seat, laughing as Arden walked out of earshot towards the bar. 'I guess having him around does have its perks.'

'Don't push him, he's only young,' Kiras warned.

'Young? How many had we killed by the time we were his age? I only asked him to get me a fucking drink.' This was a harsh and cruel part of the world – treating men as babies would only delay the inevitable; a painful death.

Bones. That's what they said in the Borderlands. Once you're gone, all that would be left is bones.

'I'm just saying. Don't push him.'

'Sly is right though.'

Sly leaned back in his chair, shocked at the unexpected back-up from Socket.

'Maybe we do need to push him a bit more. He's part of the tribe now. It's dangerous enough for him with those eyes; it won't do the boy any harm to toughen up a bit. He's a warrior and he needs to know our ways,' Socket suggested.

Sly thought for a second about trying to hide how smug he felt at the moment, then he thought, fuck it.

'You can wipe that fucked up grin from your face, Sly Stormson. And you might want to make a note of the time and day 'cause I'm sure that's the first time Socket has backed you up,' came the biting reply as Kiras folded her arms, displeased with being on the losing side of the argument.

'That's 'cause most the time he's talking complete and utter shit,' Socket added with a smile of his own. Kiras snorted, a dash of liquid flying out of her nose. Now it was Sly's turn to fold his arms in displeasure.

'Laugh it up. Now where the fuck is that kid with my drink? I'm getting thirsty...'

The door burst open and a booming voice sounded through the Hall, causing all inside to turn their heads and pause from their merriment.

'Men of the Borderlands! Make way for your leader! Saul Giantsbane!'

The room cheered for the beast of a man entering the room. Some rolled their eyes, still struggling with having to follow the arrogant bastard.

Sly just raised his jug and carried on drinking, 'I wouldn't make way for that fucking cunt if a fire consumed him.'

'Ah, Saul on fire. We can only dream, eh?' Kiras laughed, giving him a joyous nudge with her elbow at the thought.

We sure fucking can.

This isn't as bad as I thought.

Arden grabbed the drink and looked past the sweaty, cluster of men and women filling the room, searching the best way past them. The room buzzed in excitement, all in attendance eager to discover the cause of the meeting.

Saul entered the room, barrel-like chest leading the way through the crowds. The man gave him the creeps. He had never seen him up close before, blonde beard thick with dashes of grey, his dark eyes wild and constantly moving, searching his surroundings. He passed Arden on his way to the front, Raven and Baldor following, both giving him a nod of recognition and flashing warm smiles ahead of a trail of mean looking thugs – most of whom seemed intent on making certain that everyone in the room could see how big and mean they looked; chests puffed out in imitation of their leader, glowering at anyone stupid enough to cast an eye upon them. The number of assholes in the Borderlands always astounded Arden, and these were the biggest assholes of them all.

There hasn't been a single fight break out yet though. Sly seems to be doing better than expected.

He looked out once more for his allies and decided to brave the walk through the minefield of bodies who stood in his way, carefully stepping away from those who gave him looks of contempt or challenging glares.

Growing up in the Borderlands, you become accustomed to having space all around you. Freedom to move as you please. This environment felt stifling for the free warriors. The only times they would usually be this close to anything would be during fighting or fucking, and Arden didn't want any involvement in either right now.

He turned to head back towards Sly, drink in hand. At that moment, he bumped straight into the sweaty back of warrior twice his size. Arden's face froze in horror as he helplessly watched the liquid pour onto the back of the beast of a man. What were the chances that this man would be the kind to shrug it off with a laugh?

A great, rough hand pushed against his chest, preventing him from moving forward. An ally of the man he had just soaked. Arden craned his neck to look up at the man's face, to see a mouth without a full set of teeth.

'You need to watch where you're going, short stuff,' the man grunted, the corner of his mouth twitching slightly.

Slowly, the soaked warrior turned around, face as red as hell and slug like eyebrows dragged down low on his forehead. Arden peered up at the man's face and saw a slow, yellow smile break out. No warmth. More of a promise of death.

A group of men with him grinned and grunted at each other like animals, anticipating what may come next. Arden recognised the men as some of the group that had followed Saul into the room – not men to be messed with. His heart thumped faster, blood rushing throughout his body as he panicked. The man scratched a white scar on his head and stared maliciously at him.

'I just need to get past to my friends please...' Arden managed to murmur, his throat drying.

'We're all friends here! Why don't you join me and my buddies for a bit of fun?' A deep, booming voice seemed to shake the room.

Such a tempting offer.

Just my luck. First fight of the day and it has to involve me.

He looked around for an escape route, but another member of the group had blocked his retreat, a hand placed on his weapon at the hilt. *I knew I should have waited outside.*

For a big man, he moved fast. Arden didn't even see him roll his fist back before it crunched straight into his nose. The bone snapped as he fell to the hard ground, his arms splaying out to break his fall but only managing to claw at the boots of some of the other warriors watching. He screwed his eyes up in pain and felt for his nose. Broken. He felt the swelling already as his eyes watered, vision blurry with only a watery, orange glow in front of him. He blinked a few times but no more. Too painful. Too sore. The room swam in front of him as he sat up.

'Not one for talking much are you? Well, as it happens, neither am I,' growled the first man, smile fading as he reached for his sword, eager to join in. Arden felt a stab of fear, but he froze, unable to defend himself.

'Must be your lucky fucking day then,' came a voice behind Arden's attacker.

Arden exhaled as he saw Sly staring at the scene, a playful look on his face.

'Stay out of this, Stormson. This don't concern you. We're just having fun with this poor excuse for a man.'

'Everything about you concerns me, you fucking cunt. Leave the kid alone.' Sly warned, eyes darting between the men in the group as they all stood as one, ready for trouble.

'Poor excuse for a man? Someone say my name?' Kiras twirled her twin daggers, cocking her head to the side and running her tongue across her teeth.

The scarred warrior looked at his companions and then back to Sly and Kiras, knowing the numbers were in his favour. 'What are you two gonna do about it?' he asked with confidence.

Everything happened so fast, the action blurred before Arden's eyes. Sly flicked out a dagger and stabbed it straight into the scarred man's chest, a direct killing blow. The man closest to Arden fell next, a slash across his throat opening an escape route for the blood pumping out of his soon to be unmoving body. Kiras laughed as she spun and swiped up with her curved blade, in an instant slicing away another man's arm.

The others were too slow to reach for their weapons, their brains struggling to deal with the rapid change in their situation. Sly grabbed Arden with a rough hand and threw him into waiting arms.

'Just stand there,' Socket whispered, calmly watching on, wrinkled but firm hands holding Arden still, 'they're enjoying it.'

Arden took the moment to take in his surroundings once more, hand covering his bloodied nose as the red liquid streamed down into his mouth with a taste of iron, dripping onto the wooden ground. The whole room had fallen silent, fixated on the fight. Sly and Kiras stood back-to-back in a circle of vengeful warriors, weapons in hand, covered in their enemies' blood. Sly gave the room his infamous, yellow grin.

'Which one of you fuckers is next?' he asked, causing them to glance at one another, none of them wanting to approach the obviously crazy and ferocious beast bating them.

The first one to reach Sly placed an arm on his shoulder and raised a fist back to hit him square in the face. Sly welcomed the impact. Arden watched in horror as he saw him lick the blood dripping from his broken nose into his mouth and gave a bloody smile.

'That's it. Just what I wanted...'

He swung an elbow back and Arden heard the crunch of a second nose breaking, a muffled, protesting yelp and the thud of a body hitting the floor. The man that had bloodied Sly now had a look of intense fear on his face and his moment of hesitation was all that Sly needed. He grabbed the man around his neck, stamping on his foot as he did so. As the man's frame lowered, Sly raised his right knee straight into the warrior's face. Three crunches later and a bloody mess lay on the floor, barely recognisable from five seconds earlier.

Sly turned to another assailant and tackled him to the floor, punching him in the face a few times before turning his dagger on him, 'You and your pals better keep your fucking mouths shut next time or I'll get a little souvenir for my troubles.' Sly pressed the dagger against the man's mouth, pushing it hard against the corners of his lips until his eyes rolled back and he fainted.

Kiras had picked up the single limb that she had cut away. She flopped the arm around with a grin on her face as its owner shook with sobs on the floor, cradling the open wound by his shoulder.

'That's enough!' came a roar from behind Arden.

The waves of warriors parted as Raven stepped through the crowd towards the culprits, Saul scowling behind him.

'Quite the performance,' Saul growled.

Arden turned slowly to see Saul walking towards them, a shadow passing over his face, every muscle in his body tight and eager for action. Sly gave his best bloody grin and ran a hand through his wild, untamed hair. 'Just a little scuffle to get the juices flowing. Nothing to worry about.'

Kiras used the dismembered arm to give a little wave.

'I disagree. Taking down a group of my men for no reason is definitely a concern of mine.' Saul cracked his knuckles and took a step forward, dropping his grin.

Raven coughed loudly, turning attention to himself, 'I don't think there is any need for more violence today. I can deal with this Saul.'

'Make certain you do, Redbeard. Come on boys, I feel as though a breath of fresh air is needed. The stench in here is fouler than a demon's breath.'

He walked past Sly and spat on the floor, his men following him out of the door. Sly made to follow them, dagger in hand but then Arden saw hands grip both of his shoulders. He turned to see Raven and Baldor, both grim-faced, standing either side of the bloodied warrior.

Arden cleared his throat, eager to thank Sly and Kiras. Without their help, it would be more than a broken nose.

'Don't say a fucking word kid. I was bored.' Sly sloped back to his corner, eyes once more looking out for any further signs of trouble. Arden left his mouth hanging open – unable to say anything to his unlikely saviour.

'You're part of the tribe,' Kiras smirked, dropping a cold, lifeless hand on his shoulder and staring at the bloodied warrior as he walked away. 'I think he likes you.'

CIVILIZED JUSTICE

A blistering sun stabbed down through the tall glass windows of the Hall of Justice, one of the largest rooms in all of the United Cities of Archania, casting dark shadows into the mammoth room and across its many whispering occupants. The room felt warm and stuffy, packed in a way it had not been in many years, all anticipating an infamous day before them and wondering if the rumours in the city were true. Katerina Kane hooked a finger under her collar and pulled, feeling the sweat pooling around her neck.

'Autumn has been delayed by the wrath of summer's tail it seems!' one woman screeched, fanning herself with a vigour that made it appear as though her arm would fall off at any given moment. The effort she was applying to the action was almost certainly making the issue of the heat worse for her plump body, not to mention the inordinate number of frilly layers she had chosen to wear. Looking good had always been more important than feeling good. It had always been that way in the Upper City.

Kane tried to remember the last time she had seen her fellow citizens this animated. Elderly men and women who had hardly uttered a word to each other were now forgetting to take a breath between their frantic conversations: some were gesturing in an angry manner, eyebrows lowered toward dark eyes and arms waving in all directions with each heated word; others shared disappointed shakes of their heads, while a fair few seemed to spend most of their time with their mouths open in shock at the rumours permeating throughout the room.

Nobles from the most powerful houses in the Kingdom dressed in their extravagant, pompous finery were just as curious as the few villagers in their scruffy, ragged and ripped clothing who had managed to gain entrance into the large hall, brought together by a fascination for gossip and drama.

Sir Dominic had his usual fawning followers hanging onto his every word as he regaled them with the popular tale of his heroic stand against the Borderland invaders years ago. 'Must have been a hundred of the hairy bastards rushing through the gate towards me. Was I scared? Almost shat myself in all honesty!' he roared, hands flailing around, dropping an obscene amount of whiskey from his navy flask. His eyes sparkled as he cackled along with his adoring fans. They knew the story. Everyone knew the story. 'But I didn't run away, no. I stood, back straight, hands tightened around the greatest broadsword in the North and I gave a mighty roar. The scared looks on their faces gave me hope. They were just beasts, not men. My city would not fall, not this day. Not while blood still ran in my veins!'

Kane wondered, not for the first time, if it was still blood running through his veins. The amount the man drank must have influenced the blood-to-whiskey ratio inside him. He was positively pickled almost every time they met. Even meetings on the High Council were tainted with the stench of stale alcohol whenever the knight breathed. The hero of Archania took another swig from his flask, licking his lips, completely unaware that he had splashed another load onto his tight, silken charcoal shirt; tight enough to show that he had slowed down his training and spent a bit too long enjoying the various buffets and drinks that were thrown his way by admirers. The shirt creased around his midriff in a slightly unflattering way, but his face still shone with an effortless beauty, untainted by his vices. His dark hair fell loosely to his shoulders, streaked with grey in a way that gave him a distinguished look that many of the ageing men of the capital yearned for. A beautiful man, but not much between the ears, unfortunately.

Kane sighed as she scanned the room, blocking out the eager chat from those basking in anticipation of the mock trial. She made a few feeble attempts at polite conversation with others but in the end, everyone seemed to pick up on her glum mood and now only Kane sat in silence on one of the many wooden benches in the room.

'Lady Kane, an honour.' A thin, wiry man dressed all in black offered muttered apologies as he pushed through the crowds and hailed Kane with one raised hand, taking one of the few gaps that always seemed to surround her at such events. He had what looked like a permanent crease settled between his eyebrows as he chewed at his nails.

'Please, Matthias. You've known me long enough.' There was no need for such formalities between friends. 'Your nails.' Kane spotted the edges of the man's fingers, swollen and bloodied. She may be retired but old habits die hard. Everything needed an inspection. Everything was evidence.

Matthias blushed and hid his hands in the deep pockets of his dark cloak. 'I want to stop biting them but that's the problem with bad habits – bastards to break out of.'

Kane lifted a measured hand and grabbed him tightly around the chin, ignoring the scratch of stubble against her finger and thumb as she turned his face towards her. She stared deep into his eyes – deep, brown circles around black pupils that he had not been born with. Beads of sweat began to drop down from his forehead. Kane doubted it was to do with the heat. 'In this light, that trick is incredible,' she admitted, releasing his chin. 'Always surprises me.'

Matthias gave a nervous giggle. 'Ella's doing this time. Didn't just marry for looks, did I? The way she can hide the gold is a gift to our kind. Haller taught her how to do it – drains her for a while so that she needs a good nap after but it's worth it. Especially on a day like this. They're baying for blood out there, you know?' He anxiously poked a thumb back towards the tall, wooden doors at the rear of the room.

'Of course they are. Higher taxes, the strange weather, the land shaking at least once a week. And now this incident,' Kane whispered, pointing to the raised stage at the front of the hall. 'No surprise that the people are panicking.' Kane couldn't blame them. People had a fear of the unknown. Always had. It's why folk always seemed to shit themselves in the dark. Much better to spend time in the light where everything could be seen. Kane wasn't one of them though. She'd lived most of her life in the shadows, plunging her hands into the filth of Archania and dragging whatever could be found into the light where it could be seen in all its true glory. Half the cells beneath the Palace swarmed with guests cursing her role in their current living situation.

'Bet you long for the days when all people used to moan about was the horror of a female Inspector leading The Watch?' Matthias muttered as he glanced around nervously, not wanting to meet anyone's eyes in case they spotted his deception.

'Nostalgia has a strange effect on memory. I don't long for the rotten fruit being lobbed in my direction. Or the random attacks in the Lower City. Retirement suits me.' It was bullshit and she knew it. She missed the thrill of the chase, the challenge of catching the deviants. She missed the danger, the uncertainty of making it home. She missed being important.

Matthias managed to find a piece of nail that he hadn't yet torn off and nibbled at it, to Kane's disgust. 'They're going to hang him. I can feel it. The decision has already been made. How could he have been so foolish, Kane?' he whispered, his face going a dark red and his whole body shaking with fear for a young man he had known so well.

'Be calm Matthias. We don't want this getting out of hand. We all have our limits; I'm afraid young master Tate has reached his earlier than expected. He knew the consequences if he would be caught. You all knew the consequences. I always warned you this would happen,' Kane replied, perhaps a bit harsher than she intended.

Kane took out her handkerchief and handed it to Matthias to mop his sweating brow, as he struggled to control his growing panic.

'I should have kept a closer eye on him. He's been distant ever since his father died. Should have known something like this would happen. I need some fresh air.' Matthias made to move from his seat, but Kane held out a hand to stop him.

'Now is not the time to leave. We must stay throughout. If this is to end badly, we need to stay and witness; he made a grave mistake – leaving this room now will not change that.'

Matthias seemed to relax slightly at her words and nodded, running a hand through his lank, dark hair and taking his seat once more. Kane squeezed her friend's shoulder for strength.

Matthias had grown up alongside Tate in their order, barely five years older than the young mage, of course he would take things in such a hard way. Kane could only offer him support and use his experience in such matters. *What else can I do? It is my duty to be here as a member of the High Council of Archania. I must witness this to its end, for better or worse.*

Kane snapped out of her thoughts as the others on

their bench stood as one; elderly men taking off their hats and squeezing together to make way for the late addition who had just entered the hall. A beautiful, elegant woman with raven-black hair framing sharp but warm features on her pale face.

'Excuse me. Thanks. Sorry for the interruption,' she whispered as she made her way over to them.

'Late, as usual,' Matthias whispered back, instantly relaxing as his wife joined him on the bench.

'It takes time to look this good you know?' she replied, flashing her beautiful smile. 'You're a strange shade of green, my love. Are you well?'

Kane placed a hand on Matthias' back and leaned towards Ella. 'Your husband will be fine. Your beauty is making him weak at the knees, like all men.'

Ella blushed, cheeks blossoming into roses as she turned her emerald eyes towards Kane. 'Oh Katerina Kane, if only men were as careful with their words as you.'

'I'm afraid the path from brain to mouth seems to go on a slight detour through another organ for men. A most disheartening issue with our species,' Kane replied with a laugh.

'That cannot be denied. It is good to see you again.' Kane leaned forward as Ella kissed her softly on each cheek, catching the scent of her enticing perfume.

'And you, my dear. I'm just sad it is under such unfortunate circumstances. Your eyes...'

'A simple trick,' Ella whispered. 'Gold isn't exactly in fashion right now.'

'Are you hiding it for them, or for you?'

'Does it matter?'

'Your happiness is what matters.'

The excited whispers came to a stilted stop as the large, powerful doors swung open and an important and purposeful looking man entered the room. He strode forward down the aisle, between the rows of benches filled with the elite and bourgeois people of Archania, all keen to witness the day's proceedings, all focusing intently on this silver haired man.

His long, magnificent, crimson robe trailed behind him, its blood red hue broken up only by his long, silver hair falling straight down to the middle of his back. His colourful gem rings glimmered on each hand as the sunlight from the circular glass window at the front of the room caught the majestic jewellery. The sign of the White Sun clearly showed clearly on his right breast, the insignia of his Church, and the sign of the Empire of Light.

Kane stared into the man's icy blue eyes – blue circling gold pupils – as he passed. She thought that beneath the mask of sorrow that the man had chosen for this occasion lay an intense feeling of hatred and contempt, as always. Mason claimed to know the terrors of magic and its misuse; following his teachings was the only way to salvation.

Many of the audience gave a short bow as he passed, showing respect for the leader of the most powerful church in all the Northern region. Barely ten years had passed since Mason D'Argio had arrived in the city but in that time he had amassed the biggest group of followers in all the land, and now many considered him to be on par with the King for influence in the powerful nation – some even whispered in the shadows that he may be the true power in these lands.

A dangerous man, for certain. An evil man, perhaps.

'Do you know what the worst thing was about the war with the Borderlands?' Kane whispered. Matthias and Ella leant towards her, careful to make sure no one else could hear. 'It gave this monster a chance to dig his claws into our country. We were on our knees, willing to accept any kind of support. If only we could go back ten years...'

Kane watched as Mason stared down the aisle with that all-knowing look of his.

She popped the buttons open on her collar and wiped the sweat away with her thumb.

Kane struggled to hold back the hatred from her face. This man and his cult – if it could still be called that – seemed more dangerous than any of the other organizations that had existed before he had come along. The speed of its progression frightened her, as did the way that the other religious leaders seem to fade into the shadows as Mason and his followers preached of the brilliance of the Empire of Light: an Empire that consisted not only of an alliance of the three great Northern cities but also a union of three of the four largest Eastern Kingdoms, Kingdoms that were now governed by the ways of the Empire and their oppressive beliefs.

She looked at the shaking man sitting next to her and squeezed his hand. Magi wanted freedom but these were dangerous times for practitioners in the Northern region. Unless you were a part of the Empire, magic use was banned. A small pocket of magi resisted but the Empire was closing in, looking out for any form of disobedience. That's why Tate would stand in front of this crowd of fools today.

Mason reached the end of the aisle and turned to face the room; hundreds of faces focused on this one man, eager for any words that may slither out from his silver, forked tongue. He gestured for everyone in the room to take their seats before offering them all a smile that didn't seem to reach his cold, blue eyes.

'My brothers and sisters. I do apologise for my late arrival. It has been a long and quite stressful day, and I thank you all for your patience.' Mason took a deep breath and paused to look out across the silent, packed room, revelling in his power. 'It is with a great sadness that I have called for a meeting here today, in this Great Hall, the Hall of Justice. I am here to tell you all of a great *injustice* that has happened beneath our very noses here in Archania. A trial must be held, and a fitting punishment delivered.' *A trial? Is that what you're calling this? A punishment has already been chosen, there will be no trial. Just a mockery, a feigned attempt at a justice system set up by the corrupted leaders of the system.*

'Bring in the defendant.'

A hushed silence gripped the crowd as they sat up, straining to get a closer look at the door opening at the back of the room, commoners and nobles alike striving for the best view.

Two soldiers, fully armed, with their chins pointing as close to the ceiling as they could, walked into the room, flanking a weak looking blonde-haired young man, shaking with fear as hateful eyes burned into him. Light shone into the room, reflecting from the golden orbs that marked him as a mage.

Cries rang out in the hall as men and women spat, screamed and cursed at the young mage. One elderly man near Kane stood from his seat, bellowing obscenities, face warping into a deep shade of purple. How his heart was able to stand the pressure was beyond her understanding. Maybe that was the point. These people seemed as though they didn't have a heart.

Kane felt hers stop for a second as she watched the trembling figure, noticing the bruises and deep gashes that covered any piece of bare flesh exposed by the tears in the rags he had been given as a feeble attempt to protect his modesty.

Tate stared down at the floor on his journey to the lonely, wooden chair next to where Mason stood, casting dark glances in his direction. *He's defeated. He knows what is about to happen. And there is nothing any of us can do.*

The utter helplessness of the situation paralysed her. As stupid as he may have been, young Tate didn't deserve this. He was just a boy who had wanted to say farewell to his father – surely that wasn't worth punishment, just education.

Mason raised a hand to silence the muttering that had broken out from the crowd at the condemned man's arrival. 'Many in this room will know the man that is sitting here next to me. Tate, son of Tyson. This man has been brought here today to answer for a grave crime. We live in a beautiful Kingdom, where people feel safe in the knowledge that there are laws in place to keep them from harm. We are not like the tribes in the Borderlands who wander about in sin, giving in to their base desires without a thought for their neighbour.'

A few in the crowd, along with a large, fat man with a magnificent curled moustache sitting next to Matthias, started cheering at this statement. Manipulating an Archanian crowd couldn't be easier; put down the Borderlands with a few words to confirm their ideas of superiority over the neighbouring nation. Nothing more.

'One of these laws is incredibly simple. Do not touch the Sky Plane.'

Kane felt a trickle of blood escape her mouth, her teeth finally tearing through her lip, nerves mounting with each moment as the crowd bobbed their heads as one, sharing their outdated views with anyone who would listen. Matthias slid down in his seat, took out a pair of reading glasses from a pocket and tried to concentrate on cleaning them as though his life depended on it. Ella had closed her eyes, concentrating on her breathing to stave off a possible anxiety attack.

'Only a few deserving individuals are gifted with the ability to use magic, to touch the Sky Plane. They are picked by the One to use their gift for the advancement of the world he has created. If any other attempts to use magic, we all know what would happen. Complete chaos,' Mason said, his voice lowering to a dark whisper that still seemed to carry itself to the back of the room.

His cult had claimed that any use of magic by the unworthy could bring about the end of days – the destruction of Takaara. They spoke of a time when magic had been freely used;

a time of the birth of Archania. Individuals had grown in magical power to the point where they believed themselves to be gods; arguments had broken out between rival factions, each claiming that they held the secrets to magic and the way that it should be used. A war had been fought. A war that had decimated world's population.

Magic use not relating to religious purposes for the One God had been banned throughout the Empire. Now, those wishing to use magic needed to either be accepted by the Empire of Light as having a divine birth-right, or they operated in secret, like Ella, Matthias and their associates – pushed into the shadows by the iron fist of the Empire and forced to hide their gifts.

'This man was caught by members of my personal guard, attempting to use magic for his own personal gain. He has admitted his guilt and now all that needs to be decided is his punishment, which is why all you fine law-abiding gentlemen and ladies are here today.'

He flashed a wide smile at his audience, his perfectly straight, white teeth gleaming down at them. 'It is indeed a sad day for our people. A young man with his whole life ahead of him, free to follow his Lord and advance our people in almost any way that he desires, has chosen to meddle with an art that he does not fully understand, and so endangered us all.' Mason walked slowly to the frightened young man and placed a hand on his shoulder. Tate looked up into his eyes, fear lining every atom in his body.

Mason returned the look with utter coldness.

'Only the faithful may touch the Sky Plane, child.'

'I just wanted to see him one last time,' Tate whispered almost to himself. 'I never had a chance to say goodbye.'

Cries rang out from the angry crowd, their ignorance and hate frustrating Kane. These were the people she had spent decades protecting, defending them from all kinds of horrors. It made her sick.

'Hang him!'

'Burn him!'

'Traitor!'

Matthias covered his ears with his hands and dropped his head, unable to look at his young friend while the wild cries of the baying crowd rang out all around him. The faces of the crowd seemed suddenly distorted, red with anger and frothing at the mouths. They were like animals, losing all facets of their humanity as they behaved as one in calling for the death of the single, lonely, young man before them.

Mason raised a jewelled hand and asked for calm, 'In this Hall of Justice, justice shall indeed be served. The common man cannot grasp the power of magic and it is only through a connection with the One God that the lucky few, such as myself, can wield its force. If all such as yourself attempted to do as this man did and connect with the Sky Plane to wield a power you cannot comprehend, then the land would once again become scarred as it is in the Wastelands! Since the Purge of the Guardians, magic has been unpredictable, unbalanced, chaotic. With no Guardians to control the flow, it is left to those few, such as myself, to ensure that impetuous magi are punished. It is a burden I bear with great pride, but also, great sadness.'

More cheers and cries rang out through the hall, the crowd swept up in the carnival atmosphere. Kane focused on the young man sitting alone, hoping for a way to lend him strength through his darkest hour. Matthias sat with his head bowed, a hand now covering his eyes as his body shook. Fortunately, he was ignored by those around him, so focused were they on the spectacle before them.

'I have met with the King himself and a few other select advisors. As a group, after a lengthy discussion, we decided on the best course of action.' Kane held her breath, knowing what would come next but praying that she was wrong. 'The boy must burn.'

Mason held out his hand. From the side, a russet, reddish brown-skinned man with thin, dark paint lining his eyes stepped forward with a long, wooden torch, flames dancing in time with the roars from the audience. Mason took the torch and placed the flames against the wooden chair, ignoring the screams and pleading from the young man who shook violently.

'Please, no. Anything but this! Anything but this!' Tate screamed.

Kane raised a hand to her mouth in horror as the flames began to lick at his skin, the smell of burning flesh filling the air. Through it all, she could still hear the calm voice of Mason D'Argio.

'This hurts me more than you, child.'

Liar.

She turned away from the horror, closing her eyes. She couldn't escape the smell, or the crackling of the flames, or the screams that pierced her heart.

A moment later, she opened them, staring at Ella.

There were no tears in the magi's eyes. Just a cold, still fury. A futile attempt to block out the screams left her in a cloak of despair. The screams would haunt her sleep for years, she knew it. Through it all, she couldn't remove her eyes from Ella. Something needed to happen, it had to. A change. For good or ill, she didn't know. But *something* was going to change.

And then the earth shook.

The swarm of excited people filed out of the Hall of Justice, a gross mirror image of the crowds that piled out of the theatre barely three streets away at the end of each week. Kane was horrified to see the laughter and carefree looks on many faces of the men and women exiting the building and finding their way home, back to normality. Or maybe this was normality for them. They had sat there and watched on as the boy burned. A few cheers had broken the stunned silence, followed by shouts of support for Mason and his cronies. None had dared to call out in defiance of what they saw. To her shame, Kane counted herself among that number. The consequences would be swift and severe. She knew that only too well. Lord Tamir had stormed out in protest; his thoughts on the Empire were known to all in the Kingdom. It would only be a matter of time before Mason found a way to silence him and his blasphemous ways.

Ella and Matthias walked slightly ahead of her at a brisk pace, voices low and heated.

'I told you before. Haller doesn't have a clue. The damn fool is willing to let this Kingdom slide into despair and ruin. I've heard of others, others with more... proactive ideas; ideas that can save this Kingdom before it goes too far.'

Ella twisted her head around, looking out for any who may have been listening. She caught Kane's eye and smiled weakly before leaning towards her husband. 'Now is neither the time nor the place to be having this discussion.'

'It never seems to be the time or place with you. Swift, decisive action is needed to halt the decay. Mark my words.' Matthias' voice had an unfamiliar stern, determined tone. Kane guessed that watching a boy burned affected everyone in different ways. Pain. Death. Adversity. All were known to mould men in different ways.

'I understand, but we need to be careful. His followers

are everywhere and they're not exactly merciful. We just watched Tate – young Tate – burn to death!'

'Do you think I need reminding?' Matthias said through gritted teeth, struggling to keep his voice low and even. 'I'll see you back home.'

'Fine...'

'He okay?' Kane asked, catching up with Ella as Matthias stomped off in the direction of the Lower City.

'He will be. Rough day.'

'Understandable.'

Kane allowed the silence to linger, giving Ella the time to sort out her thoughts. Sometimes, not saying anything was the best course of action: words had a horrible way of making things worse in certain situations.

'Fancy taking a couple of horses for a ride? Been a while since I felt the wind in my hair,' Ella asked, face lighting up at the thought.

'I'm sure I can move a few things around,' Kane winked. 'Where shall we ride?'

'I know a place, past a small village outside of the city. Top of the hill gives the best views of the Kingdom.'

'Lead the way.'

* * *

She'd missed this. The wind whipping across her face, green fields a blur either side of her and the sheer freedom of the ride. It was pure bliss, a reliable way of ridding her of any dark thoughts and worries from the day. The ride allowed her to escape the difficulties of the city and focus on the beauty around her; the joys of the world, of Takaara.

'Good girl,' she said, leaning forward and patting the mare on the side of her neck before pushing her weight into the saddle and giving a gentle pull on the reigns. The world stopped racing past as they eased back into a gentle trot. Kane looked up the dusty path leading to the top of the hill and grinned wider than she had for some time. The sun was beginning its descent behind the hill as Ella jumped off her horse, resting her head against the animal in recognition of their bond. The warm evening glow cast a beautiful light upon them both as Kane reached them.

'Some horse you've got there. You could enter her into the races and I wouldn't bet against her!' She was only half joking. The animal's speed had shocked her to begin with, making it impossible for her to keep up with her raven-haired friend. 'Could earn some serious money with an animal as talented as she is.' Kane slid off her own mount and patted the mare on the neck once more before leading it forward with the reigns. 'Thank you, girl. Not so slow yourself...'

'Had them both since they were foals. Sisters. If you think they're fast, you should have seen their father! Fastest stallion I've ever seen. Dad made more money with him as a stud horse than he ever did as a merchant. Best business decision he ever made,' Ella said proudly. 'I wouldn't ever want them racing though. The jumps, the whips, the pressure. They're like family to me.'

'Palomino as well, gorgeous colour. Two of the best-looking horses I've seen.'

A minute later, they were on top of the hill. Kane led her horse to a sturdy pine tree and loosely tied the reigns around its base. She rummaged around for a moment in her leather bag before finding one of the apples she had discovered earlier on her ride. 'There you go girl. Enjoy that.' The mare eagerly munched on the apple as its hooves relaxed, enjoying the break.

Kane turned and strolled through the verdant meadow, eyes falling on the beautiful cinquefoils, rambling roses and lavender around her. A cacophony of colour on display in every direction.

'Amazing isn't it?' Ella said. 'So peaceful and calm. Do you know what this hill is called?'

'Hangman's Hill.' Kane sat down next to her friend, gazing out at the Kingdom she called home as the light of the day began to fade. 'This was where criminals would be brought to face the justice of the King.'

'Know it all,' Ella gave her a light-hearted push and laughed. 'Aleister used to bring me up here. Said it was his favourite place in the whole Kingdom. Feels like a lifetime ago...'

'It's incredible that a place once known for such horror is now filled with beauty and wonder.' Kane looked down from her lofty height at the vista opened out before her. From this vantage point, she could see the city of Archania in the distance. The walls surrounding the city were unable to obscure her view, allowing her the chance to gaze upon the domed palace beside the Hall of Justice; the green Upper City Gardens sprawled out in the centre.

'The view is second to none,' Ella said, following Kane's gaze. 'It's amazing how a short ride gives so much distance to what is happening down there. It all feels so... insignificant from up here.'

Around the city were small villages filled with the backbone of Archania – the farmers, the merchants, the families that had lived generation upon generation in the shadow of the great growing city. To the West, she could see the coast, ships moored in the docks awaiting their next journey across the Emerald Sea. 'Distance gives us a clearer perspective on things. How are things with you and Matthias?' She blurted it out, unable to catch herself before the words escaped her lips.

Ella sighed and fell onto her back, eyes looking up at the wispy clouds passing above them. 'Difficult,' she said to the sky. 'He's a good man, I know that. But the tension in the city is causing problems. Matthias wants us to do one thing, I want another. We're pushing in different directions and feeling more distant than we have since the wedding.'

'There are ups and downs in every relationship. Your ability to ride the waves that come with marriage will decide your destination. My husband and I would have blazing rows from time to time. Through it all, we knew that we loved each other, and that was what mattered.'

'I know. Things just don't feel... right.'

'Like they did with Aleister?' Ella sat up, frowning at Kane. 'Be honest with yourself. Does his shadow fall on your marriage?'

'I don't know!' Ella cried, falling back onto the grass and beating the ground with her fist. 'I loved him, so much! And then he left, and to do what? To travel distant lands, fight in wars that didn't concern him and fuck whoever the hell he wanted to!'

'He was young. We all believe there is more to life for us than what is in front of our eyes. The sun always seems brighter in the next land. We all make mistakes.'

'But he had me. Wasn't I good enough? He broke my heart...' Ella's voice faded into the evening as the sun fell below the horizon. 'I've never forgiven him.'

'You married Matthias: perhaps it is time you do forgive him.' Kane shifted over, looking down at her fallen friend. 'You need to make a decision. There is only so much emotion one person can hold; like a river pushing against the banks, ready to break free. Either you hate Aleister for leaving you and destroy the relationship you have with Matthias, or you let it wash away and dedicate your time to Matthias. Either way you will lose something, such is life, but at least you will be able to move on.'

'You're right, of course you are.' The sun set on the Kingdom as lights were lit throughout the villages and the city below them. 'I have a decision before me.'

'I've always found that decisions are best made after a good sleep!' Kane said, standing up and wiping the patches of mud and grass that had attached themselves to her trousers. 'You ready for a night-time ride?'

Ella sat up, face breaking out into a smile. 'Last one back buys the drinks?'

'We both know how that is going to turn out...'

'I'll have a firewhiskey.'

ONE LAST CASE

It has been a long time since I've been here. A long time since I've seen something like this. Not long enough unfortunately. Katerina Kane stared at the cold, recently deceased man that had just been fished out of the lapping, dark water. The moonlight cast an eerie glow on the proceedings, with only the gentle splashing of the waves against the many wooden ships moored at the docks making a sound.

'Who found him?' she asked the Inspector, still studying the familiar corpse, tears filling her eyes. Only her years of training and experience kept her voice from breaking as her eyes found the soft, lifeless brown eyes of the man she loved.

'Local sailor. Said he felt the ship hit something, thought he may have pulled too close to the shore, and when he checked, he found this, floating. He yelled to some passing members of Mason's men who happened to be walking by and then got him out. Couple of others on the ship were witnesses,' replied the monotone Inspector. 'I know you haven't been active in some time, but I thought it best to give you a call as soon as possible. It's not often folk like him wind up like this, and I remember you talking about him fondly.'

'Thank you, Inspector Marlin, it is greatly appreciated that you contacted me so soon.'

Kane examined the face closely, looking into the lifeless, dark, open eyes as closely as she dared. Wrinkles at the corners of his eyes spread out like tributaries – a sign of a happy man, Kane's mother had once said. The mask of his final face was one which Kane had never seen before, one of shock. She had known Braego for over eighteen years, ever since the Borderland warrior had first come to Archania. At first, Kane had mistrusted the man. He was always getting into bar brawls and drawing unnecessary attention to himself, keeping The Watch on high alert. Only after the man had risen to the position of Royal Weapons Master – partly due to his help in foiling an assassination attempt on the King's life – had Kane taken the time to get to know the man behind the bluster. In all that time, she had never seen him look even slightly distressed. He took everything in his stride. It was one of the reasons she had fallen for him.

She had found him rough, uncouth and prone to random outbreaks of absurdity, as expected from their Borderland neighbours. What she hadn't expected was how refreshing she found him. Their friendship had grown, the warrior's unique outlook on life helping with a great many of her cases, and their relationship had blossomed into something more. Casual, but intense and refreshing. Kane had welcomed the warrior's company and had recommended the man to be Head of the Royal Guard. The council had decided against this, keeping him in the position of Weapons Master instead; a role more suited to his skills apparently. Fear of anything associated with the Borderlands kept Braego from rising higher, not that he cared. He offered her a shrug of his broad shoulders as Kane fumed at the injustice of it all.

'Has anyone else been informed of his death?' she asked, already knowing the answer.

'Mason D'Argio is the only other. I believe he is in conference with the King as we speak.'

As I suspected. That man is kept informed of everything. If only a fly had been harmed today, I'm sure he would already be well aware of the incident. Kane's shoulders slumped, a sad shadow passing through her as she looked once more at her pale friend, staring at the single-entry point on the man's bare chest, the sole clue as to the cause of death. *Who could have done this to you Braego? This was no fair fight.*

Kane had seen the warrior take down some of the most dangerous criminals in the city – men who had wanted to test their might against the Kingdom's apparent best warrior. All had failed in seconds, unable to withstand the ability of a man raised in the harsh conditions of the Borderlands where it was kill-or-be-killed. Kane had never expected to see the man defeated. Now, she needed to discover how, and why.

Of course, distrust in foreigners infected the blood of

this city. The people of the Kingdom took pride in any meagre achievement of one of their own, but anything done by an outsider would be resented. Many in the city had protested the rise of the rough, fearsome warrior, believing the position he took should have been given to a deserving Archanian. Their fear of the uncivilised Borderlands, due to longstanding bad blood between the nations, may not have helped. *Hell, even other Archanians are being turned on lately it seems.* The picture of a burning youth flashed into her mind. She shook her head. These were dark times to live in. Dark times indeed.

'The single-entry point seems the right size for a small blade. Perhaps a member of the Assassins' Guild has been paid for their efforts?' Marlin suggested, looking at her for a shred of praise for his poor estimation.

'None of the Guild would ever lay a finger on someone attached to the palace. They are talented, not stupid. If they were caught, the Guild would be crushed by an army within days. This was the work of something else, something much more deadly,' Kane replied, unable to tear her eyes away from the unfamiliar, shocked look on her Braego's face.

She had seen many dead bodies over the years. Some were contorted in the worst imaginable ways. Others seemed as though they were only sleeping. There was no pattern to it.

'Get a team over here to look for any more clues regarding the cause and time of death. I have someone I need to urgently speak with.'

'You want to work with us on this one, Kat? It'd be understandable given the circumstances; to be honest I don't know where to go next for the answers.' Marlin scratched his head. A good Inspector, reliable. A wise replacement for her. But he didn't have the nose for the job; the ability to sniff out the unexpected, to go with his gut feeling. It's what separated the very good from the best.

'Just ask some questions, trace where he had been, where he was going; the usual. Keep me updated, I'll do what I can to help but we need to keep it off the record,' she warned, giving her successor a stern look. 'Your boss will not be keen on me getting involved.'

'Of course, Kat,' agreed the Inspector. 'I'll leave you out of any report.'

Kane turned and strode down the docks, her boots echoing off the damp, wooden boards as she made her way back towards the Lower City in the moonlight. A familiar pathway loomed before her, branches from old trees creating a natural arch to guide her and offering little protection from the start of the soft rainfall. The rain fell on the leaves surrounded her before dripping off in larger quantities and falling on to the ground, beginning to create small puddles by her boots.

The end of the archway loomed before her when a dark figure stepped before her, obstructing her path.

'A bit late for a stroll around the docks, wouldn't you agree Katerina Kane?' a menacing, gruff voice called out from beneath a dark hood. The moonlight caught the pointed edge of a sword as he drew it from the scabbard at his hip; a promise of violence.

Kane took a breath and drew her own trusty falchion, eyes not leaving her adversary. 'I enjoy the quiet, peaceful nature of the city that the night offers,' she replied, rolling her fingers tighter round the sword hilt's red leather.

'You were once the highest-ranking officer in this city, we both know that the only peace that night-time has to offer is an everlasting one. Your friend Braego can attest to that.' A flash of white teeth could be seen under the shadow of the hood, baiting her into the first move. Kane had survived enough dust-ups to be tempted by such a gesture.

'What do you know of his death?' she asked. Only the sound of the rain answered her. 'Coward!' she spat in defiance, anger rising.

A choking sound croaked out from her opponent, startling her and forcing her to take a step back. 'What devilry is this?' she muttered to herself.

The would-be assailant stumbled forward as his sword fell from his grip and clanged on the ground, lying in an ever-growing puddle. He retched and struggled to breathe while on his hands and knees, all the threat of violence leaving him.

Kane stepped cautiously forward, weapon leading the way. Better to be safe than sorry.

'Stay where you are, Katerina Kane. He will die without your interference.'

Kane spun on the spot and pointed the curve of her blade at the voice that came from behind her. Another robed figure, this one female by the sound of her rich, melodic tones.

'Another shadowed enemy,' she whispered, cautiously looking over her shoulder at the first foe, his face now pressed against the wet ground, body twitching.

'I am not your enemy, Kane,' answered the woman's voice.

'Then who are you?' she snapped, sword still raised, unwilling the trust the newcomer.

The robed figure raised her hands and lowered her dark hood, moonlight shining on the dark blood-red hair that fell past her shoulders.

'We share a mutual friend. Aleister. You saved his life once, consider the debt repaid.'

'Aleister hasn't been in Archania for over five years, there was no debt,' Kane replied, unwilling to lower the sword yet, mistrust informing her every movement. Aleister had not departed on good terms with her; the thief had chosen to ignore all advice that Kane was willing to offer and decided to choose his own path in life. The last Kane had heard of him had been wild rumours in a tavern spoke by drunken fools telling tales of the leader of a fabled mercenary group – The Red Sons.

'He never forgot. He's kept an eye on you all this time.'

It had been meant as a comfort, but for a proud woman like Kane, being told that you had been watched for many years unnerved her.

'How did you kill him?' Kane asked, tilting her head towards the corpse behind her, wanting to steer the conversation towards more important matters. She relaxed slightly, body loosening but still unwilling to lower the sword. *You can never be too careful in this city.*

'Poison dart. Simple, yet effective,' she nonchalantly replied.

Kane looked at the body slumped on the ground and the sword lying in the puddle and found that she couldn't deny that. 'The work of an assassin.' She raised an eyebrow.

'I'll take that as a compliment. And a thank you,' came the cryptic answer with a theatrical bow.

Kane thought back to her friend's body. 'Do you know what happened back in the docks? My friend Braego...'

'Magi,' came the blunt reply before pointing at the body on the ground, 'he was one of them. Wouldn't surprise me if Mason's lot had a hand in it. Beyond that, I can't help you.'

Kane sheathed her weapon. Just as she had expected. She looked up towards her saviour but only shadows flickered over the wooden boards. Kane sighed, alone in the city with so many questions.

* * *

Kane knocked on the wooden door three times, then stood waiting for the owner to respond to the late summons.

'One moment!' At least she was awake.

Ella looked flustered as she opened the door, her hair messy and standing up on one side, her face slightly red. *I suppose it is quite late.*

'Kat. What are you doing here at such an hour?' she whispered, pulling a cream robe tight around her and tying it at her waist before motioning for Kane to enter the room and take a seat.

'My apologies, Ella. I know that it is very late and I would not have disturbed you unless I had deemed it most urgent.'

Kane considered herself lucky to call Ella and her husband friends. Ella had been a wide-eyed lover of justice, eager to follow in her heroine's footsteps. Kane had encouraged her love of the law and equality as she had grown up, keeping in touch, even when Ella chose another path – looking after her father's famous horses. Animals had a lure that even the law could not beat.

'Where is Matthias?' she asked. A man in his position of power, through sheer will and kindness instead of bribery and treachery was rare; councillors often found themselves dripping in lies and deceit. The ladder to the top had many greedy, often blood-soaked handprints smeared on it but none of those belonged to the husband of tired looking woman sitting opposite her. Matthias was a good man, if a little boring at times. Ella's eyes had once been attracted to another, but Matthias was the safe pair of hands that she needed.

'He's in bed. It's been a long day,' she answered.

Kane scanned the room, an old habit. Her eyes were quickly drawn to a bottle of Archanian whiskey, 'A little late for a drink, wouldn't you agree?' she said, raising an eyebrow.

'Like I said – it's been a long day.'

'Again, I am sorry for the disturbance.'

'There is no need to apologise; I couldn't sleep anyway – although, for future reference, I would prefer these visits at more desirable times of the day. Thankfully, Matthias is a deep sleeper,' she replied, a weak chuckle forcing its way out of her as she rubbed her tired eyes once more.

Ella grabbed another glass before they both took a seat. She filled the glasses up before asking, 'Your favourite if I recall correctly?'

Kane nodded, adding her thanks, 'Nothing beats it.'

The pair of them sat in silence for a moment in the dim candlelight, shadows flickered between them as a slight breeze swept through the open balcony door.

'So, what brings you here at this hour?' Ella asked, breaking the silence.

Kane stared intently at the glass, swishing the dark liquid around before knocking back the fiery drink.

'Braego. The Royal Weapons Master. His body was fished out of the water near the docks earlier this evening,' Kane answered, watching Ella for any sign of recognition.

'From the Borderlands, wasn't he? I'm sure your list of suspects is longer than the Lapret River,' she said.

'You'd think so – foreigners don't do so well in the Kingdom. This is different though; he's been here a long time – people know who he is; know who he is friends with. There has to be more to it.' Kane banged her fist on the table, letting anger get the best of her for once.

She chastised herself as Ella paused and turned her head, obviously listening out for any sign that Matthias had been woken from his slumber. A moment passed before she seemed happy that he had not woken.

'You were friends with him.' She didn't pose it as a question.

'He was a good man. One of the best in the Kingdom.' Kane answered, lowering her head before taking another drink. 'Or any kingdom for that matter.'

Ella squinted, mouth slightly open. She knew that Kane had left something out, but Kane was thankful that she didn't have to explain, not now.

'Cause of death?'

'A single wound to the chest.'

'Motive?'

'Xenophobia, jealousy – many and none all at once I'm afraid; nothing concrete as of yet anyway.' Kane shrugged.

'Why me?'

'You know why.' The light of the candles gave Ella's golden orbs a haunting glow.

It had been a long time since Kane had found out about Ella and her abilities. Having a talent for sniffing out information and following wherever any shred of evidence would lead her meant Kane chased up any possible thread relating to a secret order within her beloved Kingdom.

At the time, consumed by a burning fire, her one goal kept her focused on uncovering a mysterious death in the Kingdom. Colleagues had long since given up, believing the case not worth the time and dedication required. Kane had to prove them wrong. She followed the case to its end. Along the way she bumped into a young man – a young, fearful man with a gift.

Kane had watched in awe and fear as Matthias had displayed his blossoming abilities, a stalling tactic that gave him enough time to explain his situation to her, and offer his assistance in the case; the case others had deemed unsolvable. Kane allowed him to use his ability to scry for the information, the attempt almost killed him, but it gave them their answer.

The killer wasn't a mage. Just a normal man. A man with a love of pain and torture. The truth hurt almost as much as anything else. A great man had died and for what? He had become the plaything of an evil, remorseless killer. No one deserved that.

Kane could still remember the frustration she had felt; the desire to solve the case had almost driven her mad. Eventually, justice had found the man – a serial killer. The dungeons became his home. Every now and then, Kane would visit him, ask him questions, trying to understand why he had senselessly killed the innocent. All she would get in response was laughter. One night a group of men associated with Mason D'Argio had come knocking on her door. They told her to keep quiet, to halt her questions and move on. When she had put up a fight, they threatened her husband. Kane did what anyone would have done. She did as they asked. A year later, her husband was dead.

Life could be a right bitch at times.

From time to time she would still visit Matthias, asking for his advice even though she knew the mage would resist any questions directly linked to any of his associates. Kane wasn't a fool. She knew there were others, she just didn't know who. The fire didn't burn as strong now though; she found that to be honest, she couldn't give a fuck. As far as she was concerned, it wasn't anyone's business what people wanted to do in their own home, it was only when others were involved when she would step in and start asking questions.

The two had built up a business-like relationship – one that had strengthened when Kane had introduced the young mage to the woman sitting across the table from her now.

'I suspect, as you've probably guessed, that there was an... unusual... element to his death. Something someone like myself can't quite place her finger on.'

'And you think I can help?' Ella asked, downing the rest of her drink.

Kane shut her eyes and took a deep breath. When she opened them again, they watered, blurring her vision. 'He was my friend Ella, a good friend. More than that, in fact. I am not here as the former Inspector Kane; I am here as Katerina Kane. I need your help, please.'

Ella relaxed in her chair, clearly thrown off-balance by the sudden honesty and rare, pleading tone that she heard in Kane's old, croaky voice.

'I am so sorry, Kat. I am so caught up in my own issues that it seems I am entirely unaware of the suffering of those around me. I shall do what I can to assist in your investigation.' The purposeful tone in her voice reassured Kane.

'He was not killed by an ordinary warrior or drunken fool in Archania; the wound was too precise. I have heard of such attacks – magic users who use their talent to kill with a great degree of stealth.'

Ella shifted uncomfortably in her chair, a nervous grin creeping across her face. 'When I started on this path, I never would have dreamed that people would abuse their gift like this. Young and foolish. So much has changed since then.'

'You're still young. Still a fool too.' Kane let slip a wry smile.

They shared a laugh, pausing to let the warmth of each other's company pass over them.

'I can ask a few of my... friends, see if they have seen or heard anything. I'm afraid there is little else I can do. Things are tense in the city at the moment... Tate...'

Kane placed her hand over Ella's and allowed her a moment to compose herself, understanding the pain that she must be feeling.

'Anything you can do will help but I must insist on one thing – you are not to put yourself in danger! Just check with your lot and try to rule them out. Then I can go for the others,' Kane told her, steel returning to her voice.

Ella leaned forward and wiped her eyes, staring at her

as though she did not know the woman sitting opposite. 'You cannot mean...? You know what will happen if you go in that direction. D'Argio and his men are too powerful. If they are involved, it is best you stay well away. You saw what happened today...'

Kane ran a hand through her mop of brown hair and stared across the table at one of the few people in the Kingdom she could call an ally. 'I have lost so much, Ella. My husband was murdered, I've been given a mock council role to make up for them stripping me of my position and now Braego, one of a decreasing minority that I could name as a close friend, has died. If Mason or his men had anything to do with what happened to him, I will make sure that they pay. You have my word.' Kane was not put off by the fear on her friend's face. 'Mason D'Argio will have made a dangerous enemy, one with nothing to lose.'

'Tread carefully Kat. Too many people in the Kingdom have... disappeared, of late.'

'I know, I know. Don't worry about me. You ask your questions, and I'll ask mine. Anyway, it is time I was leaving. I am truly sorry for the lateness of my arrival. Please give my best to Matthias – we must speak again in less... dark times.' She stood from the comfortable chair, her old knees creaking. *If only I was ten years younger! This would all be so much easier!* She saw her younger ally wearily get to her feet, her hand moving straight to a pain in her back and she thought, no, perhaps it would not.

'Have there ever been times that are not dark? I think such times are limited to the fairy tales told to young children.' Ella placed her hands on her hips and swayed to the side, stretching out her sore muscles. 'If there is anything I can do, just ask. No matter what happens in this city, you will always have friends here.'

Kane opened the door quietly. She turned and hugged Ella tightly – her flowery smell a reminder of better times. 'Please take care of yourself,' she implored.

'You too, old lady,' she muttered back.

Kane walked out, into the cold, empty streets and took a deep breath, wondering how many more she had left. The moonlight cast a strange glow over the beautiful city and her eyes were drawn to the city square in front of the Grand Palace. She closed them and saw again the way that young Tate had tried his best not too scream as the flames wrapped him in their deadly embrace – the crowd of people had treated it all as a fun day out in the city. Tate had done his best, but the pain must have been unbearable. None would have been able to withstand it.

She had seen death before. People died all the time from all manner of different things; peasants in the Lower City could be seen dying at any time from disease and starvation; she had seen more than one man die through injuries suffered from horse riding accidents in the Upper City, and she had once been unfortunate enough to witness a suicide from a crazed man with a knife in a local tavern she had liked to frequent in her youth. Death was a part of life. But to watch a boy burn for the crime of attempting to reach out to his late father was something that would never leave her.

She contemplated heading home, back to her double bed where she could stretch out and attempt to forget the pain of the day. There was no chance of it happening. Not even in her sleep would she find solace. The flames would be that much clearer when she closed her eyes. She leaned back and gazed at the dancing stars sparkling in the night sky. The crescent moon frowned down at her, guiding her path through the empty streets.

One final mission, one last case.

For Braego.

THIS IS THE BORDERLANDS

Arden squirmed on his bench, wincing as he carefully pinched the bridge of his nose with a finger and thumb, wanting time to pass him by as fast as possible so he could get out of the loud, testosterone-filled room and out into the open air. He made sure to stay close to those he could trust, and away from any warrior looking to use him for an unpleasant, warped sport.

All four tribes were present and accounted for and watching them drink and laugh together in the Great Hall for the first time in what felt like an age should have been pleasing to a man born in these lands. It was not.

He had never felt like a normal man of the Borderlands – he didn't lust for blood or honour, and he would never revel in the harm of anything else. He would hunt from time to time – a necessity for his survival – but he would not take pleasure from the pain of another creature. His eyes informed others of his difference in an instant. There weren't many with golden pupils in the Borderlands. Anything that made you different usually led to death in these lands.

Four tribes gathering felt rare; the need to constantly test one's strength against an opponent meant that gatherings between the tribes were not generally the best idea. The actions of individuals such as Saul and Sly only made things worse, but tonight felt like a special night and the usual stupid antics associated with such an event were being kept to a minimum, thankfully. Only six fights had broken out, including the one that had led to Arden's broken nose.

'Try not to touch it so much. Socket snapped it back

into place, it looks fine. Just... swollen.' Kiras giggled as he winced once more.

He looked at his new friends and felt comfort in their presence. An absorbed Socket exchanged war stories with an old warrior from Bane's tribe, his barking laugh loud enough to startle the dog asleep beside his feet. The poor canine stood to attention, head moving from side to side in anticipation of attack. A few scratches on top of his scruffy head put him at ease once more and Arden smiled as he saw him slowly drift off into a peaceful sleep.

On the next table Kiras playfully teased Baldor. Each time the mammoth warrior looked away from his drink, she would pour a small amount into her own and when he turned back, she would laugh at his confusion as he slowly scratched his head. She caught Arden's eye, so he tipped his head and grinned like a child. She winked and continued her little game.

Baldor finally caught on and decided to enact his revenge, stealing his friend's drink and downing it in one quick motion; the volume of his belch on putting the drink down shook the hall, and many of the men within it paused and stared at the great warrior. His booming laugh bounced through the room, contagious to the rest of the warriors, and the nerves in Arden's stomach eased slightly. Baldor gave a startled Kiras a kiss on the top of her head before calling a young maid over to fill up their glasses for another round of drinks.

The good feeling within the room even extended to Sly. The scarred warrior threw a set of cards across a table busy with drinks of all kinds. A few members of the other tribes sat with him, eyes glancing from the cards to the wild warrior. Arden stood up and moved over to sit next to him; Sly only offered him a small grunt of recognition – no barbed remark, no warning to move away. A small victory. He let Arden watch him as he cheated the others out of whatever they were using to bet with. Arden noticed a variety of small daggers placed in a pile on the table nearby and felt that next time he saw Sly outside of the hall, his ally would have new weapons to add to his already vast collection.

Suddenly, a horn blasted through the room followed by a wall of silence. Saul stood in the middle of the room, glaring at all in attendance, daring them to give him reason to explode. The unpredictable warrior cracked a grin and raised his hands in the air.

'It has been an age since we all last sat in this hall

together. The greatest men of our realm are gathered here today, warriors who have proven their worth on the battlefield a countless number of times and spilled blood for themselves, their family, their tribe, their people, their honour!' Saul grinned and ran a hand through his long blonde mane as the crowd cheered. 'We have been called here by a man you all know well, a proven warrior. Listen to what he has to say, it will affect every life in this room. Lend him your ears for just a moment, and then the festivities and fighting can commence once more!' he bellowed, his roar echoed by others in the hall. Arden saw him stare intently at Sly, the dangerous look greeted with a smirk. Bad blood existed between those two like a cracking wall of ice about to break, and Arden didn't want to get caught up in the mess when it collapsed.

The roars drifted away as Raven stood in front of the wooden throne at the far side of the hall and raised an open palm to ask for silence. Saul took his seat and clicked his fingers at a nearby maid. Her eyes widened in fear as she rushed a huge goblet of wine over to him. He snatched the goblet without even giving her a second glance. She scuttled off into the shadows as he began to pour the drink right into the huge chasm of his mouth.

'It is rare to see such men here together. Sly, a warrior with perhaps one of the bloodiest and manic reputations in the Borderlands.' Raven gave them all a wide grin as they cheered while Sly raised a dagger in the air, acknowledging his leader. 'Bane, the first man from a southern kingdom to rise to chieftain in our lands and someone known to have bested nine barbarians on his own after they dared to wake him from his slumber.' A large bald man with skin as black as the night sky stood at the back of the room. He flicked his wrist towards Raven at these words and laughed at the memory. His golden pupils flashed in the light, giving the warrior a strange look, like the sun shining in the night sky. Arden felt a thrill of excitement in his stomach. He'd heard tales of Bane. A southerner, a mage, and a chief. A rare combination. 'Kiras, the most fearless woman in the Borderlands or any other realm that I have seen.' She waved and gave a small bow to the cheering crowd. 'And Saul, a master swordsman whose name everyone in the Borderlands and beyond knows to fear – our leader and a great warrior.' The biggest cheer yet rang out as tankards were raised, ale sloshing everywhere in the room, but no one seemed to care. The famed warrior only sat in his chair, eyes fixed on Raven, face impassive.

'Our people are not known for our love of each other. We do not waste time pretending that we are something we are not. We are warriors who fight for ourselves, for our family, for our tribe. Now, I have brought you together to fight for more than that.'

Silence choked the room to such an extent that Arden thought he could see some people struggling to breathe with the tension that had been left behind in the wake of Raven's words. None of the warriors were drinking, many were standing, eyes fixed on Raven. Saul narrowed his eyes, drink almost forgotten in his huge hand as he sat pondering the words of the man before him.

Things could have been going worse; at least no one had attempted to kill him yet. A minor miracle considering the environment.

'Last week, a group of warriors – myself included – scouted a region looking for clues to a few recent disappearances. We found wolves eating the leftovers of a kill,' Raven informed them all.

'Nothing unusual about that!' One of Bane's men called out. 'They are wolves! They need to eat!' Raven patiently waited for the laughter to die down before continuing.

'Usually I would agree with you Greybeard. This was no normal patrol though. We were barely fifteen miles from where we are drinking and laughing right now; part of their meal still bore the mark of the wolf.'

Urgent muttering broke out at these words and a few cautious looks were cast towards the door, as though they felt that at any minute the wolves were going to run in and attack them while they held their meeting. Saul shifted uncomfortably, rubbing his knuckles at the thought of a member of his own tribe being bested by one of those creatures.

'The corpses we found were fresh, but they were not killed by any wolf.' Arden felt that he would be able to hear a feather drop in the room at that moment. All eyes faced Raven, listening to his every word. 'Barbarians, my friends. Men, women and *children*. All killed by a group of barbarians.'

A wall of noise erupted as curses were roared and vows spat from every corner of the room. Arden winced and raised his hands to his ears, unable to cope with the insane volume. Need to get Borderland warriors riled up? Mention the barbarians.

'Let's kill 'em and be done with it!' one of the warriors bellowed to much agreement from the others.

'For too long have we let them build and settle in the Far North. Kill every last one of them!' More roars. Raven raised a hand. Silence.

'Brothers and sisters. Today, we make our decision. The Barbarians are growing desperate, roaming too close to our lands. Lands that we have fought for. Lands that many have died for!' He had them right where he wanted them now. Arden always appreciated a good speaker. It's why he loved listening to bards – people who could draw an audience in so that they were willing to follow whatever nonsense they might spout. 'We killed most of the Barbarians that we found on our patrol. But we left *one* alive...'

Low whispers broke out as the warriors looked around the room, tightening their fingers into balls and looking for the Barbarian. Saul stood up from his seat. 'Cray, bring him in.'

All heads turned as one to the back of the room. Arden spotted a grim warrior. Shaved head, folded arms and a face that looked as though it had been squashed by a battering ram more than once. His wide, squashed nose barely seemed to stick out from beneath his dark, beady eyes. He unfolded his arms and pushed open the wooden doors.

A harsh wind could be heard biting through the hall as the warriors waited with bated breath; waiting for one of their mortal enemies to enter the room. A moment later, Cray had returned, rope tightly in hand. He walked forward between the many benches and tables, followed closely by a haggard, frightened man with wild hair and even wilder eyes.

In an instant, the room erupted like a volcano. Wine, ale, saliva, fruit, bones – even a mangled boot – all flew through the air. The Barbarian shirked away from the missiles with not a trace of anger on his worn face. No malice. Arden couldn't believe this was the man who had tried to kill him. The man who had killed Dakkar. He seemed half the size and nowhere near as intimidating. Only pity was left inside Arden as he stared at the defeated man.

The missiles and curses continued all the way to the front, some even hitting Cray as accuracy had worsened with the copious amounts of drinks the warriors had got through already. He just shrugged them off, barely seeming to notice the impact.

The missiles stopped as they finally reached the front.

Raven took the rope as Cray sidled off into the shadows, arms folded once more, a splash of red wine spilled down his brown overalls.

Ovar, the son of Erik looked around the room, searching for something. Then he found it.

The Barbarian's eyes met Arden's and the archer froze on the spot, unable to tear his eyes away from the man who had tried to kill him. Such a sadness lurked behind those dark eyes that Arden eventually had to look away before it consumed him. He was a warrior now. Part of the tribe. He did not know pity.

Or at least, he shouldn't.

Raven pulled on the rope and Ovar fell to his knees, tied hands unable to prevent him from falling. He crawled his way back up to his feet. Laughter. Arden couldn't take it. He stood up from the bench and stormed towards the door.

'Not yet kid. Gotta watch the show,' Sly muttered, hand against Arden's chest. 'Sit.'

Arden sat next to him, ignoring the curious glances from the few warriors who had torn their gaze away from their enemy. 'I can't watch this!' he seethed through gritted teeth, leaning towards Sly.

'Then close your eyes. If you leave, you won't have any eyes to close. We don't have a chance to choose kid. Gotta sit there and watch, or at least seem to. This is the Borderlands. This is how it is.'

Ovar leant back onto his legs now, rocking on his knees, eyes unable to focus. Arden wondered when he'd last been fed or given water. He shuddered at the thought of how much he had suffered since being captured. *If only the fucking arrow had killed him!*

'This here is the maggot who killed Dakkar!' Raven roared. Warriors in the room yelled their disgust, their tributes to Dakkar. Half of them probably didn't even know him. That's what happened when a crowd of people are joined by hatred; they seem to just go along with each other – a hive mentality over all sense and logic. 'His people killed innocent men, women and children.'

'We killed the men. A couple of us warned him against killing the kids. Didn't listen...' Ovar muttered to more roars.

'Your people have trespassed on our lands and killed our people. I promise, it will be the last time. This is the Borderlands!' Raven yelled into the hall. Ovar only swayed back and forth on his knees, barely able to stay vertical. 'My friends of the Borderlands, my brothers and sisters. We go to the Far North. We go to war!' More roaring. Arden felt sick.

Saul stood. A hush fell over the room as he patiently stepped forward, boots tapping against the wooden stage; his every movement carefully chosen, like an actor around the firepit telling his story. Saul slowly drew his huge, famed crimson broadsword, Deathblow. Arden's eyes met Ovar's one final time. He thought he saw a smile, or maybe that was a trick of the light as the flames danced their haunting jig.

Arden closed his eyes, but he couldn't escape the deep thud as Ovar's head hit the ground. He couldn't escape the cheer that greeted it.

He opened his eyes, feeling the bile at the back of his throat as his stomach turned.

'This is the Borderlands. This is how it is,' Sly repeated. 'Here, this helps.'

Arden took the jug of ale offered to him and leaned back. He gulped over and over as the drink continued its path down his throat. There wasn't enough room; some of the liquid overflowed and he felt the ale cascading down his chest. He didn't care. Finally, the jug emptied. He slammed it onto the wooden table, smirking as Sly widened his eyes and ran his tongue across his cracked lips.

'I want another one,' Arden said, holding back the gas rising in his throat.

'That's more like it.' Sly barked, throwing his head back and thumping him across the back. 'This is the Borderlands.'

Waking up from a nightmare is usually a relief. Sure, there's the few moments when you're uncertain of what is going on as your brain struggles to grasp reality and put it side to side with the fiction that had just been invented during sleep. Unfortunately for Arden, this wasn't fiction.

He groaned, suddenly aware of the aching throb in his head. Not a piercing pain; a thick ache that assaulted his head at once. He felt another ache, this one all over his nose. Suddenly, he remembered it all. The nightmare that had been the night before. The broken nose from the fight. The beheading of Ovar. The ale. The card games. Sly destroying him. Stumbling to the empty barn. Crying as he saw the blood-stained beam.

Eventually, he had crawled into the shadows, curled up

in the scratchy hay and passed out. He opened his eyes, squinting at first as the light from the morning stabbed at him through the open door at the front of the barn. He closed his eyes and crawled further into a corner. Today was a day of rest and recovery. He didn't plan on moving at all.

A moment later, the heavy thud of boots made their way into the barn. He struggled to open his eyes but failed, managing only to make the ache in his head worse.

'Don't worry, it's empty,' a familiar voice said over the howl of the wind. 'Close the door behind you.'

'Couldn't we do this somewhere else, Raven?' Socket. Arden knew that voice. He froze in the hay, not wanting to be seen in this embarrassing state.

'This is top secret. Just between the two of us, for now,' Raven answered.

'I got goose bumps all over,' Socket replied sarcastically.

'Bane passed on some news earlier,' Raven said, ignoring the older man. 'My brother, Braego. He's dead.'

Arden heard a high-pitched whistle. 'Shit. Didn't think he would ever die. Especially living in that soft city. Who's watching the kid?'

'That's the problem. I need to go and sort something out. The King's ill, things are changing. I don't like it, not one bit.'

'What you wanna do then? Want me to go with you?' Socket asked.

'Nah. I need you to take the boy north with Saul's lot. Get him to Korvus, he'll know what to do with him. Can't take him south. If he's recognised in Archania, there will be too many questions. No point risking it.' *Who were they on about?*

'Haven't seen that bastard for a while. Should be fun. Who you taking?'

'Sly, Bane, Baldor. Kiras can go with you to a point; she's friends with the boy. He'll trust her.'

'Makes sense. Want me to tell the boy anything? He's old enough now. Don't want to leave it too late.'

Raven paused. 'Not yet. Being the heir to the throne is a burden many struggle to bear. I know that... Throw in the Guardian shit and he'll fuckin' kill himself.'

'As if he doesn't have enough to deal with, those golden eyes of his cause enough problems without all that shit.'

'This is the Borderlands, we all got our shit to deal

with. Come on, let's get out of here before they realise we're missing.'

Arden waited until he heard the door close behind them before he felt safe enough to breathe again. He sat up, ignoring the pain and opening his eyes. Blood pumped with each thump of his heart against his chest, increasing the ache in his head.

Heir to the throne? What the fuck did that mean?

He rolled onto his side, barely able to move. The vomit burned his throat and his eyes bulged as his previous night's meal choked him on its way back up. Never again would he drink with Sly. The pain was too intense. He couldn't even remember what they had been talking about. He closed his eyes, head thumping as he tried his best to stay still and accept the darkness.

THE DIRTY WORK

The drop in temperature forced Cypher to pull his robes tighter around his skinny frame as he bounded down the stone steps, heading deeper into the palace's darker, seedy side. *Surely someone could light some fires down here occasionally? Am I not doing the dirty work of the realm? Why should I have to endure such an inconvenience when I am providing a service that few others in the land would come anywhere near?*

For five years Cypher had been the man called upon to find answers and information from prisoners in the name of the King of Archania, and for five years he had been refining his skill in the ways of asking the right questions.

Torturer they had called him. Monster. Beast. And a few other names that weren't so nice. He liked to think of himself as an artist – underappreciated even though none could claim to be better at his craft. People always wanted to listen to the stories of heroes as they run around killing and fighting in wars. They didn't appreciate the blacksmith, working day and night to ensure they had the correct equipment. The falchion. The sabre. The axe. The helmet. The hammer. The list was endless. He was like that blacksmith. He provided the foundation for those glorious stories. He was the one getting his hands dirty.

He ran his fingers over the scratched, wooden handle of the hammer that hung constantly at his side. *Of course, any artist needs the right tools for the job*. The hammer usually worked when being used by a professional and Cypher really was the best in his line of work.

He reached the bottom of the stairs, lips curling at the

chorus of screams that greeted him past the black, rusty iron gates – a song he cherished more than any other. *I guess that someone else has arrived to work early today. No need for me to warm them up then, I can get straight into the fun.*

'Oooohhh…' He breathed in, throwing his head back and pursing his lips as though kissing a lover. 'My favourite. I can feel the music coursing through these bones of mine,' he muttered to himself, clicking his fingers, eyes closed, feet gracefully stepping forward in a rhythm only he could feel.

Cypher grabbed the keys out of his pocket, tunelessly whistling as he found the right one for the gate and opened the familiar, creaking door that led into the dark, dingy tunnel. More screams. He locked the door behind him and reached out for a candle from the wall to his right. Once he struck a match against the stone wall, shadows danced in the flames as the chorus continued in the background. *Beautiful.* He continued his dance towards the welcoming screams, unable to keep a smile off his old, worn face.

The heat from the flame and the sound of the screams made him feel at home. This was where he felt most comfortable. This was where he could create his finest works of art. He peered in through the barred doors that he passed, looking at the starved and tired prisoners locked away for crimes against the Kingdom. He could see their ribs, sticking out like grotesque xylophones ready to be played.

The prisoners were all broken of course, it never took long for it to happen. First, they would deny any crime they were said to have committed, then the fun would begin. They would start off defiant, trying their best to fight their way out or spitting at the jailer to prove that they weren't going to lie down easily. Then the hammer would come out. Answers followed. If not, then Cypher had more tools that could be relied upon, more instruments to create his masterpiece. They would all break, guilty or not.

Guilty. Such a strange word. Most of these men and women that were huddled in the shadows of their cells, covered in their own piss and faeces, were not guilty. In fact, most had no idea why they were dragged from the street in the dark of the night and forced to respond to questions they could never truly answer.

Cypher's job ensured the Archanian people knew to live in fear of the consequences of crossing those in power. From time to time, he and his team of talented individuals would stumble upon someone actually guilty. These prisoners were treated differently, publicly. The boy Tate had barely spent an hour in his cell before Mason D'Argio had personally come to look for him and drag the tearful young man up from the dungeons and into his own questioning chamber. Not even Cypher knew what happened in there, but none of them would ever last long. Begrudgingly, he had to silently admit to himself that if anyone could reach his own level of artistry in this field, Mason and his eastern ally T'Chai would be top of the list. A distant second and third perhaps.

The screams grew closer and the feeling of excitement rose inside Cypher. *This thrill has kept me feeling young these last five years.* Every torture was different. Unique. They may end the same, but it's the journey, not the destination that holds the joy.

He reached the wooden door and pushed his slight frame onto his toes so that he could look inside the room. A young man cowered in the corner, his arms held out across his face in a futile attempt to protect himself from the giant of a man standing over him, knuckles bruised and bloodied.

'Glad to see your enthusiasm for the job has not diminished Zaif,' Cypher called through the door with a laugh.

The brutish man turned around. Bent nose, lank, dirty brown hair that fell to his chin and a smile that displayed many of his missing teeth, 'It's good to be back you son of a bitch. Been too long.' He walked over to the door and pulled the iron bolt across to allow Cypher to enter the room.

'How long has it been, Zaif?' asked Cypher as he shook the massive hand offered him.

Zaif stroked the stubble on his chin and thought for a moment, 'Must be two years since I got sent east. A good change of scenery but it's made me miss this place like crazy. Things are better here. Simple. Colder,' he stated with his gummy grin.

Cypher chuckled. His apprentice hadn't changed one bit.

'Please help me.' The man in the corner crawled over to Cypher, hoping that the newcomer may be of some assistance. How wrong could a man be?

It gave him a chance to give the man a proper look for the first time. Bruises and blood coated almost every inch of his face. Both eyes were swollen, and his jaw hung slightly loose and to the right.

'I see you still enjoy hanging out with the pretty ones, Zaif.' Cypher swung a boot straight into the man's nose and felt bone crunch. The beaten man squirmed on the ground; muffled cries broken by a harsh cough.

'So, what's the story with this one, Cypher?' Zaif asked casually. He hadn't even found out why this one had been locked up and he had already caused this mess. He learnt from the best. A feeling of pride burst into his chest – just for a moment. Cypher pushed it away.

'The man you are currently looking at is a low-born scumbag. He has lived his life in the Norland lower city. He has robbed many people, raped possibly hundreds of women, murdered a few I suspect,' Cypher said, as though trying to sell a prize racehorse. 'Oh, and he likes to dabble in magic. I've been told that we should play up the mage thing. Big plans. We need this one to go well, written letters and everything. Need it as convincing as possible.'

More lies to keep us and the Archanian people entertained. Complete and utter bullshit as usual. Cypher loved it.

'I can work with that.'

'Please,' begged the prisoner, 'I wasn't even born in a northern region. I am from a smaller city to the West; I am a missionary. I only wanted to spread the message of The Four. Never in my wildest dreams would I want to hurt anyone. A friend told me this Kingdom was a tolerant and open-minded one.'

A preacher. Now we have the real reason for why this man is here. Any person who enters the Kingdom with tales of the old Gods and ideas that differ to the Mason D'Argio's and his allies always seemed to end up in here, on charges of rape and murder. Quite the coincidence you could say.

Cypher knelt down slowly and stared the man straight into his eyes, 'Where are your Gods now? Why don't they strike us down for attacking you if you are so innocent? I am afraid that in these lands, there is only one God. Let me tell you, He does not give a fuck about your life.'

'My God has four faces. He is true and just. He will not interfere in the lives of men directly,' the prisoner snapped back. A little bit of fight. Obviously more fun could be had with this one.

'Oh, my dear fellow, I can see we're going to be good

friends, you and I. Very good friends indeed. The Four have a temple here, still, in the Lower City. A relic of a time long past.'

'Why do you behave in such a barbaric manner? Do you not have any feelings for a person suffering an injustice?' the prisoner continued, tears falling from his bruised and swollen eyes.

'Not really. It's our job to ignore that kind of bullshit. You're guilty. There is no injustice,' Cypher explained in a matter-of-fact manner.

'Curse you!' he spat blood through his broken teeth directly onto Cypher, 'This is not the end.'

Cypher stood and took the tissue that Zaif held out for him and wiped the blood from his face. 'Of that you can be certain, my friend. This is most definitely not the end.'

He raised the hammer and brought it down with all his strength directly onto the man's right knee. The sound it made mixed with the screams of the prisoner sounded like the greatest piece of music to Cypher's ears. 'This, is just the beginning.'

'Weaponry advances at a rate faster than anything else I can think of, certainly faster than we humans are progressing. There is a weapons room on the second floor of this majestic building. Every wall in the room is lined with weapons that have been gathered from various parts of the known world: spiked clubs from the savage Borderlands past the Great Lake; scimitars from the Sunny Eastern Empire; even a bow made from human bone believed to be from the jungle cities of the deep Southern Kingdoms. Every society since the dawn of time it seems have been able to create weapons intended to defend or conquer. Civilization progresses at a slow pace, quicker in some areas than others but this is always second to the advancement of weapons. Violence and the tools for violence are the most important areas to focus on for our species. The story of Malaris the Third, one of the greatest kings in our history, springs to mind; I'm sure you have heard the tale numerous times.'

Cypher knelt next to the broken man. 'Outnumbered against a bunch of savages that had ambushed him on the road to his son's birth, it seemed as though the man that we know as our greatest ever leader would die before his legend could even begin. Only by chance had Malaris been ambushed by Barbarians not versed in the way of bow and arrow. Twenty archers were able to defeat one hundred of the filthy bastards and the King managed to make his son's birth and become our great leader. I digress. The lesson in this story is that weapons may advance at a rate faster than anything else in the known world but when I want questions fucking answered you can take your clubs, your scimitars and your bows and shove them in a place that would be... most uncomfortable. I have this.' Cypher flipped the hammer in his right hand and grinned at the broken man as tears continued to fall down his face. 'This is my tool, my instrument, and it always gets the job done. Time is irrelevant. You start giving me the answers I want right now and we can miss out any more nastiness. Or I can make the next hour seem like the longest of your life and then I'll force the answers out of you. Either way, I win.'

Cypher focused his gaze on the man's face, and he noticed his mouth twitch with the effort of trying to speak.

'You can have your answers,' the prisoner mumbled, beaten.

Cypher turned to Zaif and laughed at the look on his friend's face; it was comparable with taking away a child's favourite toy and replacing it with cow dung.

'Apologies, Zaif. It appears this one has a bit of sense. Of course, if we don't like the answers then I believe it will be play time once more.'

The giant man cracked his huge knuckles and gave a menacing growl; a bit theatrical, but in this line of work, the theatrics often worked best. The prisoner's eyes were bloodshot and bruised but still they allowed the release of yet more tears. His body shook with sobs. Now, they could get somewhere.

'Where is the land of your birth?'

'Norland.'

The hammer struck the inside of the prisoner's knee and his body swung ninety degrees with the force of the blow. Screams rang out once more and Zaif threw his head back and laughed like he had just seen the funniest thing in his life.

'I must inform you that I am to be referred to as "My Lord" during this special question and answer stage of our time together. Failure to do so will result in more blows. Am I understood?' Cypher asked the traitor.

Zaif clapped his hands and hooted with more laughter. Always one for enjoying the show. Cypher loved an appreciative audience; it was always so hard to find one down here.

'Yes, I understand.' Cypher coughed and raised the

hammer, 'My Lord.'

'You may see it as an insignificant thing, but I assure you, it is the little things that are essential in this line of work. Now, where is the land of your birth?'

'Norland, my Lord.'

'Why have you come to Archania?'

'To spread a message of hope and love, my Lord,' he mumbled.

Crack. The hammer swung again. More laughter. More pain. Wrong answer.

'You came here to preach your message of hatred and sow seeds of doubt amongst the people of Archania. Why have you come to Archania?'

'To preach hatred and sow seeds of doubt, my Lord.'

'Correct. Are you ready to accept your punishment for following a false God and attempting to spread your heresy?'

'I am ready to accept my punishment, my Lord.'

The hammer swung a final time, landing a strong blow across the jaw to prevent any more answers and sending the prisoner into a sleep he did not know whether he would wake up from.

'Well Zaif, time for a short break I believe. We've earned it. A good day's work.'

He grinned and led the way out of the cell. 'You haven't lost your touch, Cypher. You were born for this.'

Born to torture and kill? Born to strike fear into men and women whether they were innocent or not?

'We all have our roles to play, I suppose. Our roles are infinitely better than that bloody mess on the floor.'

'Let's grab some food. All this fun makes me hungry.'

Torturer. Monster. Artist. All need food.

'Why do you still eat here, Cypher? Surely you can afford to eat somewhere better, in the Upper City. Somewhere less—' Zaif muttered.

'Shit,' Cypher butted in through a mouth full of bread and meat.

'Well, yeah,' Zaif agreed.

'Keeps me humble. Don't ever want to forget where you're from, do you?' Cypher added with a wink.

He'd grown up in the Lower City, surrounded by the muck and filth that seeped into all corners of the hideous area.

The Lower City is where he'd begged for scraps of food, where he'd seen his drug-addled mother kill his father, where he'd watched as she took her own life, where he'd been taken in by whores and thieves, where he'd taken his first life. The Lower City is where he felt at home.

Zaif flicked a dead fly from the table with a look of disgust. 'Could do with a wipe over or two.'

'Part of its charm. Maybe you've got used to a different way during your time in the East?' Cypher suggested.

'Perhaps. It's a very clean empire. Punishments are harsh for those who do not take care for the land,' Zaif explained.

'Bit of dirt never hurt nobody,' Cypher claimed. 'But I suppose it gives them more reasons for torture. Can't complain with that.'

Cypher took a swig of the dirty water and looked around the dilapidated tavern. It was filthy. Nothing wrong with that. He even thought he saw the hurried scurry of a rat in the corner of the room as it squeezed through one of the many holes in the wall. Even the rats wanted out of the dirty tavern.

A clatter from behind informed Cypher that the tavern had some newcomers. Rare. This place was usually dead at this time. It was one of the things he most enjoyed about it. Peace and quiet.

'Are the others here yet?' Cypher heard one of them ask in a low voice. Curious, he looked to his left, over his shoulder and at the bar. A couple of figures were leaning against the bar, each dressed exactly alike – black robe with a black belt on which rested a small black pouch; black leather mantle underneath a black balaclava; short black hat with a circular rim running all the way around their heads; black gloves. And most distinctive of all, a black mask with huge black circles for eyes and a large protruding beak-like nose. No prizes for guessing their favourite colour. Cypher recognised the outfit, though he hadn't seen it being worn in a good few years.

'Plague doctors,' Zaif muttered.

'But where's the plague?' Cypher asked.

'In the back, they're waiting,' the barman said to the newcomers. 'Usual drinks?'

'Aye, and a bit of meat. We might be a while.' A rough voice. Lower City accent. Local.

'Consider it done,' the barman agreed with a short bow.

The men headed past Cypher and Zaif, the first one tapping the wooden floorboards with a long, thin, black cane with a golden sun at its head.

Cypher couldn't help himself. 'Gentlemen!' The two figures turned and faced him silently, beaks pointing towards him. Cypher assumed that meant they were paying attention. 'Is there something we should be aware of? Something we should be worried about?' he sang out to them, hands out in front of him, eyebrows raised in mock confusion.

'Cypher Kellin,' the one with the cane answered, voice slightly muffled through the mask. Cypher dropped the look of confusion. The man knew him. Cypher wasn't holding the best hand right now and he hated it. 'One such as yourself should always be worried.'

'It's Zellin. Enlighten me,' Cypher grinned at him, eyes lowering, staring straight up at the masked figure. 'I do so love a good story.' He leaned forward, elbows resting on the cracked, wooden table.

'Have you not heard the cries of Takaara? The shakes that threaten to tear our world apart? Perhaps the palace dungeons are immune to such suffering.'

'The palace dungeons are nothing but suffering, my dear fellow. The cries of the guilty must be drowning out these shakes, or perhaps they are causing it!' Cypher scoffed. Zaif chuckled along, enjoying the show.

'You can laugh, but you can't block out the pain this world is going through. This land is diseased, broken. There is a plague, and we, The Doctors, are here to heal it.' The dark figure slapped his hand against his companion who let out a short squeal before standing up straight once again.

'A plague, you say? What plague is this?' Cypher began to thoroughly enjoy himself, easing into his role and running his tongue around the inside of his cheeks. Madness had always been one of his favourite abnormalities to play with. Like a child with his first toy sword.

'The plague of the rich, the powerful. For too long, the whims of the few have destroyed the needs of the many. A great healing is on the way. The Doctors will ensure it!' He banged his gloved fist on the table. Cypher stayed as still as stone. Beautiful. Such passion. He had to admire it.

'You must be young. I remember this land suffering. The war. The fighting. The death. An *actual* plague – maybe you remember the one that took our dear Queen's life? I remember it all. I miss it. Those were the days, eh? Today, there is none of that. You complain about the rich and the powerful. I grew up fifty paces from this tavern. Son of a whore addicted to faze. Now, I work in the Upper City, I have enough gold and silver to do whatever the fuck I please. If these peasants and filthy beasts want a better life, then tell them to get their lice-addled bodies out of the gutter and go and grab it!'

The man brought his black mask to within an inch of Cypher's face, leaning as close as he dared. Cypher could smell the man's stale breath seeping through the material. He dropped a hand below the table and chewed at the corner of his mouth.

'There is a war. A war between those who have, and those who have not. The King is dying, there are rumours that his children are bastards, not even of the royal bloodline. Men and women are being burned alive. This is a different kind of war to the one you and your kind are used to. I promise, we will win Cypher Zellin. We will win this war.'

'A war against those who have, means a war against the royal family. You realise that?' Cypher asked, running a hand softly up his thigh.

'We know exactly what we are doing, *torturer*.' The man spat back, the stench of his breath smacking Cypher in the face.

'Good, as long as we understand each other.'

The hidden blade shot up from under the table and straight through the man's neck; the leather proved no defence. Cypher slid the blade out, stained with blood. The man tried to raise his hand to the wound, but he moved too slowly. Cypher jumped onto the table and stabbed again. And again. And again. And again.

The Doctor dropped forward onto the table, blood seeping out from the wound and through the cracks in the table. Cypher looked down at his blood-stained hands and smirked, running them over his face as he closed his eyes and breathed in.

'Oh God, oh God, oh God.' The other Doctor had backed into the corner, falling to the ground and cradling his knees with his arms, rocking back and forth. The commotion had alerted the men in the back room. Five Doctors poured out of the room, all in black, of course.

'The Gods don't listen; I can assure you of that.' Cypher smirked.

'Please, no more,' the barman whimpered behind his barrels.

The Doctors paused, masks aimed up towards Cypher, weighing the situation as they looked from him with his red blade, dripping onto the lifeless body beneath him, to the silent, monstrous Zaif, standing now, huge sword gleaming in the dim light.

'You must all be The Doctors. I hear that you are here to heal the land!' Cypher roared with a laugh, swaying back on the table with glee. Today had turned out even better than he had expected. 'If that is true. Start with him.' He leapt off the table, throwing a silver coin to the barman who just continued to shake behind the bar. 'Apologies for the mess. Won't happen again.'

BELONGING

'Two days feeling that rough? Shit, one morning of a hangover is bad enough. What were you drinking?' Kiras chuckled.

'Honestly, I can't remember much of it.' Arden shrugged as she laughed at him and hit him on the back. He tried his best to not show her the pain it caused. He was a warrior now. Time to act like it.

'I'd have a shred of sympathy for ya, but you were warned! Only Baldor can drink with that mad bastard!' She was right. He had been warned. Didn't make the pain any less. Just upped the regret. She winked, pulling her wolfskin hood up as she stepped out into the calm, cold village. 'Let's find the old man, he'll want to get moving soon.'

Arden attached his worn, oaken bow to his sling and pulled it tight so that he could feel it resting against his back. He looked at the daggers left forgotten on the log next to him. An image of Sly with mad eyes, snarling and hungry for blood, popped into his head. *You can never have too many daggers, kid. Never.* He picked one up, small with a black leather grip and a curved tip. It slotted with ease into a gap in his belt as looked up to see Kiras grinning at him.

'What?'

'Nothing...' she answered. 'Let's go.'

Thankfully, the wind had finished its usual barrage and Arden managed to pull up his hood, lined with white bearskin to combat the cold. He didn't mind the harsh conditions of the Borderlands but an icy wind felt like a right bastard at times; cut the cheeks worse than a knife.

Wooden longhouses wore hats of white from the week's worth of snow that had fallen in the past two days. Groups of women from the village were craning up to remove the sword like icicles threatening to fall from the edges of the slanted roofs above the doorways. A few of them waved in greeting and shouted joyfully over to Kiras as Arden paced behind her. To the women of the Borderlands, she was a hero. A beacon of strength who reminded them that this was not a man's world but one for everyone.

One of the women, barely older than Arden he thought, red cheeked with long, white blonde hair offered her own greeting to Arden, winking and licking her lips as he passed her by. He swallowed hard, mouth suddenly dry as he attempted a response. All he could force through was a dull grunt and a meagre nod. Still, she giggled as he felt the blood rush to his cheeks. And to other parts as he noticed her curvy figure.

'Shame we're off fighting with the men when we could be kept warm by beauties like her, eh?' Arden almost fell over as Kiras stopped in front of him and flashed her eyes to the flirtatious woman. 'He'll be back soon ladies. A few scars maybe, but more than able to carry out some hard labour...' The women roared with laughter as Arden looked away, attempting to hide his embarrassment. 'Nothing young women love more than a warrior back from his first true battle. At least that's what I've been told,' Kiras whispered to Arden, smiling at his horror.

'Is that what you think?' he asked her, concentrating on the cold to fight away the hot thoughts running through his head.

'Me? I'm all for fighting amongst the men, but when I'm home, nothing beats a warm bed with a new woman. You'll see! Homecoming is always the best part of any raid or war.'

Arden looked over his shoulder at the rosy-cheeked woman. Her sea-blue eyes still followed him. He wondered if they'd meet again and if she would look at him the same. Maybe he'd be back, covered in scars. Maybe he would be missing a limb or an eye, like Socket.

Maybe he wouldn't come back at all.

'I hope I get to see it.'

'You will. I'll make sure of that. And remember,' she pulled him in close and leaned into his ear conspiratorially, 'if it's too dangerous, look the other way and run for your fucking life!'

Perfect way to raise the spirits.

'So, what's Socket doing at the moment?' he asked, moving the conversation away from anything uncomfortable for a change. He hadn't seen the old archer for the last couple of days – a mix of him busy organising the trek and Arden fighting what felt like an everlasting battle against the alcohol still trying to kill him.

'Met with Herick – leader of the Bear Tribe. His people live closest to the Barbarians, so he wanted to pick his brain before we head off.'

Herick. Arden had heard of him. Always late to battle. His tribe had more women than men and he allowed most to join him in battle. 'Was Herick there at the gathering the other night?'

'Nah. Late. Some of his tribe were there though. You'll like them. Some right beauties.'

They reached a short, stone bridge that curved over what was usually a running river. As winter approached, the river had frozen, sunlight sparkling down onto the ice and making it glitter as though it was a floor paved with diamonds. Children slipped and slid across the ice, showing no fear that it may suddenly crack and send them to a cold, watery grave.

'Let's ignore the bridge. The river looks more fun today,' Kiras suggested.

To disagree would be to show a hint of cowardice, to show that he wasn't as brave as the small children playing their games fearlessly. 'Sure it's safe?'

'Nope.' She jumped from the snowy path onto the ice and grinned as her dark boots allowed her to glide for a moment. Arden sighed and followed her. His arms flailed wildly in panic as both feet reached the ice. He steadied himself and tried to ignore the stifled laughter from Kiras.

'Should have just used the damn bridge...' he muttered.

'Nah!' Kiras cried. 'Look at how much fun everyone is having!' She waved to a couple of kids gliding past, shoes adjusted with short blades to allow for easier movement. 'I've been bugging Neres, the blacksmith, to make me a pair for ages. He just tells me to grow up. Same argument every year...'

'And yet, you never do...' Arden tried to turn but the movement just made him look as though he was suffering a seizure. Eventually he managed to rotate enough to welcome a newcomer – dark skin and golden pupils.

'Bane...' he whispered to himself as the tribe leader

walked towards them before hopping with ease onto the ice, similar to any who had been born and raised in the Borderlands and not in the stifling heat of the South.

'You know my name, and I know yours, Arden – the mage who is not a mage. Our kind have a way of standing out, do we not?' Bane pointed at his glowing eyes with a knowing smirk.

'Good to see you, Bane.'

'And you, Kiras. It has been too long since our paths last crossed.' The two warriors clasped forearms tightly in the traditional Borderlands greeting.

'Well, we've got a whole journey north to enjoy together. What fun!'

The dark-skinned warrior tilted his head and sighed. 'Alas, the gods have decided our time together is shorter than that. I will be journeying south. My family are in need of me. My father will soon be on his way to the Sky Plane. He will appreciate my return to help him on his way.' His voice dripped with dutiful regret. 'It has been many years since I have seen my family. This must be done.'

'Sorry to hear that. What's wrong with the old man?' Kiras asked, face softening with pity.

'Black lungs. Been coughing up blood for close to two months now, according to my brother's messages. Probably longer; he's a stubborn fool, if he knew that illness had consumed him, then he would have kept it from us. Even the Gods' plans pale in comparison to a stubborn old man at times.'

'Must run in the family,' Kiras laughed.

'You think I'm stubborn? It's a shame you won't get to meet my father. To him, I am as open as a Northern whore.'

'And twice as pretty, I'm sure.'

'I have The Four to bless for my good looks.' The warrior winked, rubbing at his smooth chin with pride.

'I didn't think people in the Southern Kingdoms followed The Four?' Arden said, confused by the words of the tribe leader.

'Most follow the two Gods – of Order and Chaos. My family have never been ones to follow the majority.' Bane chuckled.

'Do you ever regret leaving your family?' Arden's thoughts turned to his mother, the woman who had raised him and cared for him his whole life. Would he have been able to leave her for a new kingdom as Bane had done?

'There's no regret. I had the joy of a childhood with my family, and the experience of learning the ways of the Borderlands as a man. The two cultures have combined to create the man you see before you today, good and bad. I cannot regret who I am,' Bane answered. 'I see the pain in you, Arden. You are unsure of yourself. Remember, those golden eyes are just golden eyes. In the same way my skin is just darker skin. Do not let the words of others define you. Take pride in who you are, make your own decisions. Regret no part of you.'

The words hit Arden like a wave, amazed that the tribe leader had cared to say so much. He thought about the suffering and hardship Bane must have been through on his journey to the Borderlands. He couldn't hide in the shadows. He embraced the light and made something of himself. Damn what other people say, takes real balls to do that.

'Well, our journey may be short but let's make the most of it. Crossing the river?' Kiras asked.

'Yes. Neres needs a reminder to have a weapon ready for me by the end of the day. I've never met such a lazy blacksmith...'

'Too busy making these shoe blades for the kids...' Kiras muttered as a few circled her, cutting the ice up into a ring around her. 'If this breaks, you break,' she warned them, pointing beneath her and smiling as they giggled and raced away.

The trio walked in a line, Arden cautiously trying to keep up with the other two who seemed as sure-footed as if they were walking together on a grassy pathway on a summer's day. As always, Arden just didn't feel comfortable, as though he didn't belong here.

They reached the end of the river and he gave a quiet, relieved sigh, stepping back onto the soft, fluffy snow. He looked at Bane, plucking up the courage to ask him a question he'd wanted answered for a long time. 'Can you use magic?' his voice as quiet as a mouse but without the howling wind, he could be heard.

'In a way,' Bane answered carefully. 'It is... complicated. I am gifted with the ability to cast certain spells. Simple ones. I can shine a small light; help start a fire; increase my strength slightly. But all of it comes at a cost.' Bane warned.

'What cost?'

'Magic requires energy, like most things. The energy

either comes from within, or from the land around you. Our understanding of this energy transference comes from the Four Great Mages, said to be descended from the Gods themselves. People abused the gifts they had been given and it almost destroyed Takaara, scarring the land and creating the chasm that runs south of the Heartlands. Following the destruction, Guardians were born. Powerful magi dedicated to healing the land and balancing the flow of magic. Like everything, the best of intentions lay the foundation for misery. Those in power often abuse their gifts – that's what led to the Great Purge. Magic is not to be meddled with.'

Arden had heard similar stories before. Stories about the Heretic Mage, the one who had turned against the others who believed themselves to be descended from the Gods. He alone had been aware of the folly of their use of magic. He alone had prevented the dying of the world. 'Do you know why I can't use magic? Even though I have these eyes...'

Bane gave him a pitying look that instantly made him regret the question. He didn't need pity; he needed answers. 'I am sorry, Arden. I do not have the knowledge you require. Though, believe me, magic does more harm than good. You are not missing out.'

But he was. If he had no magical ability then why did he have to walk around looking like this, standing out wherever he went, trying to hide in the shadows but never succeeding? He just wanted to be normal, like everyone else. Was that too much to ask?

'Here we are,' Kiras said. The smell of molten iron and coal dust wafted through the air as they reached the doorway, already able to feel the heat from the burning forge. Arden embraced it, eager to get out of the cold.

'Neres Smith. That better be my blade you're making...' Bane warned a small man covered in black dust and wearing a long, leather apron. Around the room, in every nook and cranny, were the widest array of weapons Arden had ever laid eyes on. Axes hung on the blackened stone walls, daggers and swords lay discarded and scattered around the floor and three buckets overflowed with iron arrowheads. Other weapons Arden hadn't seen before were scattered in various areas of the hot room – circular weapons with sharpened points sticking out, a double-bladed staff that was taller than him. Sly would have loved it in here.

'Quit your whining, southerner. Yours is finished. Even

did the runes you asked for on it. Proud of it, I must say,' the blacksmith grinned, showing white teeth between his dust covered lips. 'This here is some shoe-blades for one of the little ones. They love it on the ice.'

Kiras frowned. 'Where are mine?'

'Grow up, little lady!' Neres barked back, causing all four of them to laugh. 'Socket's next door with Herick if you're here for him. Having a drink, last time I checked.'

'Perfect, we'll see you both around. I want them shoe-blades, Neres!' Kiras grinned as she headed into the back room. 'Come on, kid. Let's grab a drink. Maybe just the one for you though...'

The familiar feeling of bile rose up his throat at the thought of another drink. Even the one would be too much right now. 'Just water, I think.'

'Smart.'

'Not so smart. Tried to pour ale down my missing eyehole the other night. Remember that, boy?' Socket roared as they entered the darkened room. He sat on a wooden bench by the fire pit, ale in hand. Next to him, a pale, a slender man with a shaved head gazed unblinking at Arden.

'I can't remember much of that night,' Arden told him, head throbbing at the memories, or lack of them.

'Probably for the best,' the old man said with a smile that let him know he wasn't in trouble. He let go a deep breath and followed Kiras to the table.

'Herick the Late,' she said, sticking two fingers up at the young serving girl making her way over. The girl spun on the spot silently and went to grab the drinks.

'That name will never fade will it? Even as you are walking in here after me. I must be dubbed "the late". In all the battles I have fought, only in three have I been late,' the tribe leader grumbled back, running a hand across his shaved head. He had a warm face, one that seemed easy to trust. Just a small, white scar beneath his bottom lip gave him away as a warrior with a past.

'They are the three that people remember.'

'They seem to forget that all three were won because of me; these warriors never seem to listen when I remind them,' he said, playful annoyance crossing his face.

'Where were you during the gathering?' Kiras asked him, arching an eyebrow knowingly.

Herick squinted at her and grinned. 'Late.' They burst into a chorus of laughter, warming the room.

His tribe was different to the others. They lived on an island to the north east of the Borderlands, a challenging environment that truly tested the character of the men and women who lived there. The ones who survived the difficult lifestyle were ready for battle – men or women.

'How is Baldor?' Herick asked.

'He hasn't changed. He's the same Baldor you knew growing up,' she answered.

'I was hoping he would be here. We have only briefly crossed paths recently. He's a good warrior. A good man. Our tribe misses him.'

'Well, you can't have him back. He's ours now.' Kiras laughed.

Herick raised his hands in defeat and leaned back with an easy smile. 'He's happy. That is all I ever wanted for him. He belongs with your tribe now.'

Kiras placed her hands behind her head, obviously sharing that same feeling. 'He should be coming over in a bit. Raven's currently giving him a few details about the mission south.'

'It is a shame that he is not coming with us. The idea of him being so far from the Borderlands rattles these old bones.' Herick shook his slender frame at the thought. 'Our people aren't meant to stray too far from the homeland.'

Raven's name brought a memory coursing back into Arden's head. Lying in the straw. A secret conversation. An heir to the throne. He rubbed his hands against his warm face and scratched at the thin layer of stubble on his chin. Maybe it had been a drunken dream. A hallucination brought on by the alcohol and his fresh guilt. The sound of Ovar's head thudding against the wooden floor played once more in his mind.

'You okay, kid?' Herick's lowered, emerald-green eyes seemed to bore deep into Arden as he stared at him, as though he could hear the thoughts going through his mind. He felt suddenly uncomfortable, pulling at the collar of his shirt and craning his neck from side to side, feeling a small, series of cracks.

'Yeah, long few days...' He managed to meet Herick's eyes for only a moment before turning away.

'Going to get longer,' Herick muttered, not willing to avert his own gaze. 'I heard you're coming north with us. The

Far North. Blistering winds and deathly cold. The Land of Endless White. Birthplace of the Gods, some say. My home – and the home of our greatest enemy.'

'Everyone claims to live where the Gods were born. Most of it's bullshit,' Kiras jumped in with a laugh.

'One of us has to be right. They had to come from somewhere. A land of pure white. The Great Lake. The Mournful Giant. Those things weren't made by no human, girl,' Herick warned.

Arden had been past the Great Lake only once before. A hunt. Not a successful one. Had to turn back. Too cold, even for him. He'd wanted to go further, to see The Mournful Giant – a legendary stone statue said to be over two-hundred feet high. Those who had seen it had claimed it as the greatest creation in Takaara, a watchful guardian kneeling in the snow at the edge of life itself. Some suggested it was a memento of the time of the Gods; a watcher left by those who came before. Others argued that one of The Four had been frozen in The Endless White, tasked with looking after those who came after. Who knew the truth? That was one of the problems in these lands – lots of big talk, not a lot of evidence. For every claim, there were ten others to dispute it.

'Even the Barbarians believe they are descended from The Four,' Socket snorted as he took a drink.

'The only way that is possible is if they shit the lot of them out. Huge, hairy shits.'

'So, we're going to the Far North to wipe these shits away?' Kiras giggled.

'Off the face of the world, my dear.'

'Why?' It seemed like a simple question. So simple Arden felt unsure why no one had asked it before. 'Why should we wipe them off the face of the world? What have they done that is any worse than us?' The words rushed out of his mouth before he had time to catch them, as though possessed by another; hearing his voice but not controlling the words. The looks around the room informed him that it wasn't a question they had expected.

Herick shuffled in his seat, getting comfortable and lifting his dirty boots onto the table with a heavy breath. 'How long have you lived in the Borderlands, boy?'

'My whole life.' Arden thought he caught a look of annoyance flash across Herick's face as the chief's eyes flickered towards Socket.

'Of course.' In an instant he had relaxed, face warm and welcoming again. 'And how many times have you come face-to-face with a Barbarian?'

Arden thought for a moment. 'I'm unsure,' he said, thinking. 'A couple of times each cycle there would be a raid of some kind, nothing serious. A few injuries, sometimes a death. I've seen more people die at the hands of warriors in my own tribe than at the hands of the Barbarians.'

It was true. He'd seen vicious men. Men who fought. Men who killed. Men who raped. Men who enjoyed all of it. Why were they so different from the Barbarians? It all just seemed so... unfair. He thought of Ovar; the look of utter dismay and fear on his face. He'd had a father, a mother, a family who loved him. Did they deserve to be left without him? Did anyone?

'How many cycles have you seen?'

'Fifteen. Nearly sixteen,' Arden answered, voice cracking under the withering gaze of Herick.

'Fifteen, shit. The next winter will be my fortieth. Do you want to know what I remember from my fifth winter?' Arden didn't, but he had a feeling finding out couldn't be escaped. 'Things weren't so good with the South, the Barbarians thought they would use that to their advantage, attack us while our eyes were elsewhere. It worked, in the beginning. My people were the first hit, and the worst. One of the earliest memories I have is of their attack. Happened in the middle of the night under a new moon. Pitch black it was, until the fires. Oh, the fires, can't forget those. You remember, Socket?'

Socket nodded along, face impassive. 'I remember the fires.'

'Burnt most of our village. Stabbed the men in their sleep. Smashed the heads of the young against the rocks on the coast, blood dripped into the seas – so much it seemed to run red. They weren't focused on taking prisoners. Woman of all ages were dragged from their beds – some were unconscious by the time the skinning started. Five cycles. I can still hear the screams when I close my eyes, screams mixed with laughter. Do you know what hurt my father the most? It wasn't being dragged naked across the stones, it wasn't when they cut his arm off in front of his only son, it wasn't even when they sliced my mother from between her legs, all the way up to the top of her head. It was when they left. They could have taken our island. We didn't have the strength to fight back and they had the strength to take it. Do you know why they left, boy of fifteen cycles?' Herick leaned in close, face lit orange by the flames.

Arden could only shake his head, body shifting closer as he held onto every word being said, drawn into the story.

'They left because they had finished their fun. That's what it is to them. Fun. Our warriors may enjoy some of the nasty stuff but deep down, we are farmers, we are family men, we have our homes, our dreams. The Barbarians live for suffering, for death. They may as well worship the God of Chaos himself. They don't care for order and progression. Only pain and death. They belong in the ground, only bones. They are a hideous joke left by the Gods, an accident, one which we must rectify.' Herick leaned back, downing his ale in one. All warmth had left him, leaving a cold, grey man, aged with worry and grief. 'Does that answer your question boy?'

Arden nodded slowly. But he wasn't sure it did.

UNWELCOME

Being back in Archania after so long away had to leave its mark on Aleister. Too many years away for him to just slot back in and have everything be normal. The first thing he noticed was how wet it was. He hadn't realized how used to the strong heat and dry seasons of the East he had become. Grey skies loomed overhead, blocking out the sun and promising yet more rain. The day before had been the opposite – searing heat. It made no sense. Had it always been like this?

A cold and wet wind blew through the docks as he made his way across the wooden boards, looking out for any sign of an old friend. He took a deep breath in and welcomed the sharp air that blew into his lungs. An old sailor lay down by his feet and mumbled under his breath, holding out an empty bottle in his shaking hand before crouching over and vomiting all over the wooden floorboards.

He was home.

A familiar buzz swarmed about the docks as busy sailors prepared for their next voyage and others dragged in fish from their last journey, loading their wares onto carts sat waiting for them. Not one of them cast a glance at the drunk sailor now passed out in his own vomit.

He walked along the waterfront and tried to ignore the disgusting smell as he passed the barrels and carts loaded with fish. The only smell he could compare it to of late, was of old corpses, something he remembered all too well, unfortunately. He had come back home in the hope that he wouldn't have to be around that smell any longer, but the memories were all too fresh. One day at a time.

He greeted anyone passing with a small tilt of the head, hoping to make this a friendly stay, but grunts and lowered brows were the only response he received. Years ago, he would have taken offence at such a response, but no longer could he be that immature young boy. He was back home and turning over a new leaf. That's the phrase they used in the Heartlands anyway.

One sailor spat at his feet as Aleister passed him. As fast as he could, he kicked the man in the back of his right knee and whipped out a small dagger, curved hilt wrapped around his fists with iron spikes sticking out above the knuckles. He held it close enough to the man's neck to draw small specks of dark red blood.

'Apologise,' he commanded in a low voice.

The sailor took a moment to grasp what had happened before uttering a small cry and following the order. A pool of sweat dripped down his dirty face, leaving clear tracks between the filth.

'Now fuck off and leave me alone.'

The sailor jumped to his feet, rushing away as quick as they could carry him without a backward glance.

One day at a time.

Aleister headed towards the city. Everything seemed the same, but something gnawed at him, an uneasy feeling that wouldn't let go. Greyer perhaps. He put it down to the weather, but he couldn't shake off the feeling that something didn't feel right.

His Darakechean boots splashed in the puddles as rain began to lash down on the grim city from the angry clouds above. A canopy of trees offered a small hope of shelter from the rain and he planned to make his way over to them, when he heard a shout from behind.

He turned to face six angry, dangerous looking men, all staring at him. The man he had threatened stood with them, pointing at him with a look of hate on his face, his hand pressed against his wounded neck.

'Is there a problem, gentlemen?' Aleister asked, as though the earlier incident hadn't happened at all.

The biggest one at the front walked forward and spat on the floor. Dirty habit. 'You hurt one of my friends. Threatened him with a knife. Cut his throat.'

Aleister struggled to stifle a laugh at the surprisingly high voice from a man of his frame. 'Just a little cut. A shave.

Nothing to get all worked up about,' he replied, moving his coat to one side and placing a hand on the hilt of one of his scimitars.

'You could have killed me!' the sailor cried out.

'Yeah, I could have. How nice of me not to. I guess you just struggle showing your appreciation. You're welcome, anyway.'

The men cracked their knuckles and tried their best to look as menacing as possible. After the things he had seen and the places he had been to, he found it cute.

He drew his first scimitar and pointed the curved blade at the biggest one, smiling as he did so. The most vital parts of a fight are the beginning and the end; Aleister needed to make them aware that he felt confident in being able to end this fight, even six against one.

Weapons scraped against scabbards and belts – tattered looking rusted swords and a couple of chains. No crossbows, always a relief. He stepped forward and noticed the worried glances that a couple of them cast at each other. They weren't up to this fight; most likely they were just following the big guy out of fear. He was probably some big shot around the docks who you don't say no to and who wants everything his way. There's always one. Take him out and the rest would fall.

He jumped forward, not allowing his opponents to form any kind of defence, slapping the big man on the neck with the flat of the blade and stepping back, laughing as he did. He wanted to embarrass the bastard, not kill him.

The brute howled with rage and ran at him, waving his weapon wildly in the air with no thought of form or restraint. Comfortably, Aleister stepped to the side and grabbed the man's right arm, hitting his elbow as hard as he could and locking his arm. The sword flew harmlessly out of his hand, landing on the ground five feet away. The crack that sounded made even Aleister wince. *Maybe I did that a little too hard...*

The others hesitated, caught between helping their leader and not wanting to die. Always a tough decision. He knew their next move before they did.

'I'd take the chance to run. You won't get another one,' he warned, growling as low as he could; theatrics could be the difference between six men dying today and one being injured.

As one, they turned and ran back towards the docks, only glancing back sporadically to check on the big man down on his knees.

'Now, you've got a choice,' he started, sword pointed at

the man's neck, 'You can stand up, pick up your sword and we can finish this here and now, ending in your death and an unsolved mystery for some hard-working Inspector. Or you can get up and follow your friends; I'll promise not to kill you unless you cross me again. What's it gonna be?'

The man stared up at Aleister and sighed in surrender. His right arm fell limply at his side – with any luck, it was a clean break and would heal properly in time. He stood slowly and gave one last look at his lonely sword before choosing the correct option and racing after his friends. Aleister sheathed his sword and watched him flee.

'You've been in the city barely half a day and you've already made friends.' Cold steel kissed the back of his neck as he bit his lip, chuckling in recognition at the soft voice behind him.

'What can I say? It must be my charm and good looks.'

'You must have changed a lot since I last saw you then. Still easy to creep up on though. You'd be dead now if I was anyone else.' He had missed that voice – he realised that now – more than he thought he would.

'If you were anyone else then I wouldn't have let you creep up on me,' he answered.

The sword moved away from his neck and he spun around to see a beautiful face framed by dark, red hair. 'You're still too cocky. Didn't draw your other blade.'

'Didn't need to. It's good to see you, Zaina.'

'It has been too long,' she agreed. 'Five fucking years, old friend.'

He was home.

* * *

'Three pints of your best ale please, sir.'

'Of course, Master—'

'Aleister. My name is Aleister. This place has changed a lot since I last ordered a drink at this bar. Last time I was in Archania I believe this pub was owned by a jolly, round man by the name of Darius?'

'Aye, Darius before I took over. Was offered the place by a member of the Church when he died,' explained the barman.

'Died? A shame. How did he go?'

'Burned. Damn mage.' The barman spat on the floor and went away to fill up the glasses.

'A mage? I'd known him for years. His eyes...'

'I know, they'd worked a way around it. Getting more tricksy, the little bastards.'

Aleister took the opportunity to scan the shithole he'd walked into once more. It had been five years since he had last been in Archania; five years since he had a drink with a man named Darius, a man he had been able to call friend. The place back then had been vibrant and full of energy, regulars would welcome newcomers into the bar with kindness, warmth and a pint of the finest local ale. Time, it seemed, had not been good for Archania.

Of course, the Lower City had always had its... rustic charm. A derelict beauty that only the few could really appreciate. Rats, disease, blood, a stale smell of sweat – gave it character in his eyes. Something those in the Upper City failed to grasp. Character. Too many places looked the damn same, wanting to fit in with whatever style was deemed the most important for the season. That wasn't what he wanted. He wanted the filth. He wanted the stench. He wanted... this.

Suspicious looking men huddled together in small groups in the shadows, crowding over their own drinks as their eyes flitted about to anyone that they deemed new and strange. The only men that seemed to hold any bit of happiness and warmth in their actions were the old blokes sitting together on a round table in the middle of the inn; a game of cards and long lives full of experience had distracted them from any of the pettiness and distrust that others in the room seemed to cling onto. Their laughter pleased Aleister in this dark place and reminded him of the sad fact that times were indeed changing.

He couldn't complain about the surroundings too much though; this wasn't even close to the worst place he had been in. A mercenary had to accept work where he could find it and that meant going into places most normal folk wouldn't even dream of.

Ariel and Bathos certainly seemed to be comfortable here, perhaps happy to just be off the road for the first time in a long while. Ariel swung gently back on her chair while picking some chicken out of her teeth with a small dagger whilst Bathos shared his smile with the room, only receiving nervous glances in return. The big man thrived on the anxious looks of others. He felt at home in places like this where the lack of light and dark atmosphere allowed him some freedom to be himself. Put him in clothes made of silk and ask him to dance with a beautiful woman as part of a well thought out distraction plan and he ran for the hills. *Darakeche would have gone so much smoother if he had just put up with it for one night!*

'Three pints. Make sure you and your friends aren't causing any trouble. We don't put up with no funny business round here,' said the bartender returning with the three ales.

'Thank you, good sir, and I assure you we understand this is the last place for funny business to be had.' The barman frowned at him so Aleister flashed a wink, grinning back. 'If there is any chance you could bring over three glasses of Archanian firewhiskey to mine and my friend's table, I would be most grateful. The Gods blessed me with only two hands.'

The bartender lowered his eyes and muttered something that Aleister could not hear, but he got the gist of it. *Strange how matters of religion can make even the best of men prickly. And this was not one of the best of men.*

He walked over to his table, three drinks in hand, nodding to those that spared a glance towards the arrogant newcomer. *I do always enjoy a warm welcome.*

'Enjoy the fruits of our labour once more, my friends.'

Bathos roared gladly and Ariel patted Aleister on the back as he sat down. The three of them raised their drinks, sharing their relief and happiness. Finally, they were off the road and able to enjoy the comforts of warm shelter and good ale.

Aleister lifted his arm from the table and looked at his white sleeve, freshly coated in blood. 'That is, what I think it is, right?' he asked the others.

'If you think it's blood, then yep, definitely,' Ariel said with a chuckle.

Aleister shrugged, unconcerned as he took his first sip and grimaced slightly. *Well, not exactly good ale.* Can't complain. It had been a long time since the trio had last drank from anything other than a lake or river. A fire blazed near them and the table of old locals cheered loudly, drinking and playing their games.

Ariel drank heartily and exhaled with a grin on her face. 'So, brother. Any ideas on where our next adventure will take us?' she asked with excitement.

Bathos leaned in and whispered conspiratorially, 'Do

you already have a plan, Aleister? Surely there are people in Archania that require our assistance? I mean look around you, this is not the Archania we left five years ago. There is a darkness here.'

Bathos was right. The land they had left all that time ago had its problems, but the people had seemed happy, they were united. Problems with the Borderlands had seemed like a distant memory ever since one bearded man with a massive sword had convinced most of his men to stop attacking neighbouring kingdoms. People were not living in fear and they were proud to be ruled by a kind and just King.

They had mourned the untimely death of their Queen but had looked forward to a bright future, with two Princes in line to continue the good work of their father. Aleister hadn't seen the worth in staying in the Kingdom, but he never thought that he was leaving a country during a downward spiral.

'Did you notice the men following us?' Ariel asked. 'Looked like The Watch, similar uniform apart from that White Sun. And you know where we've seen that before.'

'We'd all heard the rumours. The Empire is getting its claws into another Kingdom. I'm not surprised really. Like a plague taking over.' Aleister didn't like it, the Empire of Light was moving north, but why?

'Reckon I might know the reason we were followed,' Bathos muttered, glancing around the room. Aleister followed his glance, spotting the pattern Bathos had noticed. All eyes were looking their way. Not blatantly, it was subtle; the look men gave when they didn't want to get caught. All of them looking at Ariel.

'Can't be your beauty...' Aleister joked. Ariel landed a soft punch on his arm as he laughed. Then she pulled her hood up over her dark hair that fell either side of her sky-blue eyes.

'I don't think it's me...'

Aleister looked past her shoulder and spotted a lone figure in the corner, sipping her drink with two hands wrapped around the goblet. Her golden eyes shone in the few rays of light that broke through the boarded-up window. 'The Lower City has been the home of magi forever. As long as she doesn't use magic, it's not a problem. They can't be mad at you for what you're born as.' He wanted to sound certain, but he wasn't sure he did. Some of the looks were mad, angry. Some scared. Aleister knocked back his drink before standing up. Time to sort out this little issue.

'Hey, assholes! This way,' Bathos and Ariel rolled their eyes as one, shielding their faces from the embarrassment. Nothing to be embarrassed about! He was clearing things up. They should be happy. He waited until he had the full, undivided attention of everyone in the room. 'I was born in this here beautiful city, left five years ago, along with my sister and best friend. We're here to have a drink and relax. However, if you're going to make this young woman uncomfortable for being a mage then I guess our day of relaxation is over...' He brushed his cloak to the side ever so slightly, allowing the onlookers a glimpse of his gem encrusted blade. 'This is Soulsbane, forged in the time of The Four themselves. Those killed by it, don't pass on to the Sky Plane. Want me to add you to the list of lost souls? Just ask.'

'Damn mages 'ain't welcome here,' a voice muttered in the shadows.

'This is *Archania!* Magic was born in this Kingdom,' Aleister scoffed.

'Well, it can die here too.'

He sat back down, frowning. Bathos just stared at him, eyes wide open. 'Was that necessary?'

'What?' Aleister shrugged.

The mage caught his eye and smiled, silently thanking him with mouthed words. She finished her drink, stood from her seat and marched out of the tavern.

'Magi are the reason the world is breaking!' Aleister snapped his head round to glare at an angry-looking fellow at the back of the room, leaning forward from the shadows to offer a glimpse of his scarred face. Half of his nose missing. 'We should be rid of them all. Then the world would be whole again.'

Aleister closed one eye and grimaced, cocking his head to the side as he stood up. 'Let me get this straight. You believe that the world is breaking because magi are being born? Even though you worship The Four? Gods who could wield all kinds of amazing and terrible magic in these lands. That right?'

The scarred man spat at Aleister's feet. 'We don't follow The Four no more. There is only the One.' The man pulled at a chain on his neck, thrusting forward the image of the White Sun.

'Does this man speak for you all? Are you all so brainwashed that you're following this new god? Archania has always followed The Four. This is where they landed first from the Sky Plane. Now you follow a cult who allows their own members to use magic but no one else?' He couldn't believe it. What had happened to the Kingdom to lead them so far from what they had been?

'Aleister...' Bathos muttered darkly, getting to his feet and moving in front of Ariel as she backed away from her own chair.

'I think it's time you leave...' the barman suggested, grabbing a sword from beneath the bar. The whole atmosphere had shifted. None of the men now looked scared or uncertain. They were all angry. They'd been pushed by his words. Good work. He noticed the sharp weapons in hands – no magic to them, but just as deadly.

'And take that fucking magic sword with you.'

'I'll ram it through your fucking throat if you say one more word...' Aleister threatened, stepping forward.

'Brother,' Ariel pleaded. 'Let's go. It's not worth it. *They* aren't worth it.'

He felt Bathos tug at the back of his robe and lowered his hands in defeat. 'Fine. I'm leaving. Zaina said things had turned to shit. I'll have the firewhiskeys to go.'

'Of all the places we've travelled to, that is in the top five of worst welcomes we've had,' Aleister moaned as they left the tavern. 'In our home, our own *home!*'

'Don't worry about it, let's head to the temple. Need to relax,' Ariel suggested.

He couldn't stay angry, not when she brushed it off so easily. It just wasn't fair. It never had been. Most countries were suspicious of magi and Aleister understood that the United Cities had a complicated history with magic, but this fear and hatred together felt dangerous. No one was in control of being a mage, just like Aleister wasn't in control of being born with pale skin. Why would the accidents of birth be held against anyone?

'Reckon we should lie low here for a while, Aleister?' Bathos asked as they strolled through the bustling streets.

'That debacle back in Darakeche may have ended in our favour financially but we have more enemies than ever, and the Greencoats will not be quick in forgetting our part in their embarrassment,' Aleister reminded them, pulling out his flask of whiskey and taking a swig.

'Our part? If I remember correctly their embarrassment was all because of you and your actions!'

Aleister felt the blood rush to his face as his sister and best friend laughed at the memory.

'Yes, well, we work as a team and you were the one that started all the commotion anyway, Bathos. I was just taking advantage of a situation that had, er, *arisen*, shall we say.'

'Fair enough Aleister. If anything else seems to "rise" during an important mission, then I suggest you take a moment to gather your thoughts and remember that we are working as a team,' Ariel warned him jokingly.

'Of course…' Aleister lifted the flask and finished off the rest of his drink, using it as an excuse to hide from his laughing friends. The burn reenergised him. Darakeche had been a close one but he wouldn't change a thing about it.

'No remorse. No regrets. Right, Aleister?' Bathos punched him on the arm and grinned. Familiar words.

'No remorse. No regrets,' he agreed.

No remorse. No regrets. Was that really true though? He thought of the people he'd left behind on his swashbuckling journeys. The people who had woken up one day to find him gone, not knowing when he would return. *If* he would return. He loved the image of the brave warrior out to defend the needy, but he just felt like a coward. A coward who always ran away when things were too intense.

Tons of remorse. Tons of regret. Didn't exactly roll off the tongue.

'Looks like we've found a man in need,' Bathos nudged Aleister, raising his huge, sculpted, muscly arm and pointing ahead of them, through the crowd.

Aleister stretched up on the toes of his shiny, new boots, pressing them against the cobbled path. The crowded market street hummed with the general buzz of too many people in too small a space, as usual. People of the Lower City haggled and argued between the shadows of the wooden buildings either side of the street. He always thought it cruel of the architects who had designed the city to build a straight path in the Lower City that had a clear view of the Palace and the Upper City high up on the hill above them. Dangling the forbidden fruit. Giving the poor people a glimpse of what they couldn't have. Some claimed it to be aspirational. A goal for them all to see – complete bullshit in his mind.

Suddenly, the buzz of the market faded into a sinister tone. He could hear the commotion before he could see it.

Shouts and yelling mixed with mean cackling and whoops of joy.

'Go back to where you came from!'

'We don't want your kind here!'

Familiar cries, no matter the city you were in. That was the way of things.

The three of them did what they had always done. They picked up the pace and walked straight towards it.

The crowd parted with ease – a quick touch on the shoulder from Aleister; Bathos' large shadow towering above them; a flash of Ariel's shining white teeth.

An audience had gathered around a group of four men: young, drunk. Men, women and children were screaming them on as they danced around a dishevelled man down on his knees; trousers ripped down his right leg, three of his shirt buttons scattered onto the cobbled floor and only one shoe. The other flew through the air, followed by the laughter of the mob. The Eastern-toned man barely moved, exhausted from the cruel game, aware that he was not going to win.

Aleister swaggered forward, jaw tightly set as he stared at the four men. With one swift movement, he caught the shoe on its next journey, taking it from the air and heading straight to the man on the floor. He glanced from the corner of his eye, sensing movement.

'What do you think you're—'

The thud of a fist cracking into the man's stomach reached Aleister's ears. He shot a glance over to see a man vomiting at Bathos' feet. Some of the vomit dripped into his messy, wild, blonde beard. Not the best of looks.

The whoops and cheers had stopped now, leaving only a sharp, chill in the air that had nothing to do with the temperature. Everyone expected more violence. Aleister wasn't in the mood. Not today.

'Your decision,' he said to the three advancing men, smiling as their eyes glanced at the intricate weapon swinging from his hip. 'Your souls will forever be damned.' They passed confused looks at each other before looking towards their fallen friend, still shaking in the shadow of Bathos.

'Not worth it. Unless you want him to cave your skulls in. He's done it before. Not pretty...' Ariel said, wagging her finger.

They grumbled and tried to look angry. Saving face as they kept their distance from the warriors, Bathos allowing them to pass by and pick up their fallen friend. He coughed, releasing a last amount of vomit from the back of his throat.

'Nothing else to see here. Go home to your families,' Aleister said to the crowd. They dispersed into the shadows, aware that their fun for the evening had ended. He turned to the Eastern native, still on his knees, and held out the shoe. 'Yours, I presume?'

'Mamoon be with you, my saviours.' He had a gentle voice – soft, but well-spoken. Aleister stared at him as he raised his face, looking up at the three of them.

His light brown skin and shaven head were signs of his Eastern heritage; he was a long way from home. Beneath his deep brown eyes, were two symmetrical, horizontal scars. White, in contrast to his darker skin. 'Where are you from?' Aleister asked, pointing at the scars.

The man chuckled, placing his bare foot back into his shoe and standing up, wincing as he stretched. 'The scars? I am from the east, a village near Darakeche. But I follow the Southern Gods. Order and Chaos as one. Mamoon watches all.' He ran a finger across each scar and pointed towards the dark, grey clouds looming above in the night sky.

'Have to take your word for it,' Aleister muttered. 'From the East but following Southern Gods. I take it this isn't your first altercation?'

'Mamoon likes to play his games, to test his people. In many places, I am not – how you would say? – *welcome*. I am Harish.' He bowed low.

'All the Gods like to play their games. That's why we're all in this fucking mess. Aleister.' He held out his hand, but Harish just shook his head. 'You'll take my help but not my hand?'

'It is not allowed. My people would look down upon me.'

Aleister rolled his eyes, glancing towards his sister. She looked away, laughing as she slapped Bathos on the shoulder. He grinned along. The joke of religion. Bringing people together and separating them since the dawn of time.

'What are you doing in this city? Surely there are better places for your people?' Aleister asked, curious as to why a sheep would walk so openly into a lion's den.

'I come to bear witness to great things. The Empire in the East has shunned my people, betrayed us. My dreams led me here. Mamoon wants me to witness the wonders of the North and cement his place within it.'

'Well, Harish, that all sounds wonderful. Hope your night improves.'

'Many thanks, Aleister. Mamoon be with you.' Harish bid them farewell, limping off into the shadows.

'Still want to head to the temple?' Bathos asked as the crowds began to mill about them once again.

'Sure. Time to ask some questions.'

A FINAL WISH

Paintings of the various rulers of the Kingdom hung on the walls of the corridor. The eyes of the Kings and Queens of Archania followed Kane as she made her way to the King's personal chambers. She took her time, giving each one of the six-foot images her undivided attention as she made her way to her destination. The proud, honourable men and women that stared back reminded her of a happier past. She chuckled as she spotted the grandfather of the current King, the infamous King Borris. Tales were still told of him and his everlasting appetite. The painting didn't do the tales justice but even here the buttons on his regal jacket looked ready to burst. The statue he had commissioned in the Lower City overlooking The King's Square was much more flattering but, in the words of many, nowhere near realistic. A monument to a fat King with a well-drilled army looked after by better men and women. Somehow, he had managed to live a long life until his very non-regal death – choking on his own vomit after one of his weekly Great Feasts. Of course, that had been hushed up; he had died peacefully in his sleep apparently, the hundreds of onlookers were all liars. His army that had conquered two neighbouring kingdoms and forged the alliance that came to be known as the United Cities of Archania, that was his great legacy. History really was written by the victors after all.

Kane reached the final painting and took her time to look at every inch of the perfect representation of her old friend. The painting showed the current King as he had been when their friendship had been blossoming; he was strong and powerful, unrelenting with his adversaries and he would never second guess himself, confident in his own abilities as a ruler and knowing that whatever path he chose to follow would be the correct one. This was the King who had defied public opinion (and that of his advisors) to appoint a young, inexperienced Katerina Kane to be the Chief Inspector of Archania. The King who had made the toughest possible decisions in the one belief that the best interests of the Kingdom were always in his heart.

What went wrong?

Only rarely would Kane be called to the King's personal chambers these days, but in the past, of course, barely a day would pass without the two of them sharing an hour or two together, speaking about the issues of the day and generally just relaxing in welcome companionship.

The decline began after the war. The plague had been devastating; thousands died, the Queen being the most prominent casualty, passing away shortly after the birth of their second son. Mikkael had panicked, as many would do in his situation, it had been the first time that Kane had ever seen the proud man at a loss for what to do.

Indecision almost led to his downfall. Riots broke out in the streets, voices filled with rage demanding that something be done to stop what seemed like a curse upon their nation. Mikkael withdrew to his chambers, hiding himself away, hoping to stay in the shadows while his world crumbled around him.

He had still sought the advice of his closest and oldest friend, allowing Kane behind his barriers, but most of the time he was a shell of his former self, refusing to eat or even play with his two sons.

The days he spent in discourse with Kane grew less and less as soon as Mason came onto the scene. The zealot had, coincidentally, arrived at the perfect time. The Kingdom had suffered from a rise in the number of magic-related incidents and the general public were on the edge of revolution. The King could not assure them that he would put a stop to the crimes; crimes that, were the rumours to be believed, had brought the death and disease with it.

D'Argio had swept in from the East, a region that had escaped the deadly plague, and recommended harsh punishments for any activity related to magic that wasn't for his own purposes, and followers flocked to him and his cult. The greater his cult grew, the more time he seemed to be spending with the King. In the last decade, Archania had become almost unrecognisable to what it once was. Kane had been shifted from her role as Inspector to a token role on the High Council. Not that her opinion ever mattered. Mason decided what was best. Everyone either agreed or were shut down.

At first, his harsh methods were frowned upon by many in the council but most were soon swayed to his way when they saw that the people of Archania felt more comfortable when they were getting into bed at night, knowing that they were safe from activities of a shadowy faction of magic. Only Lord Tamir felt uneasy around the man, distrusting his harsh methods and honey-soaked words.

Twenty feet from the closed door, guards on either side, Kane spotted an unwanted person leaning, inspecting the shining, armoured staff. The King's eldest son, Asher. Kane slowed her walk and bowed.

'Katerina Kane.' The Prince gave that annoying fucking smirk of his, the one that may have well been plastered onto his pale, smug face. 'Good to see you managing the walk to my father's chambers without the aid of a stick. Archania should be proud to see your resilience in the face of old age.'

'Prince Asher. Good to see that you have lost none of your charm. Archania will be proud to have such a witty, intelligent man to sit on its throne one day. Hopefully not too soon though...'

The mask slipped for a fraction of a second; a shadow passing over the young man's sharp features before slipping right back into place. 'They will be proud. I will be the greatest King the United Cities has ever seen. There will be statues of me throughout the world, not just this shitheap of a Kingdom.'

'It's always so warming to hear a prince speak of his Kingdom in such a way. I'm sure your loyal subjects would be queueing up to kiss your feet if they heard such beautiful words.'

'You're on borrowed time, Kane.' The mask fell completely, smashing to pieces as the shadows took over. 'My father has some strange sense of loyalty towards you for some reason. Once he is gone, your time in Archania is over. Mason has warned me against you: the old guard. Two feet rooted in the past with no will to step over the line to ensure progress. Stay in the shadows of the old days, Katerina Kane. The Light will find its way without you, and when it does, you'll be nowhere to be seen.' Asher's face quivered with intensity as those sunken eyes of his stared furiously at Kane. The tantrum of a petulant young boy. She'd seen worse.

'I shan't get myself too worked up about it; like you said, I'm a frail, old woman. Best to just take things day-by-day.' She flashed a smile at him, only further enhancing his foul mood.

'Out of my way! I'm late for my meeting with Mason.' Kane allowed the Prince to barge past her, twisting her shoulder back slightly to soften the intended blow. She grunted on impact, but the smile didn't fade. She wouldn't give Asher the satisfaction.

The Prince's relationship with Mason had always worried her; he'd been young and impressionable when the preacher pressed his claws into the royal family and refused to let go. Asher's younger brother, Drayke, fortunately had the common sense to see through the welcoming, charismatic front and peer into the darkness lurking behind. Common sense, sadly, had never been gifted to the next in line to the throne.

Kane had often thought of having a harsh word with the young man but it was rare to see him without a member of the Empire of Light at his side, usually Mason's right hand man, his champion T'Chai, and the Eastern warrior was not a man to mess with. Braego had warned her that T'Chai was a well-known warrior in other places in the world and not liked by many, only feared. *Now Braego is dead. My list of friends is growing thin.*

She took a deep breath before smiling at the guards on either side of the door to the King's room and waited as the pair of them turned the ornate handles and opened the door. They took their time, casting suspicious glances at the old woman. The sun crest on the left breast of their armour showed her where their allegiances lay. Every corner of Archania seemed infected with this madness; it was becoming difficult to escape the religion's stranglehold. *But escape it I must.*

It felt good to see the King on his feet, staring out through the window at the land he ruled with a glazed look in his eyes. Too often he had been confined to his bed or chair. But clearly, the King was worried. Kane knew him well enough to understand that a darkness plagued her friend.

She walked over to him before standing to attention and bowing, 'My King.'

Mikkael turned slowly, as though each movement could cause him harm. His face was drawn, and large, dark shadows sat beneath his eyes. 'Kat, my friend. Thank you for coming. I know we haven't spoken enough of late.'

'I live to serve, my King,' Kane answered with another

bow.

'How about we cut the formalities and talk as openly as we used to? Call me by anything but my actual name and I'll have you banished from this Kingdom. Perks of being a King,' he said. This time his smile reached his tired eyes; a smile that Kane had not witnessed for an age. Finally, there is my old friend.

'So, I can't call you King but you sure as hell can act like one? Am I clear on that?'

'Correct.'

'Okay then Mikkael, the lines are drawn.'

'Please take a seat, I'm hoping this won't be a short conversation. That is unless you have anything else to do? If so then I shall use my position to force you to stay here,' he said to Kane with a smirk, before falling foul of a sudden coughing fit. His mood seemed to improve but his health did not. He was as pale as a sheet.

Kane returned the smile but worry silently ate at her. It had been so long since her friend had behaved like this. She hoped the feeling would pass as the air of familiarity took over. She took a seat at the table and hid her pained look, watching Mikkael struggle to walk over to his own seat beside her.

'What is wrong, Mikkael? Speak plainly, like we used to. You do not look well.'

'Stating the obvious there aren't you, Kat?'

She frowned as she saw any sign of warmth and playfulness fade from Mikkael; his shoulders slumped, and a look of utter despair seemed to fill his entire being. The bags under his watery eyes seemed to darken and all energy left him in that moment. Kane tightened as a bow before the arrow is launched, anticipating the next words.

'I'm dying Kat. I have weeks left, at best. Nobody knows, so I'd be grateful if this stayed between us for now. It will be soon, but I still have enough time to tell those I love and prepare the Kingdom for when the time comes.'

Though she had prepared herself for this, Kane fell suddenly silent, at a loss for any words to comfort her dear friend, staring at Mikkael. She knew that she should say something, maybe a few comforting words, let him know how sorry and upsetting this was, but she couldn't. She just sat there as the silence and the situation wrapped itself around her like a pair of dirty hands, choking her so that she struggled for breath.

Some friend I am.

'Need some time?' Mikkael asked.

Time. Me? Like I'm the one that's dying. Come on Kat, speak!

'How long have you known?' she managed to croak at last, her own voice sounding unfamiliar with the pain she attempted to hold back. *That friend list continues to fade, will it soon be just myself alone wandering this foul abyss?*

'Around two months. The boys already know, along with a few select others. They've both taken it in their stride. Asher still bounds around the kingdom as though he runs the place. Drayke has been slightly more subdued. The guards have noted that he has been attempting to slip their watchful gaze and wander off into the city at night. He's a good boy though, checks on me every day and he's even taken up playing King's Run to spend more time with me. It won't be long before he's wiping the floor with me! I remember you being a fair hand at the card game yourself...'

'It has been a while since these hands have even touched a deck of cards, let alone played a game of King's Run!' Kane chuckled. She paused, seeing the sad look on her King's face. 'It would be an honour to share another game with you though, perhaps another time. This is just a lot to take in.'

'I know it is and I'm sorry. But a true leader understands the need for continuity. I want my family and my Kingdom to carry on as normal; stability is the greatest gift I can give them before it's time. In fact, it's one of the reasons I needed to speak to you. I know your feelings on Mason. You haven't openly attacked him, but I know you Kat, possibly better than anyone and you've kept a closer eye on that man than most in the Kingdom.' Mikkael paused for a while, coughing harshly before raising a hand to stop Kane getting out of her seat to help. 'I can deal with it. When Mason arrived here, he helped me stabilise this Kingdom. In gratitude, I have perhaps allowed him too free a reign. The people of the Kingdom have attached themselves to him while I have just wallowed in the shadows, content with staying out of the light that Mason bathed himself in. My sons have even chosen to follow him closer than myself and the gap between us now is too great for me to close.'

'There is one son who I believe isn't his greatest fan,' Kane said.

'Drayke would make a great King one day, given the opportunity,' Mikkael mused. 'He allows himself to listen to others but think for himself. I'm afraid I can't say that for his older brother. Should have always expected differences between them. At first, I thought my guidance and the help of those in the Palace would put them on similar paths. It seems as though blood does tell, in the end.'

'Mikkael...' Kane whispered, instinctively glancing over her shoulder, aware of the conversation's direction.

'Let me finish. We who know the truth, must be able to speak of it, just this one final time, Katerina,' Mikkael pleaded, tears glistening in his eyes. Kane swallowed hard, fighting back tears of her own as memories that had been locked away for so long struggled to the surface. 'Drayke would never be like Asher. Asher is of my blood. Drayke is not.'

Kane sat in silence, letting the tears drop silently down her face. They had sworn to never speak of this again. It would be too difficult. Too dangerous. She felt her heart breaking and a feeling of despair washed over her. 'Do we tell him?'

'That is not my decision anymore, Kat. It is yours, and yours alone now that Braego is dead. He is *your* son.'

Kane's body convulsed with sobs as she covered her mouth with a shaking hand, unable to escape the errors of her past. 'Was it the right decision?' Kane asked, staring into space with raw, bloodshot eyes.

'You would have been an outcast if you had kept him. Mothering a baby with a warrior from the Borderlands so soon after the war. All three of you would have been lynched or burned,' Mikkael stated. 'No, you made the right decision, Kat. I am certain of that.'

'We could have run away, started a new life.'

'Do you see Braego as a man likely to run away from a problem? He was proud. A warrior. He cherished the moments he had with Drayke, teaching him to fight, secretly teaching him the ways of his people. Braego is dead, but I promise, he lives on with that young man!'

Kane was thankful for that. 'I am glad.'

Mikkael coughed again, placing a tissue against his mouth. Kane thought she saw a patch of red as he quickly pushed the tissue away and out of sight.

'There is another reason for wanting you here today, Kat. When we took your boy in, our Kingdom was on the brink of disaster. You believed my real son to have died, along with his mother. This was a lie.'

Kane sat up, folding her arms and listening closely. She remembered the exact discussion fifteen years ago. The tears and pain as Mikkael had informed her of the death of his son. 'I was in the Heartlands; you'd told me to stay there throughout my pregnancy. The pain of that time has never left me, I fear. You looked so heartbroken.' Kane felt betrayed, how could this have been a lie? What had happened to the boy? The real prince.

Strength seeped back into Mikkael at this last statement, as though the words themselves reminded him that he had something that needed to be done before the end. 'This country has been at peace for a while now, the Borderlands too. Their leader, Reaver Redbeard came to Archania. We were able to speak as two men aiming for a brighter future for our people, for our sons. We've had a peaceful period with the tribes and no matter what happens, I need that to continue.'

'If there is anything you need me to do, old friend, then I swear I will do it.'

'There is something. I need you to understand that what I am telling you now is this Kingdom's greatest secret and something that I am not proud of.'

'What is it?' Kane asked, eyes narrowing with suspicion.

'This nation is ancient, and its history is a rich and long one. There is one aspect of it that Archania is most well-known for – its history with magic. There is a whispered legend that was passed down by my wife's family. After we met, courted and fell in love, she told me the tale. It involves a power struggle with some of the greatest magi in history and battles and bloodshed. All nonsense of course. Or so I thought.'

Kane passed him his drink as he fell once more into another coughing fit. 'Take your time.'

'We had our first child, Asher. Perfectly healthy, a normal baby boy. We were so proud. Then we were graced with our second son. His birth was difficult, as you may remember. Reaver, as leader of a neighbouring nation, travelled here to wish us his best for the future on the birth of our little prince. His eyes gave him away. Bright, golden pupils that glinted in any light. Beautiful. Our little baby son.

'You can't be serious?' Kane protested, bristling at the revelation. Golden pupils meant only one thing. 'Your son was born a mage?' She knew the implications of such a revelation in a land that hated their kind. A member of the royal family being born a mage would have tipped the land over the edge and into the flames.

'There are powerful lines of magic that run through a few families, said to be descended from The Four themselves, such as the one my wife was born into. They keep it a secret too, as it is dangerous. There are people who want to abuse the power and twist it for their own gain. During every age, Guardians are born – fabled protectors of Takaara, born to balance magic with the world's life force. Unfortunately, Guardians can be corrupted. They are human, after all. Their power can be twisted and used to destroy – such as the times before the Great Purge of the Guardians.'

'Mikkael, what happened to your son?' Kane cried.

'Reaver knew in an instant what the boy was. He knew the tales; they had been told by men in the Far North and he knew what the boy meant and the trouble he could cause. The boy is a Guardian. His power will be unbelievable. It is a power said to be able to destroy whole cities if used incorrectly. He'd be hunted. He'd be killed. I couldn't have that happen to my son.' Kane softened as she heard the pain in her friend's voice. They had both done what they thought was best for their children, no matter how hard that may be. 'Guardians were said to have almost died out after the Purge. A few are said to live alone in the corners of the world, working in secret to alleviate any damages they find in the life flow of Takaara. My son would grow up in the Borderlands in a small village while your child would be raised as a Prince of Archania.'

'Drayke...'

'I have raised him as my son, and I love him with all my heart.' A hard edge returned to Mikkael's voice as he spoke of his adopted son. 'You must believe that. I am his father, even if it is not by blood.'

'Does Mason know? Does anyone else in this Kingdom know?'

'He doesn't know. My wife, Reaver and I decided that the less people who were involved, the better it would be.'

'And Raven?' Kane asked. 'Reaver's son?'

'He knows. He has made sure that the other child is kept away from Archania at all costs. I couldn't risk my people recognising anything in him.'

'The other child? You are on about your son, Mikkael.'

'I raised two sons. Drayke and Asher – they are mine. I don't even know the name of my second son, though I have thought about him every single day of his life. I will be judged by The Four soon enough, only then will I know if what I did was right,' Mikkael grabbed a piece of fruit from the silver bowl on the table and shrugged his shoulders before taking a considered bite. 'Kat, I have one last wish, before I die.'

'What is it?' Kane asked.

'I want to see him, the boy I gave away. I am going to the Borderlands.'

'You have weeks to live, and this is what you wish to do? Embark on a perilous journey further north to see a son who you have not known since he was a baby?' Kane became suddenly aware of the increasingly high pitch of her voice; awareness was one thing, stopping it, quite another.

'I've made my decision. I'll give my family a day or two for the news of my illness to settle in and then call a meeting. Balen is already aware of my condition, I thought that his knowledge of healing could be used, but sadly we have not been able to find a cure.'

Disappointed with the change in conversation, Kane grimaced but bit her tongue. She knew better than to push her luck with the King. In his current state it would be best to let the man rest and continue this conversation later.

'Are you certain there is no chance for recovery?' Kane asked.

'In all the books Balen and I have been able to read, the only known cure lies in the use of magic,' Mikkael replied, taking another bite out of his fruit. 'Ironic, I know.'

Kane lowered her voice to a whisper, 'Surely there are exceptions to each law, Mikkael. You are the King, and this is your life. Your life dammit!'

'And as King I have an obligation to set an example to my people – to not break the laws laid down for my Kingdom. Magic can only be used for worship and even then, only by the chosen few. Those laws are in place for a reason. If I don't hold myself to the highest of standards, then I have no right to rule over even the lowliest of peasants. You know this Kane,' he finished sadly.

'I know. It doesn't mean I like it. Sometimes I wonder if our laws need updating. If using magic is so dangerous, then why is anyone allowed to use it?'

'It is our link to the Sky Plane, the only link. We need people to keep that alive but if more people were allowed to share that link then chaos would ensue, and it would be easier for them to track down the other child. Trust me Kat, like you used to.'

Looking at the frail, sick man before her and thinking about all that had just been said, she wondered if she would ever be able to trust anyone ever again. She sighed and pushed away the dark clouds forming in her mind. Her old friend was dying and, right now, nothing else was more important to her. 'I just want to help.'

Mikkael smiled and a hint of his younger self found its way onto his wrinkled face. 'Then perhaps you would care to join me in a game of King's Run? I'll go easy on you the first time.'

'You wouldn't dare dishonour me in such a way...' Kane grinned back, glad to see a bit of energy flow through her King, her friend.

'Then it is your loss...'

'We shall see!' Kane laughed before falling silent, cherishing the moment between them. 'Thank you, my friend. Let the game begin.'

POWER AND CONTROL

'That was the best night's sleep in an age,' Cypher said to himself, opening his eyes and staring up at the open wooden beams above him. Sunlight peeped through the cracks in the thin walls but today, he greeted them as welcome guests and not invasive intruders. He'd thrown the sheets off the mattress stuffed with straw he kept on the floor – too hot, unusually hot for this time of year. He smelt of damp sweat and dried blood. Beautiful.

It had been the first time that he had killed outside of the dungeons in some time. He hadn't realised until after just how much he missed the thrill, the buzz, the adrenaline rush of taking a life out on the streets. He couldn't hide behind his job or Mason in the Lower City. At any moment, one of those idiots could have drawn a weapon and ended his life. That's what Cypher missed most – the unknowing, the uncertainty. The will he or won't he. He'd felt his heart bursting from its cage as he took the man's life, each thrust more satisfying than taking a new whore for the first time. That's what Cypher missed the most – the power, the control.

The look of fear on the barman's face was priceless as he cowered behind his bar, staring up at Cypher as though witnessing one of The Four jumping out from the legends. He had become their avatar, smiting the unworthy, covered in the blood of his enemies. That's what Cypher missed most – the respect, the adulation, the knowledge that he was deadlier than all others.

He remembered the joy of wandering the streets of the Lower City, knowing that he had the skill to kill anyone he wanted to. He could hide it well, born in the shadows, they were his ally, his partner, his lover. He'd thought about joining up with the Assassins' Guild, more money and prestige. It wasn't for him, he had decided. Being told who to kill, who not to kill. It was all just so... *boring*. He liked being his own man, hurting who he wanted to hurt, going where he wanted to go. That's why he had come back, a reminder of how far he had come. No longer the free man able to do as he pleased.

Had his life improved or worsened? He couldn't tell, not in that moment.

A knock at his door interrupted his musings. 'Spoil sport,' Cypher murmured to himself darkly, sitting up from his makeshift bed and dragging a shirt over his stubbled head and placing his arms into the appropriate holes. He danced to the door, humming a tune to himself, enjoying the blissful morning sunshine that managed to find all the holes and cracks in the ceiling of the shack he had once called home.

'Zaif,' Cypher said, swinging the door open to find the torturer on the other side, an impatient look on his face.

'Cypher. Why the fuck are you here?' Too loud. Too angry. Unnecessary. 'Why aren't you in the Upper City instead of this fucking... shithole.' Zaif's eyes darted around the room, clearly unimpressed.

'I find it refreshing to return here,' Cypher answered, turning to allow Zaif a good look at his old home. 'Simple? Broken? Perhaps. Real? Definitely. Every man needs to look into his past in order to move forward.'

'For fuck's sake Cypher, we need to get to the palace. Mason wants to speak us,' Zaif sounded panicked, voice slightly higher than usual. Not at all professional. He'd been in the East. He should know better. Cypher narrowed his eyes at his old friend and tapped the creaking, wooden floorboards with his bare right foot three times.

'Do you know how many bodies I have buried under here?' he asked, enjoying the flicker of disgust in Zaif's eyes at the comment. 'I don't. Lost count. Double digits though, I reckon. Used to chop them up into little pieces to begin with, made it easier to get rid of them. After a while, when I realised that no one was even close to catching me, I thought I'd just bring them all here, make it easier for the Inspectors, make it into more of a game.'

'Weren't too good at it in the end though, eh? Got caught, didn't ya?' Cypher felt the familiar rage boiling in the pit of his stomach at the reminder. One little mistake, one stupid mistake. That had caused his downfall. Who knew what would have happened if he hadn't fucked up?

'One mistake, Zaif. *One* mistake. I could have killed almost anyone else in the Kingdom, barring royal family, and I probably would have gotten away with it,' he said with sadness.

'But you didn't. You killed Davrus Kane, the Chief Inspector's husband.'

Cypher winced at the name, as though the sound of it burned. 'Davrus Kane,' he spat. 'Davrus fucking Kane! My one mistake.'

'Well, you're making another if you don't put some trousers on and come with me. Mason *commanded* your presence. We gotta go!'

Cypher ran his tongue across the front of his teeth, enjoying the soft, morning film that coated them. How dare that bastard *command* him. That's what Cypher missed the most – the freedom, being his own man.

Yes. That's what he missed the most.

Mason's tower wasn't subtle. A white tower made with Eastern ragstone that stood in contrast to the rest of the Palace – a Norland limestone that had been painted a bright yellow. Mason had never been one to blend into the background. He wanted to be front and centre. Cypher couldn't blame him.

'Those towers are all over the place in the East. The White Empire, that's what the locals call it. Reflects the heat apparently, makes it more bearable to live there,' Zaif explained.

'Sounds a joy. I'll have to go there sometime. Paint the walls with some of my favourite red.' Cypher grinned up at Zaif, but it wasn't reciprocated. Something felt off about him today. Not his usual chirpy self. Slow to smile. Quick to rebuke. Not his usual self at all. Had to keep an eye on him. Cypher's gut had got him this far, now wouldn't be the time to ignore it.

The tower had its own entrance. Going through the main Palace entrance wasn't necessary. That's just how Mason liked it. He had his own power; it wasn't dependent on anyone else. Cypher had always had respect for that. He had always been envious of that.

Zaif knocked on the tower door three times. It swung inwards. An elderly guard peered at the two of them carefully, a suspicious gleam in his old eyes. 'Cypher, the torturer. You may enter,' the old man croaked, allowing Cypher to skip past him. 'And who is this?'

'Zaif. My apprentice. Been out east for a while. Finding himself, you know,' Cypher chuckled and winked.

'Don't worry about me, I'll be up later. Mason wants you alone first,' Zaif muttered, turning away with a salute. 'See you later Cypher. Have fun.'

Cypher frowned. If he disliked one thing, it was other people knowing about something that he didn't. The guard slammed the door shut before taking his seat once more. Cypher sighed and stared up at the circular stairway leading all the way up inside Mason's Tower. 'He's the fucking mage. Should come to me,' he grumbled to himself, placing a scruffy boot on the first stone step.

The first hundred steps weren't so bad. They were steep, but manageable. After that, his thighs burned with the effort. Even in his youth, he doubted he could have done the whole journey pain-free. He placed a hand on the wall and continued his ascent, one step at a time. His breathing came in long, deep breaths through an open mouth, heart beating faster than normal. Each step ate away at the respect he had for Mason. By the time he reached the top and saw the gleaming, white door with the familiar symbol of the White Sun carved into the centre, he wanted the man dead.

'Late.' Mason sat at his desk, flicking through an old, dusty book. The pages looked as though they might fall apart if touched too heavily. T'Chai stood at his side, leaning over him to look at the pages.

'Stairs,' Cypher gasped through rough breaths.

'Yes. Stairs,' Mason repeated with that arrogant annoyed tone that he had mastered.

T'Chai looked at Cypher, displaying the black Eastern lining around his eyes that flicked out at the edges. The two of them stared at Cypher as he caught his breath, golden pupils gleaming in the sunlight shining through the circular eastern window.

'Zaif told me that you wanted me,' Cypher began, annoyed with the lack of urgency. He'd climbed those stairs, come all the way from the Lower City. The least they could do was show some common decency and tell him the reason for the summons.

Mason closed the book carefully, pulling a drawer open towards him and placing the book slowly into the it before closing it again. He dropped his elbows onto the wooden table and drummed his fingers together, light glinting from the huge gems on the fingers of his right hand. 'Zaif came to see me yesterday evening. He had an interesting tale to tell. A very interesting tale indeed.'

Zaif. The little errand boy. Back from the East and now behaving like them. Betrayal. Backstabbing. Snide behaviour. Cypher pushed down the swelling of pride in his chest and managed to feign a look of annoyance appropriate for such a time.

'Quite the orator, is Zaif,' he managed to say without laughing.

'Quite. I called you here as I thought it would be best to get your side of yesterday's events,' Mason informed him, business-like. T'Chai just stood there, like an Eastern statue, emotionless.

'Well,' Cypher walked forward, grabbing an ornate, wooden chair and spinning it in front of Mason before sitting, smiling all the way. 'I woke early, the night terrors get me bad, you see...'

He loved to see Mason rub his temple, pausing to draw a deep breath. 'You know what I want to hear, Cypher Zellin. Get to the part where you were in the tavern. I do not have all day. Some of my business actually has an impact on this Kingdom.'

'The tavern? In the Lower City? I have a vague recollection of the events.'

'They need to be crystal clear; do you understand me?' Mason snapped, cheeks turning red as the blood rushed to his face. Too easy. 'I want a full report. You mustn't forget, *torturer,* you are merely a tiny cog, in a large, well-oiled machine. A cog that can be replaced, like that.' Mason snapped his finger and thumb together with a crack that echoed around the room. 'Do not test my patience. You will find it in low supply.'

Cypher crossed one leg over his knee and grinned. 'Wouldn't dare. Zaif and I were enjoying a well-deserved break in an up-and-coming establishment,' Cypher started, putting on his best palace accent. Even the King would be proud. 'In stepped a few disgruntled locals. Long story short, I killed one of the fuckers and put the fear of The Four into the rest of them. Barman was pretty shook-up too,' Cypher added with a flash of his teeth.

'We don't speak of The Four here. There is only the One,' Mason warned through gritted teeth.

'Maybe for you, I've lived here my whole life. Old habits die hard, I guess. Every foreigner passing through the Kingdom seems to have their own spin on the Gods. Through it all, there's always The Four.' He had never been a religious man. If there was a god, or gods, they had a perverse sense of humour. He'd heard tales of the Southerners worshipping a God of Chaos and Death. Maybe that was the one for him. Or maybe he just worshipped himself too much. Either way, he knew any mention of the Gods would rile up the religious leader.

'Why did I have to hear about this from Zaif, before

you, Cypher?' Mason asked, throwing a dark item onto Cypher's lap.

Cypher picked the item up, holding it before him, scanning every inch with the thoroughness of an Inspector. The black mask of The Doctors stained with dark blood. A delightful memory. Made him warm inside. 'Guess I was just busy.'

'This isn't the first time I've heard of these *Doctors*. At first, I thought they were just disgruntled peasants. An annoyance, but one I could deal with, like swatting flies. Zaif's report paints a different story. They are meeting up in secret in the Lower City, plotting to take down the Kingdom. They are a threat that we must deal with.'

'They're a few people playing dress-up to feel better about their lives. Trust me, I grew up in the Lower City. I know what it's like to live without knowing when the next meal will be available,' Cypher said, dismissing the claim with a wave of his hand.

'How pitiful. The problem is that I don't trust you. There was a time when I needed you; a means to an end. We have reached that end, Cypher Zellin.' Cypher's eye twitched as his head cracked to the side.

'What the fuck are you saying, mage?' Cypher bit back, spit flying onto the table. He stared at Mason but spotted the slight shift in T'Chai's stance, aware of the change in mood. 'And choose your words carefully.'

'Am I supposed to feel threatened?' Mason smirked, turning to share a laugh with T'Chai. 'You're a killer, Cypher. Nothing more. We have more skilled workers available now, workers we can trust.'

'There's no one better than me,' Cypher hissed. 'I guarantee it.'

'Sure about that?'

Cypher craned his neck around, clapping his hands together and chuckling at the newcomer, grinning as though he had solved a difficult puzzle. 'Of course! Of course! Zaif! Back from your little journey to the East. Taking my place, my job.' Cypher clapped even louder, laughing in his chair and banging his feet against the stone floor.

'That's right. The apprentice is now the master,' Zaif said.

Cypher stood up. No point arguing. The decision had been made. He wasn't an idiot. He would have his revenge. But it would take time. Careful planning. The best decisions aren't made in the heat of the moment, even if the best murders sometimes were.

He held out his hand to Zaif, who stared at it like it was a trap. 'Not gonna bite you, Zaif.' Eventually he took it, cautiously shaking it. 'See, I'm not a bad guy.' *I'm a fucking artist.*

'Cypher,' Mason called. Cypher turned to face him, lips curled into a mad grin from ear to ear. 'I don't want to see you in the Upper City again.'

'For your sake, I would hope you don't...' Cypher muttered under his breath, opening the door to leave.

The air sucked out of the room, nearly knocking him over. He looked down at his arm, hairs standing on end. The door slammed shut, pieces of the wood splintering and flying off down the staircase. Cypher turned, unimpressed. Mason's pupils were no longer golden, but red, blood red like the trickle dripping from his nostril.

'If you ever threaten me again, I swear to the One God that I will rip that pathetic soul from your body and ensure it spends an eternity in Chaos being pulled apart bit by agonising bit,' Mason spat, his usually cool exterior slipping ever so briefly.

'Sounds like a good time,' Cypher replied, disappointedly pulling the broken door open.

He had expected so much more.

* * *

Kane bounded up the steps two at a time, her breathing heavy with the unusual physical exertion and realising that she perhaps had spent too much time sitting around and drinking lately. She prayed that she would not be late; the stares from the other council members could almost be felt as a heat wave, attacking any latecomer who crashed into the Hall of Justice, and Kane did not want that, not today.

Admittedly, it was not really her fault. She had been enjoying a break, walking with Ella next to a nearby lake; with the weather so nice she thought it the opportune moment to spend some time outdoors. At least until Matthias came running towards her, panicked and waving his arms. When the poor man had finally caught his breath, he had informed her that an urgent council meeting had been called and she had better hurry there as quickly as she could.

Leaving the unfortunate Matthias with his wife by the lake, she had raced to the council chambers, cursing her bad luck.

She squeezed past the open iron chamber door and into the council room, silently promising herself to cut down on the bad food she had been eating of late and closed the door behind her. The noise of the door closing echoed around the room and all the members of the High Council turned to face her. Stern looks adorned all their faces and her mumbled apology fell on deaf ears until an unexpected member spoke, surprising Kane, with powerful, regal tones.

'Better late than never Katerina. Take your seat, now we may start.' The King winked.

The King.

In the council chambers.

The King.

Sitting down opposite her.

For council meetings the King usually preferred a quick recap from Mason or Lord Balen. Nervous glances from the other councillors meant that they must have no clue why the King had sat with them. Kane thought she had an inkling.

She took the last empty seat at the round table and stared at the faces of the men and women sat with her. Both Balen and Tamir looked their usual selves – stern and elegant, ready to serve their nation in whatever way they could. Tamir's eyes shifted darkly to the man across from him: Mason D'Argio. Tamir had always struggled to accept the fact that the religious leader had a place on the High Council. He had always argued that religion had no place in the politics of the nation; a view, unfortunately, not shared by the majority.

The members of the High Council were people who had served their country with great distinction. Some had been soldiers who had served in the War with the Borderland tribes; others had bought their position, their power due to their apparently bottomless pockets. Only one link existed between them all – all came from noble houses. All except two: Mason and Kane.

Apart from D'Argio, Kane was the most recent member of the council. After Lord Arkas had passed away beneath a particularly vigorous prostitute, most of the council had felt that the spot should be taken by a younger noble, someone with a clean record and a strong love for their country.

Some of the council had voted against it but she had gained enough support for the motion to be passed. Balen especially had spoken up for Kane, claiming that he would personally recommend her over the other men and women available. The fact that Kane's father had died in the War with honour certainly helped a few of them warm to her. She may not be from a noble family, but she and her family had certainly served their country, no one could deny that.

Others may have grumbled and never truly accepted her, but they had no choice but to let Kane sit with them during their vital discussions. Not long after, Mason took the time to get to know her, to find out all that he could about her. He hated the unknown.

'Fabulous to see you, Kat.' Sir Dominic's familiar waft of whiskey breath brought a wince to Kane's face as the knight leaned over, whispering into her ear. 'Should be an interesting meeting with old Kingy actually here. Been quite some time hasn't it?'

'It has.'

The knight wore an outrageous cloak: a shimmering silver piece trimmed with gold to match the triangular buttons holding it together in the centre. The white fur wrapped around his neck and shoulders looked as though it might have been taken from a Borderland bear, but she couldn't be certain and didn't want to engage with the man any further.

'I know what you're thinking. Had it made by one of the best tailors in the land at a surprisingly small cost. The wonderful fellow claimed it was an honour to make something for the hero of Archania; the man who held back the wave of savages threatening to end life as we know it.' Dominic gave what he thought must have been a modest shrug, but to Kane it looked as though he was revelling in the praise, as always.

'Wanted to give it to me for free, but I wasn't having any of that. I'm an honest man, an honourable one. A knight. Wouldn't want people thinking I accept freebies. Think of the gossip!'

'It doesn't bear thinking about,' Kane muttered, praying it was the end of their conversation. Dominic snorted, nodding his head and rocking back into his chair.

An old habit, hard to break, reared its head as Kane sensed the usual tension between two of the councillors. Mason had that content, all-knowing look on his face as usual. He stared straight at Tamir before leaning to his right and whispering in the ear of the man beside him, the man that led his personal guard and his champion – T'Chai. The dark-skinned soldier stifled a chuckle and Kane noticed Tamir's face redden as the blood rushed to his head in anger. They loved to annoy the righteous council member whenever they could, aware of his dislike for them.

General Dustin Grey, leader of the King's army and owner of the most fabulous moustache this side of the Emerald Sea, coughed and stared at Tamir, catching his eye and calming the situation. The other members of the council seemed not to notice; they were seasoned old men and women, with a look about them that said they were not long for this world and didn't care. They had lived through war, disease, famine, poverty and everything else that could be thrown at a nation. Nothing would come as a surprise to them. One had already dozed off with his eyes open, a thin layer of drool dripped down onto his chin. High Council indeed.

'Thank you all for coming at such short notice. I know that you all lead such busy lives, bettering this Kingdom,' The King said, raising an eye at the snoring councillor. 'I appreciate all of your hard work and service to your King and Kingdom.' The King sat once more, coughed into his fist and then took a sip of the water. Kane thought he looked more drawn out; his pale skin clung close to his usually bulky frame and he had constant dark shadows beneath his eyes, as though he had not slept for days. Maybe it was just the knowledge she had been cursed with; knowledge that had given her sleepless nights.

'Lord Balen, I believe you had some news for the council to begin with.' Kane winced silently as Mikkael doubled over, coughing into a fist whilst grasping for a handkerchief with the other. He waved away the doddering councillor, Lord Balen, as the old man attempted to offer him support. 'Please, do not be alarmed, continue.'

Balen gave a concerned glance at their King before lifting his eyeglasses from the string around his neck and placing them onto his crooked nose before shuffling the parchment in his hand. 'My King. Lords and Ladies, my fellow councillors. Grave news from the East and South I am afraid.' Could news be anything but grave in these meetings? 'We are expecting a new wave of refugees from the East. Hostilities have erupted once more in the Dehar Region. Men, women and children who are not converting to the Light of the One are being...' Balen's eyes flickered to Mason as he coughed nervously, unsure of how to phrase his next words. '... asked to move on.'

'Politely, and not at the end of a blade?' Tamir snapped, arching an eyebrow at the news. He'd never been an admirer of the East and their ways. He had his opinions and even if he felt isolated from others, he'd stand his ground to the end. Kane liked him.

'They have been offered alternative accommodation within the Empire. It is up to them if they choose otherwise.' Mason smirked from his seat, flicking his unusually long tongue across his thin lips. Tamir kept his eyebrow arched.

'As always, Archania City will welcome these newcomers with open arms, but we must be aware of the tension and issues that come with such a move. We will be adding to The Watch and their training will be overseen by both General Grey and Lord Tamir. I pray that our citizens do us proud. In the South, there are rumblings of war. Our sources suggest that the Boy King has become fed up of sacrificing men and women to his God and he wishes to mobilise his army in the pursuit of honour and glory. Whilst he may be far from us, we must be aware of the dangers of a young King with a lust for battle. As always, our spies will keep us updated with any changes.'

'In better news, in Darakeche, the Sultan's daughter has announced her betrothal – she is to wed Princess Sara of the Heartlands. Though the date has yet to be confirmed, the King and his two Princes will of course be invited to attend the ceremony in Mughabir as honoured guests.' Kane offered Balen a nod as the elderly councillor took his seat once more. He had served his Kingdom for over four decades, slow to anger and quick to smile; a necessary voice of reason battling against the passionate High Council.

Kane's eyes darted back to the King as he stood from

his seat, breathing heavily as he looked around the circle of men and women before him. 'Thank you, Lord Balen. As always, your words are welcomed and appreciated.' Affirmative mutterings all around, even a curt nod from Mason. 'My sons will be delighted to attend such a union.'

'This great Kingdom is always prepared for the worst. Remember when we kept the marauding savages from the Borderlands at bay, beating them back to where they came from? I remember. I was there. If this Boy King fancies squaring up to a man, then I promise you, he will suffer the same fate as the savages!' Sir Dominic banged his fast on the table, flashing his pearly whites at all in attendance as his dark hair whipped behind him with the impact.

'Thank you, Sir Dominic. Your patriotism and loyalty to our Kingdom is, as always, heartening.' The King cleared his throat as Dominic bowed his head, content with the praise, like a puppy being told that it had been a good boy following the instruction to sit. 'Lord Balen, you also wanted to update the council on matters of finance, I believe.'

'Ah, yes,' the old councillor stifled a cough and re-arranged the spectacles perched on the edge of his nose. 'Trade has suffered of late in the Kingdom. The cost of sending a small force to Norland to put down the troubles caused by an influx of sailors from the West has grown beyond our initial assessment. Though our work has been successful, a small number of Archanian soldiers will stay in the city of Norland to ensure that there are no further difficulties.' Nothing unusual there. Norland had long felt forced into being a part of the United Cities and longed for their freedom from the Union. Kane couldn't understand why anyone would argue against their strong cries for independence. 'In addition to this, farmland to the south of our city has fell into disrepair. The older generation of farmers have, due to natural causes, passed on and it seems the next generation are not so keen to follow in the family footsteps. This has had an impact on the goods coming into the city and until it is sorted, we must trade with the Heartlands, Causrea and Austrea, to ensure that we have enough food to feed our citizens. All-in-all, the mood in the city is not optimistic. Though, I must admit, the problems are easily solved, and our future is brighter than such issues make it appear to be.'

'The farms can be offered to those loyal to our monarchy. A simple solution,' Sir Dominic stated, as though he alone had thought of the solution that should have been obvious to all in attendance. 'As for Norland: cut the head off the snake and watch the body wither and die. Give free reign to the soldiers and show the treasonous fools what it means to stand against our great city.'

'Violence will be met with violence. It has always been the way with Norland,' Kane sighed, annoyed with having to repeat herself. The Norland problem has spanned a generation, its argument a tiresome one. 'The city needs to feel part of our Kingdom. Right now, they feel like a bastard son, watching from the outside with no one listening to their wants and needs. If they are to be a part of this Kingdom, we must treat them with respect and honour; give them a voice on this council.'

'Katerina is correct,' Tamir said, similarly bored with the discussion. 'Though, I'd be shocked if you will all agree with her. This council clings to individual power over the greater good of the Kingdom – it has always been the way.'

'You step over a line, Lord Tamir,' The King warned, glowering at him.

'Apologies, Your Grace. I just tire of hearing good ideas fall into the abyss as those who are sworn to improve this Kingdom behave as though such words fall upon deaf ears.'

'Each matter must be taken into serious consideration by all members of this council. I demand it.' The King's stern, dark eyes glanced around the whole table. It was good to hear but enacting such a demand was nigh impossible. That had always been the way.

'Of course, Your Grace,' Tamir bowed, temporarily caving into the words of his King.

'Now, the reason I am here.' Mikkael sat up straight, proud and dignified. 'My reign has been a difficult one, no one can deny that. A King's role is to protect his people, to allow them the opportunities to better themselves. That's what my father told me on his deathbed. I'm not sure I have accomplished that.' He raised a hand at the automatic murmurs of denial. 'War, plague, high taxes – The Big Three, that's what he used to call them. The three problems that could besmirch the name of a leader and feed into rebellion and riots.'

'None of which were your fault, Your Highness. Bad luck. Unfortunate circumstances,' Balen offered, glancing around the table for nods of support. Kane agreed. Mikkael had certainly ruled in a difficult period of their Kingdom's history, that couldn't be denied.

'Perhaps. This is certainly a volatile age we live in, the world trembles beneath us as the mountains spit fire and death above. I was hoping to see us into a better world, one of less fear and darkness. Sadly, I will not have the opportunity.'

The room fell deathly silent. No more nervous glances. Just sad eyes all aimed towards the gaunt leader, cheekbones sticking out sharply from his face, as though they were about to stab through his paper-thin skin. They all knew he had been ill. That didn't mean they were prepared for this. The snoring had ceased, all were paying attention to the King's words.

'Your highness...' Tamir started. He stopped as Mikkael raised a hand, struggling to continue.

'It has been an honour to serve as the King of the United Cities of Archania. The greatest Kingdom in Takaara. My time is short. Asher will soon take over as King. My final wish is to fulfil a promise I made to an old ally. I will be heading into the Borderlands with a few trusted members of my guard. I do not believe I will be able to return in time...'

'Your Highness!' Grey snapped to attention, shooting up from his seat like a poised arrow, ready to be fired. 'It would be an honour to escort you, one final time.' A pompous man. A proud man. But his heart was in the right place. He loved his Kingdom, and his King.

'I, too, would be honoured to journey to the Borderlands. Though I do fear my presence may raise tensions with our neighbours. They will not have forgotten the name of Sir Dominic!' The man really was such a pompous fool. How he had managed to keep back an invading force was known only by him and The Four.

'My thanks General Grey and Sir Dominic, but I need you here. Asher will need you here. I have written letters to each of the great rulers explaining my situation. The Empress in the East, Sultan Mahara of Darakeche, Queen Alexandra in the West, the Banks in the Heartlands. Even one for The Boy King in the South.' Kane grinned as she watched the outcry at these words. Spit flying everywhere, fists banging on the council table, faces turning purple with rage. General Grey's moustache looked ready for take-off from his fury-filled face. Kane just sat there, trusting her King, her friend. 'I know what I am doing. The South have caused us no issues, no matter what rumours we hear,' Mikkael said as the roars faded. 'To the Borderlands, there is no letter. I will personally carry the message. I ask all of you for one, last favour.' Each member of the council sat up straight.

Kane stared unblinking as Mikkael met her eyes. 'Look after my sons. Look after my Kingdom. Be better than I have been.'

UNLEASHED

'We won't be long. Bit of business to attend to and then we'll be able to join you. You won't be missing out on anything. Listen to Socket, there's a reason he's managed to live to such an old age!' Raven's humour to deflect Arden's questioning wasn't effective but he didn't see the point in probing any further as Raven released the hand from his shoulder.

'Sure. I'll still be here when you make it back,' he replied robotically.

'You will be, and you'll have stories of your own to tell. This isn't a simple raid. A battle with the Barbarians will mean tales and songs for the ages!' It was like watching a child on his Sun Day, teeth shining bright in the light of the midday sun. Arden wasn't sure they were the kind of songs and tales that he wanted to be a part of. *Thud*. Ovar's head. *Thud. Thud. Thud.*

He shook his head and blinked a few times, trying to reset his mind. Socket had warned him not to go into battle without a clear mind. No distractions. The smallest mistake will lead to death. Lead only to bones. And no one wanted to be bones.

'Raven... I have some questions that I want to ask.' He breathed in slowly, stretching his fingers out and opening his mouth to speak.

'Not now. Not here.' Raven's voice sounded higher than usual, eyes darting all around as he scratched behind his ear and winced. 'When I'm back from the South, we can sit down. You can ask me anything you want, and I swear on the Four, I'll answer your questions as best as I can.' Not exactly what he wanted, but he knew he wouldn't get a better option. He nodded, shifting his pack further up his back to ease the strain on his arms.

'Hope you've got more weapons in that pack than your shitty, little bow.' Sly growled as he trudged through the snow towards them, a hint of a smirk on his grizzled face. 'Not all of those Barbarians are gonna be in the distance waiting for your arrows. Some'll want a close-up kiss and a little poke.' He jabbed a finger against Arden's ribs and gave a deep chuckle, displaying more of his yellow teeth than necessary; warm, foul breath hitting Arden in the face and forcing him to step back. Calling Sly filthy would have been an understatement of epic proportions. His mud-stained boots stomped through the snow which looked even whiter than usual in contrast to the dark stains on his clothing. His shirt was ripped in various places – each with a story of their own no doubt – whilst his thin, olive cloak flailed against the harsh northern wind. Through it all, he still managed to carry himself with the air of a person who had just taken a huge shit and expected you to eat it, and even thank him for it after. Maybe ask for seconds.

'Easy, Sly. Give the boy some space. Doubt he wants that kind of attention. Not from you anyway!'

Sly snapped his hand round and turned his grin on Kiras as she stepped gracefully across the snow. 'He loves it. Just giving him some final tips before the big day. Wouldn't want him getting caught with just his cock in hand when they rush towards him.'

Arden gulped, unable to think of anything other than Ovar's filthy body on top of him, hands clasped around his throat. Ovar. *Thud.*

'He's got me and Socket. He'll be fine. No worries. Right, kid?'

Arden blew the air out from his cheeks, welcoming the distraction. 'Part of the tribe,' he mumbled to the rest of them.

'Yeah well, Dakkar was part of the tribe too. Don't forget what happened to him...' Sly muttered darkly.

'You best get going, Baldor is waiting for you with Bane and the other one,' Kiras informed them. 'Look after him, he's big, but he's a softie really.'

'Tell that to the poor souls who get crushed beneath that mighty Warhammer,' Raven said, waving and turning to leave. He caught Arden's eye and offered a last, knowing grin, a reminder of what he had sworn. Arden raised a hand in farewell.

Sly leaned back in toward him as the others began to move away, keen to start the journey before the weather worsened. Storms in the Borderlands were not pretty for men on the move. Best to get away quickly and make good ground.

'Be careful, kid. You're heading to the Far North. That ain't no place for the weak. You're one of us now. Time to prove it.' Arden nodded for what felt like the hundredth time, sure that his neck would begin to ache. 'Keep an eye open at all times. It ain't only the Barbarians to look out for.' He winked, slamming a hand against Arden's arm. 'You're part of the tribe, kid.' Sly turned away, leaving Arden standing alone in the snow.

The men of the Borderlands bundled themselves through the snow; occasionally one or more of them would break out in a robust and vulgar song, sang as out of tune and as raucous as possible. At other times, the harsh wind would carry vicious jibes between different tribe members, attempting to annoy other dim-witted men. Pretty much every time the man receiving the jibe would either return the verbal blow as best he could or, if his brain could not work fast enough, they would let their fists do the talking. Great warriors. Poor talkers.

Arden thought he could see the testosterone floating in the air like a fog, following the large gathering of warriors as they worked their way further north, looking for anything to kill. He at least felt certain that he could smell it. If they didn't find something soon, he worried that they would turn on each other. Chances were, he'd be one of the first in line.

'Furthest you've been?' Kiras asked as they marched through the snow, sun glistening off the calm waters of the Great Lake in the distance.

'Not yet. Used to come out here hunting a few years ago. Wasn't allowed past the lake though. Too close to Barbarian territory,' he answered, thinking back to his old fishing and hunting trips. Only the strongest and most resourceful animals were able to survive this far north. Such harsh, inhospitable conditions were not designed for life to thrive. That was true of the humans living there as well. Anyone with a bit of sense moved south the first chance they could get, where the weather slightly improved, snow only fell ninety percent of the time, and a tribe would be able to offer you protection if you could prove your worth. The ones who stayed were different. Built of sterner stuff. Giants among men who towered over others. Hairier, bigger, meaner, in most cases. The Barbarians took pride in the fact they were the ones who stayed, the ones who were able to make a home where none were meant to – a middle finger to The Four.

Arden had always just thought they were mad bastards. Ovar had changed that. Ovar didn't seem mad. At least not as mad as the warriors Arden fought next to. Ate next to. Slept next to. He just seemed like a normal man. A man who had killed. A man who had lived. A man who had a family waiting for him back home. A man who had lost his head because he had been caught.

'I've been a few times. Baldor likes it up here. Stopped coming after his Mum passed on, though. Didn't want to be reminded of her.'

'You're close, aren't you?' Arden said, seeing a rare sadness in her eyes.

'He's my best friend. A big brother. It's not often you come across folk who will put your safety ahead of their own up here. Usually it's every man and woman for themselves. Dog eat dog. Baldor ain't like that. If I'm struggling, he'll move the fucking mountains to get to me, and I'd do the same for him. He's a ray of sunshine in a world of grey clouds is that man. No one better.'

Arden had to admit, for a man of such towering strength and brutality, Baldor had a gentle nature rare in these lands. 'Herick likes him.'

'Sure does. Practically raised him after his father became bones. Took a liking to his mother, that sure helped, but it's difficult for anyone not to like the great bastard. I think Herick expected Baldor to take over when he finished being chief or became bones himself. Bit of a shock when he decided to join up with Raven,' Kiras said.

'And why did he do that?' Arden asked, curious.

'He has his reasons.' Her voice let him know there wasn't room for further questioning on the matter. Arden didn't mind. If Baldor had his reasons, then that worked for him. Pushing it would get no results. That would be a fool's mistake.

Arden curled his toes up inside his black, sealskin boots, fighting against the cold and trying to get some feeling back into his numb toes. With each step, the snow crunched beneath his boots, reaching up to his ankles. The soft, white flakes continued their slow descent from the heavens, seemingly endless this far north. He pulled his ragged cloak tight around his body and blew out the warm air from his cheeks, thinking to distract himself from the lowering temperature.

'You ever think of heading south?' he asked Kiras, wondering himself why he hadn't just left the freezing North before now.

She scratched the stubble just above her ear and scrunched up her nose as she thought about it. 'Thought about it once or twice. I'll always listen to a tale or two from the merchants who travel this far north. Can't help but feel a bit of excitement and longing when they speak of the jungles of the South or the wonders of the West. I sometimes think that I'd love to just see a bit of colour, instead of this endless white sheet around us. A bit of green maybe. I reckon that's why there's so many murderous fuckers up here. Starved of colour for so long they end up just cutting each other to get a bit of red.'

'Why don't you just leave then?' What was there holding them back? Was there anything that he would stay for in the Borderlands?

She shrugged. 'This is what I know. Sure, it's shit at times. But it's comfortable. I've got Baldor. A warm bed most nights. Food and drink. Can't complain. It's more than some folk have. And if I left, Baldor would follow. He wouldn't want to, but he'd still go if I went. That would make things difficult for Raven. A chief needs his trusted allies. With the two of us gone and Dakkar bones, he'd be left with Sly, Socket, and you.' Kiras grinned at him. 'The old man can't have much longer left. Reckon you and Sly could rebuild with him?'

The thought alone terrified him. 'I reckon Sly would kill me if there was just the two of us.'

'*Pppsshhh*. He's a big softie really. And he likes you,' Kiras said, waving her arm in the air to signal Socket as the hooded archer trudged back through the snow along the lines of men towards them. 'You'd already be dead if he didn't.'

The Mournful Giant. The Borderlands had never been a land many eagerly visited. What was there but the endless snow and threat of death? Arrogant warriors who wished to make a name for themselves would sometimes make the journey. A few merchants looking to make a profit with less competition. Now and then a Southern fool looking to escape their own lands after committing a crime where only distance would save them. The only other reason for people visiting the volatile lands stood right here before Arden. Looking up at the impressive landmark, he had to admit – this was worth the trek, worth the danger. Herick had spoken truthfully, if ever proof existed of the Gods' impact on the land, it stood here.

Two-hundred feet tall, the statue, a bluish-grey colour, seemed to be wearing a crown of clouds. Arden arched his neck upwards in awe, eyes wide open, ignoring everything else as his hood fell back from his head and snow dropped cold and wet onto his face.

'Impressive, ain't it?' Socket tapped his bow against Arden's hip and pointed up at the colossal structure. 'Damn thing reeks of magic. Shame the old ways have been forgotten. Your kind could do some amazing shit. Imagine what else we would have been capable of...'

'Not really my kind.' He might look the part but that's where the similarities ended.

'They're your kind, boy. You've got magic in you. Your eyes tell me that. Don't matter if it can't find its way out, you still got it in you.' Socket poked him again with the scratched, long, wooden bow. 'Maybe it's like a big shit and you just need a decent push to let it out one day.' Beautiful.

'Why do reckon this thing is here?' Arden asked, moving the conversation away from his inadequacy.

'Who knows what those crazy bastards were thinking? A warning to others. A gift to the Gods. A statue just to show what they could do. No idea.'

So many secrets had been lost to history. Now only remnants were left of the abilities of better men and women, those capable of creating wonders of the world in the blink of an eye. Since then, tribes were slowly trying to piece together what they could, trying to get back to the glory days when the Gods walked the land of Takaara. Arden couldn't see the point. The Gods had left the world for a reason. It was their land now, for good or ill. It was time to be the best they could be, without comparing themselves to such behemoths.

'Definitely made by a guy,' Kiras commented as she reached them, smirking up at the statue. 'No woman would feel the need to build something like this.'

Socket chuckled but Arden couldn't work out why. A private joke perhaps. The two of them walked on in the shadow of the giant, following the still-moving train of warriors barely glancing at the great creation. Arden took one last look up at the statue before struggling through the snow to keep up with the others.

'Reckon we're close?' he asked Socket, looking at the weapon in the old archer's hand.

'Shouldn't be,' Socket muttered, head turned towards him. 'But you never know. In my experience it's always best to have something in hand to kill a bastard.'

'We'll make it through the mountains in about two days. Then we'll need to be ready,' Kiras added.

Arden looked up at the line of mountains in the distance, peering through the fog and snow. A dark shadow lay at their feet, a sharp contrast with the pure white of, well... everything else. 'What is that?' he asked. Kiras looked ahead, hand resting on her forehead to block out the light.

'It can't be...' she muttered to herself.

Arden felt his stomach drop as though he'd been pushed off one of those great mountains. The men ahead of them were scattering now, running to various positions and drawing their weapons. A few shouted but the wind carried their voices off into the distance.

'Grab your bow, kid. We need high ground,' Socket growled, eyebrows dropping as he stared into the distance with his one good eye. A horn sounded, cutting through the growing wind and alerting the warriors of the impending danger.

Arden looked around as chaos gripped the tribe, those at the back suddenly aware of being on the edge of battle. The ground seemed purposely built to frustrate archers. Too flat. Strong wind.

'You okay, kid?' Kiras asked him, grabbing her weapons and giving them a familiar spin. Her voice startled him, and he turned to face her with a shocked look on his face. He stammered, unable to regain his composure, answering her as fast as he could.

'I'm f-f-fine.' Cold. Too damn cold. At least that's what he told himself. Definitely not just nerves...

'You ready for it, son?' Socket asked, eye flashing towards him. 'If not, then you need to get somewhere safe. We've got minutes until they're on us.'

Arden looked back at the swelling black mass of soldiers heading their way like a black sea crashing against the coast. 'I think so. I'm just unsure how effective I'll be with this wind. Need higher ground.'

The constant wind picked up with its mention, gaining volume in response to Arden's comment but Socket seemed comfortable enough, 'Use the first shot for range, second to adjust for the wind. After that I'm sure you'll be fine. Chances are there'll be so many of the bastards you'll struggle to miss. I won't be too upset if they take out a few of these idiots truth be told.' Socket laughed, nudging Arden mischievously and nodding towards some of Saul's men racing past.

Cheers broke out amongst the main group ahead of them and Arden looked up to see a burly, blonde warrior strolling through the group and towards the trio.

Kiras sighed. 'Great. It seems like Saul wants to grace us with his presence.'

The leader gave them his wicked grin, his eyes flashing at each of them in turn before resting on Arden.

'It's nice to see all of Raven's pack together. Even the young pup,' he said with a malicious stare. Arden dropped his eyes to the snow at his feet, checking his worn boots, unable to hold the warrior's gaze.

'What do you want Saul? Not that we aren't as grateful as always for the opportunity to exchange pleasantries with you,' Kiras remarked with a smirk, 'but there appears to be a battle breaking out.'

'I've always loved feisty women,' he said, licking his blue lips. 'There's always a place for you in my tribe girly. You're a wolf through and through, I reckon!'

'Why are you here Saul?' she asked through gritted teeth. Arden bet she had images of her twin blades slicing through the warrior's body flashing through her mind.

'Another time, maybe. The time for blood is upon us earlier than expected! The Gods must have been impatient for our victory. This is a good omen!' he roared. Arden glanced again at the soldiers in the distance, unable to make out their number. He wasn't sure he agreed with him.

'They knew we were coming. Why else would they be this side of the mountains?' Kiras spat, disgusted with the turn of events.

'Could be that they had the same idea as us,' Saul said, shrugging his huge shoulders. 'Who gives a fuck. Now is our chance to destroy the bastards once and for all. Looks like they've all come for the party.'

'How many?' Socket growled.

'They outnumber us three to one. We'll slaughter them and be back on our way home in no time, old man. Of course, if you need to stay up here and rest for a while then I'll be more than happy to escort Kiras home.' Saul rubbed his chin as he looked down at her.

She placed a hand on her blade as his eyes undressed her in the way that had become all too familiar to her, 'Watch your step Saul,' she warned.

'I'll be watching yours.'

She kept her eye on him he brushed past her, walking through the snow to give the good news to the other warriors.

'A stray arrow from either one of you would make me one very happy girl. Just saying.'

The horde of Barbarians marched through the snow, Arden's eyes fixed upon them, numbers beyond count. Three to one at a guess. This wasn't going to be pretty. 'Think we'll have enough to deal with as it is...'

'Find Herick. In the heat of the battle, you want someone close that you can trust. Better than that tricky cunt,' Socket said as he kept an eye on Saul, wallowing in the cheers of his men as he sauntered past. 'Don't want anything happening to you, girly.'

'Ah, you're making me blush,' Kiras replied in mock embarrassment. 'Then Baldor will find him and tear him to pieces. Make sure you're there for that,' she added sadly, thoughts turning to her friend.

'You're a great warrior. It's been an honour. May our ancestors watch over you when we are gone.'

Arden watched as the two warriors clasped forearms and locked eyes, sharing a mutual respect, each knowing that this may be the last time they meet. Kiras turned to Arden and offered him that easy smile of hers. It was amazing how at times like this she was able to be completely at ease.

'Stay safe kid. Look after this old bastard. Don't do any stupid shit. Remember, dead heroes get the songs, but wise cowards stay alive. I know which one I'd rather be. Now go, get into your positions. I'm sure Saul will want the fighting started before the light fades. That's if those fuckers even give him a choice.'

'I'll make sure I do that,' Arden replied, wondering if he would see the woman again. This must be the way of the warrior. Goodbyes came far too often. He thought of Dakkar. He thought of Ovar.

He strode after Socket, heading away from the Barbarians who were now close enough for their horns to be heard. 'Where are we going?' he asked, struggling to keep up in the heavy snow as he pulled his bow from his back and checked the taught string. It made a satisfying twang that informed him that it could be trusted.

'Remember I mentioned high ground...'

Arden followed Socket's gaze as the old man stopped in the snow and arched his neck up. 'Oh fuck...'

The Mournful Giant glared back at him.

A wave of nausea crashed over Arden as he leant against the stone, fingers sliding into one of the perfectly carved grooves between layers of hair. He perched comfortably on the giant's shoulder but the power of the wind at this height made him uneasy.

Socket sat, feet dangling over the edge next to the two ropes that had assisted their climb. They swayed in the wind, dancing rhythmically. 'Decent view from up here, doubt they'll be able to reach us, but we'll sure get a few of them.' The experienced fighter twirled an arrow around in his hand, peering at the iron arrowhead to ensure its efficiency.

'What's the delay?' Arden asked, wanting to concentrate on something other than the terrifying height. Thoughts forced their way into his mind, of what it would be like to fall from here down into that wide blanket of snow. 'Not that I mind...'

'It's an important battle. Looks like they're acknowledging the old ways...' Socket called to him. 'Lining up, leaders face-to-face, weighing each other up. It's mental. The aim is to get into your opponent's head, gain an advantage that way. A scholar called Paesus used to believe it was the most important part of the fight.'

'You agree with him?'

'Nah. Most important part is the end. Standing over your opponent's corpse.'

It made sense. Arden knew which one he would rather be.

He could just about make out two figures pacing through the snow between the two armies who had halted their march, just out of range of the archers. The wind died down, apparently aware of the magnitude of the day's events. 'Should make the shooting easier,' Arden said, eyes not leaving the two figures in the snow.

'Let's make each shot count. Don't wanna be heading down there once the battle is in full flow. Nothing worse than an archer feeling heroic,' Socket advised him.

Arden had no intention of making his way amongst the wild warriors below. He could see the tips of the spears in the vanguard glimmering in the daylight, readied for the fight ahead. A horn sounded once again across the icy wasteland. A huge roar erupted from men of both sides – Tribesmen and Barbarians alike. Two armies coming together as one for a shared love. Battle. Warfare. Bloodshed. Honour. Glory. Whatever you called it; all Arden could foresee was death.

He watched as the line of archers at the back of the army lit their arrows with the burning torches scattered behind the last line of warriors. A warning flurry fell short of the first line of Barbarians but they had their range.

'Take your shot. Don't worry about hitting anything specific. Work out how far you can land a shot. There's enough of them out there for us not to miss for the next few hours.'

Socket was right. A wall of Barbarians lined up for him to hit. Every arrow had to land on at least one of them. Skill and accuracy weren't as necessary as he had been told. This was contrition; being able to withstand the length of the fight. They had the numbers. The Borderland tribes would need to outlast them, outfight them all.

He picked up an arrow and pulled it back with the string of his bone bow. One eye closed, he peered down the shaft and past its iron head, praying that it would find a destination that would kill its target swiftly. A slow breath. A tightening of his fingers. And then... release. He tried to follow its trajectory, but it became lost in the wealth of arrows flying over the battlefield. He thought he saw its descent near the first line of Barbarians but couldn't be sure. Don't stop. Just shoot.

He paused as he reached for another arrow, eyes fixed on the lines of men racing towards each other across the snowy plain. Their roars could clearly be heard, even in his vantage point up high. Spears stabbed, swords slashed, and shields thumped against the men on either side. Arden stood transfixed, in awe of the number of warriors clashing beneath him.

'Look any longer and you might as well make a painting,' Socket barked, knocking him out of his trance. 'Fire some fucking arrows, kid!'

Wanting more range, he pulled his bow up to ensure he didn't hit any of his own side, horrified at the thought of hitting Kiras and Herick. Not that he would be able to tell from this height. The arrow flew high into the air, curving as it dropped amongst the Barbarians. Any one of the cacophony of screams could have been because of his arrow but he had no way of knowing. Arrow number three. Shoot. Shoot. Shoot.

Both armies gave their all, clashing in a messy crowd of weapons, limbs and blood. Arden could barely make out which men were on his own side. He nocked another arrow, leaning forward to spot his next target. Suddenly, he felt his boot slip forward against an icy patch on the giant's shoulder, flinging his body forward, his bone bow dropping from his hands as he lunged for the rope hanging from the side. Both the bow and arrow fell into the melee beneath him along with the arrow.

He missed the rope at his first try, clutching at thin air. Air rushed around him as his body began to topple towards his inevitable demise. This was it. A lame death. An embarrassing death. Stupid idiot. Slipping on the shoulder of a statue. Maybe his fall was why the giant was mourning.

He made one final attempt to reach out for the swaying rope, hoping against hope that he would make it. His heart jumped as his right hand gripped the rope, pulling his body hard and slamming him against the stone statue. He pulled himself close against the rope and sighed, breathing heavily as his whole frame continued to swing against the giant. The roars of battle were closer now. Deafening. Looking up to the heavens, he could just about make out Socket, pulling hard on the rope. Heading back up was impossible. Not now. The only way was down, into the bloodshed.

He crossed his legs over the rope, slowly dropping one burning hand beneath the other and shimmying down his lifeline. Ten feet from the bottom, he jumped from the end of the rope, landing hard against the snow, knees buckling. No time to wait.

Dragging himself up from the snow, he searched for a weapon. His bow lay nearby, snapped in two, worthless. Socket had given him that. No point blubbering over it now. *Grab something. Anything to defend yourself.* That's what he would do. He reached into the inside of his cloak, pulling out a large, curved dagger. Better than nothing.

'You here to fight or to carve the dinner?'

Arden's eyes snapped to Kiras as she danced through the crowds, twin blades cutting through anything that moved. Quick, graceful slices through stomach, leg, neck. The right side of her torso covered in red. A large gash above her right eye released a stream of dark, red blood. Her breathing sounded ragged and slow, but she kept that intense, powerful, menacing look in her eyes as she stomped straight across to him, stepping over a couple of fallen warriors.

'Destroyed my bow...' he muttered weakly in response, glad to see that her still alive.

'Then grab one of these,' she said with an air of exasperation, reaching down at her feet and ripping a long, worn sword from the grasp of a lifeless body and flinging it his way. He raised his hand instinctively and caught the leather handle, testing its weight and grip. A bit heavy, but it would have to be good enough. It was that or death. Simple.

'Thanks.'

'The fuckers were prepared for us. Gonna have to retreat soon. Be ready. Kill anything that moves,' Kiras warned, turning back into the deadly crowd, blades arching in their deadly dance, although Arden felt they were moving slower than before.

He bounced on the balls of his feet, urging himself forward, not wanting to let her down. Fingers flexed around the leather grip as he raised his sword with a roar of his own. He wasn't going to scare anyone else, but he had to do it, giving courage to himself as he watched a huge, burly tribesman fall to the snow, blood spluttering from his mouth with a final cough. A Barbarian, flaming hair long and wild, stood over his victim, noticing Arden and grinning as he heard his roar.

'I see they bring their boys now. You will count as half a kill!' His eyes were wide with bloodlust, one hand bringing a small bloodied axe in an arch through the air.

'You'll count as two for me!' Arden yelled back, shaking with fear but not wanting to show it.

He lunged forward, eager to do something. Anything.

Laughter rang in his ears as fell to the side; sword swatted aside with ease as his face smashed into the cold snow. Other warriors fought on around him, oblivious to his struggle. 'I will teach you a lesson today boy.' The Barbarian's voice boomed at him, as deep as the Great Lake itself. 'It is a shame that you will not live to learn from it.'

The fall jolted a memory, a piece of advice from Sly.

Arden's body tightened with rage as he clung at the snow, turning and throwing a ball of ice straight at his attacker. A headshot. Right between the eyes. Another laugh.

'Your aim is good, boy. But that will not help you today. It will not help you ever again.' Arden fought against the man's grip as his fist tightened around his collar, pulling him from the ground and raising him high into the air above all others. His blade lay forgotten on the ground. Useless.

The first blow to the stomach took all the wind out of him as the handle of the warrior's sword landed beneath his ribs. He tried to draw a breath, but his body wasn't responding. The next strike rocked him and sent the world spinning, hilt striking against his temple. Lights flashed around his vision as he swayed in the Barbarian's grip, helpless.

Eyes burning, he realised this could be his very last chance to fight back before the darkness consumed him. He swung a boot with all the force he could manage. Nothing. Completely missed. That same, annoying laughter. More burning in the backs of his eyes. This must be what it was like to die. He heard steel clatter against the ground, the sound coursing through his head. A hand squeezed against his throat, sucking all life from him. This was it. The end. He opened his eyes, aware that this may be the last thing he would see. Dark clouds had formed overhead, blackening the world. A spark of lightning cut through the sky a second before the roar of thunder.

'Your eyes...' The Barbarian's voice had a hint of panic. Must be delusional. Lack of oxygen. A fond thought to cling to as he passed onto the Sky Plane with his ancestors. 'Red...'

Arden jerked in the Barbarian's grip, feeling a sickness well up from deep inside him. He felt it threaten to rip his body in two as he tried to scream, but he hadn't the energy to manage it. His feet hit the floor and the rest of his body buckled as the warrior loosened his grip. Arden blinked as the heat and the sickness rushed up towards his head. He closed his eyes and then opened them slowly. The fight rumbled on but the Barbarian had frozen, mouth wide open, eyes staring at Arden. The world seemed suddenly red beneath the black clouds. Arden sucked in a deep breath, fingers clutching at his bruised throat as the energy tore at his small frame. Climbing to his knees slowly, he felt his heart beat faster than ever before. His whole body jerked, arms flailing wide and head swinging back, neck snapping in pain as he released an almighty roar.

The world continued to flash red as the thunder boomed around the open, snowy plains. Arden fell once more – weak, exhausted, unable to move even his fingers. His ear lay against the snow, the world on its side. He could see the Barbarian, mouth still open, eyes crying rivers of red. None of this made sense. But it didn't matter. What mattered was that he could rest. He closed his eyes, not wanting to see any more of the red.

The roars of battle had stopped. Only silence. He relaxed at once.

Now he could rest.

DEAR FRIENDS

The light of the moon crept through the clouds and onto the colossal statue. If there was one thing generations before had been good at, it was building shit. It may not have been up to the standard of the wonders of The Floating City of Causrea or the Blind Watchers in Darakeche – but for the Lower City of Archania, a fifty-foot bronze stature of The Fat King Borris was something to be marvelled at. Of course, the statue wasn't fat, that wouldn't do at all. Here he seemed elegant, regal, victorious, slender and handsome. A reminder of the legacy he had left behind, fist clenched in front of him while his other hand raised the standard of the newly-formed United Cities of Archania – Norland, Archania and Starik, three red lines meeting in the middle of a white background. One King to rule them all. It was to be admired. It was to be adored. It was to be loved.

It was covered in pigeon shit.

'Been a while since we've been in the King's Square,' Ariel said, hands on hips as she gazed up at the dead King. 'Good to see Old Borris is still standing. Temple looks in good nick too.'

Aleister had to agree, the Great Temple brought a flood of memories rushing back. 'It's like we never left,' he muttered to himself, staring up at the great domed building. The limestone pillars, three on either side of the colossal open doorway cast long shadows in the moonlight.

'Been a long time since I've confessed,' Bathos admitted, scratching at an itch on the back of his neck as the three of them strolled towards the Great Temple. 'Could probably be a while.'

'Don't think we've got that long, big man. We'd be here for a few cycles if you list everything.' Aleister smirked as they stepped in through the tall, open wooden doors. Nothing different there. That had to be a good sign.

'Erm... guys, are you seeing what I'm seeing?' Ariel asked, one eyebrow raised as she looked at Aleister and Bathos.

The familiar marble columns ran down either side of the temple. Sculptures of The Four were dotted around the cavernous building depicting the old stories Aleister grew up on. The Fight in the Clouds. The Rise of a Nation. The Fall of The Four. The Great Purge. Old tales. Familiar tales. Past the columns and statues in the nave, up the white steps leading to the central dais, an old friend stood talking to some strangers. Less hair than normal and that which remained had turned completely white. A few more wrinkles around the wise, old blue eyes that sparkled in the light shining around the room. Elder Morgan shook hands with a man; one of a group of people in quiet discussion with him. His dark robes matched theirs, but one major difference stood out.

'Why would they be wearing a healer's mask in here? There's no plague,' Aleister muttered to his allies, slowing down as they reached the steps. Morgan's eyes flashed to the three of them, widening in recognition. A huge smile beamed onto his face as he realised who they were.

'Even the most lost and damned can find their way back home to The Four,' he called out to them, arms wide open, welcoming them. 'Please, my friends, we shall meet tomorrow, usual time,' he said to the masked men. The group looked over at the trio, weighing them up as they made their way slowly down the steps and past them. At least that's what Aleister assumed, difficult to tell what lay beneath the masks.

'Making new friends?' Aleister asked, unable to prevent his lips from curling up as he accepted the hug.

'Always. Old habits die hard,' Morgan answered, pushing him away to take a good look at him. 'It seems they aren't the only things that die hard.' He prodded at an old scar at the side of his neck; Aleister had forgotten about that one.

'This little thing? Eager whore in Duhail. Nothing to write home about.' He brushed it off with ease.

'By what I heard, you didn't find anything to write home about.'

'She said that?' Aleister winced at the thought of her.

Push it down. Push it away. A lot of time had passed.

'Broke my niece's damn heart. Married now though, good guy too. Upgrade from the last one.' Morgan cackled and pushed him away, greeting Bathos and Ariel with enthusiastic hugs and shocked comments about how much they had grown. 'I remember when you were knee high. How the tables have turned…' The Elder looked up at Bathos, laughing once more at the giant of a man. 'Why don't we have a seat and some wine? Come, we have a lot of catching up to do!'

Elder Morgan lived a simple life. He'd served The Four as a Young Boy, then a Father and now as an Elder. He'd grown up in the Lower City, survived the plague, two wars and a riot. He'd lived a life, that was certain. Part of that life had included taking in a young brother and sister, recently orphaned. He was the reason Aleister and Ariel were still here and not dead in some ditch.

'What was with the plague doctors, Morgan?' Ariel asked as he ushered them into the leisure room. Aleister sat down on his usual creaky chair facing the only entrance – old habits die hard. The room was bare, as it should be for an elder. The only extravagances Aleister could see were the usual: books of all kinds lining the walls, floor to ceiling, and an old, unopened bottle of Causrea Red. The old man hadn't changed, it seemed.

'Healers. Not for an actual plague. All figurative. Think themselves clever,' Morgan said as he grabbed glasses from an old, dusty cupboard. Could do with a good clean in here. 'The city has changed since you left. Maybe not here, in these four walls, but out there, something is brewing.' He poured them each a glass, raising his own in salute and taking the first sip to their health. 'But it is good to see the three of you. Bless The Four.'

'And you Morgan. We have been gone for too long it seems. The world is changing. I take it you felt the rumble of the land earlier? It's a warning, something is wrong,' Aleister insisted. He'd seen countless horrors over the past few years: men committing acts of unspeakable villainy, children starving in streets, the burnings… yet, a shadow lurked behind it all, a darkness waiting to pounce on Takaara. He couldn't work out why, it was just a feeling, deep down in his gut. He'd been around long enough to know when to trust that feeling.

'Something is wrong. This Kingdom, this whole region

of Takaara, it has a history going back to when the Gods walked the earth, their feet stepping onto the same grains of soil as our own. This world is crying out, it's in pain, dying,' Morgan said bitterly. 'The King is ill, Mason D'Argio and his men are steadily growing in power, and faith in The Four wanes throughout the city. These rumbles in the ground are no mere coincidence. This city was founded by men of such power and magic that it is almost incomprehensible for us mere mortals. However, their descendants are stifled, muzzled – forced to hide in the shadows. The world is fighting back whilst breathing its last few breaths. If we listen, we might just be able to save it.'

Aleister rubbed the scratchy stubble on his chin, weighing up the pleading words of the Elder. When he left Archania, he had such lofty dreams and high hopes. Now, he wasn't sure what he had. His life. He was thankful for that. His sister and closest friend. Two of the greatest companions he could wish for. But he wanted something more. To live for more.

'What can we do to help?' he asked, pulling his shoulders back and sighing with the cracking of his back.

Elder Morgan gave a smirk that Aleister had never seen before. His weary face changed in the light of the candles and took on a wholly different tone to what he was used to. 'My dear boy, I was hoping you might say that.'

The legs of his chair scraped against the floorboards as Morgan rushed out of the room, begging for patience. Aleister shrugged his shoulders at the silent, questioning gaze of both Ariel and Bathos. He'd never seen the Elder in such an excitable mood.

The old man rushed back in and threw something onto the table before them, grinning ear-to-ear. Ariel leant forward and picked the item up, holding it high in the air so that the light of the candles bounced off the black mask.

'Why do you have the mask of a plague doctor, Elder Morgan?' Aleister asked, intrigued. His friend was full of surprises today. 'New line of work on the side? Not making enough as an Elder?'

'Bah!' Morgan snorted. 'If money were of any importance, I'd have been forced to give up this role long ago. As I said, Takaara is crying out, we must listen, and some people in the city truly are.'

'The healers. These plague doctors?' Ariel answered.

'Yes. A small group, but one with the intention of not going quietly into the night. They mean to make a difference, to stand up for what is right, to bring honour and glory back to the fallen Kingdom – because, make no mistake, this Kingdom has fallen far beneath what it was once accustomed to. Once, it was the jewel in the crown of Takaara. Now, it is a forgotten Kingdom. East, South and West move forward with each cycle whilst we stagnate, to be left in their dust. It isn't right, we must act!'

'And how do you suppose we should do that?' Aleister asked, pouring the wine down his throat as his eyes glanced towards Bathos. The big man could read danger brewing like no other. He sat there, staring into the flames of the candles, lost in their wild dance.

'Once the King is gone, Mason will be the true power in the Kingdom. The United Cities of Archania will for all intents and purposes be part of the Eastern Empire. It will be less than a cycle before it is made official, weeks if they are confident. We'll be forced to fight in their proxy wars against the South and West, taken apart bit-by-bit until there is nothing left of us. We'll be sitting ducks, waiting for an attack from all sides. Hell, the Borderlands may even try to finally do what they have threatened to for so long.'

Aleister stayed silent. He'd heard the rumours of this Mason D'Argio. He'd seen the power of the Eastern Empire. He couldn't argue against anything the Elder said. As his sister had always liked to say, '*If you've got nothing useful to add then keep your damn trap shut*!' and so he did.

'There is only one course of action that we can take. Aleister, Ariel, Bathos, my dear friends.' Aleister felt one side of his lips raise in amusement as the Elder stood and raised his half-empty glass to each of them, knowing what he was about to say and unsure if he could think of anything crazier. 'I am asking you to join me, to join the healers, these *Doctors*. To join...' He downed his drink in one go and gasped, eyes widening with a dramatic flourish. 'The Revolution!'

Guess they'd made it back home at the perfect time.

Aleister stood, raising his own glass and ignoring his sister as she covered her face with one hand. 'Don't say it Aleister...' she muttered.

'We'll hear you out,' he said, his grin wide enough to make his cheeks ache, 'on one condition.'

'Anything.' Morgan's eyes gleamed bright in the light, giving him back some of his youthful vigour as he grasped at the hope that his old friends would help him.

'I need an address...'

'I fucking knew it.' Ariel shook her empty glass in the air and sat up, face grim and stern. 'I need another drink.'

The sun fell beneath the city walls, casting a red hue over the land as Aleister strolled through the city, ripped paper in hand. The handwriting was messy and uneven, but he could read it well enough. He was heading in the right direction. Or at least, he hoped so.

It had been five years since he had walked on the paved pathway leading towards the Palace. Five years since he'd passed the Great Fountain of The Four. Mud and rotten fruit stained the faces of the marble figures as they sternly pushed their hands into the middle of the square they created, linking them together. Dirty water circled them and every now and then a jet of water would squirt high into the air and then drop back to the pool at the bottom. Not the best symbol for the Kingdom.

Passers-by stomped along the pathway, not even looking his way, lost in their own problems. He glanced to his right and grinned as he saw a few couples making their way towards the gate that led to Lovers' Park. So many memories. So much had changed since then. Yet, so much was still the same.

Five years was a long time to be gone. Gone from his home. From friends. He'd thought about returning, to see the old faces and share a drink with the few people whose company he had enjoyed in his youth. Every time he had thought about it, he'd convinced himself that there was something more important for him to get on with. Archania could wait. The old faces could wait. The drink could wait. He'd not realised that life would move on, not just for him, but for everyone. Returning home wouldn't mean slotting back into the same routine. Things had moved on, no matter how familiar the parks and the pathways were.

Aleister had left as a boy, side by side with Ariel and Bathos, taking with them nothing but some crude weapons and high hopes. He was returning a young man, better weapons but lower hopes and shoulders weighed down by the horrors he had witnessed. The big, wonderful world he'd hoped to see wasn't what he had expected. He'd escaped Archania to get away from death, disease and hatred. Seemed as though it had all followed him. Each of the four corners of the world weren't far enough to escape them.

He reached a crossroads as the sun became fully submerged under the horizon, at rest for the night. He looked at the wrinkled paper and sighed before looking back up at the Palace, the pathway lit by candlelight. He turned to his right, the path less lit. He puffed his cheeks out and sighed, letting his lips vibrate with the motion. No point waiting any longer. He placed one foot in front of the other. The right path it is then.

Security wasn't as he'd expected. A couple of inattentive guards circling the outside of the buildings but nothing more. He looked at the piece of paper one more time and then at the number on the wooden door, framed with gold swirls. She'd done well for herself. That's for sure. He knocked twice, his heart thumping hard in his chest. If only his old buddies out East could see him now. Aleister the coward – scared to even knock on a door. Where was the Aleister who had led men into battle? The Aleister who had defied royalty in Darakeche? He wasn't here, that was obvious. But if he wasn't here, then who was?

'One moment!' Her voice as soft and melodic as he remembered. Five years hadn't changed that beautiful voice of hers. His heart thumped quicker, threatening to burst straight out of his chest. Not the best way to go.

The door sprang open revealing a familiar, beautiful face. Raven-black hair fell loosely to her shoulders. Red lips popped out from her smooth pale face and her eyes widened as she realised who was at her door. Her eyes. They were different.

'No gold...' Aleister muttered. When he had left, she had been a girl on the cusp of womanhood, beautiful and innocent. Now, she stood in front of him as a woman fully blossomed. None of her beauty had faded with age but the innocence wasn't quite as pronounced. It had been replaced by an elegant, regal stance. It only made her even more stunning in his eyes.

'Hey Ella.'

Her face darkened as her eyes lowered, lips pursing tightly together. Aleister opened his mouth but his lips were too dry, tongue too terrified to reply as he realised his mistake. 'Five years. Five fucking years with not one word and that's the best greeting you have?' she said through gritted teeth as her eyes stung with tears, voice growing steadily higher with each word.

Aleister raised his hands, palms facing her. 'I know.'

'You know? What the hell do you know, Aleister?' she screeched. 'Do you know how I cried every single day for a month after you left without a word. Do you know how I waited for a year for any word about you, worrying that you had been killed?'

'No.' He didn't.

'No. You don't.' He saw the slap coming. Could have dodged it if he had a mind to. It stung but he deserved it. He rubbed his cheek softly, eyes not leaving hers.

'Not the first time you've hit me,' he said, risking a small smile.

'If you're anything like the boy I used to know, it won't be the last.' The corners of her lips twitched ever so slightly. She opened the door further and stepped back.

Aleister walked straight in.

'I've missed you, Ella.'

She slammed the door shut behind him.

He welcomed the burn as the liquid raced its way down his throat, warming his whole body. 'Difficult to get out east, Archanian firewhiskey.'

Ella just stared at him blankly, full glass still resting in her hand on the table in front of her. 'Why didn't you say goodbye? Or write?' She didn't sound angry, that's what hurt the most. He wanted the hits, the violence, the shouting. He could deal with that. This sadness, disappointment; he didn't know how to handle it.

'I thought it would hurt too much. If I went to see you, if I tried to say goodbye, I wouldn't leave.' Aleister stared at his empty glass, unable to meet her sad eyes.

'Would that have been such a bad thing?'

Would it? Looking back on what he'd been through, there'd been some highs and lows, laughs and tears. He looked up at her and finally met her golden eyes. It wouldn't have been so bad. He'd throw it all away to be with her for one second.

'Maybe not.' Pathetic.

'How's your sister? And Bathos?' she asked, changing the subject.

'Still sickeningly in love. They wanted to come and say hi but...'

'I get it.'

They sat in awkward silence, each unable to say the

words they wanted to. Aleister scratched at the stubble on his chin and looked around the room. 'Nice place you got here.'

'I'm lucky. Matthias has a good job.'

Aleister winced at the name, as though the sound of it alone was able to pierce him. 'You're happy?' he asked, unsure if he wanted to hear the answer.

Ella swished the alcohol around in her glass before throwing her head back and downing it in one. She had changed. She gasped at the expected burn and sighed, staring straight at Aleister, as though she could see his fears. 'He's a good man. Kat recommended him. Mother likes him too.'

Aleister cleared his throat to hide his amusement. 'Good. That's good. How is the old bat?'

Ella smiled. That one action sent his heart soaring and his lips mirrored hers.

'You don't have to ask. I know how much of a cow she was to you. She's fine though. Still moaning, keeps asking when I'm going to give her grandkids.' She smirked.

'I bet she was happy when I left.'

'Most people were. You were a pain,' Ella laughed. Aleister joined in. 'The thief who claimed to only rob from those who could afford it. She was glad to see the back of you, but she hated seeing me sad.'

The joy faded from his face as he saw the sadness in her eyes. 'I'm sorry. You didn't deserve that pain. I was young and foolish.'

'It's in the past now,' Ella said as she poured another glass for herself and then for Aleister. 'Life moves on.'

'It does,' he agreed, though he painfully wished that it hadn't.

'Did you realise your dream of forming your own mercenary group?' Ella asked.

'I did actually. You might have heard of them,' Aleister replied with a wink, proud of at least something he was able to accomplish away from Archania. 'I founded The Red Sons.'

It landed like a bird's shit.

'Who are they?'

'Seriously? The *Red Sons*?' Aleister asked, confused. 'We helped put an end to the year long siege of Darakeche. Stopped an all-out war in the Heartlands. You've never heard of us?'

Ella's shrug stabbed him through the heart. Or at least

through his inflated ego. 'I must live a sheltered life all the way up here in the United Cities. Word doesn't reach us so easily. Well done though. I'm sure you did very well!'

Aleister's shoulders dropped. 'Thanks,' he muttered. 'We even made our own symbol. Some fool mixed up the phrasing of our name, his common tongue wasn't so good. Still looks cool though.' He pulled back the sleeve of his silk shirt and thrust his wrist forward.

Ella smirked. 'Mother would hate that,' she said as she looked at the red circle with eight even beams reaching out from the centre. 'Was it painful?'

'Not too much. Felt like being stabbed. Little stabs, anyway,' Aleister answered as he sat back and pulled his sleeve back down.

The conversation ceased, pausing over a chasm, waiting for either of them to say what they really felt. Aleister's mouth was dry, palms sweating. He had a million things to say to her, but his body just wouldn't respond. Through the long journey north he had tried to put his thoughts and feelings into some sort of coherent speech but words in this matter had failed them. For a moment, he wished he was as proficient in speaking as he was with the blade. He just wanted her to understand what she meant to him. What she had always meant to him.

'Why have you come back?' It was blunt. She deserved an answer, but Aleister wasn't sure that he had one.

Because it was painful to be away from her? Because every night he closed his eyes and all he could see was her face? Because his hopes of a life of freedom were just the dreams of a naïve young fool?

All of the above.

'Remember when we would just sit by the lake in Lovers' Park? The sun would be low, and we'd just stay there, enjoying each other's company. I loved those moments. We'd share stories about the heroes from all the kingdoms around the world; men and women who had courageously defended the weak and innocent, fought against horror and corruption, stood defiantly against those who would stamp on the little guy.' Aleister slunk back into his chair and gave an incredulous laugh. 'That's all they were. Stories. Out there,' he said, pointing out of the window, 'there are no heroes. Just people trying to live their life, trying to survive. We were naïve, they were just fantasies of a fool. Out there, all we found was blood and war. Death and destruction. There are no heroes. Only survivors.'

He leant back in his chair, blowing out his cheeks and running both hands through his long, dark hair. His foot tapped furiously on the floor under the table.

'I don't believe that,' Ella said, almost a whisper.

'You might not. But it's true.' He had been out there. He knew the horrors, the dangers. The truth.

Ella just shook her head. 'I've lived my whole life as a mage in a country that hates and shuns my kind. I've hidden it, where I can. Pretty good at it now actually.' She placed her hands over her face and when she removed them, Aleister could no longer see the gold. She was just like anyone else. Except a million times more beautiful. 'There aren't many of us in the city. Most live in the villages further away, out of sight where we can't be easily seen. But the ones who do live here, we meet up, in secret. We work on solutions to our problems. We help and support each other. A young boy called Tate was burnt to death last week. Hadn't been thinking properly since his dad passed away. No other family left. They tortured him. The killed him. He wasn't a survivor.' She downed her second drink and slammed the glass on the table. 'He was a fucking hero.'

'Ella...'

'You need to go,' she commanded, voice hard and even. 'Matthias will be home soon.'

Aleister stood up, chair scraping against the wooden floor. He'd pushed her enough. The door creaked open as he pulled the handle, daring one last look at the forlorn figure sitting on her own at the table, empty glass in hand. 'Can I see you again?'

She paused. To Aleister, the world stopped in that moment; pausing to take a deep breath before a plunge into deep waters.

'Yes,' she sighed.

He breathed again as the world restarted once more.

JUST THE BEGINNING

'Why would they build such a thing so close to the border? Temples are usually built in the heart of their city, not all the way out here. It's almost as close to us as it is to them,' Baldor said with a confused look on his face as he gazed up in the shadow of the monstrosity.

'I'll tell you why. They want to piss us off. Fucking southerners,' Sly spat. 'They think they can build their damned temples right in our face and just expect us to accept it.' He didn't like it. Not one fucking bit.

'Having somewhere warm to stay for the night will be an improvement. Can't turn our noses up at it,' Raven said. 'Anyway, it's in their land. No problem with it in my opinion.'

Sly stopped in his tracks and faced Raven. He sounded less like a tribe leader as each day passed. 'We're hardened warriors. I'll sleep in the fucking snow if it means I can tear this shit tip down.'

'We don't need to fight battles on two fronts Sly,' Bane cautioned him. Too much caution. That was his problem. For a warrior who wore the ears of his victims on a chain around his neck, he sure liked to think about things a lot.

Sly grumbled to himself and trudged off once more towards the temple, wishing that he was heading into battle with the others, fighting the Barbarians face to face and covered in their blood. That's what real warriors did. They didn't head off in the other direction, tails between their legs, away from battle and off on some dumb, pointless mission.

The journey was getting distinctly more boring by the day. Each day, as they trudged away from the mountains and snow of their homeland and towards the green forest lands of the northern region, Sly felt more uncomfortable, uneasy. Raven and Bane were spending most of their time discussing the politics of the continent, Cray was as silent and distant as usual, and Baldor withdrawn and upset. Probably missing his favourite bitch. Although, he had to silently admit that even he had spent some time thinking about Kiras – at least she led with her weapons.

'How's it going, Baldor? Your first journey away from the Borderlands,' Raven called to his friend.

'Not bad,' he grunted back. 'Bit warm for my liking.' He shrugged his massive shoulders, causing a small amount of rainwater to fall off them. The giant warrior had ice in his veins; that's what you get for being raised on an island on the edge of the icy cold Far North. Reckon he didn't even see a fire in his youth. This must be boiling hot for him.

'It'll only be getting warmer I'm afraid. This'll be good for you my giant friend. Look, even Cray seems to be having the time of his life here.' Cray just grunted and carried on straight past Raven, causing Bane and Baldor to chuckle along with Raven. Sly just watched. *Still waiting for the cunt to snap*. They all snapped. He made sure of it.

'So, what's the plan, Raven? We going straight past the temple?' Bane asked, looking over Raven's shoulder at the large building behind him.

'We'll scout it out first, see how many people are around. Then I say we go have a word with whoever is in charge and find out where we can crash for the night. Some extra food for the journey would be helpful too. I'm sure Sly will be able to politely sort that one out for us,' Raven explained, drawing up a corner from the scarred side of his mouth.

'I always thought it would be Cray that had the silver tongue of the group,' Bane said with a deep booming laugh. 'Well, let's waste no more time, I'm starving!'

His eyes stared up at the unique building ruining the landscape. A monstrosity forcing itself upon the world and yelling at all around to stare and gaze in wonder and awe. Sly had never seen a structure like this before. The height of the building was at least six times the size of the average warrior. Who would need a building to be so tall? This whole thing was just a waste of resources. Six white stone pillars had been built to hold the building up while the roof had a downward slant on either side that Sly assumed allowed the excess rain that the area was accustomed to, to run off its side. Decent craftsmanship he had to begrudgingly admit. Still a fucking waste.

'Why is this being built here? It is too close to the Borderlands,' Sly wondered out loud, his voice echoing throughout the wide space. 'Surely they have temples closer to where they live.' Building this close to the border was a risky move for the United Cities. While fighting between the Borderlands and the United Cities of Archania was incredibly rare at the moment, the two sides didn't exactly see eye-to-eye on most issues and many of the tribes would see building a great religious monument so close to their homes as an act of aggression. His people didn't take kindly to acts of aggression. 'They're getting cocky, Raven. Too fucking cocky. They need to be taught a lesson,' Sly suggested, already knowing what the reply would be.

'I'm sure there's an explanation. Let's not be too hasty,' Raven cautioned.

'Hey! What do you think you're doing?!'

Raven sighed as he saw three men running towards them. Sly gave them a grin, letting them see his crooked, yellow teeth as he placed one rough, scarred hand on the hilt of his weapon. Time for the introductions.

'Don't be alarmed, southerners. If I'd have wanted you dead, you'd all be dead by now,' Sly said, giving his best chilling laugh and pulling out a dagger to scratch at an itch on his lip. Perfect way to put them ease. Works every time.

'Please, wait! We mean you no harm. We are just weary travellers passing through,' Raven called to the men, their attention immediately turning on him. *Shame*, thought Sly. *Could have finally had some fun on this trip.*

'And who exactly are you?' asked the one in the middle, staring at Raven as he strode towards them. The three men were all in working attire: scruffy and beaten clothing. Obviously, they were working on the final stages of this building.

'I am Raven Redbeard. A tribe leader of the Borderlands,' Raven said with pride, stopping just in front of the three men and Sly.

'And I'm the King of Archania. Pleased to fucking meet you.' The three workers laughed together and patted each other on the back at their great wit.

Sly twirled a dagger in his hand and looked towards Raven for the signal. A silent shake of the head stopped any bloodshed. *Just keep talking you southern fucks. Even his patience can wear thin.*

Raven's warmth dropped as all sign of gentility left his face, replaced with a look of thunder as his face went almost as red as his beard, voice lowering almost to a whisper, 'Take me to whoever is in charge here or, I promise you, my friend here will destroy you so completely, this lovely temple here will be known as the Red Temple throughout the whole of the known world.'

How he managed to keep his face straight, Sly didn't know. One of the men seemed to piss himself on the spot, another started backing off in an instant, while the cocky prick who had spoken first attempted to mumble some form of apology.

'Speak up or I start cutting,' Sly added, lips widening with each passing moment. 'And to warn you. I like to start with the fruits...' The horror on their faces was precious as they followed his lowered gaze. The journey was beginning to improve.

'High Priestess Dianar is inside the next room, inspecting the building, I shall take you to her.' The three men stumbled over each other in their haste to rush into the building. Cray followed them with Sly right after, still with a dagger gripped tightly in his hand. Just in case.

Bane smirked. 'Remind me never to piss Redbeard off!'

Sly paused at the door and motioned for Baldor to walk through ahead of him.

'Finally, a building big enough for your freakish form to fit in, big guy.'

Baldor only grunted in response, his eyes searching the cavernous building, not even a hint of joy on his face.

Sly wondered what it was with these southerners. They always tried to build these grand, fancy monstrosities, attempting to show off to the rest of the world, to impress god knows who. As they had just proved, you can build whatever you want, but it is what a man can do on a more primal level that truly counts when you want respect, when you want power. Of course, in his opinion those three fucks should be sliced up into small pieces right now and not leading them to some bitch priestess of theirs. Still, threatening to paint the temple red was a pretty good plan. Raven seemed to be getting a touch dramatic in his role of late.

Sly liked it. Dramatic and brutal. Much better than his peace speeches. Much more fun.

What Sly didn't like was being taken to their leader. A High Priestess, they had said. The south had always been soft, but they were reaching new lows. What kind of soft, weak willed woman ran a place like this? Probably an ugly one. Dog ugly. What Sly knew of the South, it was usually the ugly ones that wanted to be involved in religion; the pretty ones have far more interesting things to be involved in.

He passed what seemed like over a hundred wooden benches either side of him. Light streamed in through five circular holes in the ceiling, the biggest one shining directly onto a stone altar at the front and centre of the room. *Love to see the effect on a rainy day. Stupid fucks.*

'If you would like to take a seat, I will be delighted to inform the High Priestess of your arrival,' said the funny prick from earlier, struggling to meet any of their eyes before rushing off quickly into a darkened room behind the unadorned altar. *He'd learn his place. Stupid, little cunt.*

Grabbing a seat on one of the benches next to Cray, Sly sighed and placed his muddy boots against the bench in front of him, stretching his arms out as far as he could. Bane took a seat behind him, whistling some song he knew, out of tune. Raven paced down the aisle, peering around the large room with keen interest. *Better be thinking of the best places to hang these cunts. Ain't nothin' else to look at in here.* The whole place wasn't good enough to Sly for anything but stacking bodies. The bench creaked slightly as Baldor sat down next to him, not used to the weight.

'You haven't been eating all our food have you, you great brute?' Sly chuckled.

'How about I eat you and then we won't have to waste food on you?' Baldor replied, the shadow of joy threatening to break out onto his face. He looked as out of place as he always did; taking up too much room and constantly looking as though he wanted to be anywhere but here. *Can't fucking blame him; he's happier with his hammer and a good fight. He's a warrior, always will be. Not sure if I could say the same about the rest of 'em.*

Raven and Bane dropped deep into conversation – looking around the new structure and commenting on the paintings that adorned the room. Most of them seemed the same: men in robes burning or having their heads chopped off; stern-looking men pointing at things. *They want people to be scared. If they want to do that, they need to do better than paintings. Only blood,* real *blood, can make a man afraid.* Not that Sly knew anything about that.

Minutes passed by slowly, the unfinished temple silent apart from the odd cough from one of the workers stood at the back of the room, sheepishly apologising every time he did so. Sly tapped a dagger restlessly against his thigh. It didn't help that Cray just sat right there, not moving a muscle, constantly staring at the altar with a grim look on his face.

'Not a fan of religion, eh talkie?' Sly ask him. Cray turned his head and looked at him, frowning.

'Not a fan of control,' he turned his head to look back at the altar before spitting on the floor before him.

Sly looked over at Raven and Bane, both paused their conversation at the rare, spoken words. The man was a mystery to them all. None of them liked him. He was Saul's guy. Distrust was natural – they didn't have to explain it. They sure as hell didn't have to feel bad about it. This was the tribal way. It always had been. Men under Saul's command could not be trusted. An unspoken truth.

Every time Cray spoke, it always seemed cryptic. This man was hiding something and until Sly could work out what it was, he would be sleeping with one eye open.

Footsteps echoed from the darkened room behind the altar, interrupting the silence that had taken hold of the room. Sly faced the darkness and saw the mouthy worker leave the room, his eyes fixed on the floor as though he did not wish to face any of the warriors in the room. Still terrified. Behind him came a woman seemingly bathed in light. Her golden gown ran down to the floor and flowed majestically behind her. Light seemed to cling to her very being.

Sly gave Baldor a silent nudge, licking his dry lips as he looked upon her face, at her sharp, beautiful features and long, waving, golden hair. It had been a while.

She had a surprisingly commanding aura about her for one that seemed so young and beautiful. Didn't seem past her nineteenth year by Sly's reckoning, and yet he could see by the stern glint in her green eyes why these men took orders from her.

'Greetings men of the Borderlands. I am High Priestess Dianar. I apologise for your long wait, we were not expecting guests for a few weeks at least. As you can see, we are unprepared for such company.' Her voice was strong, proud and flowed almost like the sound of a river. This woman had power.

He had been a friend of Kiras' for enough time now to be aware that women can have a power similar or greater than that of men, but that was raw power, a power familiar to him. This was different. This was majestic. This felt like magic. He shook his head and moved his finger once more to the hilt of a dagger. He'd been around enough to know the dangers and risks involved in magic – he'd seen men break, turning from brave heroes into dribbling wrecks. It couldn't be trusted.

'This wasn't a scheduled visit. We didn't intend to intrude upon you and your... gracious workers.' Raven gave the men a withering look, pausing for a moment as they cowered at his words. 'In fact, we were not aware that such a structure had been built so close to our lands. I am Raven, leader of a tribe of the Borderlands. My fellow travellers and I are heading to the city of Archania; I need to speak to their leader. We only hope that we can have a dry floor to sleep on and some warm food for the night and then we shall be off.'

Any warmth fled from her face at these words. 'It is within our borders; we do not need to let you know of every development we care to take on. You could learn from this place though, once it is ready for visitors. Our God of Light can watch over all that seek to leave the darkness.'

'Leave the preachy shit, little girl. We prefer the darkness. Can we have the food and rest or not?' Sly snapped, bored with the conversation already. He hadn't come here for a sermon. If these fools couldn't give anything but words, then it was time to move on.

Dianar's composure seemed to leave her for a moment as she flashed a menacing look at the rude guest. Then her mask returned.

'Of course, you may. Enjoy your night here. Tomorrow you must leave for Archania.'

With that, she turned her back on them all and made to leave the room without a backward glance, all traces of welcome going with her. 'Get our esteemed guests some hot food and show them where they can stay. Make sure they are gone in the morning,' she told the uncomfortable men she passed, her cold voice carrying through the large room. The workers gave quick, fearful looks at their unwanted guests, not able to work out what would be worse: having them stay for the night; or having to force them to leave in the morning.

'Subtle Sly. Subtle,' Raven said, shaking his head.

'You know these religious types, Raven. They're all cracked in the head. We weren't going to get anything good outta her apart from the food and a dry night. Still, I'd like a bit more. Wonder if she's had to take any of those vows these God-fearing women love to harp on about. Wouldn't mind stepping out of the darkness for that. She's got some fight in her,' Sly replied with a wink.

'Sometimes I wonder how you struggle to make friends, Sly.'

'Sly's right though, Raven. These religious types can be dangerous. Do we even stay one night? Let's get the food and leave. That woman makes me uneasy.' Bane shook his body, as though it would rid him of his thoughts.

'Some woman scaring a leader of a Borderland tribe, Bane? What the fuck's up with that?' laughed Sly, throwing his head back and slapping Cray on the back, angering the warrior.

'Most of our people know that Kiras could take you in a one-on-one fight, Sly, so maybe it's not best to get into that.' Bane replied with his own laugh.

Sly frowned but left it at that, grumbling to himself. 'That woman is man through and through, let me tell ya. She's a freak. No shame in losing to that one.'

Sly scratched his beard and turned away, his thoughts centred on the majestic woman who had just dismissed them so easily. She was so confident in herself, so comfortable in her power and surroundings. She felt she deserved her position and she wanted to make sure everybody else know it. Arrogance. It reminded him of Saul. He didn't like it one bit.

'Things are changing with the South. They're getting bolder. Building a temple so close to our border is no accident. I don't trust 'em, especially these zealous kinds,' Bane answered gravely, his thoughts obviously falling on a similar path.

'We still need to warn them about the Barbarians and see if there is any kind of help they can offer us. We'll see how things stand as soon as we get there. It's possible not all of the south has been swayed by this shit,' Raven replied.

'Doubt it. These southerners are fucking fools. Mark my words, this is just the beginning,' Sly remarked darkly.

Baldor grunted his affirmation. He knew it. They all knew it. Just the beginning.

'Are you sure about this, brother?'

Aleister splashed the finger length blade in the bucket of water before placing it against his right cheek, drawing the blade slowly down his skin, careful not to draw blood. The scrape of the blade made a satisfying sound as it ripped the short stubble away; his first clean shave in Gods know when.

'As sure as I have ever been.' After the shit they'd been through over the last couple of years, he wasn't about to let his sister rain on his parade. 'How come you're so against it? I thought you liked her?' He caught the roll of her eyes in the round, reflective piece of metal perched upon the wooden table leaning against the damaged wall. There were multiple holes scattered throughout the wood and if he listened closely, he could hear the scurrying of what he hoped were small footsteps of mice. The room was sparsely furnished, but he liked it like that. A small bed, low table, metal mirror to check himself by and a couple of buckets to be used as he saw fit. Not a room for royalty but a damn sight better than what he had been used to on the road.

'You know how much I like her. That's not the problem.' Her arms were folded tight across her chest with her dark hair pulled up tight into a manageable bun. Not exactly the image of reassurance he wanted. 'Her husband will not be best pleased. And that's putting a positive fucking spin on it.'

'Well, that's why he doesn't need to know,' Aleister responded, wincing as the blade cut a small spot on the edge of his chin. He rubbed his thumb against it and wiped the blood away. 'Anyway, we're not doing anything wrong. Just two friends meeting up to catch up on lost time.' He'd always taken pride in being able to convince people of what he wanted. That comment didn't even convince himself.

'If you're not doing anything wrong, then why does he not need to know?'

'Lectures from my little sister aren't as fun as they sound you know?'

'Lecturing my big brother isn't as fun as it sounds you know?'

'Liar.'

'Just a bit.' She sighed and strolled over to him, placing

a hand on each shoulder and forcing him to look her in the eyes. 'Be careful, Aleister. She's a good woman. Think about what is best for her.'

He sighed, throwing the blade into the bucket with a splash and blowing his cheeks out. 'She is a good woman. The last thing I want is for her to be upset and hurt.' This time he was convincing. This time he believed it.

She released him, strolling over to the open window, watching the sun set behind the slanted, wooden buildings of the Lower City. Small rays of light fought to sneak in, leaving a trail of dust motes dancing in the air. 'I don't know why, but I just feel like something bad is about to happen.' Aleister instantly readied a mock rebuttal but the tone in her voice made him halt and think for once.

'It's the first time we've been back for years. The first time in a while that we've paused and taken a breath. It's normal to feel a sense of dread, especially in this dive.' The couple in the room next door began shouting again, as if on cue. 'At least we're together. Together, we can get through any shit.'

He walked across the room, ensuring that his bare feet missed the upstanding, rusty nails he'd almost caught himself on the day before. He placed a hand around his sister's shoulder and stared out onto the street. Screaming merchants, cheeky children, the odd fashionably-dressed gentlemen attempting to keep to the shadows on their way to get their latest fix away from prying eyes. This city sure was special.

'Something just isn't feeling good. It's right in my gut – a sense that we're walking into danger. I haven't felt this way since we left Darakeche.' She placed her hand on his, eyes glistening with tears she dared not allow to roll down her face. She was strong. She always had been. Strongest out of the three of them and that was a sure fact.

'Sure it's not just the salted pork from yesterday?' he asked with a snort, allowing her to elbow him in the ribs with barely a move away. He deserved that jab. 'This was meant to be a good break for us. Away from the endless fighting. A chance to reset. If you're not feeling good, then we don't have to stay here. Another couple of days, then we can go.' He said the words, ignoring the pain in his chest as they left his lips. He wasn't ready to leave so soon. Ready to leave the city again. Ready to leave her again.

'Let's see how things go. Maybe it's just me...' she

whispered to the darkening city.

'Come on,' Aleister said, dragging her away from the window and pushing the broken wooden shutters closed to block out the view from their room. 'Bathos will be waiting for us. You know how uncomfortable he gets sitting in a tavern on his own. He'll either be drinking the tavern dry or caving in some poor idiot's head. Bound to be one or the other.'

'That's why I love him,' Ariel answered, exaggerating the fluttering of her eyelashes.

'Me too.'

'Promise me you'll be careful tonight, Aleister? That you won't be an idiot.' She turned her eyes towards him once again, eyes he'd struggled since a young age to ignore. It was the big brother in him. Big softie more like.

'Don't know if I can promise that, little sister. But I can promise things will get better for the three of us.' He stopped for a moment, hearing the smash of glass against the wall next door. Things were escalating. 'This is just the beginning...'

Aleister raised his trusty, tattered, olive green flask to his wet lips and threw his head back. He welcomed the burn of his throat as the liquid slipped down past his tongue and on its way through him. It steadied his nerves. Calmed him. As if he needed calming to meet a woman. This wasn't like him. He was confident, cocky even, some would say. Now here he was, walking down the moonlit street, hands shaking and needing a calming drink to think straight. This wasn't any old woman. This was *the* woman. He knew that now, even if he wasn't willing to admit it to his sister.

He placed the flask back into the inside of his leather jacket, marvelling at how it had managed to survive the past couple of years. It had been a gift from a renegade soldier from the South. He'd been shocked to hear that Aleister had left his tent to join battle without a flask to steady his hands. Aleister had accepted gladly, eager to make new allies. Later that day, his new friend lay motionless on the ground, an arrow through his neck. It was a wake-up call, a reminder of the frailty of life on the road.

Smoke filled his nostrils as he continued down the cobbled path, jumping out of the way of a horse and cart passing by loaded with merchant wares. He looked up and saw the smoke seeping out of one of the larger wooden buildings in this part of the city. It wasn't the harsh smell of smoke caused by burning wood, it had an odd flavour, easy and welcoming.

'Got some new brands in this moon if you fancy it?' Aleister twisted to face the speaker, a scantily-clad woman with long, curly red hair that fell bouncing onto her huge bust. 'If that's not your thing, could always try something else.' She pulled the lower part of her skirt up, grabbing at the frilly, laced material and showing off a bit more leg than necessary. She offered him a wink and a lick of her overtly red lips, just in case he didn't understand the meaning of her words.

'Not tonight, I'm afraid,' he answered with a devilish grin.

'Your loss, honey,' she muttered back, dropping the skirt and leaning against the iron door frame. Lady Sofia's Rooms of Pleasure were still thriving if the noises coming out from the open windows were anything to go by. Good to see the old professions were still thriving in Archania.

'Still a hit with the ladies...'

Her hood cast a shadow over her face; plump, red lips caught the moonlight in a way that made Aleister pause and catch his breath. He didn't need any guesses to know who had snuck up behind him. 'Ella.'

'Enjoying being back?' she asked, nodding over her shoulder at Lady Sofia's.

'Hasn't changed much,' he replied. 'From the outside,' he added, pulling at his collar as he suddenly felt hot. 'Walked past it loads back in the day.'

'Hmm...' Ella groaned. 'Come on, follow me. There's some people I want you to meet.'

'You've piqued my curiosity.' He followed her, half a step behind as she wove through the busy crowds, gliding through them with the air of someone who knew these parts well. Impressive. When they were younger, Ella had only visited the Lower City to visit her uncle or Aleister. It was a place to be feared for her, a place too erratic and unpredictable for her to be comfortable. Now she was leading him with ease through some of the seedier parts of the streets. 'You've changed since we last walked these streets.'

'Grown up. Life has its way of forcing you to do that,' she replied with iron in her voice that only added more questions to his list.

Ella turned sharply down a dark alleyway between two

decrepit, seemingly abandoned buildings. Even in this run-down part of the city they stood out as pieces of shit. Nothing interesting or worthwhile of note. Maybe a few users might find a good spot inside to hide away from the world and embrace their dirty habits away from prying eyes, but that was it. The smell of piss filled Aleister's nostrils as they walked through; a sign of what the locals thought of this place. A small, ginger cat stood in front of them, fur raised as it spotted the two of them encroaching on her territory. It calmed down as they walked on by, but its suspicious eyes stayed on them all the way through to the other side of the alleyway.

'Your friends live nearby?' he asked, daring to breathe in through his nose again as they reached a side road. There were less lights in the windows of these buildings. Without thinking, his fingers found the hilt of his sword, ready for danger. Experience had gifted him with a nose for danger, for trouble. This place was trouble. He couldn't imagine Ella walking these streets alone.

'They have a need for secrecy. *We* have a need for secrecy,' she said, her green eyes flashing at him from under the hood.

'Matthias come here?' He regretted it as soon as he said it, as though his name was a curse word that shouldn't be mentioned between them.

'Not for a while,' Ella muttered through gritted teeth. A tale for another time, but Aleister knew when to bite his tongue and shut the hell up. He was itching to find out more but now wouldn't be right. He was alive because he knew patience, when to strike. To take opportunities when they were available and not force them. A stab of guilt sliced through him as he thought of Matthias. He pushed the thought away. Not his problem. Not yet anyway. 'We're here. Keep your mouth closed unless you're asked a question. Use your eyes and ears instead of your tongue,' she warned him. He couldn't keep a naughty smirk from forcing its way onto his face. 'Very mature...'

In the shadows between two decimated wooden buildings stood a hooded figure. Tall frame, wide shoulders. He leant casually against one of the buildings as though he expected to be there a while. Aleister quickly sized him up – a good size for a fighter. He certainly wasn't lacking in food like most of the Lower City citizens. The figure stepped forward as Aleister and Ella approached, standing carefully in front of a small stone frame. As they walked closer, Aleister spotted a glint of moonlight against an iron door within the frame; unusual compared to the wooden doors often found in these parts. A door designed to ensure difficulty in getting in, or out...

'Follow The Four,' Ella said, clasping arms with the guard, head held high as she flicked her hood down onto her shoulder, revealing her raven-black hair. The guard nodded and released her, stepping aside and pulling at the handle on the iron door. It opened upwards, revealing a stone staircase, light flickering from further below. 'He's with me.' She aimed a thumb at Aleister, and the guard nodded again, staring straight at him.

Aleister held his gaze, looking into the man's eyes as his golden pupils flashed in the light; a mage, like Ella. He looked over at his companion and her eyes flashed in response, pupils glowing – no more deceit and deception. She was as more beautiful than anyone he had ever seen. He watched as she stepped carefully onto the first stone step, motioning for him to follow. He breathed deeply and pulled his jacket closer around his body, brushing his hand against the sword at his hip for reassurance. Then, he followed her down into the basement. Halfway down the stone stairs, he heard the iron door slam shut above him, echoing through the tunnel.

No turning back.

BROKEN

White everywhere. At first, he thought it was the snow, the frozen wasteland of the North, the true North. An endless ringing in his ears grew in volume as Arden struggled to open his eyes. They felt heavy, weighed down and too sore to open. It couldn't be the snow. Lights flashed through his eyelids, reds and oranges mostly. He tried to open them again. No luck. Too heavy. Too sore. Too painful. He tried to focus on his other senses, needing to feel something, anything.

No sound, just the ringing in his ears. No sight, only flashes of colour amongst the darkness. He tried to concentrate on what he could feel. Instantly, he regretted it. Pain attacked every available nerve as he attempted to move his fingers. His head pounded with each beat of his heart, thumping again and again, each beat bringing with it a new horror.

Cold air rushed in through his nostrils along with the smell of blood. Great. He tried to remember what had happened, but it only made his head thump worse. Not worth it. Could be dead, though, this didn't feel like death. Too cold for death. Damp, soft snow crunched beneath him as he tried to roll over onto his back. It hurt like hell. Everything hurt like hell.

'Take a moment, kid. Easy,' a familiar voice advised him. Socket. He was alive. He sucked a deep breath in, coughing as the cold air rushed through, chest feeling as though it was breaking with each movement. 'Easy, I said.'

Arden tried his luck again, lifting his eyelids slowly. A bright light pierced his eyes, forcing him to raise an arm to block its path. He blinked a few times, trying to focus on Socket's face as the old man crouched over him. He looked concerned, his good eye cautiously looking over him like a broken bow, checking to see if it could still be used.

Arden sat up slowly, surveying the scene around him. It was carnage. Bodies lay all around in the snow, twisted at awkward angles. Patches of blood stained the white ground. A few survivors stumbled through the bodies, one mumbling to himself, eyes wide open in horror as he looked at his fallen comrades.

'Socket, what happened?' Arden asked, horrified at the scene before him.

The way Socket's eye twitched made Arden wince. 'What do you remember?' the old man whispered, leaning back to peer at him with his one good eye.

Arden struggled to piece together the scenes from his memories before he had fallen to the snow. 'A Barbarian attacked. There was red, red everywhere. Thunder ripped through the world and pain tore through every inch of my body. It felt like the end of the world, the end of everything.' The words should have felt stupid being said aloud in the presence of others; he should have reddened with embarrassment and fell into an uncomfortable silence. That's what should have happened. But it didn't.

With each word, Arden knew he was speaking the truth, though he knew how it must sound. The Barbarian, eyes streaming red tears down his face in silent horror popped into Arden's mind. He looked across the broken vista before him and his chest grew heavy, guilt growing to a point that threatened the rhythm of his breathing.

'It was me wasn't it...' Not a question. There was no need for a question. He knew. Of course, he knew. For his whole life he had felt cursed by his eyes and lack of magic. Now, the true horror of what he had actually been wishing for had come crashing into his world. This was magic – unshackled, rampant, destructive.

'You can't beat yourself up, kid. This wasn't your fault,' Socket offered, resting a hand on his shoulder.

'How can it not be my fault?'

'You didn't know what you were doing...'

The bodies were a mix of Borderlanders and Barbarians. There had been no favourites in the attack, no bias towards one side or the other. A shiver ran down his spine at the thought; the lack of discrimination in his magical outburst terrified him.

'Kiras?' he asked, not knowing if he wanted to hear the answer.

'Safe. She's safe.'

He released a deep breath and lay back in the snow, staring up at the white sky above. A silver lining in the storm clouds swirling over him. She was safe. He hadn't killed her. 'Where is she?'

'Both sides were spooked. Saul called for a retreat; needed to regroup to decide what happens next. Kiras decided to go back, keep an eye on him,' Socket answered as Arden sat back up from the snow.

'And the Barbarians?'

'What's left of them trudged back towards their home. Neither side wanted more bloodshed today. For once, they'd had their fill.'

'And what are we going to do?'

Socket grabbed Arden's arm and dragged him to his feet. It took a moment for his eyes to focus. When they did, he wished that they hadn't. From this vantage point, the sea of bodies was almost worse than he had feared. More red than white covered the ground ahead, evidence of the nightmare becoming a reality.

'A friend of mine lives further north from here. He has more experience in this field than anyone else I know. If anyone knows how to help you, it's him.'

'And what if he doesn't know what to do?'

Socket faced him square on, jaw set and one good eye staring straight at him. 'Then we pray to The Four that we figure something else out. If he can't help you, only the Gods can.'

Arden's eyes hovered on the mass of destruction lying in the path leading further north. 'Don't suppose there's another way to get there?'

'This is the only way,' Socket said, stepping in front and leading the way through the snow. 'You think it looks bad, wait until the smell hits you...'

Socket had been right about the smell. Half a day later, the reek of death still clung to Arden's clothes and gear as they neared a small village. He fought back the constant urge to vomit, praying for somewhere to clean himself and rest for the night. As they neared the village, Arden felt uneasy, unnerved by the silence. The dark of night had gripped the village, clouds obstructing any light trying to force its way through. Yet, no light could be seen inside the wooden buildings. No candles. No flame. Nothing but darkness.

'Strange folk live in these parts, kid. Keep your wits about you. No one lives this far north without having a screw or two loose...'

Arden bit his tongue before asking about Socket's friend living further north. The old man must have his reasons for wanting Arden to meet him. That had to be good enough. Arden spotted his ally gripping the hilt of the sword at his side. The old man caught his eye and growled.

'Visibility ain't good enough for the bow. Best be ready for anything.'

Arden locked his jaw and breathed out long and slow, feeling for the long dagger hanging from his leather belt. He'd seen enough blood and death to last a lifetime but that didn't mean he wasn't ready to defend himself. He'd survived this far, there had to be a reason for that.

The eerie silence permeated the village. The dreadful reek of death grew stronger as Arden reached the broken wooden *welcome* sign. He heaved, struggling to fight back the vomit rising from the pit of his stomach. Lifeless bodies littered the streets, a morbid decoration of horror. A day filled with death had given way to a night unwilling to offer any respite for Arden.

Socket dropped to the ground and inspected one of the corpses. There was an eerie stillness to dead bodies that Arden knew he would never get used to it. It was more than a body at rest; it was the complete lack of life that unnerved him the most. Peering over Socket's shoulder, he saw a small body of a young boy. He guessed that the boy had barely made it to his sixth cycle. Now he was food for the earth. Bones, as they said in the Borderlands. Where is the sense in that, the sense in any of this?

'Barbarians have passed through here on their retreat. Easy game for them. No defences in a village this small. Simple folk. They didn't deserve to die. We need to be on our guard, they may be close.'

'If they are, we'll make them pay.' Arden gritted his teeth in anger and swallowed, struggling to hold back his emotion, wanting to scream to the heavens for all the good it would do. He'd seen the horrors of death, the fact that these Barbarians had fled from battle only to inflict such pain and suffering on innocent people made his blood boil. Now he wanted vengeance. Now he wanted blood. A deep throbbing began behind his eyes, heating up second by second.

'Stay calm, kid. Your eyes...' Socket muttered, a look of fear passing over his face like a shadow. 'We need to look for any survivors. However slim the possibility is that anyone is alive, we must at least look.' Arden stayed silent, unable to speak for the moment. The throbbing stopped, his mind focusing on the carnage in the village.

Walking through the rubble and destruction, he forced himself to look at the bodies, making sure that they were in fact dead. The horror of the sight kept his eyes fixed on each of them, unable to look away. He stopped and hunched over, his stomach turning. The day's food rushed up his throat with extreme force. The vomit flew out of his mouth and onto the snowy earth. As his mouth filled with the bile and vomit, a small piece found another exit, burning a path through his nostrils. He coughed as he choked on the acid, throat sore from the effort of forcing out the burning liquids.

Socket waited patiently for him, a look of pity on his old, wrinkled face. 'Take your time. This must be very difficult for you. No matter how many times I've seen this, it's always a bastard.'

Arden coughed, spitting out the last bits of vomit that were caught in his throat and mouth. They crept through the darkness of the village, eyes darting everywhere for any sign of the perpetrators. Some of the bodies were young men his own age, others looked older than Socket; all had perished together. No distinction was made for the dead. It appeared that death had no preference for age. All ended up in the earth at their time. Good or bad, there is only one destination. Only bones.

'What village are you from, Socket?' he asked the old man as they entered an empty patch of the village, no longer having to look at the bodies or smell the stench of the death of those around them.

'I entered the world not too far from here actually. The Far North has always held a place in my heart,' Socket answered.

'When was the last time you were home?'

'I am unable to visit and have not been able to for what seems like an age.'

'Do you miss it?'

'I used to. It was a lifetime ago though, Arden. Time can change a lot. Mountains will rise and fall; Kings will live and die; everything will fade. It may not help now but even the pain you are feeling right now will leave. It may not completely vanish, but you will be able to manage it. You will be different for it of course, but it is up to you how this will shape your future.'

Arden coughed again. He did not know how to answer Socket. The old man seemed a mystery to him. He had heard tales of the expert archer since he was a small child, tales told barely feet away from where they now stood. He was a legend, a myth, a puzzle.

They passed a blacksmith's forge and he fought back the urge to be sick once again. A naked body was bent over the forge, deep, red blood dripping down the inside of the figure's legs, a sign of the torture that the poor woman had suffered prior to her death.

'We need to find these sick bastards,' Socket said bluntly.

'We can't let them get away with this,' agreed Arden.

'I don't believe you have a choice,' came a growl from the side.

Arden snapped around defensively but he knew it was pointless. Ten separate archers were focusing their arrows on the pair of them; they were helpless and outnumbered.

Socket laughed.

'What are you laughing at, old man? This shouldn't be funny for you,' the apparent leader of the group said, his face contorting as the laughter echoed through the eerie village. He seemed oddly familiar to Arden, a big hulking figure. A man who seemed to have far too much brawn and too little brain.

'It is certainly not funny. Destroying a village, killing and raping innocent people is certainly not funny. It is the work of cowards,' Socket said calmly, displaying his missing teeth. The hulking figure took a step forward, balling his fists and breathing heavily through his nose.

'I would hold your tongue if I were you. This village was weak, insignificant. You should envy them. They are in a better place now. We may have had some fun with a few of the... more suitable ones, but they were sacrificed for the good of our kind.'

'And what kind may that be? Rapists? Murderers?

Cowards? All of the fucking above I reckon,' Socket spat. The bows were pulled back, all now aimed at the old man.

'I think I'd shut your old man up, boy. He's gonna get you both killed,' the stupid one warned Arden, pointing at him with a giant sausage-like finger.

'You've killed everyone else here. What's two more?' Arden said, despair setting in. He moved his right hand slowly towards his hip, closer to his concealed weapon; something Sly had suggested before leaving south with the others. One of his better ideas. If he was going to die than he was going to die on his feet with a blade in his hand, like a true warrior. This town deserved some sort of vengeance, no matter how small that may be.

The memory of Sly prompted another reminder. He did know this man, this was the bastard who had wanted to fight him back at the meeting, one of Saul's men. They weren't Barbarians.

'You're from the Borderlands. Why would you do this?'

The bastard moved closer to him; faint signs of recognition flashed across his face. He pointed his blade at him, eyes twinkling with recognition. 'I remember you. Fucking snot-nosed kid from the Great Hall. It would have been easier if you had died that day kid. It would have been a blessing.'

Arden forced himself to look at the mutilated body by the forge and raised an eyebrow. 'Was that a blessing too?'

'My boys seemed happy enough. There were a few screams, I won't deny that. All for a good cause. We've made new friends. There is no room for the weak, you will not be missed.' Arden raised his weapon and the arrows snapped back against their strings, ready to bring an end to the unexpected meeting.

Arden sped his hand towards the blade as Socket acted simultaneously. They moved as one to attack the killer closest to them, eager to kill the smug bastard before they passed into the void. Arden thought he was quick, but he was not quick enough. He felt the impact of knuckles crushing into his cheekbone. He dropped to one knee with the blow before staggering back to his feet.

The second blow hit harder. His back slammed against the ground, snapping his head back to the earth with a jolt. He lifted his head, vision blurred as he looked for Socket. He could hear the roars of a fight but not the whoosh of arrows that would have meant certain death for his ally. He blinked, focusing his sight. Socket had taken two of the bastards down, but he had reached his limit. Not every story had a happy ending. Two of the warriors were taking it in turns to hit the old man in the stomach while another held him tight, arms locked high at the shoulder, defenceless. The last one ambled over towards him, taking his time, enjoying the certainty of his victory.

'You should have just kept walking, boy. There's nothing this far north but death for you.'

Arden coughed, blood spewing from his throat as his enemy leered over him, a dull sword grasped gently in his grip. 'Fuck you,' he spluttered, wanting to die on his own terms. If this was the end, he wasn't going to give this bastard the satisfaction of cowering in fear.

The foul grimace fell on the man's face. His dark, lank hair fell loosely as he loomed over Arden, legs spread either side of him. His sword thudded into the snow next to Arden's head as he released his grip before tightening his fists into balls, black eyes fiercely staring into Arden's. 'I'm going to enjoy this, mage.'

A tooth tore from Arden's gums as the first strike smashed into his face. There was a numbness at first, no pain, just a void of any feeling. Then the world came crashing back in like a wave following the tide. The whole left side of his face felt as though it was on fire. The next strike was worse. The curved bone beneath his left eye blew up in an instant, cracking on impact. He struggled to see, left eye swelling fast whilst his right struggled to stay open; his whole body screamed for relief, wanting to shut down and recover. His head rocked back and forth, his body jerking as he suffered a further blow. More blood flew from his mouth as he turned onto his side, saliva laced with blood dripping out onto the snowy ground. He attempted to crawl away instinctively but a boot to the stomach put an end to those plans. His hands snapped to his stomach, blocking what felt like a broken rib as the air rushed out with the kick.

Through his eyelids, Arden thought he caught the flicker of a white light flashing across him.

Then, the attack stopped. Silence choked the village once again.

He lay there, breathing ragged and distorted, body working in overdrive to keep him alive. He wanted to see what had happened, to make sense of the break in his torture. Opening his eyes barely helped. One side of his vision was black, the swelling beneath his left eye blocking his line of sight. The vision from his right eye blurred and warped as he strained to see in the darkness. For a moment, he thought he could see two figures – tall with hair as white as the snow at their feet. One thing was certain: no one stood over him now.

His head thumped with the pain from the flash and the ringing in his ears completed the disorientation for the young warrior. A deep breath filled his lungs with the cold, crisp air. He struggled to open his eyes again and gasped, his vision slowly returning in his right eye. Struggling to a sitting position, he groaned and pulled an arm across his sore ribs, pressing against them tenderly. Broken.

Most of the group were as still as the villagers had been, as lifeless as their innocent victims. His vision focused a moment before his hearing returned. A couple of the bastards were crawling about, struggling to move and screaming out in pain. Arden moved his head slowly, holding it with one hand as he looked around for his saviour.

Socket seemed fine. A small dagger hung in his right hand, blood stained and glinting in the dim light from the moon creeping through the clouds. Fresh blood dripped from its edge as he pointed it towards another of their crawling attackers. Beside him stood a robed figure, white hair flowing down to his shoulders while he held onto a staff for support.

'You should probably finish that one off, sonny. Call it courtesy or something,' the newcomer said. His voice seemed imbued with the strength of a mountain, old but unwavering. He leant on his staff, but Arden felt support wasn't its purpose. The voice had power; this man had power. 'I'd do it quickly, else he'll just bleed out and that's not one of the best ways to go.' Golden ringed eyes flashed towards Arden as he spoke.

A mage.

'Nothing more than he deserves,' Arden snapped, in no mood for mercy as he looked back over at the raped and beaten corpse.

'Perhaps. Though I do feel that the more we behave like these beasts, the less of an example others will have to follow. It is your choice, of course,' the mage said, shoulders shrugging as his lips twitched seconds before launching a disgustingly large ball of saliva through the air past his thin, blue lips.

Wincing as he stood, Arden paused, taking a good look at the injured man who had mocked him. Crouching down next to him, his blood turned cold as his eyes fell upon the man's face. Blood dripped from his eyes, streaming down a pale, moon-like face. He coughed and spluttered as a drop of blood dripped past his parted lips. Arden held the dagger against his throat and paused. Taking the life of another this close felt wrong, intimate even. He didn't know this man; didn't know what path had led him here. An image flashed through his head of the man sitting at a table with a caring wife and children. The image faded into one of Ovar, begging for release. Another flashed through his mind of the dead villagers and that was enough. He stuck the blade straight through the man's throat. The thrashing lasting only a moment. His eyes went cold and lost their light even as the blood continued to run from them; a red river to remind Arden of the pain this man had been in.

'That's the last of them,' Socket sighed, wiping his own weapon against his filthy trouser leg before sliding it away absently. 'You always did have perfect timing,' he said to the newcomer.

'I try my best. You'll have quite the swelling in the morning, boy,' the stranger said, pointing at Arden's throbbing cheek. 'Shit, you have quite the swelling now...'

'Who are you and how the hell did you do...' Arden paused, arms wide and hands waving to the utter chaos around him, '... this.' He stared at the pair of them, waiting for an explanation.

'Two questions; which should I answer first?'

'His name is Korvus. He is the reason we are here,' Socket answered simply.

The seemingly weary man took a few steps in the snow, steadying himself with the black staff he held tightly with his left hand. His piercing golden eyes stayed focused on Arden before he turned his gaze on the fellow warrior, speaking in a strong and commanding voice.

'That is correct. It has been many years since last we spoke, Socket. They don't appear to have been too kind to you if you don't mind me saying.' His eyes sparkled mischievously.

'How kind of you to notice. You barely seemed to have aged a day. As usual,' Socket barked back.

'The years have taken their usual tax upon me, that I can assure you.' He paused and took a closer look at Arden. 'Golden eyes. I am blessed to be in the company of another with the gift. Forgive me boy but I must say – your face seems familiar...'

'His name is Arden. More than that we can speak of in

a more comfortable environment, do you not think?' Socket queried, eyes flashing between the two of them. Even in his weary and beaten state, Arden spotted the look between the two old men. They wanted a private conversation.

Korvus grinned, slowly nodding his acceptance. 'It would be nice to be back indoors now that the pleasantries are done with.' He mulled over the corpses barely two feet away as though deciding on his preferred piece of furniture. 'Beautiful scenery in these parts but I find that such misfortunes do seem to put one in a foul mood.'

Arden clutched at his rib, hobbling over to his new ally. 'I'd be happy never seeing this place again.'

'Don't worry, such atrocities are not permitted in my home. The defences are as strong as they have always been. As they always will be,' Korvus informed him, whistling a light tune as though he was out for a typical daily stroll in the snow, not at all concerned to be surrounded by death.

'And where is it that you call home?' Arden asked.

Korvus grinned and pointed his staff behind him. 'Why, the Far North of course my dear boy.'

Arden gave a puzzled look first to Korvus and then to Socket. Socket smirked and put a comforting hand on his back, 'I'd close your eyes if I were you boy. This ain't a fun journey, especially the first time.' Socket swallowed hard and blew hard out of his cheeks. 'To be honest, it ain't fun after that either...'

'What does that mean?' Arden asked, voice wavering with unease.

'Close your eyes boy,' Korvus commanded before slamming his staff into the bloodied ground. 'Let me take you on a journey...'

And then there was darkness.

Arden woke, squinting at the bright, afternoon sun hanging alone in the sky, not a cloud in sight. Strange snow-topped mountains greeted him as he sat up, peering across the open vista. A dark opening in the side of a mountain arched its mouth wide, welcoming him into the unknown. *Where in the five hells am I?*

The pain beneath his eye had faded to a dull ache but still felt as though he had a boulder attached to the side of his face. A slow roll of his tongue against his teeth reminded him of what he had lost in the fight. He licked at the gap, rubbing his tongue gingerly against his sore gums.

He slowly pulled himself up onto his weary feet and sighed, brushing snow from his ripped, muddy-brown trousers. 'Where do I go from here?' he muttered to himself, frowning. Every muscle in his body cried out in pain. He felt a tightness in places he didn't even realise he had.

'Finally, you're awake,' Socket said, leaving the cavern entrance and hobbling over to him with a grin on his face. 'You were out for longer than we had thought.'

'We?'

'Me and Korvus. His method of travel can be a bit difficult, especially the first time. Takes a while for the mind and body to work out what happened. Slow movements would be best for ya,' Socket suggested. 'You're looking prettier than I thought you would. Couple of scratches and scars will only add to the allure you have when we head back to the Borderlands. Scars are the stories written on the body of men. That's what Paesus said anyway.'

It all came back to him.

The old mage had saved them back in the village. Arden had seen death and torture. He had killed a defenceless man. He took another look around. 'How did we get... well... wherever we are now. I don't recognise these mountains.'

'You won't. We are guests of Korvus. No one else will be able to find this place. You will never find this place again – unless you're invited.'

'Thanks for the clear answer.'

'Nothing is clear where magic is concerned. You'd do well to remember that,' advised the old warrior. 'You should know that better than any.'

'Good to see you on your feet again, young sir. Apologies for the turbulent ride. It is something you will get used to, in time.' Korvus shuffled out from the darkness, leaning once again on that ivory staff of his, a great big, welcoming grin on his face.

'This is your home?'

'In a manner of speaking. It is difficult to explain to one so unused to my ways. A conversation for another time perhaps. Now, we have more important matters to discuss,' Korvus told him.

'Like how you killed those men,' Arden said bluntly.

'Not all of them. I remember quite vividly the image of

you thrusting a sharp, pointed weapon directly through the throat of one of them. I will not take the credit for that one.'

'How did you do it?' Arden asked, his head still throbbing from the journey; he wasn't in the mood for cryptic answers.

'It was a matter of will, desire, and a great bit of skill. Of course, a powerful, magic conductor like this staff of mine can always come in handy at such times,' he said tapping the staff on the ground, making an imprint on the snow. Arden winced, mind racing to the last time he witnessed the mage use his staff. 'Don't worry, you are safe from harm. Just don't ever fuck with me.' A dark look crossed his old, wrinkled face and Arden took a step back. A warm, hearty laugh broke the uncomfortable silence. He rubbed his forehead; maybe he'd struck his head on the journey, that would be one reason for the madness.

'Why did you help us?' he wondered out loud, still rubbing his head and closing his eyes for a moment. It was too bright. Painfully bright.

'When two travellers are squaring up against ten men who have just raped, tortured and killed most members of a village full of innocents, I usually side with the travellers. Call me old fashioned like that.'

'How do you two know each other?' Arden asked, turning to Socket, eager for answers.

'We go back a long way. A very long way. Korvus saved my life; I offered him a service in return,' Socket answered bluntly.

'What kind of service?'

'One involving a great deal of blood.'

'That's kind of how these things work. There's nothing more powerful than blood. Magi know that better than anyone, especially old, foolish ones like me,' Korvus said with a sadness in his eyes.

'You killed for him?'

'Yes.'

'Is that what you want from me too?' Arden asked directly, wanting a straight answer.

'Yes. You will kill for me, boy, but I can give you guidance and help in a way that only a few others in this world can,' Korvus offered. 'Also, I'm not forcing you to do anything, it will always be your choice. If you happen to die after choosing a different option, believe that it was nothing to do with me,' he added with a wink, leaving Arden to decide on the level of humour being applied.

'What can you do for me?' Arden asked, curious.

'I can show you your past, your present, and your future. I can make sure you head down the right path at a time when all others lead only to darkness.'

'Where will the right one lead me?'

'To chaos, and more darkness, naturally,' Korvus admitted, unapologetic, waving a dismissive hand in the air and stifling a yawn. 'But at the very least there will be a glimmer of light in the distance, something to grasp at and aim for when all else is lost.'

'Can you tell me who I am?' he pleaded, a sudden urgency rising inside him. Finally, here was his chance to get some answers. For too long he had been kept in the dark. 'Who I really am?'

The old mage's lips curled up at the corners. 'Boy, that is the very least I will do.'

PASSING SHIPS

'You might wanna peek at this. It ain't pretty though.'

Sly spat on the ground and waited for the others to join him at the top of the hill. Not often will a man see such a gruesome sight, even a seasoned warrior like him. Good work.

Raven joined him. 'Scouted the place out?'

'Tracks lead off into the woods. Small group I reckon. Ten or eleven maybe,' he answered with a furrowed brow, taking a measured guess. He looked back along the path and gestured at the line of dangling bodies, held up by the old, oaken trees that led straight into the dark forest. Four days out from the temple, about three away from Archania by Raven's reckoning. Lawless lands. On the outskirts of kingdoms, near the borders, the furthest points away from rulers and their laws, crime thrived. Killings, muggings, rapes. All kinds of fucked up shit. Most the time it was too much of an inconvenience for anyone to head out here and investigate any issues; the smart, cruel bastards knew that. They worked the system. Clever fucks. The locals might get lucky every now and then – a decent warrior passing through, maybe a disgraced soldier looking for a purpose who wanted to help. More often than not though, they would be left alone. Forced to fend for themselves and seek their own justice. Vigilante justice. Sly loved it.

'Quickest way through is to follow the bodies. I reckon we may stumble upon the architects of this fine piece of work.'

He stroked his axe and growled low as the blood lust grew inside him.

'If this is the quickest route to the city, then we go on. I won't be put off by a few burnt and decaying bodies swinging overhead.' Raven let his huge chest rise with a deep breath and stepped forward. Always the leader.

'What do you reckon? Bandits?' the booming voice of Baldor asked as he peered at the closest charred body.

'Possibly. Whoever it was they were sick fuckers. Don't know many that would hang a guy and then burn him before they're through the Black Gate,' Sly poked the feet of one of the unfortunate bastards, grinning as he swung back and forth. This was an unexpected bonus.

'You're enjoying this aren't you?' Bane tilted his head slightly to the side, a confused look on his face.

'I'm a man who appreciates the little things in life,' Sly replied, scratching his mess of a beard. 'An artist always shows respect to another artist's work, and there is no greater art than the art of war.'

'This isn't war. It's torture,' Baldor's soft voice barely carried over to him in the cold wind.

'From where I'm standing, it's one and the same, big man. One and the same.'

'Then perhaps you need to stand somewhere else.'

Sly gave his old ally a familiar pat on the back, calming him before racing off after Raven, keen to find those responsible for this bloody scene.

The thrill of a battle had reenergized him, given him that extra burst of adrenaline that he had missed, trawling through the snow and heading away from his homeland. He was heading straight into danger, into a battle with foes that outnumbered them at least two to one. Men who it seemed, did not care too much about inflicting horrifying amounts of pain and torture on fellow humans.

And he loved every second of it.

The only sound came from the crows calling out above them.

Raven raised a muddied hand to signal those behind him to stay back while he looked out from behind a tree. Sly dipped low into a crouch and stuck to the shadows. Cray continued his silence. Useful, for once.

Sly slunk forward through the narrow cluster of trees, moving away from the worn path and further into the darkness. He sniffed the air, catching the scent of damp sweat in the soft blowing wind. They were close. A scout maybe. He kept to the shadows, listening out for any sign of movement.

The way the green leaves were crushed into the soil beneath him told him that he was on the right track. He gently pulled out a small dagger strapped to his side. This needed a lighter touch than usual. If the alarm was sounded, the battle would be difficult. Chances were, not all of them would make it out alive. Bones.

Light from the moon broke in through the gaps in the canopy above him. He grinned. Leaning against a tree, one of the bandits sat with his hat covering his face, sharp blade forgotten to his side on the mossy ground. Defenceless. Asleep. Easy. Almost too easy. No fun.

He crawled forward until he could feel the warm breath of the bandit on his face. Slowly, he grabbed the tip of the man's hat and lifted it up, enjoying the sudden look of horror that passed the man's face as he awoke to such a terrifying image. Sly pushed a hand hard against the bandit's mouth and sliced his dagger across his throat. He squirmed for a moment before passing the black gate. Bones. Easy.

One more dead because of him. He placed his hands in the bandit's blood and smeared the warm liquid over his beautiful face. This would give them a fright. He always knew how to have fun with his prey.

The tracks were easy enough to find from this position. Minutes later, he could see the glow of a fire in the distance. Five silhouettes could be seen sitting close to the heat of the fire with one walking around the small camp, bow in hand. He would need to die first.

A hand squeezed his shoulder from behind. Instinct

took over. He grabbed the tight fingers and turned, fist leading the way and striking his attacker square in the face. He held his dagger high, looking down at his opponent.

'Shit me you bastard!' Sly exclaimed. 'Cray, don't fucking do that, or I'll be sending your silent corpse to the black gate as well!' He struggled to keep his voice low, not wanting to cause suspicion. He chuckled, offering a hand to his fallen ally. 'Stupid fuck.'

Cray grimaced as he got to his feet, the heat of his anger burning through his small eyes. 'Bastard. The others are finished. We move when you're ready,' he muttered. Not even a hint of joy. No sense of humour, this one.

Sly gripped his dagger, preferring it to the heavy axe, as he moved towards the light. Daggers were for stealth. Axes for fun. He paused as his tattered, muddied boots landed on a fallen twig. *Crack*. Shit. The archer ceased his patrol, eyes darting in Sly's direction. Now or never.

Aim for the eye. Wasn't a perfect throw. Never is. The dagger found its home in the archer's throat. His hands scratched at the sudden impact before his body fell with a thud on the bed of orange leaves. Sly decided he'd tell the others that's exactly what he had meant. Always better that way.

He roared into the circle by the fire, now with his trusty axe in hand. Time for fun. The axe buried itself into the nearest bandit's chest with a dull thud. No armour. No shield. Easy. Three others rushed to their feet, one without a weapon. The other two were sent to the black gate with their allies. Bane's curved scimitar slashed straight across one unfortunate bastard's chest whilst Baldor crushed a skull with his Warhammer. The unarmed bandit raised his hands. Surrender.

'Please. Don't kill me. I have a family in a village west of here,' he whimpered. It was so annoying when they did that. All big and proud with a weapon in hand but crying like a baby when faced with their maker. *We all had families. Dumb fuck.*

Sly didn't even look him in the eyes. One swing of the axe and his body dropped to the ground. No more crying. Raven joined them in the circle, eyes towards the last bandit. He hadn't even stood from his position near the fire. His face stared into the flickering flames; he knew his time was up. Calm. Accepting.

'Were you the ones who killed the villagers?' Bane asked him.

'They wouldn't accept the Light. It was necessary,' he said, voice calm and even. He believed that what he had done was right. Sly wasn't here to judge. A man has his reasons.

'Any last words?' Raven asked. The bandit didn't move, eyes lost in the fire.

'I will bathe in the Light of the One.'

Raven reluctantly tilted his head forward.

'Tell him we said hi.'

Sly's axe whipped through the air. Two more strikes and the head rolled next to the flames. Bones. Sly closed his eyes, breathing steadily as he cracked his neck from side to side. 'That. Felt. Good.'

'Hate to break it to you, but it ain't over yet,' Raven muttered. 'Lights, over there.'

Sly growled and opened his eyes, twisting his bloodied axe around in his hand and holding a small dagger tight in his other. Another group? Connected to this one? Who cared? Either way, they'll meet the same fate.

'No chance for stealth, they know we're here,' Raven told them. 'Weapons ready, get behind the trees in case they have archers.'

The others moved to cover. Sly just stood there, weapons hanging loosely at his side as his chest rose and fell faster and faster, wanting them to come, pleading for them to come.

He was ready.

He was always fucking ready.

The lights of the raised torches wove through the trees, steadily moving towards them. Moments later, a large group of men broke through the trees, forming a line and pointing their shiny spears in his direction. 'Stand down! Weapons on the ground! Now!'

He understood well enough. The languages of the

Northern region all seemed to blend into one. It sounded odd, more melodic than he was used to, but he got the gist of it. Even if he hadn't, the dark grimaces on their faces beneath their silver helmets made their message very clear. Sly spotted how clean and shiny the edges of their weapons were. Not been used recently. Probably never been used. He could take them. At least the front five. Raven could help out with the three other lines behind them. Easy enough. 'Bring it on you dumb fuckers.' He laughed as they tightened their grips and lowered their weapons, ready to strike as one. It was like watching a dance. All pompous and fancy. No real grit. No real danger for him. Boys playing at war. He'd seen enough of men like that. He'd sent enough through the black gate himself.

'Peace, my friends. We mean no harm.' Ah fuck. Raven playing the damned peacemaker again. The red-haired warrior crept out from behind his tree, empty hands held high and clear in the air. No weapon in sight. An easy target. Sly cursed under his breath.

'All of you! Weapons on the ground!' came the cry. Persistent fuckers.

Bane, Baldor and Cray followed Raven out, trusting their lives to his stupidity, dropping their weapons on the ground. Well most of them anyway. Even from here, Sly could see a few hidden daggers glinting in the firelight. Not completely stupid at least.

'*All* of you!' one of the soldiers commanded, eyes staring straight at Sly.

'Come and make me, pretty boy,' he growled back, eager for the conflict.

'Sly...' Raven warned, turning his head and raising his eyebrows.

Sly dropped his weapons with another curse, keeping a few daggers on his belt and making certain that his cloak kept them from view. He'd be damned if he was going to be defenceless against these shiny bastards.

'Who are you and why have you spilled blood in our lands?' the cocky soldier asked, eyes flashing back to Raven. Sly kept his own upon him, marking him as the first one to strike if it came to blood.

'We are warriors from the Borderlands. We are on our way to Archania. My brother lived in the city. I wish to pay my respects as he recently passed through the black gate. We were passing through the forest when we found the hanged men. We identified the culprits and brought the dead justice,' Raven informed them.

'Justice is not yours to give.'

'Nevertheless, it has been given.' Raven's voice had an edge that stoked the flames of battle inside Sly once again as he clung on to the hope that there would be more blood this night.

'So it seems,' a voice called from behind the front line. The men moved apart, allowing a newcomer to stroll through. His silver armour gleamed in the firelight beneath his deep red cloak. The man had tired eyes above dark, purple circles. He looked weary, on his last legs, yet these men treated him with respect and reverence. 'Justice is mine to give.' The old man walked wearily towards Raven, gloved hands pulling his helmet from his head to uncover thinning, white hair. 'Yet I suppose that it can be forgiven, one leader to another. You look very much like your father, Raven Redbeard.'

'He always spoke very highly of you, King Mikkael,' Raven responded, holding a hand forward which the King readily clasped in the Borderland style. The King of the United Cities of Archania. Walking through a forest, days away from his Kingdom in the middle of the night. Something smelled off.

'What the fuck are you doing here?' Sly spat, staring at the King.

His eyes glanced towards him as he released Raven's grip, one perfectly arched eyebrow raised in surprise. 'It seems we are passing in the opposite directions. My journey is taking me to a new temple close to our border. It has been too long since I have left the walls of my city. Too long since I have left even the walls of my home. The temple is a good excuse to get out and stretch my legs whilst I still have the chance to.'

'Any plans to go further?' Sly noticed a sharp edge to

Raven's question, as though he had already worked out the answer but had to ask anyway. The King bristled at the question before bursting into a coughing fit. Looked as though he was about to keel over there and then. Be a surprise if he even made it out of the forest, let alone any further than the temple.

'No further. An official request would have been sent if I had planned to cross over into the Borderlands. I am not searching for any trouble. Not at my age, Redbeard.'

Raven let it go but he still had an intense look on his face, eyes burning as they bored into the King. 'We spent a night in the temple. Your people were... *welcoming.*'

'I'm sure they were. Dianar has close ties to the Kingdom. Her father has served me well over the years. Even now, he is ensuring the smooth running of the United Cities. Here.' The old King turned to one of his men and muttered something. A moment later, the King had a piece of parchment in his hand, a red seal with the image of a sun etched upon it. 'This will be proof that we have met, just in case you encounter any... difficulties getting into the Kingdom.'

Raven exchanged a curious glance with Bane at the words. Funny choice of words from the King. Why would they have any difficulties?

'Thank you, Mikkael.'

'We best be on our way. It's a long, hard road,' the King said, snapping his fingers before placing the helmet back onto his head. The soldiers marched into a straight line, two of them moving ahead as scouts to ensure a safe passage. 'And Raven, I am so sorry about Braego. He was a good man. Trustworthy. Loyal. I couldn't have wished for a better Weapons Master. It is a loss for the whole Kingdom.'

Raven offered his thanks as the King's horse trotted forward. Two of the soldiers helped him up onto the animal. Well fed. Still would struggle in the snows near the border. Bad decision. Men living south of the Borderlands never seemed to think about these things. Too busy making sure their helmets and armour were shinier than their enemy's.

Raven stood alone, holding the parchment in his hand

as the sound of marching and hooves faded into the distance.

'You don't think he's just heading to the temple, do you?' Sly asked, pulling some tobacco out of his pocket and chucking it into his mouth as he strolled over to the chief.

'What else would he be doing?' Baldor asked, looking at Sly, brows coming together in the middle of his great forehead.

'I have an idea...' Raven grunted, pulling at his red beard in frustration.

'Not just stretching his legs then?' Bane asked.

'Old man looked like he was on his last legs. He might make it to the temple. Seriously think he'll survive in the Borderlands? Weather ain't exactly gonna help him. He'll be through the black gate before we get back, mark my fucking words,' Sly said through each chew.

'Honestly, that might be for the best. Come one, three days. Let's see if we can make it in two,' Raven urged them.

Sly spat onto the floor and picked his weapons up, grinning at them as he placed them back onto his belt, not wiping the blood that had already dried onto the blades. He stomped off through the trees, looking for his next battle.

* * *

The smell of piss filled the air. Not a problem. It was familiar, almost comforting. It reminded Cypher of the dungeons. After a while, you get used to things, no matter how bad they may seem at first. He knew that. He'd experienced that truth more often than most.

He'd slept well; sleep filled with dreams of vengeance. A shard of glass across the neck of Mason. A dagger through the stomach of T'Chai. A hammer to the knees of Zaif, the fucking traitor. That one didn't need death. Didn't deserve death. He needed pain. He deserved a lesson. Whatever Gods there were must know that Cypher would make sure that he would get it. He didn't pray for it. Didn't get down on his knees and beg for it.

He just promised it.

He informed them.

Told the Gods his plans. Plans that he knew he would carry out. They may be dreams of a night, but he would make damn sure that they would be a reality in the cold light of day. Not often would he go for a stroll through the city in the daytime. He'd always preferred the darkness, for obvious reasons. The shadows were a comfort for one who wished to go unseen. The dungeons had been filled with darkness and shadows, just enough light available for artists to see their tools, their instruments. But he wasn't in the dungeons anymore. He wasn't in the Upper City anymore. He was back down here, in the Lower City with the Palace staring down at him from the hill up high at the end of the cobbled main road, past the gate through which he was no longer welcome.

He passed Sofia's Rooms of Pleasure; the girl on the door looked as though she was about to call out to him, test her chances. The moment she recognised him was beautiful for Cypher. Mouth open and ready to call out, eyes wide in recognition and leaning slightly forward, tits hanging out as always. No sound came out of her mouth, she managed to catch herself in time. She'd wasted words on him enough. No need to waste anymore. She knew he didn't pay for that kind of shit.

He sauntered on past her, whistling a merry tune as he dodged a bucket of filth dropped from one of the open windows above him. The dirty water splashed onto some angry fool's shoes. The ensuing shouting match through the wooden shutters of the window and the large woman leaning out brought a grin to his face.

A misshapen tavern loomed over the pathway a few doors down. Not the best tavern. Bit grimy. Needed at least a bit of work but it was quiet. Discreet. Perfect for what Cypher had planned. Even more important than that, he knew the people who used the tavern. He looked skywards before entering, making certain that no one else was about to send their day's waste out onto the streets below. A glum looking woman with dark red hair stood perched against the frame of a balcony, leaning out of the open window, her beauty shining through her sad face. He smiled wider and entered the tavern, pushing the wooden doors open and rolling his shoulders to stretch the sore muscles in his back.

Two lone figures sat nursing their drinks with glum faces. Neither looked up as he entered, both lost in their own issues and miseries. Typical in a place like this. Keep your eyes down and don't let yourself get dragged into other people's business. That was the way to get by. He'd seen it all before.

The room was what you would expect from a tavern in this part of the city: dust everywhere, cracked wooden panels lining the floor, filthy glasses behind the bar and one even in the hand of a barmen dressed in black and white who scrubbed heartily with a an even filthier cloth. Admirable effort but he was certainly just making things worse.

'What can I do for ya, sir?' the barman called over, halting his work, much to Cypher's relief.

'Got an Itari Red?' Cypher asked, pulling his cloak up from his ankles as he sat back onto an old wooden chair that squeaked slightly as he placed all his weight upon it.

'Norland Red. Ain't had Itari in a while. Not since the troubles broke out just south of the Heartlands,' the barman replied with a sorry grimace.

'Ah, of course,' Cypher bit his bottom lip as he remembered a particularly fun session in the dungeons with a fool from the Heartlands. Within an hour the cretin had sang all sorts of songs about the troubles facing the duelling Kingdoms of Itaria and Venekia. Young rulers. Both ambitious. Both arrogant. Both utterly moronic by the sounds of it. The prisoner had told him everything. Then he had been burned by Mason and his men as an associate of magi. An untruth, as Cypher liked to think of it. So many had died thanks to untruths. Countless men and women burning because of him. Because of Mason. Bastard. 'Norland Red would be a delight.' Not as sweet, but it did the job.

The barman grabbed a bottle with a greenish tint and poured some of its contents into one of the less dirty looking glasses, much to Cypher's relief. Cypher pulled out a piece of silver, flipping it high into the air as the barman placed the drink in front of him. He caught the silver with a look of shock and stuttered his response. 'M-mighty kind of you to pay with silver. Not needed for a meagre Norland Red but it is certainly appreciated! I could grab the rest of the bottle for you.'

'In time. For now, take a seat,' Cypher instructed, tilting his head towards the empty seat opposite him. 'You can earn more than that silver with just a few words.'

Cypher licked his lips as he watched the barman's face change from shock to silent reflection. He knew what he was thinking. Men in downtrodden taverns in this part of the city don't get lucky often. There's always a price for success, here more than anywhere. The cogs in his mind were at work, attempting to decipher what may be required by this stranger with the silver pieces.

'What do you need to know?' The reward obviously outweighed the risk.

Cypher kept his eyes on the man as he walked to the chair – podgy stomach sticking out and forcing the buttons on his stained white shirt to fight what looked to be a losing battle to stay together; he knew the way of this world. Barman probably didn't make much money, not enough passing business in these parts. Most of the men with money would end up in Lady Sofia's with a whore and some chew rather than sit in the shadows and drink their life away. There were few exceptions, of course, as there always is. He could be easily swayed with a low bribe, nothing special was needed. Nothing over the top. Easy business. Cypher's favourite kind when not using weapons.

'I've noticed a few strange things happening in the Lower City. Odd behaviour.' Cypher stared straight into the man's soft, tired brown eyes as he sat back and laughed at the torturer's statement.

'Nothing unusual there. Strange place down here away from the fancy wigs and frilled shirts. Simpler. But strange, yes. Always been that way. Have to fend for ourselves. Don't see many of The Watch stepping down here to sort things out. We have to look after each other ourselves!'

Cypher agreed, letting the barman feel as though he had said something wise beyond his station, as though he had happened to walk into this decrepit tavern and luckily stumbled upon one of the great philosophers of our time.

'Yes, yes, indeed. But,' Cypher leaned forward, voice dropping to a whisper, forcing the barman to lean in, 'I've seen strange people. People in masks. Like the doctors who used to stroll about during the plague when it was at its worst in the city. Seen any of them?'

The barman leaned back, eyes shuffling from side to side as though nervous that the shadows themselves could see him. 'Plague doctors?' The muscles in his stubbled neck flexed as he swallowed nervously. 'Haven't seen any of those about since the plague was over. You must be mistaken...'

Cypher gave a reassuring smile; at least that was the aim. Came out as more of a grimace he reckoned, whilst placing another silver piece on the table and delighting in the fact the barman's eyes seemed to light up upon seeing it. 'We both know I'm not mistaken. A barman of your talents and warmth must be able to know things that others in the city do not, I am sure of it.' He was really slapping it on now, lathering him up to get what he wanted out of him. Perfect example of foreplay. 'Now, what do you know?'

The man's eyes never left the piece of silver as he blurted out what he knew. 'Heard they want change. Real change. Not sure who runs them, but they say he has ties to the council, in the Upper City,' he said, pointing a sausage-like finger to the ceiling. Ties to the council. That could work. He'd played enough card games to know not to give his hand away – eyes unflinching, lips immovable, waiting for more information. 'Rumours going around that the King is on his last legs. After he's gone, these doctors are planning on taking over. No more Mason D'Argio. No more royalty. Something new. For everyone. Not just for the rich and powerful. We could be a land of free people.'

Wishful thinking. No one was ever free. That's what Cypher had found out. Somehow, we were all imprisoned, unable to fulfil our true desires. 'Sounds promising. Where would one find these doctors? I wish to pledge my allegiance...'

The barman grinned, thankful that Cypher wasn't going to cause any trouble. 'Funny you should say that...' His eyes darted to a closed door at the back of the room.

'When?' Cypher asked, eyes flashing with desire. He flicked the silver coin towards the barman and sat back.

'Finish the bottle and they won't be much longer,' the barman informed him, clutching at the silver, unable to keep the glee from his face.

Cypher downed his glass in one motion and gasped, displaying all his teeth as he grinned at his newfound friend. 'Make it two bottles.'

'I know who you are, Cypher Zellin. My question is, why should we let you live?'

A reasonable question. After the last fight in the bar against The Doctors, they had reason to suspect his motives for wanting to speak to them. At the very least, this displayed the fact that the group were not being run by morons.

'Dead, I mean nothing to you. Alive, I mean so much more,' he answered. 'Your little group is cute and able to make a fuss in this Kingdom but, with my help, you can achieve greatness!' He threw his arms into the air, staring maniacally at the three men sat in front of him in their stupid plague costumes. They were a means to an end, nothing more. He would be careful to remember that.

'And what can you offer us that we do not already have? Our group's last interaction with you did not end so well, if you remember correctly,' the middle one said through his dark mask. The other two just sat in silence, motionless.

'You have heart – a will to improve this city. Many before you have had that in spades; still, they died. With me alongside you, you have someone who has lived in the Upper City; someone who has met with the higher powers that rule this Kingdom. You might not like me, but you don't need to. My knowledge of this Kingdom will turn grumbling peasants into revolutionary heroes!' He thumped his fist against the table and looked at them each in turn. 'We have a mutual enemy. Paesus says, "the enemy of my enemy is my friend." Let us use that advice to create something beneficial for the both of us. You want a revolution; I want Mason humbled at my feet. Working together, we can both get what we want. Apart, we're not likely to succeed.'

'I have to admit, we can use the help. We have willing men and women, but they fear moving on the Upper City. Having someone of your skills working with us will ensure that they know we mean business. The Doctors will be a threat known and feared throughout the Kingdom. The Kingdom will be forced to listen to our demands.'

'Demands? There will be no demands. The royal family has had their fun since this Kingdom was founded. They have been left to fester and rot along with Archania for too long. Just as a doctor must amputate a rotted limb, so we must cut the royal family out from this Kingdom. The King is leaving the city and he will not return. The sons are weak and unfit for rule. Our time to strike draws closer. Follow me and this Kingdom will be in our hands within the fortnight!'

'It's interesting you mention the Princes, one of them has been wandering the Lower City at night recently. Perhaps he may be of use to us?'

Cypher nodded, rubbing at the stubble on his chin and licking his lips at the thought. Must be Drayke. Asher loved his home comforts too much to leave the Palace, let alone traverse the Lower City. The younger Prince would be a useful tool in the revolution if caught. 'Excellent, place lookouts throughout the streets. As soon as he is seen, send word and we will attack as one. Together, we can change this Kingdom.'

'Killer. Torturer. Psychopath. These labels have followed you for many years. Such a person may be a liability to our cause. We aim for progress, for a better Archania tomorrow than the one we have today. It's true, we share a mutual enemy, but is that reason enough for us to allow such a loose cannon on board?'

'Ambitious. Determined. Artistic. Clinical. Those are the words you should focus on when making your decision. I'm not afraid to get dirty to get the job done and that's something you lot must need if you are to succeed. Your flowery notions of what is best for Archania may sound good, but I can provide the steel necessary to prove to others that you mean business. People may fear me, but they know that I can back up what I say. Place me at the edge of the sword cutting through the rope that strangles this Kingdom. Let me be the one that plunges into the filth and comes out with a better Archania. You don't need to like me. Hell, most people don't. You just need to understand that I'm necessary.'

Cypher folded his arms and breathed out. No more words. Either they accepted his offer, or they didn't. Either way, he would end up with what he wanted.

'Our cause is more important than any individual, Cypher Zellin. We all understand that. You're right, I don't like you, and in all honesty, I doubt I ever will. The tales I've heard send shivers down my spine.' Cypher fought back the urge the laugh. 'Yet, I see the value in having someone of your... status within our group. We could discuss terms but I'm not sure I would believe anything you say. All I ask is that you reign in your bloodier tendencies for only the times we deem it necessary. I will not hesitate to strike you down if you cause more trouble for my brothers and sisters.'

'A fair comment. I have one request...'

'Yes?'

'Mason, T'Chai, and a man called Zaif. All three are to be given to me if captured alive.' It appeared a reasonable request. Having the three of them under their control would mean victory. He would be able to do whatever he wanted. A new order would be on its way.

'Mason will face a trial for his crimes if caught alive. After his sentencing, you can do what you want with him. The other two, you can have your fun.'

The masked man held out a black-gloved hand. Cypher leant forward and gripped tightly, shaking it once before release.

‘Welcome to our cause, Cypher Zellin. You’re a Doctor now.’

‘Mother would be so proud,’ Cypher smirked. ‘Now, where do I get my outfit?’

BENEATH THE CITY

Four grey stone pillars stood on the edge of a great circle carved into the rough floor. Wooden benches followed the circular pattern around the room, broken only by sets of stone steps to aid in the passage leading up to the highest level in the room. From any position amongst the benches, views would be unobstructed; all could see straight into the centre of the room. Here Aleister now stood, biting his nails uncomfortably at the mass of red robed men and women gathered close by, greeting one another like long-lost friends. Three robed men glided across the room, swinging metal spheres seeping with a strong-smelling perfume that battled unsuccessfully against the stale smell of sweat hanging in the air.

'You're feeling uneasy,' Ariel said, unable to keep the humour from her voice.

'Fifty strangers in masks and robes are filling an underground sanctuary that I had no idea even existed,' Aleister replied, barely moving his lips as he edged closer to her. 'Yeah, guess you could say I'm feeling a bit uneasy.'

Candlelight cast an eerie orange glow throughout the room as the guests mingled through the stifling underground room. The white masks perched upon many of the faces of the figures wandering around were the same. All bore a look of sadness, eyebrows arched upwards and mouth curled in a deep look of dismay. Circles had been cut open allowing each wearer to see through the mask with only slightly impaired vision. Through these gaps, Aleister spotted a golden glow gleaming out.

'Magi. Every one of them,' he muttered.

'Of course they are. Why else do you think I would bring you to a secret underground meeting?'

Aleister raised an eyebrow. 'You sure you want me to answer that?' He let the punch land on his arm, smirking in unison with his old friend.

'Haven't grown up at all have you?' Ariel tried to suppress a giggle.

Aleister had to admit, even though the surroundings could have been better, he hadn't felt this happy in a long time. Looking at the woman beside him, trying to stifle laughter, her eyes glinting in the low light of the flames, he knew he had made the right decision in coming back, in coming home.

A small figure nearby turned, spotting Ella and Aleister and quickly finished up a hushed discussion with two other guests. He gave his excuses and glided over towards them; eyes fixed on Aleister. His robe was open, displaying a garish pink waistcoat embroidered with gold trees.

'My dear Ariel, what a wonderful surprise to see you!' The masked man took an offered hand and bowed low before releasing it. 'We were not expecting you. Matthias mentioned that he had er... other matters to attend to this evening.' His face flashed towards Aleister. Suspicious, most likely. It was fair enough. Aleister knew how it must look. So did Ella.

'This is Aleister. He's an old friend recently returned to the city,' she said smiling towards him. The masked man offered out a sweaty palm for Aleister to dutifully shake. 'He's the one I spoke about the other day,' she added, dropping her voice even lower.

The stranger peered over Aleister's shoulder, looking for a signal. A moment later, he lowered his hood and pulled his mask away, revealing a mop of red hair, pink, puffy skin and dazzling green eyes. 'No need for such measures. The door is locked. No one will be entering now. My name is Rude Haller. Come, join me.'

As if on cue, the others in the room followed suit. Men and women revealed their true faces; a variety of skin colours and ages scattered around the room. The only constant Aleister noticed was the golden glow of their pupils. This meeting had brought together all kinds of magi from across the realm, united in their struggles no doubt.

Aleister followed Haller to a bench on the second level, pausing only to undo the top button of his shirt, attempting to fight against the stifling heat suffocating the room. 'Shame you can't crack a window open down here...'

'The heat is a mild inconvenience, yet it is one with which we can endure. Secrecy and safety are paramount to our order in these dark times. If we must suffer mildly in the heat, then so be it.' Haller shrugged, taking a seat and motioning for Aleister and Ella to join him. 'Ella has shared some interesting tales about you. If half of them are true, then you have my respect. And that is not something easily earnt in this Kingdom.'

'Tall tales that grow larger with each telling, I'm sure. The truth is usually much less exciting to listen to in the taverns and bars throughout the Kingdoms of Takaara. I have talented bards to thank for any reputation that may travel ahead of me.' It was his usual response to such words; not entirely truthful but humble enough for the company he was in. Striking a balance between confidence and humility was important when meeting potential allies. He'd learnt that on the road.

'Still, when Ella speaks, one must listen. Her recommendation led to me allowing you in here, the first non-mage to enter. Not lightly are these decisions made. Some argued against it but we are in need of allies in Archania, and Ella convinced us of your skills and expertise.'

Aleister peered out of the corner of his eyes, biting his lip as he watched Ella shift uncomfortably in her seat. What had she told him? Tales from the Archanian bards? Whispers that grew as they made their journey from the East? How would any of that lead to this order wanting him?

'If I can help in any way at all, just let me know.'

'You've been back in Archania for just a short time. However, you must have seen the way we are being marginalised; the way those in power are treating us worse than dogs. Drawing us out on jumped-up charges and burning our kind with no reason. Crowds cheer. They cheer as though it is some Gods damned sport,' Haller spat, shaking his head with disgust. 'Well, I'm afraid my kind cannot stand back and wait for our inevitable demise. We have a right to exist in this Kingdom, as much as any other. We're going to do our best to make sure that everyone else knows that. That's why you're here tonight, Aleister. I need your advice.'

'Advice on what?' Aleister asked, resigned to the answer coming his way.

'On igniting a rebellion.'

'You're kidding,' Aleister said, rocking back and looking at Ariel, eyes pleading for an answer. Her face stayed stoic and sure. Nothing had been said that she didn't expect. 'Rebellion? You could start a civil war.'

'That's why we need your help. The Red Sons. I've heard about what you accomplished out East. You prevented the Empire from choking the life out of Darakeche. You understand war, certainly civil war. You can support us. You can give us the edge we need.' Haller's eyes were wet with emotion, wide and desperate. He believed every word he said.

'The Red Sons... we got lucky. This is different. Mason and his men are entrenched in the city, aware of the land and willing to defend it. I couldn't guarantee a victory over such forces,' Aleister admitted, shaking his head as he stared into the hopeful eyes of Ella and Haller. False hope would only lead to death. Harsh truths were necessary.

'We're not asking for guarantees, Aleister. For too long we have existed in the shadows, accepting our place on the outskirts of society. We are not demons; we are not horrors within society waiting to destroy the weak. We are normal people who exist with a gift. We cannot let this misjustice continue. We may fall, but we cannot stand still. Our time is coming. You can either stand with us, or step aside.' Haller's voice dripped with passion, clearly displaying his love for the magi around him. 'My parents raised me in a village not far from the city walls. I grew up in their shadow, curious of what life was like inside. My father was a blacksmith; made his fortune whenever there was a war brewing or a battle to be fought. He always said he would rather be poor and at peace than rich and at war. I agree with him. The problem is our people have been fighting a war in the shadows for far too long. We yearn for the days of peace: rich or poor. I can see no outcome where we are given the rights we deserve: the right to live free and in peace, the right to respect our heritage, the right to be ourselves and not hide, that does not involve a fight. We must take our time, we must prepare, and I will ensure that we do so properly.'

Aleister chewed on the thick skin inside his cheek, mulling over the words. 'You'd need a small army; the Lower City would need to stand in support of you to even afford you a chance of fighting back against Mason and his men.'

'I'm aware of that. We have support, or we will do, once the King has passed. Loyalty towards him has not passed on to his eldest son. Asher is the key to all of this; the people's hatred of the foul Prince will tip the odds in our favour. No one wants that fool of a prince to sit on the throne,' Haller spat, body shaking with excitement as he leaned towards Aleister. Ariel sat patiently by his side, eyes intent on Aleister, mouth unmoving.

Aleister sighed, silently cursing himself for even entertaining the idea. 'I'll need to speak to a few people. Test the waters. Such a task can't be engineered overnight. I'll need time.'

'And you'll have it, I promise,' Haller replied, grinning wide as he looked at Ella who burst into a smile of her own. 'We have had decades of persecution. Our patience is greater than you might think.'

'Do you have the support of the other magi here?' Aleister asked, wanting to be certain of the available resources.

'Let's find out,' Haller smirked, flicking his head back,

his flame-red hair dancing with the movement. He stood up, arms raised as he signalled for silence in the room. The horde of red-robed magi turned to face him, conversations faded away as their eyes met Haller's raised hands, palms open. 'My brothers and sisters.' His voice rang out through the dark room, clear and even. The voice of a leader. A voice made to be followed. 'It's been three years since we first gathered; we were scared, worried, shaking as we watched the Kingdom turn on us and kick us into the gutter.' Cheers rang out through the cavern at these words as the magi roared, hands slapping against backs in response to the speech. 'Our kind has been persecuted more than any other throughout the history of Takaara. Our *gift* is said by many to be the result of The Four themselves. The Gods we pray to every day and night are the reason we can do the things we do. Recently, the land has been crying out in pain. They say it is because of us, magi.' Roars of disapproval echoed around Aleister, flames of anger rising. 'No! Takaara does not cry because of us, it cries because of them: the greedy, the cruel, the evil. Mason and his Empire vow to rid this world of magi like us. Well, I say we rid Archania of them!'

The roars this time were cries of hope: of faith. Aleister recognised the signs of a skilled orator. He wasn't moved like the others. A silver tongue meant nothing in the heat of battle. Faith was no shield capable of protecting against steel. More than words were needed to convince him that this battle could be won, or that it was even worth fighting for. He looked into Ella's golden eyes and felt his own shields break down, barriers he thought had been built with care and the hardiest of materials. With one look from her, they crumbled like paper walls falling against the crashing of waves. He would help her. He would help all of them. He would go to the ends of the world just to see her face.

Even if it meant he would be greeted by death.

'Look after my sons. Look after my Kingdom. Be better than I have been.'

Those were the last words the King had said in her

presence before going ahead with the plan to travel northwards, to the Borderlands. The Royal Road wouldn't be too dangerous now the King had been convinced to take an appropriate guard, but his failing health still concerned Katerina Kane. Seeing him again would be a gift, one she did not expect to receive. Now, all she could do was follow the last words her friend had said to her.

She sat on a creaking, wooden bench, a slender oaken pipe hanging loosely from her lips as her incredulous eyes stared up at the rear Palace walls. Angry clouds loomed over the open training grounds Braego used to love so much, waiting for an opportune moment to release their downpour no doubt. A dark shadow, stocky but graceful, clambered down a tied sheet from a window high up on the third level of the beautiful building, hood raised to avoid detection. Even from this distance she recognised him; the careful movements, the wide shoulders, the gentle landing as he dropped slowly onto a grassy patch of ground beneath him.

He'd done this before.

She smirked, careful to ensure the pipe didn't fall from her lips as she watched her son through a host of pompous, colourful flowers. She stood up, holding her cloak tight to guard against the chill falling over the grounds. A quick glance upwards showed only darkness as the clouds covered the stars above. A grim night indeed.

'A bit late for a stroll through the palace gardens, don't you think my Prince?' Kane said, voice low to avoid the hearing of anyone else listening.

Even in the low light, Drayke's face was priceless. Caught red-handed, sneaking out of his room in the middle of the night by someone he considered an old friend of the family. There wouldn't be any way of getting out of this one. The shocked, open mouth hung there for one second as his mind raced through a variety of excuses. Fortunately, Prince Drayke was no fool. Lying to a former Inspector would only lead to embarrassment and he knew it.

'Wouldn't believe me if I told you I enjoyed moonlight training sessions, would you?' Drayke asked, strolling over to her with a smirk stabbing at Kane's heart. So like Braego's.

'I would believe that,' Kane said, turning her head at an angle as she watched her son. 'But I'm sure there are easier methods of travelling through the palace. In fact, I am certain of it.'

'Ah, yes. Seems you have me there. It's good to see you Inspector.'

Kane bowed, as duty called. 'Please, Katerina, Your Highness.'

'I always preferred Kat. Concise and to the point. Nothing unnecessary. Like you.'

'Flattery won't get you anywhere with me, my Prince,' Kane grinned as she saw the mischievous look fade from her son's face to be replaced with a look of acceptance. 'What are you doing escaping the Palace at a time like this?'

The Prince bit his lip and rubbed at the few tufts of fluff sprouting from his chin. He sighed and took a seat on the bench, launching himself back and spreading his arms wide over the back of the bench. Kane pulled at her cloak and sat next to him, waiting patiently.

'I'm the Prince of a Kingdom with such great history. The Four walked through Archania, as small as it was back then. Kings and Queens have fought injustice for as long as we have recorded the events. My own lessons are there to teach me that leaders must learn from the past to build a better future. We are there to serve our people, not the other way around.' Drayke shook his head, jaw locked as he struggled to find the correct words. 'Yet, as my own father's health fails, all I see is injustice. I'm a Prince with no power, Kat. My hands are tied, I feel helpless. Completely, utterly helpless...'

Kat frowned as Drayke's shoulders sagged, his whole body drooping on the bench as his green eyes stared up into the night sky, faint drops of rain falling from the grey clouds onto his pale face.

'And how may I ask, will a stroll in the middle of the night help matters?' Kane asked, curious.

Drayke's cheeks flashed red at the question, eyes

unable to meet Kane's. 'I've been doing it for a while now. There's nothing I can do in the Palace to help matters. Father doesn't seem to care; my fool of a brother only has an interest in frustrating the serving staff and disgracing our family name. The House of Albion is falling. I can't have my father, Mikkael Albion be the last of our long. It is up to me to do something, anything. I've been heading into the Lower City to see my people,' he mumbled.

The reckless disregard for safety and protocol reeked of his father. Braego's chest would burst with pride if he could see his son right now. Unfortunately, her position deemed her unable to encourage such behaviour. The trappings of position.

'With all due respect, my Prince, do you understand how dangerous and stupid that is?'

'I've seen men and women burnt in front of a cheering crowd,' Drayke muttered, eyes wide and unstaring, lost in memories most unpleasant. 'I know the dangers. You can stay here every single night if you wish but I promise, there are other ways out of this Palace, and I will find the right one to get around you. I need to see what life is like in my Kingdom, what it is *really* like, Kat. Only then can I help its people. Surely you understand that?' His eyes were soft and pleading as he turned his head to face her, rain falling heavier onto his creased hood. He certainly didn't look like a Prince right now.

'My Prince, you leave me with only one choice.' Kane sighed, lips twitching as she saw Drayke's face frown in disappointment. 'I will escort you and see that no harm befalls a Prince of this Kingdom.'

Drayke shot to his feet, followed shortly by Kane, grin reaching his ears as he jumped on the spot before pulling her into a tight hug. Kane relaxed into the hug, accepting the rare closeness to her son.

'Thank you! You won't regret it. We'll be back before first light!'

'Yes, yes we will! First light would be much too late! You listen to me and follow anything I say, my Prince. If you want to behave as though you're not a Prince then you must drop all thoughts of being in command. The Lower City can be a dangerous place, especially for one in such a position as you are in,' Kane warned, trying not to show how excited she was to spend time with him.

'You sound just like Braego. When I trained with him, he would stand right here lecturing me about the differences between royalty and the common man. He took me out once, you know, to the Lower City.'

'Did he now? The King would be furious if he found out!'

'I know! Father would hit the roof!' Drayke laughed. 'Now, let's go. I've heard people love to sit in a tavern and share tales over a glass of fine wine.'

Kane frowned and chuckled at the same time, fighting back the urge to mock her son. 'Fine wine? You haven't been inside a tavern in the Lower City, have you?'

'Nope. Tonight will be an adventure!'

'It will be, my Prince. It will be.'

* * *

The pitter patter of rain filled the air as Kane led Drayke through the Lower City. In the Palace grounds and surrounding area, it had felt easy to view the whole event as an adventure; a thrilling night with mother and son sharing a unique experience in the quiet, enchanting autumn night. Now they had reached the Lower City, the reality of the situation kicked in. Every shadow could hide a cutthroat, a sellsword, an assassin. Kane felt the familiar instincts kick in as her eyes darted around the cobbled streets, keenly aware that at any moment they could be threatened.

She glanced at the Prince, hood pulled low enough to cover his identity from passers-by. It was a blessing that most of the common folk only recognised King Mikkael and Prince Asher; Drayke, not being the heir to the throne, felt less important to the general public. His face would not be easily spotted, especially on a night like this under the cover of clouds and the night sky. Kane grasped at her own soaking wet hood, careful to avoid any recognition from the men stumbling past, obviously deep into their night's cups. Folk in these parts weren't exactly fans of authority. A Prince and an ex-Inspector would cause a disturbance that would make things difficult, that's for sure.

As dangerous and stupid as the decision now felt, she had to admit, her body rushed with excitement, thrilled with an energy she hadn't felt for some time. Her fingers found the hilt of her blade, rubbing gently at the silver as a shrouded figure hugged against a tattered merchant's stall, closed for the night. The man passed by, keeping to himself. Kane suddenly became aware that she had been holding her breath.

'Do you miss it? Being an Inspector?' Drayke muttered, eyes glancing around in wonder. It must feel like another world to what he was used to. The Palace, the serving staff, the grandeur. This was real life. Mud. Blood. Exhaustion. Sweat. Tears.

'Sometimes. I miss feeling needed,' Kane answered honestly. 'I'll never be willing to just sit at home twiddling my thumbs whilst others throw themselves into danger. Whilst I still draw breath, I'll do what I can for this Kingdom.'

'Father speaks highly of you. He trusts you. I don't think I can say that for most people. Many just want things. Titles, money, favours. You don't. You help because you want to. I admire that.'

Kane passed the lump in her throat off as a cough while looking to the side, blinking quickly to fight away the tears attempting to force their way through. 'It has been an honour to serve your father; to serve this Kingdom.'

'Will you feel that way with my brother?'

'Huh.' Kane paused, thinking of the correct answer. 'Serving this Kingdom will be even more important when your brother is in power.'

'Good response. He'll need all the help he can get. He may be a bit of a monster but he's still family. I'd hate to see him struggle. Well, not too much anyway.'

The clipped sound of boots tapping against the wet, cobbled street mixed with the rain dropping against the ground. A few curious glances came their way, eyes following the two hooded figures rushing through the darkened street, but none called out to them. An errant word or two could lead to violence in the Lower City. Sometimes it was easier to keep your mouth closed and let people be. On the other hand, some people just couldn't help themselves.

'That can't be Inspector Kane under the hood...' a voice shouted from the shadows of an alleyway.

Kane's whole body tensed in an instant, stepping protectively straight across Drayke and sliding her eyes to the ragged man leaning against the old butcher's building. Wild, wet hair; messy greying beard; a glistening scar to the side of his right eye. She didn't recognise him at all. Then again, she'd had the unfortunate pleasure of meeting many of the area's dangerous men and women. Remembering all of them would be an ability beyond most humans. 'Should I know you?'

The ragged man chuckled, glancing at his muddy boots and jabbing a dirty finger into his mouth, rubbing at a piece of gum where usually a tooth should have sat. 'We've met before, nothing memorable. Can't blame you for not recognising me; this face has seen too many winters and I've not been lucky enough to live in the Upper City like yourself.'

'I've spent enough time down here,' Kane snapped back, shoving an inquisitive Drayke back and out of sight. 'I've served my time down here. I've earned the few luxuries I now have.'

'Certainly,' the stranger agreed, forcing his tongue through the gap in his yellowing teeth as he tried to peer over Kane's shoulder. 'You've earnt much. Katerina Kane the protector. The shield of the people. Yet, you haven't been protecting much lately, have you?'

'And what is that supposed to mean?' Kane stiffened further, grip tightening on the hilt of her blade as she purposefully slid it slightly from its home. They shouldn't have come here. It was a bad decision. Careless.

'The burnings. Mason D'Argio. My nephew, Tate...' The man's voice broke as forced out the name, as though just saying it caused him pain beyond belief. Kane knew that pain. She understood that pain. It could make even the sanest of people do stupid things.

'Tate. Your nephew?'

'The boy who burned last week?' Drayke pushed past Kane before she could stop him, eyes wide and staring at the stranger. 'Please, accept my heartfelt condolences. No one should suffer a death in such a way. If there was anything I could have done...'

The stranger's eyes glistened with recognition as he stared at the Prince, jaw dropping as he peered closer at the young man. 'Prince Drayke... you are the same age.' The stranger moved a hand closer to the Prince's face before hesitating, drawing his hand back and balling his fist tight against his chest. 'My nephew had just lost his father, my brother. He was the only family I had left. Yet you all left him to burn. Who does that? His own people are too slow to react, dithering about in their meetings whilst others are rounded up. Thankfully, there are others who want to do some good. People who wish to change Archania for the better.'

'Your Highness, we should leave,' Kane suggested, mind being dragged like a carriage through the various outcomes of the situation. Most didn't seem to end very well for them. 'This was a bad decision. We *must* leave now.'

'Kane is right, but I can't let it be that easy. This Kingdom needs healers, and you can help us, my Prince.'

'How? How can I help you?'

'By dying.'

The scraping of steel echoed through the streets over the downpour of rain as Kane reacted first, dragging her son behind her and pointing the blade towards the stranger. 'You dare threaten the Prince?' she hissed through clenched teeth.

'He dares stand idly by whilst the rich and powerful destroy our way of life, burning our family. The King is as good as dead. The sons will be next. This world needs healing. It doesn't need royalty and their self-obsessed ignorance.'

'And how do you plan to do that?' Kane asked, searching for any hint of a weapon on his person and finding nothing.

'You misunderstand me, Katerina Kane. I am part of something bigger. It is not my role to kill the Prince. Mine is a lesser, more nuanced part to play. This isn't the first time we've seen the Prince swaggering through our streets where he doesn't belong.'

'*We've*?' Kane repeated.

The stranger grinned, breathing deeply and puffing his chest out. 'He's here! The Prince is here!'

Even with the continuous flow of rain splashing onto the ground, Kane heard the slamming of wooden doors opening and swinging on their hinges. Doors all along the street were being pushed open and through them came a stream of dark figures. All dressed in black, long robes flowing across the rain-drenched cobbled streets, menacing plague doctor masks covering their faces. Most had their black hoods up to protect them from the rain, whilst others wore tall, black hats. Unsheathed steel glistened in the light of the moon as Kane backed away, a strong hand clutching at Drayke's shoulder. What madness was this? 'Draw your sword,' she commanded, not allowing panic to set in. They were outnumbered and the odds were against them, but that didn't mean all was lost.

'Who are they?' Drayke asked, sliding his sword from its scabbard and dropping into a crouched fighting stance, eyes darting across the rows of enemies heading their way.

'Enemies. That's all we need to know right now. Don't hesitate, Your Highness. Strike quick and hard. Remember Braego's teaching.' Ah, Braego. How Kane would love to have him here beside her right now. An odd family gathering perhaps, but their chances would improve tenfold with the Borderland warrior at their side.

The masked men and women halted, facing Kane and Drayke in silence. The stranger had drifted away in the commotion, not wanting to be caught up in the violence no doubt.

'You're making a grave mistake. Attacking the Prince will lead to swift retribution. The King will not allow such an insult to go unpunished. You'll all be dead within the week,' Kane shouted, praying that the warning would be enough. Her stomach churned, body betraying her lack of hope.

A figure in the middle of the crowd stepped forward, rain splashing off the rim of his magnificent, raven-black hat. 'We are punished every single day. There is a divide within this Kingdom, both literal and figurative. It is time for us to smash down the wall that separates us from them.' He pointed a gloved hand at Drayke and continued. 'For too long they have been able to get away with whatever they wanted. Money we earn through hard work and labour is spent on their fancies and luxuries. They live in lavish mansions of stone and marble whilst we lose a whole street when a fire catches on one of the thatched roofs. They torture and burn our people in front of cheering crowds and expect us to just carry on. And better yet, they do it all in plain view of us. We look up from our filthy streets every day and are reminded that we live in their shadow. It can't go on. It is unsustainable for a Kingdom wanting progression. Unless you pray to The Four for stagnation, we must rid ourselves of the disease that is royalty. Tonight, we begin with Prince Drayke.'

'You'll have to go through me first,' Kane warned, gripping her sword and aiming it at the speaker.

'It brings me no pleasure to kill you, Katerina Kane. Though, it will be interesting to see if you last longer than your husband.'

Cypher had to admit, the look on Kane's face gave him a thrill that coursed through his body, warming him right down to the ends of his toes. The horror, the hatred, the sheer passion excited him almost as much as his work in the dungeons had.

'If I remember, he managed to stay on his feet for the first thirty seconds. The rest of the minute I watched him crawl across the floor. Don't worry, the rest of it was quick. Dagger to the throat. I'd spare you the rest of the details but I'm sure you remember!'

'You would be wise to keep your mouth shut on such matters, Cypher Zellin, those words may be your last.' To her credit, Kane's voice was steady, even. Most people would break at the memory of their husband being murdered. Not her. Cypher licked his lips, impressed with her resolve and strength.

'The numbers advantage allows me to say whatever the fuck I want, even in the presence of royalty.' Cypher bowed mockingly low to the Prince, eyes not moving from Kane as she shifted with his movement, obstructing a clear path to the young man. 'I must admit, I've always been on the fence when it comes to royalty. Some argue they are part of a tradition that makes our Kingdom great, historic ties that should not be severed. Others, like my new friends here, feel that they stand in the way of true progress. What are your thoughts, Katerina Kane?'

'I think if you don't back away right now, I'll have your head.'

Cypher chuckled behind his mask. 'I have to disagree. I'm no fool.' He raised his gloved hand, enjoying the theatrics. 'Take the Prince. Do as you wish with our ex-Inspector. Be careful, even at her age she will be dangerous.' Cypher spun on the spot, twirling his cape and walking through the crowd of masked Doctors who parted as he reached them. There was no point risking his own safety – one-on-one, Kane would be deadly. Let others play the hero. He would wait in safety. This wasn't his fight, his end goal.

'Coward!' Kane's voice rang through the rain behind him. Cypher turned slowly, facing her as she raised her sword, dropping into a defensive stance as three of The Doctors paced forward, drawing their own blades.

'Better to be a coward and breathing than a dead hero. Ask your husband when you see him. I'm sure it won't be long.'

Cypher reached the back of the line where the architect of this whole group stood patiently watching it all, away from any danger. 'She's a good woman, Katerina Kane. She doesn't deserve this,' the masked man said. 'King or peasant, she would defend all if she felt they deserved it. Status holds no importance in her mind.'

'You don't have the heart to kill her. That's why I'm here, remember? You can keep your distance and pretend this isn't your fault.'

'I know it's my fault, damn it! This Kingdom is worth more than any one person, Katerina Kane and Prince Drayke included,' the leader snapped back.

'Then there's no need for the crocodile tears. Progress is made on a foundation of blood and sweat. Go back through history and give me an example proving otherwise,' Cypher dared. It had always been this way. That's why leaders always had those who loved them and those who hated them. Loved for the necessary decisions and vilified for the death toll. Only the strong could make those decisions. Strong people like Cypher. He was born for this.

'I can't argue against it. I just wish there was another way.'

'But there's not. So, let's get it over with and move on.' Cypher peered through the crowd of Doctors, watching as Kane stepped back, one hand pushing the Prince away from the fight. Brave, but it would be for nothing.

'Now, this looks like a jolly meeting! Doesn't seem as though we've been invited though…' a voice called out from the shadows. Cypher frowned as all heads turned to the newcomer. His jacket was soaked through with rainwater, raven-black hair falling down to his shoulders as he sauntered across the cobbled road, sword gleaming in the moonlight as he swung it with ease in his right hand. Behind him followed a large group of red-robed figures, white masks hiding their faces.

'Shit.'

'Shit,' Aleister muttered under his breath, not allowing his confidence to fade.

'That's Prince Drayke,' Ella muttered behind her mask. Katerina Kane shielded the Prince, standing between him and the black-masked bastards creeping towards her, swords in hand. It appeared that they had arrived in the nick of time.

Aleister had no idea why the Prince would be wandering around the Lower City but whatever the reason, his night was about to come to an unfortunate end.

'The Prince must be lost,' Aleister cried, smiling to the mages lining up behind him. 'I'm sure I can escort both him and Ms. Kane back to the palace; the streets can be dangerous at this time of night.'

Kane glanced at him before returning her gaze to the three masked men approaching her. 'We would very much welcome the assistance. I'm sure this has all been a misunderstanding.'

'Excellent. Swords are not needed. I'm sure you three were merely over-excited at seeing the Prince and felt the need to ask his opinion on your recently acquired weapons. The Prince finds them delightful, but they will look much better when sheathed.' Aleister dropped the smile, raising Soulsbane high and pointing it at the nearest figure. Even with the mages behind him, they were slightly outnumbered. Thankfully, no one would be stupid enough to risk their life when the odds were so uneven, especially when retribution from the Palace would be swift and deadly.

'I'm afraid, we're not leaving until we have the Prince.' The crowd parted as one of The Doctors strolled forward, drawing his own weapon. A golden handle gripped in a black gloved fist. Quality steel, well-made and professional. This was no common cutthroat. 'I don't believe I've had the pleasure of meeting you.'

'It's been a while since I've stepped foot in Archania,' Aleister answered. 'I recognise the mask but perhaps you should take it off, seems rather impolite.'

'It's best if he leaves it on. This is Cypher Zellin, nothing more than a killer and a torturer,' Kane spat. Aleister hid his surprise. This man had killed Kane's husband years ago. The last he had heard of the man, he had worked his way into the dungeons, torturing both the innocent and the guilty.

'Ex-torturer. His father,' Cypher pointed the tip of his sword at Drayke, 'never complained about my efforts. That's behind me now, of course. Though, I am willing to make an exception or two, for a good cause.'

'What cause?' Aleister heard Haller's footsteps as he walked up beside him, empty-handed.

'To unite Archania. Its people have suffered too much.' Another of The Doctors stepped forward, placing his own gloved hand on Cypher's, lowering the weapon. His voice dripped with authority and education. Aleister would have paid good money to see who hid behind that mask.

'There are other ways,' Haller pleaded. 'We want a united Archania. Destroying each other will only weaken our cause.'

The Doctor's shoulders sagged, all fight leaving his body. 'Lower your weapons.' The three dark figures sheathed their weapons, followed by Kane. Aleister lowered his, grip still tight around the leather. This could be a trap. 'We know who you are. There are mages within our ranks, mages who feel you are not making the necessary progress. A revolution is coming, whether you want it to or not. Blood will be spilled. If we fight now, we achieve nothing. But let this be a warning, if you stand in our way again, we will not stop. Archania stands on the dawn of a new era. You can be with us, or against us.'

Cypher placed the ornate sword into its scabbard, looking around at the crowd of red robes. 'I know how you all feel. You want more. You hate how you have to live in the shadows, never showing the world your true self.' He ripped off his mask and displayed his misshapen, yellowing teeth. 'We'll send the message to all of the villages around this Kingdom: in two days' time, we'll be in the King's Square, soon to be the People's Square. If you want to see progress, join us. If not, then stay the fuck out of our way.'

Kane grabbed the Prince and marched him away, passing close enough to Aleister to whisper. 'That escort still available?'

'Always,' he replied with a laconic smile.

Aleister glanced at Ella next to him as he turned to follow the Prince and Kane. A tight grip on his shoulder prevented him from stepping forward. He glanced to his right to spot a black glove squeezing him. 'I'd suggest you move that hand before I remove it, permanently.'

'I know who you are, Aleister of the Red Sons. You made a mistake coming back here. Next time we cross paths, you'll be dead.' The voice was softer than expected. He didn't recognise it at all.

Shrugging the hand off, he spat on the rain-soaked ground. 'Many have tried. None have succeeded. Good luck.'

A WARM WELCOME

What was it with walls? The further south they headed, the more walls sprung up. Did the southerners really love being fenced in like pigs all the time? Or were they scared of their neighbours and just wanted a barrier between those who were more proficient in the way of steel? Sly didn't know the answer. Either way, it was fucking madness. The open air, the wild, the freedom of the wilderness, that's what he needed, what he wanted.

'Must have taken years to build those walls,' he said, staring up at the white perimeter of the city.

'It protects the Upper City. When attacked, it's easily defended. Those in the Lower City are less fortunate. They have to fend for themselves,' Bane said.

Sly peered from the hill, down at the grim city beneath them. Everything looked so much smaller from up here, yet even from here he could see the difference between the two cities. One seemed pristine and gleaming, the other grim and dirty. He already knew which one he preferred. Unfortunately, they were heading towards the huge wooden doorway flanked by eight soldiers standing in the shadows of the wall. 'Let's get this shit over with.'

'Halt!' One of the soldiers stepped out from the

shadows as Sly approached the door with the others. Their silver armour shone in the light of the sun: a helmet covering most of the face; chainmail clanging with every movement, obviously not the best fit; gauntlets; shin guards, and a long, white cloak trailing behind. *Never saw the point in wearing white.* Too easy to get it dirty and enemies could spot you from a mile away unless you were in amongst the snow. Sly glanced at the bottom of the cloak and smirked. Filthy. Mud had splattered up from the bottom of the cloak and ruined the pristine look the soldiers were going for. 'What business do you have in the Kingdom?'

'We come from the Borderlands,' Raven said, stepping forward and waving a hand across the group. 'My brother lived here, Braego. He died recently; we're here to pay our respects.'

A flicker of recognition passed across the soldier's face. He looked back to his colleagues and nodded up to the battlements above. A moment later, the wooden doors creaked open, allowing Sly a look at the city beyond. The sheer number of statues, even in his tunnelled vision through the open door, was overwhelming. Why would any Kingdom need so many statues? Some of them appeared unfinished, missing arms or legs.

'Braego was a good man. He'd often spend time assisting in the training of the fresh soldiers coming through the ranks. He didn't need to do it; definitely wasn't a part of his job. Most folk here don't like anyone further north; scars left over from the wars, I guess. Most liked him though. Like I said, he was a good man. You look like him.'

'I'm his better-looking brother.' Raven winked. 'I'm glad he enjoyed it here. Borderlanders don't travel well. Miss the snows and open country.'

'He spoke fondly of his homeland.' The lead soldier peered across the rest of the group, eyes landing on Bane. 'It is rare for us to receive guests from the Southern Kingdoms, especially a mage.' His eyes flicked to the golden orbs. 'I don't think we've ever had one such as yourself pass through the Kingdom with Borderland allies.'

'My parents always claimed I was unique. I trust that

won't be a problem,' Bane answered.

'Many in the Kingdom blame mages for the difficulties in their lives. I can't promise a warm welcome for you; I can't promise a warm welcome for any of you. Even after his years of service, Braego wasn't liked by all in the Kingdom. Keep your head down and I'm sure there won't be any problems.' Bane nodded his thanks. 'Now, I'm sorry but I must ask that you hand over any weapons. Only authorised personnel can carry weapons in the Upper City.'

Sly paused, hocking up a good load of saliva before letting it fly onto the ground at the soldier's feet. 'That 'ain't happenin' while I'm still breathing.' The anxious glances passing from soldier to soldier let him know all he needed to – not a clue how to respond to people unwilling to eat whatever shit was thrown at them.

'I'm afraid it's protocol. You will be denied entry into the Upper City if you choose to ignore this request.'

'Doesn't feel like much of a request if you're giving us an ultimatum.'

'Easy, Sly.' Raven slid his belt off with ease and held his sheathed sword towards the soldier before him. 'Here, we're not looking for trouble.' He did well not to glance over at Sly as he said it. 'We'll be here for two nights: enough time to pay our respects before leaving.'

The others followed his actions, releasing their weapons and handing them over. The unlucky recipient of Baldor's Warhammer grimaced with the weight of the mighty weapon as he received it with both of his gloved hands. Baldor loomed over him for a moment, a warning of what may come if anything happened to his beloved weapon. Sly grumbled, staring down at a rather short soldier who gripped his tasselled spear tighter while Sly reached for his axes. Sweat dripped from beneath the nervous soldier's helmet as Sly thrust the heavy axes into his chest, forcing the man to drop his spear and almost shit himself by the looks of it. 'I want them back in the same condition I'm handing them over. I never forget a face.'

The young soldier turned to his leader, hands crossed

over the axes and holding them tight to his chest before his eyes flashed to the stains of dark red on the edges of the weapons. 'I promise they will be well looked after in our weapons room. I will personally see to their safekeeping,' the leader said.

'We appreciate it,' Raven responded, shifting his shirt slightly to cover the small blades strapped at the back of his waist. Between them, Sly reckoned the guards had missed about eleven weapons as they smiled and led the way through the doors into the city.

'The Upper City is the pride of Archania but, knowing Braego, might I suggest heading to the Lower City for a night whilst I sort out an opportunity for you to pay your respects. He thoroughly enjoyed the taverns in the Lower City and claimed that the people there were more to his taste. The Bloody Stag was his favourite, I believe. Easy to find, all the locals will be able to guide you. It's on Market Street. Just follow the loud noises and unusual smells and you'll find it.'

'And how will you find us? We will need your assistance to meet those who worked with Braego,' Raven said, scratching at his mighty red beard.

'A group of Borderlanders, one from the Southern Kingdoms: trust me, I'll find you.'

* * *

One hour. Just one hour. That's all it took in for Sly to dismiss the Upper City as a soulless void of pretence and fake beauty. Men had walked past in white wigs, powdered faces, rosy cheeks, one holding onto a thin leash attached to what could only be described as a large, barking rat. Their clothes were too tight in the wrong places and flared out in others. Women had walked along the wide, smooth pathways towards mammoth areas of low-cut grass, only pausing to turn up their own powdered noses as they crossed Sly, disgust openly acknowledged.

'Reckon it's the smell,' Bane had said, eyes following the women as one spun an umbrella, shielding her pale skin from the heat of the midday sun. Sly had sniffed at his armpits. No different from usual. Pungent, yes. Repulsive, no. Well, maybe. 'Or it could be the scars. Or that you haven't shaved in months.'

'Their loss.' He shrugged and spat on the floor; a thick, brown mess that splattered onto the clean red sandstone pathway slaloming across the city. 'Then again, could be you scaring them off.'

Bane raised an eyebrow and shrugged in turn. 'If the colour of my skin is putting them off, then I have not missed out at all. People fear what they are not used to. I travel so that I fear less, and I help others to do the same.'

'That why ears are swinging around your neck,' Sly said, flicking a finger against one of the trophies before Bane could stop him.

'They are signs that a little fear is sometimes necessary...'

'Yeah right. You're as bloodthirsty as the rest of us, Bane. Just speak all nice, that's all.' All warriors were the same. Romantics obsessed with wanting others to view them as beasts with a heart. Paesus had written his poems about warriors who fought and killed to save kingdoms, or even to get a kiss from a fawning woman. Reality was men who had no other talents had one option. They could fight. They could kill. That was it. Some had tried other roles. Carpenters. Blacksmiths. Merchants. They all came back to this life. The way of the blade, some called it. Sly had never lied to himself though. He was a killer and damn good at it. There was no other life for him.

'Not everyone wanted this life.'

Sly dug a dirty finger in his ear, scraping at the collection of wax stored in there as he stared wide-eyed at Cray. The glum bastard had been silent for so long Sly had almost forgotten that the man could speak. 'Who the fuck put a penny in your talk box?'

'Just saying. Some of us didn't choose to live this way.'

'Still here though; still fighting,' Sly commented, scratching at an itch at the bottom of his back, right next to where the hilt of a dagger pressed against his skin.

Cray only grunted back.

With the conversation finished, Sly's ears pricked at the buzz of noise in the distance. Strolling downhill, he could look to the source of the sound. Must be the Lower City. Even from this distance, he could see the point in the Kingdom where the bright, extravagant colours of the Upper City faded away into the grim, grey tone of the Lower City. He licked the back of his teeth and grinned to himself. Finally, they could have a bit more fun.

'If Braego enjoyed it down there, then I'm sure we will feel more comfortable,' Raven said, following Sly's gaze. 'Not too much fun...'

'Can never have too much fun, chief,' Sly mocked, picking up the pace.

'There are guards and dungeons here and we have no weapons...'

'That's where the fun is,' Sly argued as they reached a border of guards with their backs towards the oncoming warriors.

Easy to get out. Might not be so easy to get back in. The guards held their spears high, barely moving an inch as the group eased past them and stepped onto the uneven, cobbled path.

Thatched roofs sat on top of decaying wooden buildings on either side of the street. A wave of unique smells hit Sly as he walked down the path: a mix of shit, sweat, piss and the stink of animals. Horses trotted every which way down the streets and into the shadowed alleyways between the filthy buildings. Dogs searched for scraps of food before getting distracted and attempting to pounce on the skinny pigeons that seemed to swarm and gather in groups in various locations. A couple of curvy women stood on a street corner, chests hanging so far out their dress it seemed like magic. This place was a hive of filth.

He loved it.

'Keep an eye out, lads. No trouble,' Raven warned, eyes

searching the shadows for any sign of attack. Good idea not to keep their guard down. This part of the city was swarming with activity. Sly struggled to grasp the sheer number of people milling around the streets: selling their wares, arguing, rushing to get to the Four knew where. The only time he'd seen such a large gathering of people was in battle: it made the hair on his arms stand up. He reached for the dagger at his back, relaxing as he rubbed the leather grip. If there was any trouble, he'd be the one ending it. Or starting it. No point ruling anything out this early in the day.

'The city has grown,' Bane said, staring around at the mass of people. 'Last time I was here, it seemed half the size.'

'Too many people. Dangerous,' Baldor added, sweat glistening on his soft face.

'No worries, big man. I got your back,' Sly said, slapping the giant on the shoulder, a struggle at that height. 'Doubt these southerners will fancy attacking you, weapon or no weapon. You're three times their size!'

'A big target,' Cray mumbled.

Sly groaned. 'I think I prefer it when you're the silent and stupid type.'

Deeper into Archania's Lower City, a square of stalls stood together as a swarm of eager buyers pushed and shoved around like flies on shit. Sly expected some of the crowd to move out of the way as the warriors walked through, shoulders back and heads held high. Most didn't even give them a second glance, except maybe for Bane who earned a couple of anxious looks before people turned back towards the wrestling around the stalls.

There was a proper smell around the stalls; Sly caught a whiff of it as he sniffed, creasing his face. An awful reek of salted fish, pork, piss and rotting flesh. Must be a corpse nearby. With so many people around, arguments were bound to break out. Not all arguments could be ended with words. There were enough shadows in the gaps between the tall buildings to dump any incriminating evidence. He reached for his dagger and gripped it close to his side, ready for anything. He pushed into an irritated-looking man who himself had shoved past three women in his rush to get to the front. No patience. For a moment, the man looked as though he was about to argue with Sly. A low growl and a wide, unblinking stare made the man think better of causing any trouble.

A few dozen paces later and they pushed out through the crowd, Baldor leading the way; funny how people appeared more agreeable to get out of his way than anyone else. The smell eased off slightly: now the wind only carried with it the smell of sweat and piss. An improvement.

'There's the tavern the guard mentioned. The Bloody Stag,' Baldor grunted, throwing a trunk of an arm up and pointing at a sign swinging out onto the street. On it was a gruesome painting of a stag's head separated from its body, blood dripping down into a puddle of red. Very welcoming.

'I'm gonna have a walk around the city. Been a while since I've walked in Archania. Don't want to waste time sitting in a tavern,' Bane said, clasping hands with Raven. 'Grab a few rooms above the tavern and I'll meet you there at sundown.'

'Turning down a drink? That's the South in you,' Sly said, passing Bane with a friendly punch on the arm as he walked to the tavern. 'Don't have any fun without me. If I hear you've punched some dumb shit on your own, then I'm gonna get pissed!'

'I'll wait until we meet up for that!'

'Too fucking right.'

'Seriously, you know what the guard said about the people here. Not too keen on mages or outsiders. Keep a low profile,' Raven warned.

'No problem. Like I said, sundown.'

Sly pushed a finger against one nostril and blew a streak of snot from the other before wiping the leftovers on his sleeve. 'I'll lead the way.'

The tavern wasn't too different from the ones he was used to; seemed like folk who liked a drink always fancied it in dimly lit rooms with a stench of stale blood and sweat. The circular wooden tables dotted around the room were surrounded by a variety of mismatched stools, most likely due to others being broken over customers' heads when talk gets too heated, in Sly's experience. The place hadn't seen a lick of paint in a while but places like this weren't meant to be pretty: they were havens for the reviled, the lonely, the angry men. Every town needed one.

Sly stalked off into the corner of the room, catching every look sent his way from the listless locals intrigued by newcomers and making sure that they looked away first. Small victories: first impressions were everything in a new place. Nothing about the locals stood out: a motley bunch of dour faces huddled around their drinks. He kicked a boot against a stool to slide it back against the corner and sat down, leaning back against the wall and lifting his muddy boot onto the round, wooden table. A few more glances. Nothing more.

Cray followed silently, slowly pulling his chair back and sitting down, his expression unchanging. Always looked as though he was walking in a field fall of shit.

'Enjoying the delights of Archania?' Sly asked to pass the time, eyeing Raven and Baldor as the landlord finally lowered the glass he was cleaning and walked over to greet them.

'Same as most of the North. Folk eat. Folk drink. Folk fight. Folk fuck. Nothing special.'

'Been around the North much?'

'Most places. You?'

'Helped take Norland when I was barely old enough to raise a sword. Snuck away on the ship as it left the Borderlands. Thought it would be a great adventure. Damn city surrendered the second day we got there. When we heard that Reaver come to an agreement with the King, we burnt most of the city and got back on the ships. Fought a bit more with the other tribes before Reaver returned. Never seen so many men pissed off. All that effort, and for what? To go back home with the news that we'd made friends with the soft bastards we'd vowed to kill.' Sly spat on the floor, placing his elbows onto the table and glancing over at the men across the room, hoping against hope that one of them would give him an excuse, any excuse.

'Thought he was doing what was right I suppose.' Cray shrugged.

'Where did that get him?' Sly asked, feeling increasingly agitated. 'A knife in the back. Bones. He messed up the moment he called for the retreat. Could have taken the whole of the North in that campaign. Instead, we shuffled back and fought for scraps with the Barbarians.'

'Thought you preferred it back home?'

'I do. Still don't mean what he did was right. The man had no pride...'

Sly sank back into his seat, welcoming the familiar silence as the anger faded away. Old wounds. Cray was right, he preferred it back home. Heading here just brought back difficult memories. He knew how things were back home. It was easy.

'Sorted a few rooms out for us upstairs. Decent price.' Raven dropped the drinks onto the table with a bang, causing the liquid to splash over the sides and seep into the cracks in the wood. 'Nothing special but better than what we're used to on the road.'

Baldor took a seat, failing to blend in with the rest of them as his large frame dominated the corner of the room. 'Be good to sleep in a bed.'

'Day one and you're already getting soft. Haven't heard you complain about sleeping rough before,' Sly said, feeling the frustration rise once again. He couldn't stop it. It was the warm, stale air. It was the sound of the market outside, seeping through the thin walls. It was being away from the Borderlands.

'Just saying, it'll be good. Only so many times a man can sleep in a blanket of snow in some cold cave that smells like shit before he starts wanting more.'

'More? Bah!' Sly spat again, drawing a few uneasy looks from the locals. 'Got a fuckin' problem with me, assholes?'

'Sly. Easy. We ain't lookin' for trouble.' Raven glared at him after raising a hand to the offended party. No more looks came their way.

'One night. That's all I'm doing, Raven. I shouldn't

have come here anyway. Should be up there, fighting with the old man and the girlie. Even the kid would bring a smile to my face right now. Better to be putting folk in graves than to be waiting to say the words over them. Braego left the Borderlands years ago, now he's dead. End of story.'

'I need to know how he died. If someone killed him...'

'What? What if someone killed Braego?'

'Then we'll kill the bastards.'

Sly dug a finger into his ear and pulled out a lump of wax. He wiped it on his shirt and stared straight into Raven's unflinching gaze. 'You're in another land, away from Saul. There's no way to get a message to him. You gonna kill here?'

'He was my brother, Sly. If they killed him, then fuck the truce.'

Cray shifted in his chair, cracking his neck with a tilt of his bald head.

'What do you think of that? Saul's dog will go running back to him and let him know if we kill any of the bastards,' Sly said, licking his lips and leaning into Cray. 'Saul's little bitch.'

He knew the blow was coming. Still, he felt the wind rush past his face as he snapped back into his seat, barely dodging Cray's attack. 'Say that again and I'll fucking gut you.'

'Ooohh,' Sly cackled, clapping his hands together as the rest of the room stared at the commotion. 'Got some fight in ya! What would you do then, Cray, if we had to do a bit of killin'? If Braego really was killed by some soft fucker in this city?'

'If they killed one of us,' Cray said, chest rising and falling with the adrenaline raging through his body, eyes wide and staring straight at Sly, 'I'll bury my own dagger in the bastard's chest. Or maybe I'll bury it in you. Either way, Saul ain't finding out.'

'My apologies for interruptin' you folk, but I overheard you talking about Braego: you on about the Weapons Master from the Borderlands?' Sly turned to face the newcomer. He'd shuffled over from a table on his own, stank of stale drink and looked well past his best years. Lank, dirty blonde hair fell in waves onto his chest and shoulders, greying slightly in places.

His eyes darted between them all as he rubbed his hands together nervously, fingers twitching with unease.

'Aye. He was my brother,' Raven said, offering a seat to the man. 'You knew him?'

'I did. Drank in here from time to time,' the man answered, declining the seat with a curt shake of his head. 'He'd sit with me when I was alone and keep me company. Kept me from doing dumb shit. Well, more dumb shit anyway.'

'He was a good man, Braego. What is your name, friend?'

'Eric.'

'Well, Eric, it is good to hear that my brother was able to share a drink with people in a kingdom that used to hate our people not so long ago.'

'He made many friends but...' Eric paused, looking over his shoulder as though fearing an attack. He leaned forward, voice lowering to a whisper, forcing the group to move closer to hear his words. 'He made enemies too. It was murder. I promise you; it was murder.'

Raven cracked his knuckles, breathing in deeply through his nose and out through his mouth. 'Who?'

'I saw him the night of his death. He seemed troubled, wasn't himself at all. Kept saying that he'd made a mistake and that he needed to make things better. I pressed him, wanting to help, like when he'd helped me. He'd shook his head; the secret was too big of a burden for me to carry. He calmed down after a couple of drinks. The last thing he said to me was that if he went missing, there was only one person to blame.'

'Tell me, Eric. Who killed my brother?'

'Mason. Mason D'Argio.'

'We don't give a shit about protocol. You either let us through nice and easy or we start splittin' skulls. It's your decision.' Sly glared at the guards as they shuffled across, six of them joining to create a barrier preventing the warriors from making it back into the Upper City.

'We have a meeting with Mason D'Argio. We passed

this way barely an hour ago,' Raven said, breathing steadily to keep his fury at bay.

'Unless you have proof of such a meeting, I must insist that you remain in the Lower City. Orders are orders.' The guard smirked back, enjoying being in control. A couple of the others swallowed nervously, clearly not as confident that orders alone would prevent the group from getting past.

'If that's your answer, then this is ours,' Raven said, dropping the act of respect. His fist crunched violently into the nose of the lead guard, blood spewing into the air as Sly launched a knee into the groin of his own opponent. He followed it up with an elbow to the back of the neck as the guard leaned forward in agony. Both men crumbled to the floor, groans of pain syncing as one.

The remaining guards clutched at the hilts of their swords, hands shaking. A shadow passed over them, stopping them in an instant. They looked up, eyes staring at the towering, silent figure of Baldor.

'He's a big guy, ain't he?' Sly nodded, patting a hand against his friend's back. 'I've seen him punch through a man's stomach and force his fist through the other side. Straight through – bones, flesh and guts. You got enough guts to stand up to him? If you do, you'll have none once he's done,' he warned, enjoying himself.

They parted like the sea breaking against rocks, moving either side of the group before kneeling down at their fallen comrades.

'We gettin' our weapons first?' Cray asked as the four of them stalked along the immaculate city street, heading up towards the centre of the Upper City. 'I reckon we'll meet guards better prepared than those fools.'

'We have what we need,' Raven said, pulling his cloak aside to reveal a couple of his hidden daggers.

'You sure you grew up in the Borderlands?' Sly asked Cray. 'I feel naked if I don't have a few blades attached.' He lifted his own cloak at the back and spun, showing him the daggers he had managed to sneak past the guards.

Clouds gathered overhead as the warriors walked through curious groups of people. They stared, pointed; some even laughed and shook their heads. All were dressed in the most ridiculous of clothing. All too tight with bits sticking out needlessly at the shoulders. Looked impossible to fight in. Both men and women wore pale make-up to make their faces look like some weird contorted version of the moon. The height of idiocy, Sly thought. He'd never be confused as a leader of fashion, but these fools looked utterly ridiculous.

The laughter and curiosity shifted as a large group of guards marched their way, sharpened spears facing forward. Word had obviously raced ahead of them, warning the guards of their presence.

'Halt!' one of them cried. Raven stopped, eyes flickering to all before him, counting them one by one.

'Nine,' he muttered, holding an arm low and to the side to ensure his group followed his action.

'Baldor could have them on his own,' Sly said out the corner of his mouth. 'Just say the word, chief.' The spears looked dangerous and even the most foolish of men were capable of dealing death with such a weapon. Still, they had overcome worse odds.

'Friends! What is this?'

Sly cocked his head to the left at Bane's voice, lips breaking into a grin as he saw the southern warrior walking up steps to meet them, a sword hanging at his side. 'Bane! Perfect timing! Knew you wouldn't want to miss out on the fun.'

Sly's face dropped as another man followed Bane up the steps. His skin was a gentle brown; his thin lips looked capable of a smirk and a grimace but nothing more. His slender but lean frame spoke of one who was quick with a blade, dangerously quick. The robes he wore were unlike any other in this city; they were loose, allowing movement. A golden clasp on his left shoulder kept his white cloak close to his body. Sly spotted a curved blade sheathed on his right hip, always close by if needed.

'What are you doing, Bane?' Raven asked, one eyebrow

raised as he too spotted the newcomer.

Bane sighed, slowly stepping forward, palms facing them and a regretful smile on his dark face. The ears around his neck wobbled as he walked their way. 'This is T'Chai. Second in command to Mason D'Argio. For now, you can say that he speaks on behalf of Mason.'

'The same Mason who killed my brother,' Raven thundered, nails digging into his palms as he clenched his fists tight as hell.

'The very same.'

'Braego found out what you will all find out soon enough.' The brown-skinned warrior stepped forward, graceful and lithe. 'You either work with us, or you are against us. Braego hid information from us for over fifteen years. Information that would have helped this Kingdom, this world even!'

'And so, you killed him.'

'Yes. I personally killed him. Easy enough: I arranged a meeting by the docks and had an old addict Braego had befriended poison his drink to slow his movement. It was a swift death, if not entirely painless. A small bit of magic helped of course. Didn't want to leave anything to chance.' His voice was even, calm, as though he was speaking to them about how his day had been, and a boring one at that. 'Of course, it was all for nothing, in his case. We know what we need to know. The boy is in the Borderlands, meeting with that old fool of a mage. Before the week is done, he will be in our hands, make no mistake of that.'

'The boy has done nothing!' Raven roared.

'No, and that is the problem. We need him to fulfil his potential if Takaara is to be saved.'

Sly squinted at Raven, scratching at his beard. What the fuck were they on about? Out of the corner of his eye, he spotted the guards creeping around them, creating a boundary. 'Take one more step and you'll be the first one with a dagger up his fuckin' arse!' he bellowed, feeling the veins in his head about to pop. He'd had enough of the talking nonsense. Now was the time for action.

'Cray...' Bane said, golden pupils turning to the grumpy warrior.

Sly felt a hand against his back and then a dull thump against the back of his head. He fell forward onto the stone pathway, hands taking the brunt of the fall. 'Fuck,' he muttered, reaching for the back of his head, the source of the pain. Already, there was blood on his hand. 'Fuck, fuck, fuck.' He struggled onto one foot before a boot met his ribs, lifting him into the air and dropping him down onto the ground once more. He heard the roar of fighting around him as the guards moved forward, slamming their shields onto Raven as the valiant warrior grasped at his dagger, blade flying left and right, but nothing landing.

Sly rolled to his left, dodging another kick from Cray. His eyes fell on Baldor. The giant bellowed and rushed into the fight, slamming into two of the guards and sending them flying onto the ground. Bane moved forward, blade drawn and ready to strike.

'Nooo!' Sly screamed as the sword sliced across Baldor's calf, first his left and then his right, felling the warrior like a great tree. Bane held the sword against Baldor's neck, ensuring that he would stay still for the moment.

The world turned red as Cray's boot met Sly's face, cracking his neck back and knocking a tooth down his throat. He coughed and spat it out along with a whole stream of blood. 'Fuckin' coward. If you wanted a fight, all you had to do was ask.'

'This way is more fun,' Cray replied with another boot to the already injured ribs. Sly doubled over on the ground, coughing and struggling for breath. Raven was on his knees next to him, glaring up at Bane who returned the look with a smile.

'Traitors. Both of you. Fuckin' traitors,' Sly spat as he fell into a coughing fit.

'Traitors?' Bane asked. 'He's the traitor.' He pointed at Raven with his free hand, sword still resting against Baldor's neck, beads of blood trickling down onto the warrior's shirt. 'His dad made a pact with Archania. A pact that has threatened our people ever since. He hid the boy from Mason and his people, knowing how important he is. If you want to blame anyone, blame him.'

'I've got no fucking idea what you're on about. All I hear is that you're a fucking traitor,' Sly replied.

'As touching as this all is. I've heard enough.' T'Chai stepped forward, drawing his curved blade in one swift motion. 'Say hi to your brother for me.' Blood splattered onto Sly's face as the blade arced across Raven's neck, his lifeless body dropping to the floor with a thud.

'Chain the big one up, the Empire will have a use for him. Lock the other in the dungeons. I'll decide what to do with him later...'

Baldor didn't move. His mouth hung open, eyes wide as they stared down at his fallen chief. 'Redbeard...'

'You fuckin' bastard!' Sly roared.

Cray smiled as he dropped his boot onto Sly's face.

Once.

Twice.

Three times.

'This council has drifted into a slumber of late, something that can be attributed to my father and his lack of focus during his recent illness. Such a lack of focus and desire to improve this Kingdom will not be tolerated whilst I am here. Any one of you can be replaced,' Prince Asher of House Albion clicked his fingers dramatically and glowered at all of them, enjoying his time on the throne, 'like that.'

'Well spoken, Your Grace. Whilst we here have always endeavoured to do what is best for this Kingdom that is so close to our hearts, we must admit that there have been lapses of late.' Mason agreed, raising a smile from the Prince and an affectionate nod. 'We must double, nay *triple,* our efforts to ensure that this Kingdom does not slide into an abyss, to be forgotten.'

The other councillors mumbled their agreement, all willing to admit that they could have done more of late. Kane nodded her own accord, cursing silently in her head that such an arrogant fool was now in charge of this Kingdom. Asher was a child in a young man's body; a child who had grown up with everyone around him being too scared to admonish him. He used his status to live a life of luxury, abusing his position in a whole host of ways. Now he sat in one of the most powerful seats in all Takaara, side-by-side with Mason D'Argio, a man he admired above all, except perhaps for himself. The future of Archania was looking bleak indeed.

'This is still the greatest city in all Takaara!' Sir Dominic bellowed, flashing that usual smile of his to the circle of councillors. Kane stifled a chuckle of her own as Lord Tamir visibly rolled his eyes and sighed, dismayed that the knight once again thought it necessary to verbalise his thoughts. 'No wars since the skirmishes with the Borderlands – which I fought in, if you remember. Trade is going well, is it not Lord Balen? The sun is shining bright and strong even though we are well into autumn. Our future looks bright, my Prince.' His eyes wrinkled at the corners as he nodded, looking for any sign of encouragement from the tired councillors around him. Balen offered a small smile but the others had drifted off, clearly uninterested in the expected outburst from the vain knight.

'Your words are truth, Sir Dominic,' Mason eventually agreed, 'yet, there are problems within this city that must be addressed.'

The murmurs breaking out across the table now mixed with concerned glances and arched eyebrows, confusion seeping through the entire room. Kane shifted in her seat and glanced at Prince Asher. His pale face was solemn, yet behind the mask, she felt as though she could see the battle being raged as he struggled to keep a smirk from dancing at the corner of his lips.

'The Upper City is a beacon of propriety and progress: exactly what we wish to display to the world. Sadly, the Lower City is a filth-ridden hive of criminals and scum that has been left to fester for far too long,' the Prince spat. 'There are rumours spreading across the city that some of the citizens are ungrateful with the running of this Kingdom. They feel it would be better if our great monarchy was replaced. With what, I have no idea. Maybe one of the peasants would like to try their hand at running the Kingdom!' The joke brought a smattering of sycophantic laughter and applause. Kane stayed silent, unmoving.

'There will always be citizens who want more, citizens who are unhappy with their lot in life,' Tamir said to the Prince, a bored look on his face. 'How do you propose they are dealt with?'

'Swiftly and with no remorse!' General Grey bristled, his moustache dancing with a comical energy. 'A threat to our monarchy is an insult to all of us who have worked to keep this Kingdom safe!'

'People like me!' Sir Dominic added, beating his chest like some kind of ape.

'A message has been sent to my sister, the Empress of the East. She is aware of our small... difficulties. If any assistance is needed, she will move with all haste,' Mason informed them. 'We will triple the number of guards in the Lower City for the foreseeable future. Any activity deemed treasonous will be dealt with instantly and with all the strength we can muster.'

Kane had heard enough. 'That will only incite further hatred and disgust amongst the people of the Lower City! They need to understand that their rulers will listen to them, that their voices will be heard. They do not need to be squashed like bugs. They are the backbone of this Kingdom!'

'The backbone?' Asher flew up from his seat, enraged. His face purpled as his dark eyes stared holes into Kane. She stayed unflinching in her seat. The rage of an immature boy was nothing to her, even one as powerful as Asher. 'These people are a plague: a disease that threatens the life of this very Kingdom. If you think they should be defended, then perhaps you should go and join them in their pits of filth.'

Kane waited a moment, mulling over the words of the spoiled brat. Her face grew hot, not with embarrassment, but anger: anger that this young, foolish, insolent man could speak to her in such a way. The heat died down as she controlled her breathing. Best not to make a decision when the flames of anger are dancing inside. She pushed her seat back, legs scraping along the stone floor, before she stood. She looked at each of the councillors in turn – some were good, some not so. All had been companions to her on the council, most were nothing more. They were all doing their best pretending that they were somewhere else. Only Lord Tamir looked her in the eyes, unblinking. His face had the look of a man with a deck of cards in hand, cautiously weighing up his next move.

'Thank you all for your support on this council. I will do as my Prince has suggested. It is my belief that each citizen of this Kingdom, regardless of birth or status, deserves to be defended. As such, I will join them, in their pits of filth. I wish you all nothing but good health. May the Four watch over you all.'

'The Four? I will be watching over you Katerina Kane.' Asher finally released that ugly smirk of his, marvelling at his own wit.

Kane reached the door before she turned back, looking around the room she had worked in for so long. Perhaps she would never return. 'Your father would be so disappointed, Asher. My heart breaks for him.'

'If you step foot in here again, it'll be a one-way trip to the dungeons. Get out of my sight.'

'Gladly...' Kane whispered, striding past the motionless guards.

SETTLING

Arden of the Raven tribe stretched his arms out wide, rolling his shoulders whilst opening and closing his fists. His body still ached, even though a week had passed since the battle. His sleep had been uneasy since he'd arrived at Korvus' home, wherever it was. Socket had continued to be vague, speaking of magic and the unknown instead of giving him an actual answer. Nightmares were becoming a regular occurrence for him. Yet again, last night, he had been visited by an old, weary traveller, blood-soaked hands reaching out to Arden, ice blue eyes wide and dangerous. Every night it was the same message. *Run! Run whilst you can!* That was when the nightmare ended, every time.

Arden blamed it his new surroundings. The castle was eerie – grey stone on the outside, dark, shadowed corridors on the inside. Its sheer size was daunting to Arden; half of his tribe could move in tomorrow and they would be comfortable, yet he'd only seen a handful of servants in his time at the castle. Korvus had told him it was better to keep the numbers down – less chance for trouble, less chance for betrayal.

Stretches finished with, Arden pulled his white silk shirt over his head and tied the laces on his brand-new boots. He walked out of the room and into one of the castle's many silent corridors. The stone floor was covered with a red carpet running down the middle of the corridors throughout the castle.

Painting and tapestries lined the walls either side of him: Kings and Queens from distant lands and battles that now were forgotten by most in the world. At least that's what Korvus had told him. The way he had discussed it felt to Arden as though this was all meant to mean something to him, as though he wasn't just filling time and making idle conversation. Echoes of Raven and Socket's lessons from his training would flash into his mind whenever Korvus began to weave his tales of the bloody history of Takaara.

Being used to cramped caves and wooden longhouses, Arden marvelled at the immense labyrinth of the castle. How anyone could navigate their way through the mammoth building and arrive at their intended destination was beyond belief. The servants were helpful, stopping to assist him whenever they saw that familiar lost and frustrated look on his face. For some reason, if he stopped worrying about where he was, his feet managed to guide him to his favourite room in the castle – the library.

'Ah, up early again, Master Arden.'

He waved at Korvus as the mage greeted him, an old, tattered book wide open in his hand as he stood next to a towering bookcase taller than any house that he had seen in the Borderlands. Arden had been lucky enough to learn his letters when he was a child, his mother sitting with him every evening and going through whatever words she could get her hands on. He couldn't claim to be a great reader, but he was proud of his ability, even if many in his homeland liked to mock him for it. There were worse things to be mocked for.

'Yeah, difficult night's sleep.'

'Nightmares again?' Korvus asked, frowning as he closed the book and walked over to him.

'Yeah. They'll pass.'

'They will. It must be strange for one such as yourself to stay in a place like this. "Familiarity breeds comfort," my father used to say. A few more days and you will be fine.'

Arden hoped the mage was right; he was sick of feeling tired all of the time. The swelling on his face had gone down but the pain lingered on. Korvus could have helped ease the pain but claimed that *'pain was a teacher second to none.'* Right now, he felt he could do with skipping a lesson or two. 'I'm sure you're right.'

'I usually am.'

'Where's Socket?'

'Out for a walk. It's been a while since he stayed here; loves the mountains, the clear air, the clear sky above him. Getting old means you appreciate the smaller details in life; you never can be sure when it will be your last chance to take them in.'

Arden raised his eyebrows at the morbid turn in the conversation. As old as Socket was, it was difficult to think of a time when the archer wouldn't be alive. 'Any one of us can go in an instant; it's not just age.'

'True, but time wears you down and develops in you a chance to appreciate what is around you. The less time you feel you have, the more you want. Life really is wasted on the young.' Korvus placed a hand on Arden's shoulder and smiled softly. 'Take a seat, I'll have the servants bring you some food. Reading is always a joyful pastime but reading on a full stomach is a wonder unmatched.'

Not long after, two servants entered the room, a small table of food perched upon a stand with four wheels creaking their way towards him. One of the servants offered a plate to Arden as the other lifted the silver dome placed on top of the steaming food. Strips of hot venison and vegetables filled his plate. The smell danced through the air into his nostrils, instantly forcing his stomach to growl. He ate the meal with a ferocity that drew nervous glances from the servants as they poured him a drink and offered him a knife and fork. No need. That's what his hands were for.

'It seems you can take the boy out of the Borderlands...' Korvus smirked, letting the rest of the sentence fade. He'd used it a lot lately. Usually, when Arden had done something that made the servants look uncomfortable.

'Where are we, Korvus?' Arden asked through

mouthfuls of meat, hoping that this time he would get a real explanation.

'Home. My home, at least.'

'Care to give me any more information?'

'Are you prepared for more information?'

Arden hesitated. 'Yes.'

The smirk on Korvus' face wasn't especially promising. The mage placed his book back into an empty slot on the bookcase and spun away, heading to the large bolted door that led out onto the castle battlements. He slid the bolt open with ease and pulled on the circular, iron handle, staring at Arden as the door swung inward. 'Let's find out.'

The rush of fresh, cold air blew through the room and hit Arden hard. His heart thumped a steady beat and he wondered, not for the first time, if he had died in the battle and this was in fact his purgatory, a state of waiting before being judged by The Four. He swallowed hard, following Korvus out through the door. He stood on the battlements, resting a hand against the cold stone and looking out across the stunning vista. Rows of snow-capped mountains ran parallel, either side of a winding, clear blue river that snaked off into the distance. Pine trees huddled together either side of the river, swaying rhythmically in time with the wind.

'Beautiful, isn't it.' Korvus stated. There was no way of arguing against the comment, no possible reason for disputing his claim. 'Untouched by man; created by the Gods, for the Gods. There's no better place in all the universe in my mind. I'm sure there are some who may field their own choices but to me, this is it.'

'Were you born here?' Arden asked, eager to find out more about the private mage.

'No,' Korvus muttered, eyes lost in the beauty before him. 'I was born in Norland. Now, it's one of the United Cities of Archania. Back then, it was just Norland, as it always will be for me. A good city: busy, a bit dirty like all cities are, but it was home. I loved it. Still do in fact. Back then, mages were still feared, but they were also respected. My father was a sailor on a merchant ship. Didn't see much of him growing up. My mother was a mage. She taught me basic magic: how to start a fire, how to ease people into sleep, how to open a lock without a key. Basic stuff.' Korvus bit his lip and scratched at a small white scar on the edge of his chin.

'I was ten cycles when it happened. Some of the locals knew my father was away. Drunk and filled with ideas of lust and greed, they broke into the house, daggers in hand. I can still remember the look on their faces. The leers, the licking of their lips as my mother stepped in front of me. She tried to fight. They struck her. That's when it happened.' Korvus' face had taken on a far-away look, lips moving but eyes dead to the world. 'I remember screaming and everything going red, then darkness.'

Arden became suddenly aware that his mouth was hanging open. He closed it, recognising the scene that Korvus had described. 'What did you see when you woke?' he asked, uncertain if he even wanted the answer. He'd often been told curiosity can be as fatal as a knife in the back.

'In my rage and fear, my mind had latched onto the last spell that I'd used. Fire. The smell was strange, like cooked meat. Four blackened corpses lay around me in the ash and smoke that had once been my home, one of them my mother's. For three days I sat there, unmoving, unable to comprehend what I had done.'

Arden thought back to the battlefield, the row upon row of corpses that lay scattered around the snowy field. Vomit flew up his throat and forced him to lean closer to the edge of the battlements, looking down at the moat that circled the great castle and breathing slowly.

'It's an old magic, that's what I found out years later. Only accessible to those descended from the greatest mages in history, the very people who shaped this world we live in.'

Arden pulled back from the edge, mouth open, eyes squinting at Korvus. The mage no longer had that glossy look over his face. He was smiling, a warm smile that Arden was only now seeing for the first time. His golden eyes flashed in the light of the morning sun. 'What are you saying, Korvus?'

'This castle exists on the spirit plane – or sky plane as some call it. It was created by The Four as a place of sanctuary, a place of learning. They knew the dangers of magic, the way in which people would turn on our kind.' The world seemed to spin as Arden's legs trembled. He held out a hand for support, pressing against the cold stone. 'You are an heir to the Gods, Arden; an heir to The Four.'

'Why, why didn't my mother tell me?' Arden stammered, head throbbing, forcing his eyes shut to block out the bright light of day.

'She looked after you, but she wasn't your real mother. Your real mother died shortly after your birth. Your father understood that you would be capable of great magic. Knowing that, he sent you away.'

'My father?' He had always been told that his father had died in a storm crossing the Emerald Sea. Whenever he had questioned further, his mother had rushed to change the topic. He'd thought she struggled to speak of it as the pain was still too much; or maybe his father had been a thoughtless brute like so many in the area. Pushing would only cause her more stress. Never had he believed that there could be another reason.

'Your father, the King of the United Cities of Archania. And he is on his way to see you.'

'Focus. Your concentration is slipping. It's simply not good enough!'

Arden wiped the beads of sweat from his forehead and bit his lip. The past week had been non-stop training, burning the candle at both ends under Korvus' instruction. As much as he wanted to bite back at the harsh mage, he'd learnt in his short time in the castle that answering back had unfortunate consequences. He absent-mindedly rubbed at his sore knuckles, taking a deep breath and closing his eyes.

'I've taught children to produce a flame before, that's how easy this spell is. All you need is concentration and the will to succeed. Let nothing else enter your mind. Focus on the flame you want to produce, let everything in your body and mind work towards that goal.'

Arden saw the flame in his mind, swaying slightly and crackling like the large fire in the Great Hall back home. Home. Not for the first time, he wondered if he had made the right decision leaving the village and heading out with Socket. His old life may have been boring, but it was a shit load less confusing.

The cane struck the knuckles on his right hand with a familiar crack. *Son of a bitch!* He spun, holding his injured hand against his stomach and bending over, breath hissing through his clenched teeth. 'Seriously? I was doing exactly as you asked!' he moaned, unable to stop himself.

'If you were doing what I had asked, there would be a small flame floating between the two of us. Do you see such a flame?' *If I did what I wanted to, then this whole room would be in flames.* Korvus stood alone in the centre.

'No, Master Korvus...'

'Neither do I. Tomorrow, we will start before dawn. Perhaps the earlier time will help sharpen your focus,' the mage's voice was smothered in disappointment. Usually, Arden would feel guilt, but Korvus wasn't the most sympathetic of trainers. Where Socket had taken his time with Arden, showing him the necessary movement and grips to improve his archery, Korvus felt the need to rush. It was as though he felt everything needed to be finished and ready two minutes ago. What progress Arden did make – little though it was – he waved away as unimportant. If it wasn't perfect, it wasn't good enough.

He stomped out of the library without a backwards glance, wanting to meet with Socket. The old archer hadn't been himself since the attack. He struggled to move; a pronounced limp obvious to anyone near. He tried to hide the injury, but Arden knew it wasn't healing the way the old man had hoped. In an effort to keep any questions at bay, he had taken to hiding up in his room, keeping away from the training Arden was having to endure. Arden wasn't going to let him keep to himself, if he had to put up with Korvus and his tough regime then Socket wasn't going to be afforded the luxury of his own company.

The corridors were quiet, as usual. He reached the door

leading to Socket's room without passing anyone else. It was eerie passing through such a mammoth building and not seeing anyone else. The silence drowned the air around him, suffocating him. He longed for the wide, open spaces of the wild and the grunts of warriors passing by. Even a curse from Sly would be preferable to this existence. For years he had disliked the hustle and crowd of men and women in the towns and villages around the Borderlands; he'd often slunk off into the shadows, preferring his own company before being forced to interact with others. The truth was he missed it. He missed the smells, the sounds, the general chaos of life around him. Without it, it all felt so empty and lifeless.

He raised his hand, banging his fist hard against the thick wooden door. Silence. He banged again, harder this time. Silence. He pressed his ear against the door, listening for any sound of life on the other side. No luck. He stepped back from the door, annoyed that Socket had left his room without coming to find him. What could the old man be up to? He tried the handle but there was no shifting the door, it had been locked.

Arden turned away, continuing his route away from Socket's room, not wanting to bump into Korvus again today if he could help it. He wasn't in the mood for any more of the fool's demands. What pissed Arden off the most was Korvus continuing to deny him any more information regarding his father. He'd claimed his father was a King and that he was on his way to meet Arden. The shock of the news had faded away, leaving a bitter taste of scepticism in Arden's mouth. The only reason Arden put up with the mage's shit was because he craved more information. Korvus knew that, played on it even. What if it was all a lie? A scheme to force Arden to stay and help the mad mage. Arden knew he had power, he'd seen that on the battlefield, perhaps the mage was trying to unleash it for himself. Still, the faint glimmer of hope that it was true, that his father was alive and on his way to the castle meant that Arden bit his tongue more often than not. A small price to pay for the hope it offered him.

Lost in his thoughts, Arden found himself facing an

unfamiliar set of stairs leading down. He frowned. There was no ceremonial rug following the steps on their descent, no paintings on either side of the wall. Just stone steps leading down to darkness. He searched either side of the corridor, looking for any sign of onlookers. Deserted.

He peered down the steps, searching for a hint of light at the bottom. Nothing. Only darkness stared back. His right boot found the first step, left followed, after a slight pause. His pace quickened as he descended the stone steps, licking his dry lips as blood pumped hastily through his veins. He reached out a hand and brushed it softly against the wall, fingers trailing against the rough, cold stone, guiding his journey down into the darkness. It consumed him as he continued, not a glimmer of light to be found. Eventually, his boots found even ground, informing him that he had reached the bottom.

He closed his eyes, accepting the darkness swallowing him. The absence of light allowed him to focus, feeling each breath enter through his nostrils and journey to his lungs with the rhythm of his chest rising and falling. He breathed out through his mouth, his thoughts a void waiting to be filled. In the clarity of the moment, Korvus' words streamed into his head; advice and instruction on how to access his power. Arden thought of a flame, one to act as a torch and light his path. It flickered for a moment, draped in shadow, threatening to die out. Arden held it there in his mind as tight as possible, the rhythm of his breathing in time with the swaying of the flame.

His eyes opened and grew wide. Floating in the air in front of him was the flame he had created in his mind. He'd done it! He clapped his hands together, astonished at his own power. For the first time in his life, he had succeeded with a spell that he had actually intended. His gleeful laughter halted for a moment as the flame darkened. He controlled his breathing, amazed as the flame grew, as though his breath was providing the energy and focus required to give it life.

The light of the flame filled the previously unseen corridor. It was unlike any other that Arden had seen in the castle; older, darker, more menacing. He found himself feeling that it might be better to walk in darkness than use the light. The walls were more rough and uneven than the upstairs, as though carved inexpertly into the very rock of the mountains surrounding the castle. As the flame neared the rock, he noticed dark stains scattered unevenly against the grey. A slow, ominous dripping sound echoed in the distance. Must be near the river, at least that's what Arden hoped it was.

He crept behind the floating flame, eyes scanning all around him.

Moments later, his eyes fell upon a door, wood rotting and broken. Fragments of wood lay at the base. This door was old, very old. There was no handle to be found, so Arden pushed against the door, cautiously peering through as he guided the flame into the room.

It was the smell that hit him first. He coughed, holding his sleeve up to his face to block the stale stench of filth reaching his nostrils. The flame hovered above a cage built against the wall, iron bars trapping an emaciated figure curled up against the wall in a puddle of piss. Arden flung himself to the ground, dropping to his knees and looking through the bars.

The figure's skin seemed stretched to breaking point against bones, ribs threating to break through. Pencil thin legs were curled up tight into the body with only a thin piece of filthy cloth to hide the modesty of its wearer. Long, wild black hair fell down, covering part of the figure's bent spine.

'What the fuck...' Arden murmured to himself.

The figure turned slowly, each movement seeming a painful one. His beard was a tangled hive of filth: dark red, dried blood staining the wild, frayed hair around his face. Black eyes squinted towards Arden; a weak hand raised high to protect them from the light of the flame hovering in the air.

'Another mage.' The prisoner muttered in disgust, mustering enough energy to sneer at Arden. 'Just get it over with.' His voice had an unexpected strength to it. The accent reminded Arden of Ovar, or perhaps it was just the cage he was in.

'Get what over with?' Arden asked, puzzled.

The black eyes found Arden's own, silently questioning him. 'I've not seen you before. Who are?'

'Arden. I'm of Raven's tribe. Raven Redbeard.'

The black eyes sparkled in recognition. 'You're a warrior of the Borderlands.' Arden nodded. 'What are you doing down here?'

'Curiosity and misfortune led me here. You?'

'Rotten luck and the will of a madman,' the prisoner spat. 'My name is Rejgar, son of Ragnar. I should not be here.'

'Ragnar!' Arden spat. The very warrior who threatened to invade the Borderlands and slaughter the men and women who opposed him.

'My father sent me on a scouting mission. My group came across a village on the outskirts of your land. Thought we'd have a little fun; seemed undefended and weak. Next thing I know, there was a flash of light, and then darkness. When I woke up, I was down here, alone but for the rats running around my shit.'

'Who put you here?' Arden asked, dreading the answer.

'An old mage, a cruel fucker with a love of torture.' Rejgar shook, saliva flying from his mouth as rage turned his pale face red. Flecks of spit caught in the mess of his beard and his eyes watered. 'Scraps of food. Drops of water. And the creep takes my blood to fuel his heathen magic. He's a fuckin' parasite, that one, believe me.' He held his arms out through the bars, giving Arden a clear look at the scars covering his wrists and forearms, the flame giving them an eerie, orange glow. 'A blood mage. Heard tales of them growing up but thought they'd died out a long time ago. Gave mages a bad name, they did. Fuckers use blood to draw energy for their own spells and magic.'

'A blood mage?' Arden had heard of the term long ago; figures of fear and horror told to children when they didn't do as they were asked.

'Aye. A corruption of the Gods. They can't draw energy from the earth, so they use the blood of those around them, sucking the very life out of people in order to serve their own sick needs.' Rejgar burst into a fit of violent coughs, shaking so much that Arden thought the poor man would break a rib.

'What is he trying to do?'

'How should I know? He's not exactly going to tell me his plans. When I resisted at first, he beat me and starved me until I had no choice but to follow his instructions.' Rejgar's eyes turned wild as grabbed at the bars and stared at Arden, body shaking with adrenaline. 'You're a mage. Open the cage, release me. I don't want to die down here in the dark. I need to be free, out in the open. Let me die in the wild, like a true Barbarian.'

'Korvus will know it's me...' Arden mumbled, backing away from the cage. He dared not get on the bad side of the powerful mage.

'Please! You're my only chance. Don't leave me down here to die.' Rejgar grabbed Arden's hands through the bars, surprising him with an unexpected strength.

'Fuck...' Ovar's face swam into focus in Arden's mind, reminding him of the guilt and regret over his death. He could have done something then. Should he do something now? 'Stay close. I'll get you out of the castle. After that, you're on your own.'

'Thank you! That is all I want.' His face lit up, yellowing teeth on full display through cracked lips.

Arden closed his eyes, finding that focus point once again. This time it felt easier, like stretching his legs before a long journey; the muscles needed were relaxed and ready for the task. He placed his hand gently against the lock, pressing the rough metal and picturing the lock opening. The click of a release threw him from his moment of introspection. Nausea swept over his body, stopping his breathing as he swayed to one side.

'Careful, friend.' Rejgar hungrily pushed the door open and pressed his bony hand against Arden's shoulders, steadying him.

'Just a wave of dizziness. It'll pass,' Arden said, waving away any concern as he breathed in slowly.

'Aye, one brought on by the magic. You new to this?'

'Fairly new.'

'I've seen it before. Vald Sickness my people call it: sickness brought on by wielding power the body can't handle.'

'Promising.' Just what he needed right now. Finally, he had unlocked his abilities only to be told that it may harm him. Just his luck.

'It'll pass.' Rejgar stretched his arms into the air, twisting his wrists. A cracking noise followed along with a sigh of relief. 'I never thought I would leave that fuckin' cell. I can't begin to tell you how many times I prayed to the Gods for death. That would be better than another week in this hell.'

'If you don't want to end up back in there, we'll need to be quick.'

Rejgar moved slowly, too slowly for Arden's liking. Not much he could do about it though. The fragile man looked as though each step was agony, the muscles in his body clearly having to re-learn their movements as he staggered up the steps, breath heavy all the way.

'Just a bit further,' Arden whispered, worried about what they may find when they reached the top of the steps. The corridors and passages of the castle had been empty earlier but there was no guarantee that that would still be the case.

At the top, Arden held out a hand to Rejgar, silently asking him to wait whilst he checked the passages around. Silence. There were in luck.

'Stay close behind me,' Arden instructed, stepping out into the corridor, eyes furiously surveying the area. Every flicker of a shadow seemed like a hammer slamming down on their hopes of escape.

Without warning, the incessant throbbing in his head returned ten-fold. He bit back the urge to scream, body shaking with agony as his back arched, shoulders pulling back as his head looked up to the ceiling. *Not now. Not now!*

'Vald Sickness...' Rejgar whispered as Arden fell to the floor with a thud. 'I'm sorry my friend, I can't go back. It will be easier this way.'

Arden lay paralyzed, muscles ignoring his cries for action, for defence. His eyes widened, pleading with Rejgar for reason, for help. The Barbarian slid a hand against Arden's hip and released the dagger from the sheath. The cut was swift, easy. A burning sensation coursed across his throat and his hand automatically rushed to close the wound, body still shaking from the sickness. His vision blurred as he felt the blood soak his hand. His eyes closed as a dark, skinny figured rushed off down the corridor away from him, racing with an unforeseen speed.

Arden lay back, his body weakening with each second. He closed his eyes and tried to breathe. A quiet sense of serenity bathed him as his ragged breathing slowed down. If this was the end, he would die without guilt, without regret. He'd saved a life: that would surely be more important than the fact his own may soon end. A weak smile found his lips as he leant back, barely hearing the shouts in the distance.

THE RIGHT THING

Aleister frowned as the sunlight creeped in through a gap between the closed curtains. Dawn forcing itself upon him, ending the dream of the night before. The sheets stuck to his sweaty, naked body. He wrestled them off and turned in the bed, locking his eyes upon the sleeping beauty next to him. Eyes closed and lips slightly parted, her breathing was heavy with small tremors of faint snoring. One of her arms hung loosely off the side of the bed whilst a smooth foot peeked out from the edge of the sheets at the bottom. How had he ever managed to leave such a perfect woman?

The emotion of the threat of rebellion the night before; the whiskeys; the years of frustration and tension caused by being apart – all of it had led to what they had done last night. He'd longed for it, the urgent kissing, her perfect body in his arms, the deep passion between them. It had been everything he had wanted and more. The only problem was that it had to end at some point. The passions of the night had to make way for the reality of day. He stood up, stretching his arms up high and yawning as he walked over to the curtains, pulling them open. The streets were quiet; most were still resting, unaware of the momentous night that he had loved more than any other.

'Morning already?' Ella squinted towards him, pulling the sheets up to hide her naked body. A shame, Aleister thought.

He could stare at her all night and day and never be bored. She dropped her feet onto the floorboards and picked up her dress that had lay forgotten on the floor since Aleister had torn it off in the night. He watched her pull it over her head, savouring every inch of her pale skin, feeling his heartbeat quicken as his blood rushed away from his head and to somewhere a bit lower… Not now. He pulled his own trousers up and rearranged himself, averting his gaze as Ella walked over to him.

'Looks like it will be a beautiful day,' he said, clearing his throat as he looked out through the window. 'Not as good as the night though, in my opinion.'

'Look, Aleister…'

He let her begin but he wasn't going to let her finish. The sad look on her face informed him of all he needed to know. 'A mistake. Won't happen again. Matthias.' He didn't have the heart for full sentences as he stared into those beautiful, sad glowing eyes.

She nodded softly. 'He's a good man, even if we do have our problems.'

'I understand.' He didn't. She loved him, just as he loved her. Damn what people would say. Damn the gossips. Damn doing the right thing. And damn Matthias.

Ella forced herself onto the tips of her toes and kissed him gently on the cheek. Her lips lingered against his skin for long enough to ignite the fire in his body once more. She breathed in slowly, dropping back onto the flats of her feet and closed her eyes. When they opened again, her pupils had changed, as black as coal, circled by the familiar green halo. The trick was designed to help her blend in with the normal citizens of Archania, but it didn't matter what colour her eyes were, she would always stand out to him.

As the door closed behind her, Aleister fell back onto the bed, staring up at the ceiling. He rolled his stiff neck to each side, wondering how he somehow felt worse this morning than he had before Ella had met with him the day before. Tasting the forbidden fruit had consequences it seemed. Who would have thought that sleeping with a married woman would make you feel like this? The conflict of joy from the night before and reality of the morning turned his stomach.

Two knocks on the door ripped him from his melancholic wondering. 'Come in,' he called out, not even bothering to move from the bed.

'Just saw Ella on her way out, looking a bit sheepish. I gather you two weren't up all night debating the modern merits of Paesus' shield formation theories?'

'However did you guess?'

He felt Bathos lower his large frame onto the bed as thick fingers gripped his shoulder in an easy, comforting squeeze.

'You think that was the right thing to do? I'm not saying it wasn't. Just wondering how you feel about it.'

How did he feel about it? Confused. Happy. Upset. Frustrated. Elated. Annoyed. All over the fucking place.

'You know how I feel about her, Bathos. About how I've always felt about her. I just feel so stupid for letting her slip away.'

'She didn't slip away, you left. You were young. You both were.' Bathos' calm, dulcet tone was meant to relax him but Aleister didn't feel like being relaxed, not now.

'It would be so different if she wasn't married. And to someone she doesn't even love!' He sat up, running a hand through his messy hair and staring at his creased shirt on the ground. He sighed. 'It's my fault. I know that. I just don't know what I should do now. I know what I want, but I don't want to hurt anyone. I don't know what the right thing to do is.'

Bathos stood up, meaty hands resting on his hips as he breathed sharply in through his teeth. Aleister knew that look. Nothing good ever came from that look. 'Hate to say it but... you didn't give her a choice when you left her last time. Maybe now it's time to let her make a decision. You've just got to respect it.'

Aleister scowled as he picked his shirt up and threw it over his shoulders. His fingers struggled with the bone buttons, continuing to divert his gaze from Bathos' all-knowing face. 'You've been listening to my sister too much, you know that?'

'She's a smart woman. She got the brains as well as the beauty in the family.' The big man smirked.

'Bastard.' Aleister clutched his jacket hanging from the wall and punched his friend on the arm. 'Let's grab some food. We've got a while before we meet with Kane. Not gonna spend it wallowing in my own self-pity.'

'Not gonna argue with that. At least we know that's the right thing to do.'

Kane stalked the cobbled streets, squinting in the light of the sun. She could feel the bags beneath her eyes like a dead weight. At her age, an uneasy sleep always resulted in a shitty day to follow. That was the way of things. No fighting against it. Her sleep, what little she had achieved, had been broken by dark dreams: swords flashings, flames rising and blood spilt. Hopefully not a sign of things to come and more of an over-active imagination playing on the events of the previous evening. She'd spent much of her time awake, cursing herself for allowing Drayke to convince her to take him into the Lower City. How could she have been so foolish? Betrayed by her will to spend some quality time with her son. In the harsh light of day, it seemed such a stupid thing to do. The Prince of the United Cities of Archania wandering almost defenceless into some of the darkest parts of the Lower City. Madness.

The King's Square bustled with its usual groups of men and women. The stalls were making coin enough to keep the merchants happy whilst a group of scattered poor, unfortunate men and women sat around the edges, begging for any bit of charity that could be mustered in the hearts of passers-by.

'Here, spend it on some food. For yourself, and the dog,' Kane suggested, dropping a piece of silver into a rusty bucket. The filthy, exhausted woman's face brightened at the sound of the coin slamming against the bottom of the bucket, echoing before settling at its base. Through all the filth and dirt, the decay of life upon her, Kane could see a beauty waiting to escape.

'Bless you, Miss. May The Four watch over,' the beggar

grinned, displaying gaps between her yellow teeth. She seemed surprised, as though such a simple act of generosity was rare in these parts. Maybe it was. Sad.

'And you.' Kane ruffled the soft fur on top of the dog's head, smiling as it closed its eyes, losing itself in the pleasure of the attention. 'Look after this one. More loyalty in these animals than you'll ever see in humans.'

Kane pulled herself back upright and winced at the clicking of her knees. Every movement was starting to feel like a chore. Where was the woman who had run every day up the watchtower staircase? Just ten years ago, she had been able to train with Braego, blunted blades, but movement as sharp as the finest swords in the Kingdom. Now, standing up caused her pain. Time was the one enemy that always seemed to have the upper hand.

She walked through the shadow of King Borris, glancing up at the stony King. His eyes seemed to follow her as she made her way through the square; it wasn't a good likeness, according to most. He was the Fat King, this stony avatar was slim, regal, powerful. It was everything this Kingdom needed right now. But all they had to guide them was a dying King, wandering through the Borderlands in the hope of righting a wrong. It may seem like the right thing to him, but Kane wondered if it was the right thing for the Kingdom. Thankfully, it wasn't her choice to make.

'Wonderful statue, don't you think?' Kane turned to see a warm smile and eyes wrinkled at the edges. A holy man. A wise man. 'Nothing like the fat brute of course, but wonderful nonetheless.'

'Elder Morgan,' Kane muttered, lowering her head respectfully to the preacher.

'Come. A beautiful day it may be, but discussions between two such as us are best handled inside. Bit of red might be available if you behave yourself.'

'I wouldn't say no to that.'

'Of course not. Who would?' The Elder winked and bade her follow him through the crowd and into his temple.

The temple was as she remembered: towering pillars, benches laid in orderly rows facing the altar, rooms either side for private prayer and discussion. The only difference she could spot was the distinct lack of worshippers: a point not lost on the holy man.

'I know exactly what you are thinking. Where is the flock? Surely each shepherd must care for its flock. Without it, he is nothing but an ordinary man. A man with no purpose.' His voice tailed off as he sighed, running a hand along the wooden benches wistfully. 'You must remember the weekly gatherings; this place was packed with more people than those that attend Prince Asher's extravagant parties in the Upper City. The King himself would come each month to call to The Four, to ask them for guidance in front of his loyal citizens. How things change.'

'Time. A right bastard.' Short. Simple. Nothing more needed to be said.

'Aye, a right bastard.' Morgan agreed. 'Come through to the dining room. The Young Boys can handle the mass of people crowding to get in.' His voice dripped in sarcasm before he waved a hand over at two of the long, yellow-robed figures standing in front of the altar.

The dining room was sparse, exactly as Kane remembered. 'You enjoy routine. Familiarity,' Kane said, eyes taking in the small room.

'I find comfort in Order, the one of the Four I can relate to the most. Although, I must admit, every now and then, a bit of chaos is needed; wouldn't you agree?' His mischievous eyes sparkled as he clutched at an old bottle of red, waving it conspiratorially at Kane as she took a seat.

'A balance between the two. That is what we are meant to pray for, is it not?'

'A balance, yes. Light. Darkness. Order. Chaos. The Four together are said to be the balance of Takaara. Yet, there will always be ebbs and flows between all. Such is the way of the human condition. Order is comfortable; however, it also leads to stagnation. Chaos brings with it a chance to change!'

He poured the wine into two separate glasses, passing

one over to Kane as he took his own seat opposite her.

'Now,' Morgan started, placing the bottle onto the dark, wooden table and sitting back in his chair, swirling the wine around in his glass before giving it a sniff, 'my people tell me that you are in the King's Square to see me. To what do I owe the pleasure of an audience with the retired Katerina Kane?'

Kane ignored the fact that the Elder knew she wanted to see him. Ignored it, but she would not forget. Old habits. Know when to use information freely given. There is a time and place for everything. 'I've been informed by a mutual friend of ours that you have connections to the group calling themselves The Doctors. We had a bit of a disagreement last night. I want you to tell me what you know.'

Morgan's eyes flashed at the mention of the healers. He licked his dry lips then sipped slowly on his wine. 'Where were you born, Ms. Kane?'

'A small village on the edge of Norland. Moved around the United Cities a bit. Father was a merchant before he passed on.'

'But you've been in Archania for a long time.'

'Since his death. I was eleven.' She remembered it well. The sickness. The tears.

'You've seen this Kingdom go through a lot. Kingdoms can be like wine. They can prosper, breathe and improve with age, like this one,' Morgan said, taking another gulp. 'Or they can be like the flesh of the dead. Left alone, it rots and decays. Let me ask you, have you seen this city age with the grace and taste of a fine wine? Or have you witnessed rot and decay?'

Kane paused, allowing the wine to swirl between her cheeks and across her tongue, thinking. Her memories would always be seen through a haze of nostalgia. She'd seen suffering, suffered herself in fact. She'd joined The Watch in the hope of being able to do some good –right wrongs, fight injustice. She'd had some success, but where had it got her? Had she helped to improve the Kingdom or just slow down a Kingdom slowly burning?

'There has been some decay,' she admitted. 'But there

is also hope. We are living in peaceful times. Our neighbours to the North no longer threaten us and there is no sign of the plague.'

'I agree,' Morgan nodded, leaning forward close enough for Kane to catch a whiff of the wine on his breath. This wasn't his first drink of the day. 'Other problems, bigger problems have grown out from the shadows. Our eyes have always leaned to the North, yet it is the South and East that have sharpened their weapons towards us in the hope of catching a sleeping giant.'

'Rumours and gossip, Morgan. My seat on the council allows me the prime opportunity to hear the facts first-hand.'

'Facts? Facts given to you from Mason D'Argio – whose sister sits on the throne as Empress of the East. Facts from Lord Balen? Facts passed on through turncoat spies now working for the Southern Kingdoms.' Kane bristled at the comments. She'd heard the rumours, sure, but this was nothing but the disgruntled moaning of citizens unhappy with their status; envy coated their words so much that they dripped with the stuff. She'd heard it all before. Still, the hairs on the back of her neck stood up as she mulled over the Elder's words. 'I know how it sounds. But trust me, I'm in a great position to judge, more than yourself. You are surrounded by sycophants and fools in the Upper City. Men and women who would rather bury their heads in the sand than admit that there is trouble brewing that could throw their perfect lives into turmoil.'

He made sense; Kane wasn't going to deny that. She'd lived for too long in the Upper City, enjoying the perks of her role on the council and losing touch with the real side of Archania, the side that she had been closest to in her role as Chief Inspector. That's why she had made the mistake with Drayke, her senses had dulled. Fool. Ineptitude had crept up on her silently, changing her for the worse. Elder Morgan was right, order had led to the rotting of this once great Kingdom. Kane rubbed at the bridge of her nose and wrinkled her forehead, feeling the threat of an oncoming headache.

'What do you think needs to be done, Elder?' she asked,

sighing heavily.

'The United Cities of Archania as we know it is on its last legs. It is best that we burn it down and rebuild from the ashes. In a figurative sense, of course.'

'And how do we go about that?' Kane arched an eyebrow, eager to hear the Elder's proposal for such a thing.

'Mason and his men are laughing at how they've been accepted into this Kingdom with such ease. They were given places of power, close to the ear of the King. Do you remember what it was like when he first arrived? A small temple in the Lower City; the citizens were intrigued but nothing more. As soon as he got in with the elite, the higher-ups; that's when things changed.' Morgan spat.

Kane's memory didn't fail her. She remembered the intrigue and curiosity of the man from the East preaching a new way of worship. He'd promised a better life, one away from plague and war. One where Takaara could heal with the right actions from its people. The citizens of the Kingdom had flocked to him in their droves.

'It was the war that started it; following that came the plague, people were ready to believe any old shit. They turned from The Four, following only the Light of the One, as Mason claims. The fools in the Upper City lapped it up, it became fashionable. No need to seek penance and restraint like before. Now, one could lavish their money on whatever the hell they wanted to and damn the people around them. The suffering of others was not their problem anymore. It was easier. Easier than this,' Morgan claimed, glancing around his bare room and sighing.

'The religious path has never been an easy one in this Kingdom,' Kane admitted. Too much self-loathing, guilt and judgement in her opinion.

'Until Mason arrived. As soon as it became fashionable, only the poorest of my flock continued the faith. Now though, the fire is burning!'

'Which brings me back to the original question: how do we rebuild this city?'

'Rebellion, Katerina Kane. Rebellion.' Morgan grinned, finishing his goblet of wine. 'The first acts of a revolution for the ages!'

'Just to speak of such an act is an offence likely to throw you into the dungeons,' Kane warned.

'I know the consequences. I also know what will happen if we do nothing. Stagnation. Rot. The death of this Kingdom. Given the choice, rebellion is the path I must take. We all know what Prince Asher is like. As King, he will be a puppet and Mason will be able to pull the strings, even more than he has been.'

'And do you believe you have the might, the men and the equipment to overcome The Watch and Mason's men? A rebellion is no small task.'

'The Doctors have resources; you would be shocked to hear what they are capable of. More people are coming into the city from the villages and the disgruntled magi will join our cause, for too long they have been mistreated and abused. The Doctors will offer them a new Kingdom, a new world, a new life!' Morgan pounded his fist against the table, shaking the empty goblet, face as red as the wine he had been drinking.

'There will be bloodshed. Innocent blood. The men on The Watch are not evil, nor are all of Mason's men,' Kane said, rubbing a cufflink gently in her right hand as she felt the fear rise in her. The consequences of rebellion would be swift and brutal, not romantic like in the stories.

'Chaos has a cost,' the Elder stated simply, eyes hard and unblinking. 'Any deaths to the cause will be regretful but it will not stop what needs to be done. They will all be given the opportunity to pick a side. I will be praying to The Four that they choose wisely when we meet in The People's Square.'

Kane had heard enough. She wanted the best for her Kingdom, but a rebellion? It went against all she had known. Order, structure, rules and laws. Breaking them meant chaos. Chaos meant death. A sense of dread filled her as she stood. 'I wish you luck with your endeavours, Elder, as always. However, I cannot condone such rash action.'

The Elder mirrored her actions, face impassive. 'I shall pray for you so that you will do the right thing, when the time comes. I may be disappointed with your decision, but I am not shocked. Let me show you out Katerina.' His face softened, suddenly he looked decades older than during his outburst. 'I'm tired, Kat. I've been fighting to protect the faith of this Kingdom and at times it has felt like a losing battle with no allies, like a soldier standing to meet the cavalry with only his trusty spear to halt the onslaught. I don't have much time left. The time I do have, I want to spend doing what I can to protect the faith. Doing the right thing. When I'm gone, I want this Kingdom to be on the path to salvation; I will fight for that with my last breath, even if I stand alone.'

'You're a good man, Elder Morgan. Surely, there is another way?' Kane pleaded softly.

'I wish there was another way. We do not have the time available for another way. We must take action,' the Eder responded, voice laced with sadness and regret. He didn't want this any more than she did. He felt forced into it. Backed into a corner with no escape. She understood that feeling. Kane respected the man, even if she didn't like what he was planning to do.

She followed the Elder from the room, closing the door behind her. Kane's eyes flickered to the sunlight shining through the open door at the end, landing on the shadows of two Young Boys whispering to a cloaked figure shrouded in darkness. Instantly, her hand fell to the blade at her side. Something was wrong. Every nerve in her body informed her of danger.

'T'Chai. What does that lapdog want here?' Morgan muttered under his breath, forcing a wide smile to reach his eyes as he strode down the aisle towards the unexpected visitor. 'Greetings, Master T'Chai! I believe this may be the first chance I've had to welcome you to my humble temple of The Four. Not as flashy as yours up the hill of course, but we do what we can.'

The warrior eyed the room with clear disgust, rolling his tongue around his mouth. 'My role forces me to enter all manner of buildings. I do so in service of the One.' His grasp of the language was perfect, barely a hint of his native accent seeping through.

Kane watched as Morgan halted, keeping his distance from the armed warrior. His golden plate armour gleamed in the light of the sun shining into the temple. His white cloak fell like a white wave trimmed with gold, echoing the hood pulled tight around his head. Her eyes were drawn to the incredible craftmanship between the plates of his armour. Even the golden iron spaulders moved with the smoothness of dragon scales as T'Chai crossed his arms, gloved hands clanging against his iron gauntlets. Two curved swords rested easily on either hip, pearl white scabbards hanging tightly onto a golden belt. An Eastern weapon designed for use on horseback, deadly at close proximity. Like anything with a sharp edge, Kane guessed.

'How can I help you?'

T'Chai's beady, dark eyes flickered between the two of them, thin, sharp tongue now licking at his lips as the shadow of a smile grew on his dark face. 'There have been rumours, dark rumours, regarding ill will towards my master and the running of this Kingdom.'

'Rumours? What would rumours and ill will have to do with me? I am but a humble servant of The Four, and your master does not run this Kingdom.' Morgan couldn't help but add the little jab, drink no doubt adding to his lack of restraint.

Kane thought it would be best if the Elder spoke as little as possible. 'The Elder was just showing me out, T'Chai. Perhaps this discussion can continue at another time.' She inched forward, head held high as she stepped past the warrior; face dropping as four members of Mason's guard strode into the temple, closing the door quietly behind them, blocking out most of the light from the sun.

'It would be best if you stay, Katerina Kane,' T'Chai muttered, smirking.

Kane spotted Morgan's face drop, the blood draining from his face as he watched the soldiers rest their hands on the hilts of their swords. His mouth struggled for words silently as Kane stepped back, ensuring all five of the adversaries were in her line of sight. Poor odds but nothing she could do about that.

'This is a house of The Four. Blood must never be spilled in such a holy place. Cursed are those who commit such barbaric acts!' Morgan cried, arms flailing.

T'Chai stood motionless, unimpressed with the Elder's outburst. 'I do not recognise your strange superstitions, old man. What I do recognise is your will to usurp the King.'

'What nonsense! I have served the King all my life!' Morgan bellowed, growing more agitated by the second. Kane tried to catch his eye, force him to see sense. He was only making matters worse.

'Surely there is some mistake?' she asked, pleading with T'Chai.

'The Elder has been spotted meeting with members of a group hostile to the current regime in charge of this Kingdom. Last night, we have witnesses that claim you attended such a meeting, Katerina Kane, dragging our young Prince Drayke along for the ride.' Kane wanted to smack the knowing, smug grin from the bastard's face there and then, but she knew the virtue of patience.

'A mistake on my behalf. The Prince and I were enjoying our time, walking through his father's Kingdom when we stumbled upon an argument between two groups of citizens. Nothing more happened,' she said, words whistling through gritted teeth.

'Perhaps. Yet, the last piece of the puzzle slotted into place today. Your Young Boys were ever so helpful, Elder Morgan. They informed me of your secret meeting today with Katerina Kane. A meeting that spoke of rebellion. They will continue to serve the One to the best of their abilities, I am sure.'

'You bastard!' Before Kane could stop him, Morgan lunged forward, a roar echoing through the huge temple.

T'Chai barely moved.

Kane missed the usual squelch of blade passing through flesh and blood as the scimitar glided effortlessly through the Elder's body. Morgan's mouth widened in shock as he stumbled back, red hands holding tightly against a hole in his humble robes, steadily changing colour as the blood poured from the fresh wound.

'No,' Kane whispered, rushing to guide Morgan onto a bench. His breathing was ragged, eyes unfocused as Kane knelt next to him. 'You bastards. This is a place of worship. He is an Elder!'

'He is a traitor to his King and country. He will not be missed.'

Everything became clear. She watched the light fade from the preacher's eyes, his head drifting down onto his shoulder. She felt his dead weight drop against her, so she pushed him back against the bench as she realised what it meant to do the right thing. Rage rushed through her tired body, offering her a burst of energy she had once credited to her youth. She tried to slow her breathing, but it was like fighting against a hurricane.

Using the fresh wave of energy, she jumped to her feet, sliding her sword out of its sheath and arcing through the air towards the Eastern native.

T'Chai blocked the strike with ease, flicking his wrist to deftly deflect the attack. His face was impassive, as though he was fencing with a child and not defending himself against an experienced swordswoman. Barely a hint of annoyance flashed across his face.

Kane stepped back, chest rising and falling as her heart continued its fast beat.

'Take her in for questioning. Dispose of the old man.'

The four soldiers moved in as one, unable to circle her due to the benches either side of the room. The first attack was passable, easily deflected. They were well trained, but no experts. 'I've still got some life in these old bones,' Kane muttered, raising her sword in defiance.

The next attack was faster. Kane dropped her shoulders, blocking low before striking back. The edge of the blade glanced off the iron guards on the shoulder of her opponent, scratching the perfect armour. She readied herself for the next attack, sword diagonally sliding to the right as she peered to the left at her next opponent. A high strike, blocked with ease as she flicked her wrist to the side, pushing the blade high before stabbing at the stomach.

Almost.

She felt as though she was settling into the old groove, comfortable with the blade in her hand, giving her the old strength that had once been so familiar. It was as though she was welcoming back a limb that had been lost.

A sharp pain stabbed at her side from behind. She fell forward, dropping to her knees, sword falling from her grasp. Fool! Dropped her guard. Her hand arched back to the source of the pain. She pulled her hand back in front of her as the room swayed. Red. Blood.

'You fight well, for an old woman,' T'Chai said, walking from behind her and kneeling so that she could look him straight in the eyes. One of his soldiers offered him a white cloth. He took it and carelessly wiped the blood from his curved blade before throwing it back. 'Rest, Katerina Kane. You will need your energy.'

His fist struck with lightning speed.

The cold, stone floor rushed to meet her face and darkness welcomed her with open arms.

LIGHT AND DARK

Daylight. A Borderlander doesn't get much of it, all things considered. Even the summers consisted of grey clouds and torrential downpours. That's just how it was. No point tearing up over something you can't change. Now though, Sly realised how much he missed the small amounts of daylight he'd been given back home. The few rays that managed to penetrate the sheet of grey seemed like a gift from the Gods now. The complete and utter totality of darkness was stifling in the dungeon; all consuming, terrifying. There wasn't a lot that Sly feared but this, this was torture.

'Just give me some fucking light dammit!' he roared into the darkness, shaking against the chains trapping his wrists against the wooden beam behind him. The chains rattled, echoing around what he thought was an empty room. He slammed his head back against the wood, and again. 'Fuck.'

He'd been in bad situations before, couldn't deny that: the trouble up in Oslar after the battle; the brothel incident in Argrion; the blood battle against Edgar the Cruel. Each of them had times when he felt the end was near, that he had taken his last breath. All warriors had those moments, even him. Even then, in the worse situations he could imagine, there had been glimmers of hope, rays of daylight creeping through the suffocating darkness. Now, there was no light, no hope. He ran his tongue across his teeth, pushing against his sensitive gums and tasting blood. One of his teeth wobbled, loose enough to fall out. He forced his tongue against the loose tooth and spat it out onto the ground. His tongue rubbed against the newly formed gap, painful but pleasurable in a strange way, like so many things. He was falling apart, always had been, truth be told. His whole body ached from the beating, from the tips of his fingers down to the ends of his frozen toes. Twenty cycles. He'd been fighting for twenty cycles. Fuck. The black eyes. The scars. The broken bones. The missing teeth. How long can someone live a life like his before the body just stops? He'd seen others try to leave. Men who'd reached the end of their limits. They'd tried to start new lives – merchants, sailors, guards, carpenters. He hadn't seen any of them smile again. Not like they used to; not like when they were caught up in the battle-lust.

Sly tried to picture himself selling some rugs or a shiny piece of rock to idiots in the towns and villages of the Borderlands. Give them that winning smile of his and they'd be lining up around the corners. At least he could give them what was left of his smile. Same difference. He let out a long sigh, slowly rocking his head back against the wooden beam, concentrating on the rhythmic thud. No point changing now. He was a warrior. He'd die a warrior, even if it was in this dark, silent hell.

The lack of sleep was affecting his thoughts. He didn't give up. There's always a way out. Had to be. He arched his back, twisting his shoulder ever so slightly, trying to feel the concealed dagger. No luck. Must have taken it from him when they brought him in. Of course they did. They might be soft but they weren't stupid. He roared again into the void, wrestling against his restraints. No luck. Worth a shot.

Must be underground. No light, no sound. They had to bring him food and water soon. Didn't make sense to keep him chained up in here if they weren't going to feed him. They would've killed him if they wanted him dead, they'd had the chance. Sly promised that he wouldn't give them another chance if he could help it. The next time he saw one of those soft cunts, he'd rip the eyes out of their goddamn heads. You get a chance to kill a man, you damn well take it. Never know if you'll get another.

Hours later – or was it minutes? – his body tensed at the sound of boots clipping against a stone floor in the distance. His heart beat harder with each step, the sound growing in volume as the footsteps grew closer and closer. This was it; this would be his chance. He breathed in deeply, puffing out his chest and slamming his back against the beam once more. Just a little bit of room, that's all he needed.

Too late. A rattle of keys on a chain sounded nearby as a glimmer of light slithered under a crack in a door opposite him. Not daylight, but it was a start.

The door swung towards him as a tall figure walked his way, torch in hand, wide shoulders set either side of a thick neck decorated with a row of dangling ears.

'You!' Sly screamed, feeling the bile rise in his throat as Bane shuffled towards him, whistling. 'You fucking sell-out. Got some nerve coming in here after what you did.'

Bane set his torch into a holder fixed against another beam rising from the stone floor. He disappeared for a moment, lost in the flickering shadows of the room before entering the light once more, dragging a small oak chair with him. He spun it around before dropping onto it with a sigh, arms hanging loosely over the top as he stared patiently at Sly.

'Nerve? Nah. You're the one chained up in the dark. I can walk around like a free man. Not nerve.' The bastard sniffed, nostrils flaring as his golden eyes stayed fixed on Sly. Sly thought of what he could do with them eyes if he had a free hand and a dagger. It'd be a fucking masterpiece...

'Traitor. Come all this way with us and this is what you do? Betray us for those soft fuckers. Raven is dead because of you.'

'Soft? I vividly remember them beating the shit out of you. You may have missed parts of it after you passed out. I remember it all quite well.'

Sly hocked up a thick load of spit and launched it at the bastard. Good shot. Right on his face, dripping slowly down his cheek. The southerner flinched, wiping it away disgustingly with a gloved hand, nodding to himself.

'I expected nothing less from the great Sly. I've travelled beside you, I know you better than you think.'

'You know shit.'

'You don't give a fuck about the Borderlands. You don't give a fuck about Raven,' Bane said, jumping up from his seat and inching closer to Sly, lowering himself onto his knees, almost close enough to bite. 'You only care about one thing in this fucking world.'

'Enlighten me.' Dark thoughts danced in Sly's mind: images of his bloodied axe buried deep into the fucker's skull. The bastard would pray for death before the end.

'Blood. Battle. War.'

'That's three things.'

'All go hand in hand. And I can give you them all.'

'And how are you going to do that? Little help from your new friends?'

'New friends? Yeah. And they can be *our* new friends. Think about it. Saul as the King of the Borderlands; Mason leading the United Cities of Archania; his sister – the Empress of the East. The whole of the North will be united for the first time in history, no one will be able to stand in its way! We could march into any damn kingdom in Takaara and they would kneel or die. No other choice. Even the Barbarians would follow our lead, or they would be destroyed.'

A united North? Where was the fun in that? 'So, we join with them. What then? They make suggestions for how we run our land. Start building across the border. Introduce their ways, their fashion, their ideas into our home. We lose what makes us the Borderlands. That's what happens.'

'Is that such a bad thing? What are we anyway? A bunch of arguing fools camped out in the snow following the Old Gods who do nothing for us.'

'We? You're from the South, a world away from our

kind.'

'You know me better than that,' Bane's voice lowered to a growl. Sly had hit a sore spot. 'I've earned the opportunity to call myself a warrior of the Borderlands. I won't have some fool in a dungeon tell me otherwise.'

'That right was stripped from you when you killed Raven Redbeard.'

'He was a good man, most of the time. Made a shitty decision and it cost him.'

'Seems to be going 'round lately...'

'Don't mess with me, Sly. Raven's death is not the end of our people. There are others who can lead us into a better world.'

'And you think Saul is the one who should lead us? The *King* of the Borderlands.' Sly scoffed at the thought of the brute wearing a crown. It would be like forcing a dress on a dog.

'At first, yes. But, after that...' Bane paused, baring his white teeth. 'If someone else were to take an opportunity, I'm sure there could be a better man to lead our people into a Golden Age.'

'Raven Redbeard. He would have been the one to lead us.'

Bane nodded, a smile starting from the corner of his lips. 'Raven Redbeard. The son of the famed Reaver Redbeard. He would have been a great leader. Unfortunately, he kept something from all of us – a pact with the King of Archania without consulting anyone else. Now he's dead, someone else can rise to fill his place. That's the way of the Borderlands.'

Sly blew his cheeks out. 'That was up to him. I've no idea what you're on about. What Raven did before I joined up is his business. Only other person who might know is the old archer, but Socket is days away from here now. What do I gotta do to get the fuck outta here, Bane? I don't have anything they want. I just wanna smash someone's face in and head home.'

'There's been some... trouble, in the Lower City. The King's left the city and some of his opportunistic subjects have taken it upon themselves to call for change. Apparently, they're not a fan of the poor fucker who is next in line. Feel as though they should be able to choose their own leader.'

'Sounds good to me.' Sly saw the logic in that. It was the way it should be. The strong leading the weak. No one should be born into leadership. Gotta fight for it.

'Mason wants us to put this mini rebellion down before it becomes more of a nuisance. We get our weapons back and an understanding that if we use excessive force, we won't be imprisoned.'

'Excessive force?'

'We're allowed to kill the bastards.'

Sly thought about it for a moment. If it meant getting out of this stinkin' dungeon and into the open air, he'd kill any of the fuckers. He wasn't known for it, but he could be patient. Bide his time until he can pay Mason back for throwing him in here. A knife in the back of Bane would make him feel a hell of a lot better too.

The sound of laughter filled the corridor outside as three shadows passed through the scarce light. Sly heard a key turning in a lock before a door swung open. Must be the next cell along. More laughter as something hit the floor. Another prisoner. Must be unconscious.

'What about Baldor? He's a good warrior.'

'We both know he doesn't have the brains to work with the people he believes killed Raven. He'll swing that hammer this way as soon as he gets the chance. Best to keep him locked up in a labour camp outside of the city until everything dies down. Teach him some humility.'

Sly made his mind up. Waiting here to die wasn't an option. He'd get out and then he'd make them all pay. If he could save Baldor on the way, even better.

'Get these fuckin' chains off me and I'll kill whoever the fuck they want.'

'I thought you'd say that.'

'It's not like her...' Aleister's sister muttered, twisting her hair nervously between her fingers.

'I know. She's never late.' Aleister had known the retired Inspector for as long as he could remember. Keeping out of her grasp in the Lower City sharpened his wits like a sword on a whetstone and their relationship grew into one of respect and even friendship. Admittedly, Kane had often rolled her eyes at some of his more adventurous ideas, but she knew his heart and that's what mattered to them both.

'How long do we wait?' Bathos asked, peeking out from between the buildings and casting his gaze down the quiet side street. Even in the light of day, this part of the Lower City was emptier than an Eastern desert in the summer. The locals knew the dangers of wandering around this area. Aleister knew the dangers too. Having the huge Bathos on one side and his deadly sister on the other certainly put him more at ease than most.

'A bit longer. Give her a chance,' Aleister responded, forehead creased with worry. 'Let's just hope the delay is nothing serious.'

'Do you think it could be anything else? If word got out that Kane was with the Prince when he was threatened, then there's bound to be trouble. Mason will make sure of that.'

'How far do you think the preacher would go?' Bathos asked, strolling back towards them, unable to keep still and wait.

'He's burned a boy alive for making one mistake. I wouldn't put limitations on what he is capable of.' Aleister sighed, dreading the thought of what might happen to Katerina if Mason had got to her.

'Then you're not going to like this...'

Aleister spun on the spot, drawing his blade effortlessly with the movement and swinging it high. The clang of metal on metal sounded through the alleyway as his gauntlet bore the brunt of the reverberation.

'Zaina.' He breathed a sigh of relief and pulled his sword back, sheathing it as his two companions did the same, dropping out of their own defensive stances and instantly relaxing. 'You fucking fool. I could have killed you.'

'You wish. Saw that coming from a mile away. Thought

you were the fastest blade in the North?' Zaina mocked him, blowing her luscious, red hair from out of her eyes and sheathing her dagger in a belt tightly wound around her shoulders and hips, criss-crossed leather housing a myriad of small but lethal weapons.

'Fastest mouth maybe,' Ariel murmured, stepping forward and wrapping an arm around Zaina's shoulder. 'Good to see you, Zaina. Been too long. You look well.'

'And you. The Eastern sun has changed your skin. You have a healthy glow. I like it.'

Bathos bounded forward, a huge grin painted on his face as he dragged his old friend into a breathless hug. 'You missed out. Should have joined us.'

'Nah. Had enough fun back here. Someone had to keep an eye on things whilst the three of you went cavorting in the deserts!'

'It wasn't all fun...' Aleister said, sheepishly scratching at his scalp and avoiding her knowing gaze.

'Hmm...'

Pleasantries dealt with, Aleister felt a sense of urgency, remembering the way Zaina had greeting them. 'Katerina Kane. What do you know?' he asked, unable to hold the question off any longer.

The smile faded from Zaina's face, all warmth drifting away as her thoughts turned dark at the question. 'She met with Elder Morgan earlier today.' Nothing unusual in that. The two were acquaintances, if not firm friends. 'From what I've heard, T'Chai himself arrived as their discussion ended. He wasn't alone.'

'Zaina...' Aleister pleaded, swallowing hard as he steadied his breathing. 'What happened?'

'They dragged her out, unconscious. Beaten, bloodied, bruised. A complete mess. You know where she is heading.' The dungeons. T'Chai, the bastard. Mason's own lapdog had done the dirty work.

'On what charges?' Bathos asked, though Aleister knew.

'Putting the Prince in danger,' he spat. 'Fuck.' Zaina nodded wordlessly. Such a charge meant Mason could do as he pleased with her.

'There's something else. And I need you to keep a cool head, no matter what.'

The companions shared an uneasy glance as Aleister lost the battle against his breathing, mind working excessively as he struggled to reach a suitable explanation for Zaina's words. 'Tell me.'

'Elder Morgan...' she muttered, barely audible. 'They carried his body out for burning. He was murdered in the temple. T'Chai's men.'

Uncontrollable rage rushed through Aleister unlike anything he had ever felt before. He released a roar, punching his gloved fist clean through a wooden slat next to him, splinters flying off all around him. The others allowed him a moment to calm down. A moment to control himself as Bathos shared a gentle hug with Ariel. Morgan had meant so much to them all.

'Zaina, go straight to Jax and the Red Sons. Tell them what's happened. Tell them that I need their help. Ride with all haste and make sure they know that time is of the essence.' The embers of a plan were already sparking in his mind: revenge. He wanted the most glorious revenge the world had ever seen.

'Aleister,' his sister whispered, placing a calming hand on his shoulder, her tearful eyes nervous and panicked. 'Don't do anything stupid.'

'Don't worry,' he replied, breath rushing out through his nostrils, 'I know exactly what I'm going to do.'

They were hurting his friends, people he considered family. They'd fucked up his home beyond recognition. He'd come back expecting to see the progress his Kingdom had made; instead, he saw nothing but sadness and fear. Shadows and flame.

If they enjoyed burning so much, he'd give them what they wanted.

He'd burn the whole damn place down.

She opened her eyes, or at least she tried to. Her right eye opened a fraction, spotting lamplight flickering in a darkened room. Her left eye wouldn't budge; swollen and closed shut from the beating. The thought woke the rest of her body up from its slumber, piercing pains arching across her whole body, memories of the attack in the temple. She struggled to sit up, groaning with the small movements and feeling relieved as her back leant against a thick, wooden beam to prevent her from falling over onto her other side. Each breath entering and leaving her body brought with it a piercing pain in her ribs. At least one broken rib. Maybe more. She rested a weak arm against her ribs, steadying her breathing to ease the pain. It had been a long time since she'd taken a beating this bad. Back then she had been younger and healed quick enough. Now, she was old, tired. She doubted she'd be getting over this any time soon.

'You are awake. Praise Mamoon,' a voice carried through the darkness, startling Kane. Not that she was able to show it. She stayed stuck against the wooden beam, unable to move. 'When they dragged you in here, I didn't think you would wake up.'

'I'm undecided as to whether waking up was the best thing for me,' Kane replied, Elder Morgan's lifeless, open eyes staring straight at her in her mind. 'Perhaps it would have been best to embrace death.'

'You cannot choose death, my friend, death chooses you. It has always been so, since the beginning.' The voice was soft but deep. She struggled to place it. From the Eastern Kingdoms, if she was guessing.

'Well I'm hoping death makes its decision sooner rather than later. Life is becoming far too tiresome of late...' Kane lamented. 'It seems we may be here for a while. My name is Katerina. Kat for short. What is your name?' At least she wasn't alone. Conversation keeps the mind active; it would stop her from going mad if she was indeed going to stay here for a long time.

'Harish. I am new to the city. I was told this was once a

land of diversity and open arms.'

'Well, Harish, is that what you have found?' Kane asked, not enough energy to laugh.

'I feel as though I was tricked,' Harish said, a hint of laughter in his own voice. In the worst situations of life, if you can't laugh, then what can you do? 'I have met a few people in this city who are kind and welcoming. The majority have spat at me, hit me, mocked me and I have ended up here. Not exactly what I was expecting but my lord works in strange ways. I will consider this all part of my test.'

'What test is that?'

'The test that determines if I am welcome in his everlasting kingdom, the one that never ends.'

'Not sure I like the sound of anything that never ends,' Kane muttered. 'This city has changed. It used to be welcoming, a beacon of progress. Not anymore. Though, I am surprised people have treated an Eastern native in such a manner. These days, our Kingdom has strong bonds with those in the East.'

'Ah yes. I am of the East, but my God is of the South. Mamoon is the one lord I follow. It is why I escaped from my homeland in the first place.'

'From the East, worshipping the South and running to the North. You trying to make things more difficult for yourself?' Kane croaked, breaking out into a short coughing fit, each one sending more pain throughout her injured body.

Harish waited patiently for her to finish. 'I must follow my heart, no matter how difficult the road may be. If I keep on the correct path, I will arrive at the destination designed for me and me alone. If I waver from that path, the reward will not be as sweet.'

'That's what every religion seems to tell its followers. Put up with the shit you get in life and something good will happen when you die. Ever think that it's all just a load of shit? What if there's nothing at the end? What if this is all we have?' Kane snapped, the pain of her injuries making her angrier than she wanted to be. She'd followed The Four for most of her life, just like most of the Kingdom. Blind allegiance and routine had meant that she attended the temple service at the end of each week. Braego had changed that. Spending time with the Borderland warrior gave her a new insight into the world. His people followed the Old Gods, numerous beyond belief. He had claimed that each family prayed to a different God, but they were all connected, not competing for attention but revelling in the constant discourse between man and spirit. He had opened her eyes, forcing her to become aware that there could be more to the Gods than what she had previously known in her bubble.

'That is a depressing way of looking at life. I choose to believe that there is more. Mamoon is constantly by my side, even if others are not. He guides me through the hard times.'

'And where is he now?' Kane asked, looking around the dark cell as a wave of nausea hit her. She barely managed to hold back the vomit.

'He has brought me to you. That is no bad thing, even if I would have preferred to meet in much nicer... surroundings.'

Before Kane could respond, she noticed light flickering through the small iron bars followed by the rustling of keys. The owner found the correct one, turning it easily in the lock and thrusting the door open. Light flooded the room as a tall figure walked in, holding a lit torch in front of him, dark eyes peering into the cell.

'Lord Tamir. What are you doing?' Kane asked, pleased to see her fellow councillor.

The councillor rushed over, black cloak trailing behind him, hood up over his shaved head. 'I came as soon as I heard. Kat, what have they done to you?' His worried eyes told her all she needed to know. Her face and body were a wreck, numerous wounds and bruises painted all over her. Not a pretty sight.

'Mason's men weren't exactly kind. Tamir, Elder Morgan...' her voice dropped to a whisper as she thought of the preacher.

'I know.'

'In the temple...'

'I know.' Tamir's face hardened, words forcing their way through clenched teeth. 'They'll pay. I promise. But first, we need to get you out of here. We don't have much time before the guards I've paid off will be back.' He eased her to her feet with all caution, slipping a gentle but strong arm under hers and around her back.

'Tamir, we must help my new friend here. Harish, come with us.' She could not leave the man behind to die in this hellhole. It wouldn't be right.

'Katerina...' Tamir cautioned, voice low and intended only for her. She tried to wave away his protest but struggled with the motion.

'It is okay, Kat. I will stay. If I leave, I am afraid I will only slow you down.' Harish didn't sound sad, as though he had accepted his fate.

'Nonsense,' Kat bristled, shuffling over into the darkness, forcing Tamir to follow her, torch in hand. The light fell on the prisoner, lying slumped on the ground. Kane's face dropped, a hand covering her open mouth instinctively.

He was naked, apart from a tattered loin cloth barely allowing him to keep some modesty. His dark skin held a tapestry of burns and scars, some recent, some months, maybe years old. Her eyes fell beneath his waist, one leg lay at an awkward angle, clearly broken. His other finished at a stump just where his knee was. The wound had been cauterised with fire, leaving a black stump at the end. Harish smiled, displaying a mix of teeth and gums. He had certainly been tested.

'This is your one chance to escape this dungeon, Harish. Please,' Kane muttered, eyes watering as she looked at the smiling man on the ground, a casual defiance sparkling in his brown eyes, 'come with us.'

'I will stay. This is your path, Katerina Kane. Walk it with pride and faith. I will stay on my path, dark though it may be. You shall follow the light, though I do hope our paths meet again.' He rubbed a finger against the two white scars beneath his eyes and pointed up to the heavens. 'Mamoon protect you, Katerina Kane. Order and Chaos as one, as it should be. I have enjoyed our conversation. May our next one be in the light of the Sun.'

Tamir dragged her away, closing the door with the heel of his foot as he guided her from her cell. The corridors were empty, the usual guards nowhere to be seen.

'How did you find out?' Kane asked him as she shuffled her way through the dungeons.

'I have my ways,' he answered cryptically.

The pair of them made their way out of the dungeons, daylight teasing Kane as it creeped through the iron door leading out into the courtyard.

'Lie low. I have enough room for you to stay in my guest house; it will suffice whilst there are people searching for you. Whatever happens, stay the hell away from the Lower City tomorrow,' Tamir ordered.

'Why?' she croaked in response, eyes unflinching as they stared at the light at the end of the tunnel.

'This Kingdom is tearing itself apart.' Tamir thundered, eyes narrowed at the thought. 'War, Katerina Kane. War is coming.'

'Shit.'

* * *

Her sleep had been broken by flashes of the attack, memories racing back in the form of nightmares. Sleep would escape her grasp tonight.

Tamir's guest house was surprisingly sparse. The bedroom had a bed, a table with a small, simple chair and little else. There was a bathroom connected, with a toilet, sink and a bath that called to Kane. She twisted the metal taps, testing the flowing water with the back of her bruised hand. Hot. Good. The heat would ease her aches and pains, at least for a little while. She needed rest. She needed time to recuperate.

As the bath filled up with hot water, she let her gown slip to the floor, allowing her an unobstructed view of her broken and battered body. Numerous bruises had darkened to a blue or deep purple. The swelling around her ribs had worsened, hurting her with each breath she took. It would take some time before she was back to her best, if ever. An old body just doesn't heal in the same way as a young one.

She turned the tap off, happy with the level of water. She winced as she dipped her toes into the water, shocked by the burning heat. An unplanned groan escaped her as she lowered herself into the water, dropping everything but her head beneath the bathwater. For a moment, she lay in complete silence, embracing the healing effect of the water as her aches and pains lessened. Minutes passed, maybe even an hour before she opened her eyes. In the water, she could forget the troubles: the fights, the battles, the death. It was a world separate from reality, a shield from the pain and anguish. The problem was, at some point, she had to leave that bubble, that shield.

Kane placed her hands against the side of the tub and carefully pushed her body up onto her feet. There was pain, but the soak had eased some of the more painful injuries that had been bothering her. Now there was just a dull ache around her ribs when she breathed, an improvement, to be sure. The towel she used to dry off was soft and not as coarse as the one back home. Obviously Tamir wanted his guests to be comfortable in at least one way, even if the room he put them in was so minimalistic. Most of the prominent figures in the Kingdom had lavish guest rooms, using them as opportunities to flaunt their wealth and standing to all who stayed over. Tamir wasn't like that.

She tied her night robe around her, realising that she was in need of fresh clothes. The set she had worn when entering her temporary abode was blood-stained and filthy. In all honesty, it would be best if she burned the lot. Tamir had informed her that he would send a clean set of clothes for her in the morning. For now though, she wanted to have a peek in the closet and see if there was anything that may take her fancy. She'd never been too picky when it came to fashion: anything that fit and allowed her enough room to move with ease was good enough for her. The fashion of the day always seemed to pass her by, others may have noticed but she'd never given a shit. What a person wore never seemed important when she was doing her job; it was their actions that were the most important.

The closet extended to fill the length of the entire guest room, double doors linked together with slats that could be opened or closed with ease. Kane pulled the nearest door open and peeked inside, humming softly to herself. She flicked through the first few dresses hanging up: boring greys and browns – easy to blend it. She wanted to see if there was anything unique, anything that would stand out. She wouldn't wear it outside of course, but in here, where no one would see her, why not? All of the clothes – dresses, shirts, trousers, skirts –were fairly standard; nothing out of the ordinary. She had abandoned all hope when she spotted a small cabinet, knee-high, standing on its own in the shadows beneath the hanging clothes.

The cabinet looked old and worn, white scratches marked its metal surface and a curved lock hung loosely through a hole on its face. The last person using it must have either been in a rush or had taken the contents in a hurry and not yet returned them. Kane's surveying eye scanned the cabinet as she felt the old habits come rushing back along with a flow of adrenaline through her relaxed body.

She pulled the lock away and carefully drew back the door, sliding it towards her. Inside the drawer was a robe as black as midnight. It was tougher than the other clothes she had seen, leather.

Her head ached as the robe stirred within her blurred memories, memories that were struggling to surface in her mind. It was as though she was trying to look through a dense fog; the outline was there but not enough clarity for an answer. She picked the robe up and stood, holding it by either shoulder. Suddenly it dawned on her where she had seen the exact robe.

'Oh fuck no. This must be some kind of mistake...'

She dropped the robe to the ground, leaving it in a crumpled mess as she stared back into the drawer, her fears confirmed. Inside, she could see what had been lying beneath the robe.

Black eyes stared back at her above a crooked beak-like

nose.

'Tamir, my friend... what have you done?'

RECOVERY

'I should be getting used to this shouldn't I?'

Arden grumbled a few curses as he sat up in the bed, trying to ignore the bloodstained bandage wrapped around him.

'You should be dead.' Socket's good eye glared at him, not even the slightest hint of humour on display. 'What in the hells were you thinking, kid?'

'The guy was knocking on the door to the Hells himself,' Arden replied, moaning as the stabbing pain in his ribs flashed through him once again. 'Did you expect me to just leave him there in the darkness? He was rotting in a cage all alone. The last time I left someone when I could have helped, they lost their head. I didn't want that on my conscience again.'

'I expected you to use caution. If you had just spoken to me or Korvus, we could have warned you that the man is a vicious monster. He's been responsible for torture, rape and more murders than I can count in these parts of the world.' Socket sighed. 'And you just released him back into the world and put yourself and countless others in danger because you didn't think you could live with him being locked up in the dark.'

Arden's cheeks burnt with embarrassment, forcing back his response just in time, hesitating before getting himself into more trouble. In the cold light of day, his actions seemed rash and careless. 'I'm sorry. I didn't think...'

'That's the problem!' Socket pressed a hand against Arden's leg and lowered himself onto the bed, eyes pleading with him to listen. 'You didn't think. And that needs to change, kid. You're caught up in matters that are way bigger than you and your conscience. You're a Guardian, part of a dying race; a dying race that Takaara desperately needs! When your life is threatened, *all* life is threatened!'

Ignoring the aches and pains coursing through him, reminding him of his mistakes, Arden sat up further, shifting away from Socket. 'Well I don't want that responsibility! No one asked me to be a Guardian! Why do I have to be the one with this power? A power I can't even fucking control.'

Socket's eye softened as the old man inched closer, his shoulders dropping as the fight left his body. 'You didn't choose this. I know you didn't and, believe me, if I could take this from you and spare you the pain and suffering then I would do so in a heartbeat. Unfortunately, life doesn't work in that way. The Gods have a path for us, and we must walk it to the best of our ability.'

'What if I fall, like with the Barbarian?' The words rushed out before he could stop them, his fear spilling from him unfiltered.

'Then you get back up, dust yourself off and keep moving forward. No one is perfect, Arden. We all fall, from the lowest peasant to the greatest King. Even Guardians fall. It is our ability to react to our mistakes that gives us the opportunity for greatness. You've been thrust into a difficult station ahead of your time. You'll need to react better and faster than others, that is true. But I believe in you, kid. Wouldn't have brought you all this way if I didn't.'

Arden stayed silent, thinking about Socket's words. It had all happened so fast. Joining Raven's band of warriors; Ovar's execution; the battle with the Barbarians; travelling to the Far North – it felt like a whirlwind of events had crashed around him, turning his life upside down. 'I just don't think I'm ready for this. Korvus must agree. The old bastard has been in a foul mood ever since training began. I bet he thinks you brought him the wrong guy.'

'He knows who you are; Korvus is no fool,' Socket answered with a reassuring smile. 'These things can take a bit of time. There's no manual on preparing for life as a Guardian and there's hardly any Guardians left to question. He has been waiting up here, alone, for what feels like a lifetime, waiting for the next Guardian to find him. Finally, you arrived. Guess we can allow him a few moments of impatience and frustration.'

'Why though? Why has he been waiting here, away from the world, waiting for me?'

It didn't make any sense. Why would anyone cut themselves off from the world in such a way?

'I'm sorry. It ain't my story to tell, kid. It's his and his alone. He has his reasons.' Socket stood up with a few moans as he stretched his limbs and cracked his neck. 'I'll let him know you're feeling a bit better. Get some rest. We'll eat together tonight, I promise.'

'Thanks Socket. For everything.' Arden shut his eyes and drifted away before Socket reached the door.

* * *

'The wound's healed better than I thought it would: stupid idiot should have been killed for what he did. That shit deserved to rot in the dungeon until the end of time. Letting him loose on the world is a fucking sin I'm not willing to forgive any time soon, Guardian or not.'

'He's still young; he's not ready.' A voice sounded beside Arden, echoing around him. His eyelids were heavy, too heavy to open for the moment. He'd needed that sleep, hell, he needed more. Why were people having a conversation in his room?

'Not ready? He has to be ready. Archania is set to fall into the Empire and we haven't heard back from the Borderlands since the battle with the Barbarians. There's been two quakes in the last week and the mountain is spewing its fury almost daily. Time isn't on our side, Socket.' Korvus sounded pissed and frustrated. No change there then.

'Let me head back to the Borderlands; see what's going on. Kiras should have responded by now. It's not like her. When I come back, we can go through the last test with the kid. I want to be there for it. I *have* to be there for it.'

'Not waiting that long, Socket, I'm sorry. This is more than just you and him. Anything could have happened in the Borderlands since you left. I can't wait. You want to be there, we do it tomorrow night.' Korvus' voice was stern, leaving no room for argument.

'Fine... let me tell him. He deserves that at least.'

'The less he knows about it, the better,' Korvus answered. 'He needs a clear mind, focus. If not, this could all go to shit and we'll have to wait another fucking generation. We don't have a generation to wait.'

'I know what to do. I've had enough time to think it through. Just wish there was another way...'

'We both do. Life can be fucking shit and we both know that as well. Wake him up and bring him through for some food. He'll need the energy.'

'How's the grub?'

Arden slowly rotated the fork around his plate, lost in his thoughts of a conversation half remembered. 'What?'

'You okay, kid?' Socket asked from across the table.

'Rough sleep. Getting stabbed isn't too good for the body. Who would have thought?' He forced out a laugh and threw his fork down, leaning back in his chair and sighing. 'I just feel like shit.'

'You'll feel better after something to eat and some water. Need your strength for your training.'

'Mmhmm...' He picked the fork back up and stabbed at the piece of meat on the plate, chewing it briefly before swallowing. Should have chewed more. It scratched at his throat painfully on the way down. 'Still can't get the taste of blood from my mouth. Doesn't do much for the appetite.'

'Stop losing your fights then.'

'I'll keep it in mind.'

Socket greedily munched down the rest of his own food. No problem with his appetite it seemed. It was odd seeing the archer dressed up in fine clothes, well, finer than the tattered, ripped ones he was used to. His olive-green shirt hung loosely from his skinny frame, pulled together at the front with silver clasps shaped like arrows. Socket spotted his gaze and grinned.

Bought it in the West years ago – Causrea I think it was. Needed to get into an opera house and my usual clothes didn't seem... suitable.' He chuckled. 'Met the most beautiful woman in the world in that place. Smooth, dark skin; perfect deep brown eyes and a figure you would kill for. Funny too, she was.'

'What happened to her?'

'Plague,' Socket replied bluntly. 'Hit the West hard. The streets stank of death everywhere you went. Couldn't burn the bodies quick enough. Was too dangerous for most people to get close enough to burn the bodies. In the end, a large band of elderly men and women volunteered for the role, sacrificing themselves for the next generation. One of the biggest acts of heroism I've ever witnessed. Good people. Good city, Causrea. Didn't deserve that. Plague never came so far as the Borderlands – stopped at Archania. Some claim it was too cold. Not sure about that but, either way, we were lucky.'

The silence was an easy one – not heavy or uncomfortable. Arden chewed a few more pieces of the salted meat, swallowing carefully and licking his lips. He stared around at the rows of books lining the tall walls and wondered what knowledge lay inside the vast castle – knowledge hidden from the outside world.

'What was it like, fighting with Reaver in the Border Wars?' Arden asked, wanting to change the subject to something he had often thought about when he was younger. Growing up, tales of Reaver and the one-eyed-archer were everything. He saw the two men as heroes, legends of his homeland.

Socket sniffed and wiped a hand across his wet lips. 'I was drunk for a lot of it. Young, drunk and stupid.' Socket scratched his head and gave a wry smile. 'Everyone views the past in a way that helps them to make sense of it all, a way that helps them cope with what happened. The bits I remember were hell. Endless fighting, going to sleep and not knowing if you would wake up. Hard bastards everywhere. No point making any friends as most likely they'd be dead soon enough. Hearts of stone, Reaver used to say – that was how people got through it all, those that did. Reaver had some good ideas and some bad ones, just like anyone else. Other men had wanted to bring the tribes together; the difference between them and Reaver is that he won. That's why he had the glory. We got lucky. Managed to get through the scrapes with cuts and bruises instead of ending up as bones.

'I remember going months without a decent sleep as I'd wake up screaming, unable to escape the unblinking eyes of the latest kid I'd put an arrow through. Death is death wherever and whenever it happens, kid. Some of us are just lucky enough to make it through this life further than others.'

'I don't want that, Socket.' Arden shook his head, staring at the half empty plate in front of him. 'I don't want to wake up in the middle of the night seeing the faces of the dead. I want friends, I want a home, I want peace. I thought that's what we'd been fighting for.'

'That's the problem; we're always fighting for it. Never ends. People speak about wars as though they're in the past. Uh-uh. Wars are a constant, in this part of the world at least. Different enemies, different weapons, but same outcome. Death, grief, and a shit load of tears. Not much changes. Well, that's where you come in. Been a long time since a Guardian was found...'

'How will that change anything?'

'Gives people hope. When we had the Guardians, we didn't have the earthquakes, the eruptions, the fear. You can restore a balance. Can't make anything worse, can ya?' Socket laughed, winking with his one good eye.

'How am I supposed to handle that pressure?' Arden exploded, flinging the fork onto the plate and shaking his head. 'Give people hope? Me? I just don't think I can do it...'

'Maybe you can, maybe you can't. Only way we'll know is if you give it a go. Like I said before, you fall, I'll pick you up. I'm with you 'til the end, kid.'

'Why? Why would you help me like that?' Arden blurted out, confused.

'You're the first Guardian in a generation to make it here,' Socket said as though that was enough. 'On top of that, you're a good kid. Not many of those around nowadays. Weren't many around in the past to be honest. I'm gonna die one day; when I do, I want it to mean something. Or at least, to feel as though it means something.'

'How do you think Reaver felt when he died?'

'Alone. Scared.' Socket shrugged. 'Same as most folk. Happy that the tribes were together, proud of his own son. Still didn't make his death any easier. Nothing ever would.'

'Do you know how he died?' Everyone knew he'd been stabbed, other than that, his death had been a mystery, a cause for gossip across the lands.

'Stabbed in the back,' Socket answered bluntly. 'Men like Reaver, who think big and want change, are often looked at as a problem, something to be eliminated. Not everyone agreed with his plans. Problem with the Borderlands is you've gotta always be watching your back, or a dagger finds its way there.'

The door swung open, disrupting the conversation between the pair. Korvus stormed into the room, a foul look etched on his old face, dark eyes glaring at Arden. There was no subtlety about the man at all.

'Good to see that you are up and about,' he barked. 'Let any more psychotic prisoners loose lately?'

'Just the one,' Arden snapped back, not in the mood to take any of the mage's shit. 'You should have let me know about him.'

'And you should have understood that this isn't your

home. It is mine. You are a guest and you should act accordingly. Another slip up and you are gone. Guardian or not, there are rules.'

Arden glared back at Korvus, fighting the urge to blast back as he felt the heat boiling the blood inside him.

'Now, now... there's no need to speak about this. Mistakes were made but we must move on,' Socket butted in, easing the tension, obviously uncomfortable at being between the pair of them. 'We must work together and that means understanding each other.'

'You must have used magic to release him. Focusing was your first problem, one you seem to have overcome at the worst possible time,' Korvus said, ignoring Socket. 'Tomorrow is your next test. Sleep well tonight, you will need the energy.'

'What test?'

'It is better if I don't say. Just know that failure is not an option.' Korvus spun on his heel and stormed out of the room without a backward glance.

'You're not gonna tell me anything about this test, are you?'

'Wish I could,' Socket couldn't meet his eyes, shamelessly looking down at his own empty plate. 'I know you can do it though, kid. You really can. You're a fucking Guardian for a reason.' He stood up, chair scraping across the marble floor. 'Get some rest. You will need it.'

FEELS LIKE HOME

Anticipation weaved through the crowd as it made its way through the Lower City under the light of the fading sun; grey clouds drifted lazily overhead, a silent menace. Sly kept his eyes moving from side to side, still uncomfortable at being this close to so many strangers who seemed to be getting along and sharing familiar tales with one another.

'I keep expecting them to whip out a blade and cut off a head or two. This amount of men ain't supposed to be this close together without blood, Bane.'

'It's strange for us Sly; for them, we are strange.'

'Still don't fucking like it.'

There was a lot he didn't like at the moment. He didn't like being in this dumb country. He didn't like these southern idiots. He didn't like the fact that miles away, Borderland warriors were bathing themselves in glory whilst he was sweating away in this cesspit of a city for no damn good reason. And he sure as fucking hell hated having to walk beside the two people who had caused the death of Raven and beat the shit outta him.

For a moment, Sly wondered if he had made the right decision joining with the two traitors; then he remembered the absence of light and feeling of dread that had consumed him in the dungeon. It wasn't a good decision, but it was the best one in a shitty situation.

He stretched his fingers out, feeling the usual itch as they grasped for a dagger, a blade, a broken piece of glass, anything he could use to protect himself. 'Should never have come here. Should've stayed in the Borderlands and cut open a few of those Barbarian bastards like the girlie.'

Bane grunted at the mention of the Borderlands, peering through the crowd with a wary eye, looking for something. 'Do as I say and then you can get back to her and the ice and the snow and the continuous petty fights. I'm sick of this place too you know. Too many words being spoken and not enough being done. Things are changing though. North, south, east and west: it's all changing,' he grumbled.

'Any idea on who we're turning to bones?' Sly asked, eager to keep his mind away from the surge of the crowd strolling down the cobbled streets. Too close. Not enough room to reach for a weapon and swing.

He struggled to hear any specific conversation in amongst the overall babble of the excited crowd. His fingers twitched nervously as he looked over his shoulder at the mass of people that were following them down the street.

'Bane, I've got a bad feeling about this. We're being followed.' The starlight glimmered on the edges of the spears being held tightly in the hands of a few guards standing out in the crowd.

'Of course we're being followed; we're all heading to the same place. Try to relax. Trust me.'

Sly spat on the floor in disgust and took one more look around, his eyes taking in all around him before focusing on a tavern on the corner of the street, the upper most windows of which were boarded up with broken bits of wood. 'Say that again and I will stab myself. Relax? Fine, let's go for a drink before this stabbing...'

Bane mulled over the idea, working his tongue across his teeth and cheeks. 'Not a terrible idea. Head to that tavern.' He nodded towards a building that looked as though it needed more than just a lick of paint to be enticing. 'I'll check in with T'Chai and Grey and see where they want us. Stay in the fucking tavern or the next time I see you, you'll be the one that's bones.'

'You got it, *chief*.' Sly drew out the end of the word, glaring at the traitor. Bane glowered back, undecided on whether to take the bait.

'Stay out of fucking trouble.'

Sly chuckled darkly and turned to the tavern, passing through the wave of locals heading to the square. He ignored the disgusted looks some of them gave him as they walked around him and his fellow traveller.

'You my babysitter?' Sly asked. 'Here to hold my hand so that I don't get lost?'

Cray shrugged. 'Drink.' Good answer.

'Fair enough.'

Keeping his head down, Sly peered out beneath his messy hair at the three guards in the crowd. He kept walking towards the tavern, even as he noticed one of the guards motion towards the other two and say something that was lost in the buzz of sound around them. Those around them dispersed as the two burly warriors made their silent way towards their destination. Sly lapped up the fear in some of their faces and disgust in others.

They reached the darkened street corner and Sly put his hand on the wooden door, hesitating. There was no noise in the tavern and Sly wondered if it was closed. He eased the broken door open and looked around for the guards as the door creaked; they were nowhere to be seen.

The room was dimly lit; Sly could make out two large figures huddled in the corner, their hands around tankards. Neither of them moved as the newcomers walked in. Sly looked behind the bar at a large array of bottles, many of which were foreign to him, although a few were familiar.

'It's not often I see a new face in here, though it is always a joy to see fellow brothers of the Borderlands. What brings you here my friends?' His voice was raspy, as though it had rarely been used. His beard was a black as the darkest shadow while his head had long ago lost all hope of growing hair.

'The welcoming people,' Sly answered gruffly.

'Hmm... not too bad in the Lower City, people just mill together and get on with things. Different story in the Upper City. Folk up there couldn't give two shits 'bout anyone else. Just the way it is. What can I get you?'

'Something strong. Remind me of home.'

'I got just the thing. Take a seat,' the burly man said before busying himself behind the bar.

Sly grabbed a seat, making sure to look once more at the two men in the shadows – they had continued a low conversation, their attention seemingly focused away from everyone else. Sly relaxed slightly and felt the tension ease from his body. This was more like it. Felt a bit more like the Borderlands. If he concentrated hard enough, it could almost feel as though he was back home. Almost.

The barman walked back over. Sly nonchalantly spotted a maze of scars crossing over each other on two tree-trunk like arms that were carrying the drinks.

'Here you go! Traditional Border Mead!' he exclaimed with a huge grin behind his dark beard, 'I promise, you will not find a better drink in the United Cities.'

Sly gave a nod and took the first sip as Cray grunted his thanks. The barman walked away, flinging a small, grubby cloth over his shoulder as he did so. A familiar taste, one that Sly welcomed even if it wasn't as good as the stronger stuff that he was used to in the Borderlands. It was close enough.

He used the lack of conversation to study his companion. He gazed curiously at the silent warrior as he slowly sipped his drink, dark eyes focused on the table in front of him. Sly casually scratched as his ragged beard and tilted his head to the side. 'Just me and you now silver tongue. So... now we're not with the ear enthusiast – what's the story? Why the fuck were you even with us in the first place if all you were gonna do is turn?' They had travelled to this hellhole together but Sly hardly knew a thing about him. Not usually an issue. After Raven's death, he wanted to know more about his moody companion. Couldn't hurt to try.

Sly kept his eyes on him as he took another sip, not rushing to answer the question. He respected the confidence Cray was showing, even if he could feel an impatient rage building inside him.

After what felt like an age, Cray placed his drink on the table and looked at Sly straight in the eyes. 'He wants you dead. Saul.'

A belly laugh erupted from Sly's body before he could stop it; spit flew across the room as he arched over the wooden table. The barmen and two customers stared over at the strange scene as Sly sat back up and shook his head, aware of eyes on him in the room but unable to look away from the man opposite.

'That's it?' he asked incredulously. 'The big secret mission – he wants us dead. Of course he wants us fucking dead!' he roared. 'Biggest open secret in the Borderlands. Every man and his dog knows that.'

One of the men made a motion to stand up as the volume in the room rose but the barmen signalled to him to sit down. Smart. Northern.

'I have two young daughters. They mean everything to me. If Raven messed with the understanding Saul has with this Kingdom, I'd been ordered to kill the lot of ya.' Cray punctuated his words with another sip of his drink and nothing more.

Sly sat back in his chair and puffed his cheeks up before blowing the air out and running his hand through his hair. 'Cunt. He's a fucking cunt,' he muttered, eyes never leaving the melancholy man opposite him.

Cray shuffled uncomfortably before continuing, 'Saul and Bane are working together – for a change. They want to unite the Borderlands with the United Cities. Saul will rule the Borderlands as a King, it's what he's always wanted. Raven was gonna go along with it – fulfil his father's wish of "peace at all costs". Then Mason's men went and fucked it all up by killing Raven's brother. If they hadn't done that, Raven would have gone along with it all. Saul would become King; the North would be united.'

Saul and Raven.

A King in the Borderlands.

Sly shook his head, unable to believe the words coming out from the usually silent warrior, 'I see now why you kept your mouth shut. Best way of keeping the shit from flying out. Raven would have told us the plan. He's not that much of a fool.'

'He's not a fool. He knew that the Barbarians would need to go south. The might of the Borderlands and Archania would be the only way to deter them from launching a full-scale attack. As soon as they saw the nations together, the Barbarians would cave in and we could do as we please.' Cray stated before adding, 'Raven's had enough of the Borderlands and biting his tongue. Was offered a chance to sit on the council here, an honorary member – the link between the two new best friends in the North. It's all been sorted with a few people down here. You need to get over it. Make one wrong move, I'll kill you.'

Sly kept his mouth closed, trying to digest what was being said – it wasn't like him. The more he thought about it, the more the words seemed to make sense. He'd felt uncomfortable ever since he had left his homeland and now it all clicked into place.

But there was no chance he was going to die in this shithole.

He slowly dropped a hand beneath the table and ran his fingers across the hilt of a dagger. 'Seeing as the other dog isn't here, how about we have some fun? Cause I'll tell you one thing for certain,' he leaned forward and whispered to Cray, staring dead in his eyes, 'I sure as hell ain't dying on account of you or any of your fucking family.'

Sly felt the familiar flow of battle lust course through his body as he saw the rage boiling inside of Cray. Cray's fists trembled around the tankard as he spat back, 'If it means they survive, I'll kill you right now.'

Sly licked his sharp, yellow teeth. 'Prove it.'

As quick as a flash, Sly leapt up and flipped the table onto his opponent before drawing his weapon. Cray took the blow better than expected and rolled to the side, clearly assuming an instant attack was inevitable. Sly liked to play with his victims though. A quick death was never fun. Well, that wasn't *always* true...

The commotion had proved to be enough now for the barmen to allow the two customers to step in. Sly scanned the pair of them – from the Borderlands as well by the looks of it. Big brutes with sharp blades that were drawn eagerly.

The barman sighed and shook his head as he watched the chaos unfold. 'This is why I moved away...' Sly heard him curse under his breath as the two brutes jumped into action.

He dodged the first blow and landed an elbow of his own cleanly on the cheek of one of the assailants. After narrowly avoiding a short stab from the second one's sword, he parried the next blow, roaring as the battle rage took over. *Clearly, they both don't mind going for the kill. Just how I like it.*

He twisted and carefully moved his feet away from the strangers, watching as Cray dusted himself off and readied his stance, preparing for a fight to the death.

BANG!

Sly's head swivelled towards the sound of the door crashing open. Five tall, armoured guards rushed inside – deadly lances pointed their way. The noise and commotion had obviously disturbed the locals. Sly looked at the silver armour shining in what small amount of light was able to creep into the bar. Small, white suns were emblazoned on the torsos of each of the men's armour.

The guards paused, looking at the chaotic room, lances still raised. One of them stepped forward. Short, dark hair shaved neatly at the back and sides; green eyes that darted around the room and all its occupants.

'Which ones, boss?' one of the other guards asked.

The leader looked at the five men in turn. He shrugged. 'All of them.'

'Shit.' The barman dropped low behind his bar at the comment. Useless. Sly turned to Cray and the two strangers – they all shared a dark, determined look. If they were going down, they'd do it fighting. No other way.

The guards stepped forward, no hint of fear in any of their eyes. Five armoured men with lances against five Borderland savages. They liked the odds.

Sly liked them even more.

A roar from behind the bar distracted all of them. Flashes of metal came spinning through the air. The strangers caught the swords, smiling as they turned the blades over in their hands, feeling the weight of the deadly weapons.

'You don't fuck with the people in my tavern,' the barmen threatened, throwing another sword in Cray's direction.

Sly released a hearty laugh.

'Axe?' he asked without expectation.

The barman winked.

A moment later, Sly was running his hand over the largest axe he had ever seen, 'Do much tree cutting?' he asked.

'From time to time,' the barman replied with a knowing smile.

The guards took a step back, hesitating with this complete reversal of fortune.

'What's the plan?' Sly smirked at Cray.

The moody warrior returned the smirk with one of his one. 'Kill the fuckers.' he suggested.

The closest guard lunged towards Sly, only to find his spear snapped to the side by Cray's sword. Sly took the chance to swing the axe down as hard as he could. A dull thud sounded as the iron buried itself into the neck of the fallen guard.

The rest of them backed off. Wise.

'Not so fast,' a voice muttered from outside the tavern.

Sly tightened his grip on the mammoth handle. Curious glances crossed the room as the guards slowly backed into the tavern once more. A huge, beast of a man followed them in, bloodied sword in hand. His huge body was covered in signs of battle: right eye discoloured and bloodshot; left arm seemingly incapable of movement. Thankfully, his sheer size, bloodied weapon and the vengeful look on his battered face was enough to intimidate the outnumbered guards. A look of recognition crossed the man's face as he looked around the tavern.

'There's a madness in the city tonight. Go. We'll deal with these soulless bastards,' he said, looking over at Sly and Cray.

Sly wasn't going to question his luck. He punched the closest guard with all his strength. The guard crumpled to the floor in a moaning heap. A look of hate shot up from his bloodied face as Sly walked past the rest of them and out into the city, axe in hand, pausing only to nod his thanks to burly warrior.

The streets were chaos. Blood curdling screams could be heard in the distance as Sly focused on the fires dominating the skyline. Smoke drifted lazily up from the crooked streets. More soldiers filled the streets, striking at anyone close enough to spear. Bands of locals fought back with their crude weapons, anything they could lay their hands on.

'This,' Sly nodded, feeling the muscles at the corner of his lips twitch as he closed his eyes, feeling the battle all around him, 'is more like it. Feels like home.'

Cray breathed out through his nose and marched forward. 'We need to find Bane. Get this over with.'

'Then we can settle things,' Sly spat, opening his eyes. 'I won't forget what you did to me, and what you did to Baldor and Raven. You'll pay.' He didn't want to admit it but already he could feel a change between them after the tavern fight. Sly knew what it was, even if he wasn't going to say it. Respect.

Cray shrugged. 'What's the plan?'

Sly just kept moving forward. 'Keep walking. Anyone gets in our way, kill the fuckers.'

THE PEOPLE'S SQUARE

'The forgotten. That's what we all are. Men, women and children who have lived in the shadow of a once great city that is now infested with vermin and filth. They sip their wine, devour their plays and powder their faces whilst ignoring any sense of suffering and pain that we go through down here in the slums!' Cypher paused to allow the cheers and shouts of anger to rise up together as one, fuelling those around the Peoples' Square. Mob mentality was truly a wonderful thing. 'We work our fingers to the bone in a futile effort to afford the scraps of food and water that are thrown our way from the snobs, the braggarts, the vainglorious elite. We have fought amongst ourselves: the poor, the injured, the sick, the weak... *the magi*. Yes, my friends, the magi have suffered as much as we have, if not more!'

There were a few anxious glances in the crowd around the statue of King Borris. A slight unease in the air that replaced the anger and rage for a moment. For an age, they had been told about the dangers of magi. They ruined the planet; they can kill with barely a thought; they were a danger to all free folk – to decent people like you and me. For Cypher to tell them that they too were a victim of the Upper City Elite was a drastic change. People in the crowd were having to struggle against their inherited prejudice whilst standing there amongst the people they had despised so recently.

'I know what you're thinking: they're dangerous, careless, arrogant, evil...' Cypher nodded along with the crowd before halting and wagging a finger, flashing his teeth to his audience as they ate up every word, following his lead as though he were pulling invisible strings attached to each and every one of them. 'No, my brothers and sisters. Those words describe the Upper City Elite: the very poison destroying our city. It is the royal family – including the King who has left us – it is Mason D'Argio and his sheep, it is rich, jobless fools who sit there in their high towers looking down on us and laughing at our misfortune. They are the ones who deserve your hatred, your rage. They are the ones who should be on trial, not the magi. They are the ones who should burn for their crimes, crimes against us all!'

The thousands of people packed into the square roared their approval. They were packed in tight, some swinging from the famous statue whilst others hung off balconies sticking out of the buildings overlooking the chaos. He had asked for the Lower City to join him and hear his call to arms, and they had not failed him.

Such pitiful, gullible fools.

They lapped up his every word, his every move: eager for him to fuel their base desires and primal urges. They had suffered. They had been trodden on.

Cypher just didn't give a shit.

'I won't profess to be the most caring of men: you all know my what my role was until recently. I was a part of the machine that is chugging along with no end in sight; a machine that is riding over this beautiful Kingdom and destroying its people, its true citizens. If you want what I want, the course corrected for our once great nation, then I implore you to heed the words spoken today by the people who truly love this Kingdom. Listen to their words and be brave. Believe in The Four and they will give you strength. Deny them, and you will be left in the darkness...'

He slid from the podium, cheers ringing in his ears as

he turned to face the row of masked men standing with military precision behind him. 'They'd trust you more if you took off the damn masks,' he muttered, pulling a handkerchief from his breast pocket and wiping the sweat from his forehead. Starlight lit the square but it was still warm, the sheer number of anxious and excited bodies ensured that it would stay warm even as the night sky began to grip the city.

'The masks give them something to believe in, a shared cause,' the leader responded behind the long, pointed beak. They must all be sweating their balls off in that gear. Black robes, black gloves, black hats, black masks. Dumb idea.

'I find men follow men in the long run. Familiarity is what they crave, it's comforting. They see a pair of eyes; they can believe in you. Doorway to the soul, Paesus said. Hide behind a mask and it breeds mistrust. Just my opinion, what do I know?' He patted the man on the shoulder and grinned, turning to take his place in the line as the leader stepped onto the empty podium to a resounding roar from the crowd.

'My brothers and sisters. The very fact you have all joined me here in what is now known as the People's Square, is enough to bring me to tears. Your faith, your support, your belief is what drives me to new heights, what fuels the fires raging inside me!' Cypher nodded along with the crowd once more, genuinely impressed with the start. 'I have witnessed the cruelty, the apathetic way in which the elite of our Kingdom treat the hard-working citizens of Archania. I have heard you named as the backbone of this Kingdom and I find that an apt metaphor. A Kingdom who relies on the strength of its poorer, honourable citizens to survive. They are parasites, parasites who leech off the hard work of others. I, myself have been guilty in the past of such crimes, but now, my eyes are wide open, and I can see your pain. It is a pain that I will work to alleviate, a pain that I will work to end!'

There was a tension in the air, an electricity, as the crowd shook their fists and cried out in primal rage, finally hearing their aggrievances spoken out loud. The few guards that were scattered around the square looked terrified, uneasy with the role of playing peacemakers in this cauldron of hate and rage.

'My colleague, Cypher Zellin, has joined our cause. He is aware of the need for a change in this Kingdom. And change is coming my friends. It will be an unstoppable juggernaut that will pass through this whole Kingdom. I promise, your lives will never be the same! For too long we have lived in the shadows. The flames of rebellion are rising...' Cypher waved his hand and smirked at the adoring crowd surrounding the podium, a wave of downtrodden and forgotten men and women who had finally grown a backbone in a futile effort to stand up against people much stronger than them. Futile and stupid. Not that they knew that. It was all so predictable...

Aleister rolled his eyes as the roars rang out across the square. He'd never seen the place so packed! Thousands of men and women lined the streets and packed themselves into the square around the old statue of King Borris. Many people perilously clambered onto balconies, tall buildings and the statue itself in order to get a good view of the men in plague doctor masks lined up on the podium in front of Elder Morgan's temple. Wooden boards blocked up the doorway, a reminder of the horrific act that had taken place barely two days before.

He had listened to Cypher give his histrionic speech with a constant feeling of vomit in his throat. The killer had lapped up the applause and the cries of the grand audience before him, breathing it all in like oxygen. What a load of bullshit. The torturer hadn't changed, though he now dressed like one of The Doctors, sans mask. He was keen to show his face, unlike the others. Recognition and respect were what he craved, and he was getting everything he desired as the moon shone down.

'Seems to be enjoying it doesn't he?' Ariel muttered, nudging her brother and rolling her eyes beneath her hood.

'It's what he's always wanted,' Bathos added, eyes unmoving from the bald men lined up at the back of the podium. The apparent leader of The Doctors spoke to the crowd, urging them to be the backbone of the Kingdom. Such drivel.

'Together, we can ensure that this Kingdom is free from corruption, from fear, from hate. We can strive for greatness once more! No longer will we rely on the monarchy, the Kings and Queens who look out for themselves and their rich friends. Let's trust in ourselves. Let's begin a revolution that ends with grabbing our destiny with both hands!'

Aleister winced and closed an eye, squinting from the other as he backed away from the huge roar. A particularly sozzled brute with a strong stench of body odour swayed and held a hand high in the air, wafting the potent smell from his hairy armpit towards those around him.

'Grab our destiny!' the brute roared, eyes dipping out of focus as he staggered and bumped into Ariel.

'Take our Kingdom back!' Another cried next to him.

'Grabbing a bar of soap would greatly improve the lives of all around him...' Ariel said, peering at the brute from out of the corner of her eye and shuffling in front of an unamused Bathos.

'Shit,' Aleister nudged his friends and nodded down the road to the side of them. 'Looks like the cavalry is coming. Eyes open. We don't know what's going to happen.'

In rows of four, soldiers in gleaming silver armour and cloaks of the purest white marched down the cobbled streets, flanked by spear-wielding horse riders. It appeared that the Upper City Elite had heard enough. It was time to shut down this heresy.

Two sides of the square had spotted the incoming soldiers. The thrill of being part of a group drained away as the looming threat of punishment rode towards them. Excitement faded into fear and anxiety, forcing those closest to step back and push against those closest to them. Aleister watched in dismay as the crowd lurched in waves like falling dominoes, one after another. Men and women cursed and gasped for breath as they were pressed up against others; children squealed as their heads began a slow crush against the much taller adults surrounding them.

Aleister spotted one such child and squeezed his way over. 'Here. Climb up,' he commanded, lifting the boy under the armpits and raising him up onto his shoulder. 'Climb across to the statue. You'll be safe there.' The sandy-headed boy nodded, breathing heavily as a faint smile reached his face. Aleister watched as the boy rushed over to the statue, aided by more kind-hearted folk in the crowd.

'My brothers and sisters! Be mindful! The soldiers dare not attack. Spread out and ensure that none are harmed in this crowd of good men and women!' The leader roared from behind his mask, voice breaking as he watched the scene unfold before him.

The soldiers halted near the exits, doing nothing to stop the chaos. They stood as statues, a few even chuckled as they watched their own people suffer.

'Archania!' a red-haired man roared to the crowd, familiar dazzling green eyes surveying the madness from the raised base of the statue of King Borris. Even without his red robe, Haller looked like a man in control, a man who you listened to when he spoke. A small group of frightened children were spread around him, clinging precariously onto the statue in fear of their life. 'Archania!' he repeated, this time followed by a deafening silence as all in the square turned to face him. 'We stand at a crossroads. We have a choice to make: a choice that will start us on a path to one of two destinations. We can choose to give in and go along with this Empire of Light – turning a blind eye to the suffering of the downtrodden and the poor. Or we can turn onto a new path – a path where we do not yet know the destination. My name is Rude Haller,' Haller held up his hands, a dark grin falling upon his face as wave upon wave of people in the crowd pulled out the white masks Aleister had seen beneath the city, 'and I say we cut the head off the snake.' Haller screamed, tightening every muscle in his body, face growing purple as he called for every ounce of energy in his being. The white masks stared up at him as though he was their saviour, crying out in support as they raised their red hoods in unison. Aleister wondered for a moment if Ella was amongst them, offering her support to the mage leader.

A low rumbling rose from the ground beneath them along with a huge bang like thunder. Dust blew over the crowd, forcing Aleister to shield his face. Urgent muttering broke out around him as he returned his gaze to the statue of King Borris. He gasped as the dust settled. Haller looked exhausted, panting heavily and leaning on another mage for support. At his feet lay the stone head of King Borris, decapitated. A stunned silence fell on the crowd as all eyes returned to the podium. A row of plague doctors now mingled between a row of red robed magi, red clashing with the black, white masks standing next to the hooked black beaks of The Doctors. The leader of The Doctors stepped forward as the clouds drifted gently away, allowing the moonlight to shine directly upon him.

'Your time is now. Our time is now. An Empire of Light will not stand against the Flames of Red and Black. Take back your city, take back your country, take back your freedom!' The leader paused, basking in the tears and screams of assent from the wild crowd, buoyed up once more by the charismatic men. Aleister stared silently. It was as though time had slowed down. He watched the leader move a gloved hand up to his face, watched through the wave of arms gesturing in the air, saluting the great man. The hand clutched at the bottom of his mask and tore it away, displaying a stern face and eyes swallowed in sadness. A deathly silence hung in the air as all eyes looked up at the councillor.

'Fuck...' Aleister heard a man whisper next to him, mouth hanging wide open.

'I, Lord Tamir, bear witness to the first day in a new age for our people. Do not fight for me: fight for yourselves, for your brothers and sisters. Nothing more, nothing less.' The sword sang as he whipped it from its sheath, raising it high into the light of the moon. 'Let the flames of rebellion consume any who stand in their way,' he cried, words dancing through the silence of the crowd. 'For Archania!'

On cue, a hundred magi raised their hands and

summoned orbs of fire to signal their intent.

'Ariel, Bathos! To the Eastern Road. We have to cut a path if any are to get out alive,' Aleister called, mobilising and gripping his sword as he pushed through the excited crowd.

'Shit. We really doing this?' Ariel asked, following instantly.

'It'll be a song for the ages,' Bathos smirked, easily clearing a path alongside them.

'Just make damn sure we're alive to hear the song.'

* * *

She pinched a finger and thumb together either side of the edge of her hood, pulling it lower to cover her face as the guards cautiously urged their steeds forward. Being recognised dressed in the robes of a Doctor would only add to her problems, of which Katerina Kane suddenly had many.

The crowd was ready to erupt, heat from the flames above the red-robed magi carrying across the square as the sky darkened, black clouds promising an angry storm in response to the growing threat of violence. She flinched as yet another wave of movement led to a man twice her size knocking into her, his hip slamming against her already sore ribs. As she stumbled back, her eyes landed on a familiar face forcing its way through the tangled mass of limbs and fury.

'Aleister!' She meant to shout it out but instead forced only a squeak and a few unpleasant sounding coughs. 'Aleister!' she called again, this time managing to raise her volume.

'Kat,' Aleister pushed his way through the crowd, his face mirroring the storm clouds above him. 'How did you...'

'No time for that.' She brushed his concern away with a nonchalant wave of the hand; there were more pressing matters to attend to. 'This place is going to explode. We need to get as many people out of the square as possible.'

'The Eastern Road looks like the easiest way out. Less guards. Take down a few and we'll be able to pour out like water through a broken dam,' Ariel said joining her brother. 'Bathos is readying a route through the crowd.'

Kane twisted her head and following the low grumblings of the crowd as the giant of a man eased his way through the mass of people, all unable to prevent him from passing through. 'We must be quick. As soon as Mason finds out about Lord Tamir, he will want vengeance. I dread to think what that monster will do.' She followed the trio through the crowd, attempting in vain to prevent the crush of the crowd against her already injured body. Another coughing fit brought with it specks of blood, flying from her mouth onto the hand she flung up as a shield. *Forget it. That's not important right now.*

Stones were raining down on the armoured soldiers patiently waiting at the edge of the square. The horses shuffled back slightly, alarmed by the heavy missiles coming their way. A few of the Lower City citizens had drawn weapons: a couple of axes, a hammer, one even had a sword. 'Step back or we will use force!' one of the soldiers commanded from his horse, spear pointing forward at the rabble.

'We're done listening to you! Go back to your master like whipped dogs and leave us the fuck alone!' a man at the front of the line roared back in defiance, waving his sword above his head in warning. The crowd around him echoed his roar, growing in confidence as they became aware of their advantage in numbers. They marched forward; grim determination etched on their faces. Kane peered up at the soldiers. Suddenly they seemed unsure of themselves, aware that they would have to fight to keep the mob back.

The crowd marched on, calling for blood, a chance for vengeance. Kane struggled to keep up with her friends as Bathos bounded forward, eager to reach the frontline, followed by Aleister and Ariel. She struggled for breath, clawing at those around her in a desperate effort to get forward. A dull thud froze her on the spot as the roar of the crowd died down. The first few drops of rain fell upon the mass of angry men and women as all eyes turned to the Eastern Road. Kane snapped out of her stupor and rushed forward, taking advantage of the sudden stillness of the crowd.

At the frontline stood a circle of horrified onlookers. Aleister knelt next to the man who had held the sword which now lay forgotten on the ground. The man's head rocked back and forth in a slow motion, eyes unfocused and drool escaping his lips. The edge of the spear had sliced through his neck, taking half of his throat along with it as it tore through him.

'He killed him. He fuckin' killed him,' a woman muttered through her tears, hammer hanging loosely in her hand. 'What do I tell the girls?'

Lightning tore the skies apart chased by the roar of thunder. The storm had arrived. Rain now fell like a sea of arrows on the shocked faces in the crowd. Fingers tightened around weapons or balled into fists as a wall of desperate, irate faces turned to the soldier mounted on the horse, spear no longer in his hand. She felt it may have been a trick of her hopeful mind, but she thought a flicker of regret crossed the man's face; a face that now looked incredibly young and inexperienced as the lightning flashed across it.

'They have drawn first blood,' Tamir called from the podium, pulling his mask back over his face. 'Make them pay!'

They rushed forward as one, knocking Kane to the ground. Rough boots stepped over and onto her, catching her stomach as she curled into a ball, struggling to breathe. Crying out would be useless as a cacophony of sound blasted through the square; an orchestra of noise bellowed from the sky and square as one. She raised an arm to cover her head as more boots fell upon her, the crowd eager to get their taste of vengeance. They obviously hadn't been warned of its bitter taste, one that hangs in the mouth for years to come; Kane had, though now she tasted nothing but her own blood.

'Kat!' a voice shouted in the void. She felt a hand beneath her, dragging her onto her feet. The sound of weapons clashing rang out through the square, the roar of battle in full flow, flames everywhere. 'Are you okay?'

Golden pupils. Raven-black hair. A worried look painted on a beautiful face. 'Ella, my dear,' Kane groaned, spotting the red robe her friend had draped around her. 'You have to get out of here. It's too dangerous!'

'Too late for that. Come on.' She pulled Kane's arm around her shoulder and eased her towards the Eastern Road.

The battle was intense. Bodies were strewn all over the ground. The Lower City was fighting back with all the strength it could muster, years of hurt and pain released through a cathartic swing of a sword, a hammer, an axe, a rock. She rolled her jaw, feeling the dull pain and wincing as she placed a hand against it. She felt like a jigsaw put together by a child with some of the pieces not quite in the right place.

Ahead of her was a mob of red and black, all yelling and cheering, ignoring the heat of the battle around them. 'What the...' she muttered to herself as she looked up at the beam stretching out from the upper window of the wooden building. One man threw a rope up to be caught by a child hanging out of the window. He ensured the rope caught on the beam as he dropped it back down, ready to be tied by another. The cheering crowd grew more animated and angrier as a soldier was dragged through the group. They spat and cursed, boots flying towards the captured man.

'Please! I'm sorry! I need to get back home. My mum...'

'He had two daughters!'

'A family man!'

'You fuckin' pig!'

'This is the least you deserve!'

'I say we cut him a bit first...'

It was the young soldier: the one who had thrown the spear. They wrapped the rope tightly around his neck as a woman brought forward a hammer and stared at him with her dead eyes.

'You took him from me. I'll never forgive you.'

Kane turned away a moment too late. They held his hands down as the woman slammed the hammer against them, shattering all the bones in both of his hands. His screams pierced the night before another blast of thunder cloaked them.

'We need to stop this!' Ella said, placing a white mask over her face and drawing a blade. 'Step away from him!'

'Fuck you, mage. He's ours,' an ugly boulder like man spat back through his patchwork of missing teeth, tightening the noose, ignoring the sobs from the soldier.

'We're on the same side.' Ella reminded him.

'I never said I was on no mage's side. You're like them. Act like you're better than us just 'cause you can do some tricks. Now, fuck off unless you wanna make this a double hanging.'

The mob hoisted the soldier up, two of them pulling at the rope to raise him like a flag. There were no smiles. No pride. Just a grim satisfaction. He would die slow. No snapping of the neck. Just a slow, painful choking as he struggled to draw breathe. A horrible way to go, all things considered.

'Release him!' Ella cried as Kane dropped her arm from around her and grabbed at her own sword before remembering that she no longer had the weapon; felt as though she was missing an arm.

'Don't say I didn't warn you, bitch.' The brute stepped towards Ella, smiling as he saw her hands shake, knowing that she didn't have the fight in her. 'Never done it before have ya? Pathetic.' The back of his knuckles caught Ella's face. Kane's jaw dropped, painfully. How Ella had managed to stay on her feet was beyond Kane's belief. A large, red mark stained her cheek as her face filled with fury.

The blade snapped forward in silence, gliding with ease up the man's ribcage and straight into his heart. Ella pulled it back in shock, muttering to herself. 'What have I done?'

Kane grabbed her arm, dragging her away from the perplexed man scratching at the wound as blood seeped out of his body. 'Run, we need to run!' Kane commanded as Ella sheathed the weapon, now dripping red.

'Magi! The magi have turned on us!' The scream arced through the air, punctuated by further screams and the clash of steel on steel, iron on bone. Chaos truly had taken over the square.

The soldiers had retreated, surprised by the sheer ferocity of the attack from the poorly armed and untrained citizens of the Lower City. Fires had broken out and danced across the wooden buildings, illuminating the night in horrific beauty. The howl of the wind terrified Kane; it dragged the flames further into the city, threatening to destroy all before it.

Kane picked a fallen sword up off the ground and gave two measured swings. A bit heavier than what she was used to, but it would have to do. If she was going to die in this mess, then she wanted to do so with a blade in her hand and a song in her heart.

Just like Braego used to say.

Pockets of the battle now spread out across the city – soldiers against Doctors, Doctors against magi, magi against soldiers and all other combinations combined. Logic and reason had been abandoned for the old prejudice and hate. Through it all, Kane hobbled along the cobbled streets, praying they would be able to see the sunrise.

Armour glinted in the flamelight as Aleister dodged the jabbing swords and struck a blow of his own. The flat of the blade caught the edge of the soldier's helmet, shifting it ever so slightly. Good enough. Blinded by his own helmet, the soldier was defenceless. Soulsbane sang through the air and cut through the weak chainmail, driving through flesh and organs. The man vomited blood as Aleister spun away, looking for the next attack.

Horses ran along the street, riderless and confused. The people were worse off. Panic set in on the untrained citizens; they swung wildly with closed eyes, praying that each moment wouldn't be their last. The battles became a blur of swinging weapons with only luck ensuring that enemies were hit. Aleister saw a man vomit in horror after his sword found the gut of a friend. He frantically tried to apologise and check the damage but found only a spear in the back from an opportunistic soldier.

'Ariel! Any sign of Kane?' he asked, searching the chaos for the injured woman. He'd lost her early on as the huge crush of the crowd surged towards the soldiers on the frontline.

'Not for a while. What do you want to do?' his sister

asked, wiping blood from her forehead. Not her own blood, at least.

'Not much we can do. Chances of finding her in this are slim to none. We have more pressing problems.' He pointed to the flames which were spreading faster than expected through the rows of wooden houses lining the cobbled streets of the Lower City. 'This whole place will be smoke and ash soon enough if we don't do something about it. Head north through the backstreets with Bathos and tell any mage you pass to control the flames. Their fires are causing more harm than good.' Ariel nodded and ran towards Bathos, slapping him on the arm and racing down one of the shadowed backstreets.

Aleister turned back, twisting Soulsbane in his grip and sighing. The easterly wind blew hard, catching the flames and smoke in a scene of horror for all to witness. Time wasn't on their side. The soldiers were backing away now, heading to the Upper City, keen for more support. The rebellion had fallen apart before taking its first breath. He needed the leaders – Haller and Tamir. They were the only ones who could control their people, control this madness.

The streets were less crowded now as the fights spread across the city with the army slowly retreating, allowing the fires to do their work. The People's Square was almost deserted. A few people stumbled around the broken statue of King Borris, doing their best to avert their eyes away from the lifeless bodies at their feet. The crackling of the flames surrounded the square as Aleister walked to the statue, eyes fixed on a small body near the decapitated head of old Borris. He swallowed, took a few deep breaths and looked at the unblinking eyes of the boy beneath him. He recognised the face: the same one he had helped out from the crush of the crowd. There were no signs of a fatal wound. The poor boy had most likely been trampled to death. Aleister knelt, closed the boy's eyes and ran a hand gently over his head.

'It is always the innocent who suffer in war.'

Aleister stood up, his eyes stinging with tears as Haller walked towards him, staring at the boy. 'You let them get out of control. You both did. You and Tamir. Leaders who lose control of their people don't deserve to be leaders at all.'

'Speaking from experience, I believe. Tales of The Red Sons have reached every corner of Takaara.' Aleister flinched at the memories. He'd done his best. Perhaps that just wasn't good enough. Everyone has their choices.

'That was different. They were trained, prepared. They knew what would happen if things went wrong.'

'And I'm sure that's what you tell yourself when you sleep at night.'

'What the fuck is that supposed to mean?'

'It means you are in no position to judge me on the effectiveness of leadership. You left The Red Sons to fend for themselves. Perhaps that is why they are not here to help you in Archania's darkest hour.' Haller looked down at the boy and sighed. 'Regrettable. This was our chance!'

'You released the arrow too soon. You weren't prepared. I warned you,' Aleister said, brushing a hand against his watering eyes. 'These people weren't ready for a war. The Red Sons would have arrived if we had time. A rebellion, a revolution cannot be rushed.'

'I must share the blame.' Aleister glanced to his right and spotted Lord Tamir trudging his way over, skin stained with ash and a thin, open wound above his left eyebrow. His sword scraped across the ground as though the weight of it was too much for him to bear. 'I feared Mason bringing the Empire's army to our gates. I felt this was the only chance we had. I was a fool. They are here, already.'

'Where?' Aleister asked, eyes flashing. If the Empire had brought their army, they would be able to wipe out any who stood against the monarchy. Treason was punishable by death.

'They've marched through the Upper City. A display of strength to calm the worrying elite of this Kingdom. It won't be long until we have been folded into their Empire. All is lost...' Tamir's voice drifted off at the end, all strength leaving his body.

'Well,' Haller muttered, 'I will not be taken to be one their playthings!' He pulled a dagger out from his crimson robe and stabbed at his throat, pulling the blade hard across his neck to open up a wide, gaping wound.

Aleister rushed forward as the mage fell, pressing against the wound with both hands, ignoring the stream of blood pouring over him. Tamir stood and watched like a statue, unmoving.

'His biggest fear was being taken to the dungeons and put on display as a reminder to others.'

The light in Haller's green eyes faded, shoulders slumping back and head rolling against the fall. Aleister released him, gently placing his body on the ground as the blood continued its journey, darkening the crimson robe and dripping next to the head of King Borris.

'Shame. If he'd have waited just a moment, I'd have done it for him...'

'Let's just get this over with,' Sly grunted at Cray, staring at the two men in front of the statue. They each had their swords ready, each stained with blood. They'd been busy. The one who had released the body of the fat mage looked young, athletic, ready for a fight. The other was dressed in the black robes he had seen all day – older, more experienced. Could be interesting.

'Who are you?' The younger one asked, slowly stepping to the side, toe first, then heel. Good footwork. This wasn't his first fight. Good.

'Been asked to kill the leaders of this huge shit show. Looks like that one has done our job for us,' Sly said, pointing an axe at the fallen mage. 'Now, step aside and we can kill this one and then I can fuck off back home.'

'Home. This is my home,' the older man said, taking a step forward. 'I'll defend it to the death.'

'They always say that,' Sly whispered to himself.

'Look,' the younger one lowered his weapon, dropping out of his fighting stance and relaxed, 'my name's Aleister, I grew up in this city. This isn't your fight. The Empire has caused this. These people are sick of silently watching their city suffer.

You could help us.'

'You're from the Borderlands, you don't want any part of this.' The older one muttered, keeping his own fighting stance.

'In all honesty, one fight seems like any other. Not much seems to change, whoever wins. That's always been the way.' Sly shrugged.

'Please... just step aside. The city is burning.' Aleister's eyes were full of sorrow. The fool genuinely cared about this shithole. Odd.

'Ah, you found them!' Bane strolled through the rain, barely noticing the bodies on the ground. Two soldiers of Light flanked him, swords drawn and bloody. 'And I see one of them is dead already. Kill the other two and your work is done. Home to the freezing Borderlands, never to return.'

Sly's skin crawled as Bane slapped his back. It took every ounce of energy not to kill him there and then. Home to the Borderlands. To King Saul. Not a pleasant thought. The lightning lit up the square, illuminating the headless statue, the corpses scattered and lifeless, the sadness in the two men standing over their fallen ally. Suddenly, Sly felt he could see clearly. He knew what he wanted to do. What he had to do.

Thunder struck in time with the axe, catching the nearest soldier in the throat. Poor bastard didn't stand a chance. Didn't even have time to look surprised before he dropped, clutching at his throat. Sly slammed his boot against the body and pulled the axe back out, spraying blood all over himself before swinging the weapon at Bane. The experienced warrior pulled his sword up and blocked the blow with a growl.

'Fucking bastard. Knew we should have buried you when we had the chance. Won't make the same mistake again...'

'Won't give you the chance.' Sly's eyes darted over to Cray. The warrior just stood there, sword limp at his side, eyes switching between the two of them.

Wet hair pressed against the side of Sly's face as the rain continued its onslaught. He stepped to the side, back to Aleister and the older warrior in black. Those two seemed the least likely to stab him in the back now.

Bane shook with rage, eyeing up the three of them. He put two fingers into his mouth and whistled long and hard.

'Ah, fuck...' Sly muttered, gritting his teeth as four more soldiers marched towards their position. 'Don't suppose you've got any more guys around?'

'None that will arrive with a fucking whistle,' Aleister muttered back, raising his sword and dropping easily into his fighting stance, shifting to the side. 'Lord Tamir, looks as though we'll have to cut our way through.'

'The best road, sadly, never seems to be the easy one,' Tamir responded, mirroring the younger man's stance.

Aleister jumped forward, attacking high. Bane swatted the strike with ease, smiling at the effort. The dark warrior launched his own attack, thrusting at Aleister's gut, but the young warrior spun to the side, avoiding the blade with ease. Not bad at all.

Sly licked his lips and gripped the hilt of his weapon tightly, rocking forward as he looked into the eyes of the five soldiers lined up in front of him. 'Reckon we can take all five of them, old man?'

'Reckon we don't have a choice.'

'Four!' Cray cried, stabbing his old blade through the back of a shocked soldier. The silver-armoured warrior looked down at the blade sticking out of his chest, sharp and red with his own blood. His weak, gloved hand tried to grasp the point and failed before it slid back out, forcing him onto the wet ground. 'You owe me,' Cray said, not even looking over at Sly.

'Owe you? You're fuckin' having a laugh! After what you did!' Sly mirrored Cray's actions, slowly circling the soldiers who suddenly didn't look so confident. Their fingers twitched, obviously struggling to form a plan to battle the seasoned warriors.

'Poor choice, Cray!' Bane shouted over the storm. 'Think of your family!'

'I am!' Cray leapt forward, his sword barely caught by the nearest soldier who seemed amazed by his sudden luck.

Tamir took the opportunity, dropping low and thrusting his own blade through the bottom of the soldier's back and up out through his chest before spinning and allowing his motion to pull the weapon from out of the wounded man.

'The odds are even...' Tamir said, a hint of a smile on his old face.

Sly crashed ahead with his axe held high, roaring to the Gods, eager not to miss out on the blood. All of the warriors faced off with an opponent, lurching forward with weapons bathed in blood. His strike was deflected wide, but he anticipated the defence, thinking ahead and slamming the butt of his weapon against the soldier's chin. The soldier rocked back, struggling with the blow. Sly took the offensive, not allowing a moment of rest. The soldier's eyes came back into focus as he shifted his weapon to the side and forcing a glancing blow.

Sly grinned, feeling the energy of battle take over, the familiar surge of bloodthirst that governed his every movement as his fingers twisted around his axe. He feigned high but struck low; a simple trick, yet it worked. The edge of his axe struggled through the chainmail and bit into the stomach of his opponent, compelling him to drop his own weapon. Sly spun and used the momentum to slice his weapon across the soldier's neck, tearing his throat away. He heard a weak gurgle as the blood filled the man's airways before the thud of his body falling next to the huge stone head.

Glancing past the headless statue, Sly witnessed Bane's sword barely missing Aleister, the young warrior losing concentration for a second. A second that could have cost him his life. He recovered quickly, forcing the bigger warrior back with three quick strikes, all deflected, but forcing Bane onto the defensive, something he wasn't used to.

Sly panted hard and pushed forward, eager to take out the remaining soldiers.

* * *

'Fuck!' Aleister cried, aware that luck had been on his side as the stocky warrior's blade just missed his neck. He flew forward, striking three times as fast as he could, forcing the warrior onto his heels. There was no time to think, each action a response to muscle memory and instinct. The clash of steel filled his head, but he pushed it out. Now wasn't the time for distractions; he had to trust his new allies would deal with the soldiers if he was to have any chance at defeating his own opponent.

His opponent rushed forward, dropping the evil grin and launching a series of swift, accurate blows, a necklace of what looked like ears dancing with the movement. Aleister twisted his wrist and instinctively danced across the wet ground, blocking each attack. Or at least trying to.

A burning pain tore through his body as the edge of the blade caught the skin over his ribs. A glancing strike but a strike, nonetheless. His luck was wearing thin. In his experience, there was never much of it in a battle anyway. Chances were, he wouldn't have anymore.

'You could give up. I'll make sure it is as quick and as painless as possible.' The warrior flashed his white teeth, confidence surging through his every movement.

Aleister checked his side, pressing his hand against his ribs and wincing with the pain. No internal damage. Still hurt like hell. He rocked his shoulders back, feeling the cracks in his body and allowing himself a moment to breathe slow and deep. Last chance. Don't fuck it up. He feinted left and stepped right, thrusting his weapon towards his opponent's ribs. It was deflected once more with ease. *Shit.* It had been too long since he'd been standing opposite such an experienced warrior. He'd grown rusty.

Aleister breathed in again, launching one final, last ditch attack, praying that it would land. His blade speared through the warrior's stomach, his opponent's sword hanging loosely at his side. He hadn't moved, there had been no attempt at blocking the blade. A look of confusion passed over the man's face as his eyes looked down, staring at the point of a sword sticking out through his throat, edged with his own blood. The shaven-headed warrior poked his head around the warrior's shoulder, giving a grim smile as he pulled his sword out with difficulty.

'That's for the Borderlands, you fucking piece of scum,' he muttered into the man's ear, words dripping with hate.

'Now,' the wild-haired warrior said, wiping his axe against his trousers and grinning ear-to-ear at his ally as he stood over the fallen soldiers, 'we're even.'

'I fear the battle has not yet been won. The flames are spreading,' Tamir said through panted breaths. 'We have little time...'

'Then let's go.' Aleister clapped him on the back and smiled. 'Our work is not yet done.' He turned to the two Borderland warriors, each splattered with an obscene amount of blood as they stood casually together, each wiping down their weapons as though they had completed a normal day's work. 'And what will you both do? We could use men of your... skills.'

They glanced at each other, holding a silent conversation with that one look.

'We've got business to attend to back home,' Sly grunted. 'Gonna slip out in the chaos while we can. This fight ain't ours.'

Aleister sighed, unable to argue with the logic. 'Well, I wish you the best of luck. If your path ever takes you here again, come find me.'

'Sure. Now, what's the best way back to the Torvield from this shithole?'

'Southern Gate is lightly guarded. Take a couple of horses and ride around the city back home or see if you can pay for passage on one of the merchant ships on the coast,' Tamir answered, pointing to the Southern Gate.

Another nod and they were gone, leaving Aleister alone with Tamir.

FANNING THE FLAMES

Cypher ambled through the battle-strewn streets, whistling a merry tune as he scanned the countless number of bodies that lay scattered about the cobbled streets of the Lower City. Both sides had suffered losses. The citizens of the Lower City had been ill-equipped for such warfare, whilst the soldiers of Archania had been ill-prepared for a battle against their own people. Leadership on both sides had failed. As always, it would be the victor who would write the books in such a way that the light would shine upon them, and Cypher always made sure to be on the side of the victor.

'Cypher Zellin!' A voice called through the smoke and flames. Cypher tossed the torch against the nearest wooden building and grinned as the flames took hold, attacking the wood with a startling hunger. 'It's so good to see you again, old friend.'

'Zaif!' Cypher answered, plastering his face with what he thought was a warm and welcoming smile. 'I wish I could say the same to you. Alas, if my memory serves me right, the last time we left, it wasn't on the most pleasant of terms...'

'I guess not,' Zaif replied, scratching his head and rolling his eyes into the corner as he thought back to the moment in Mason's office. 'Still, we had some good times in the dungeons, did we not?'

'Great times,' Cypher answered, nodding. 'All of those screams and cries of torment. It would be a shame to forget those.'

'I'm glad you agree,' Zaif replied, stepping forward, smile unmoving. 'In fact, I've been looking for you, amongst the bloodshed. I have a proposition: one brought to you by Mason D'Argio himself.'

'Is the preacher coming here himself, to fall to his knees and beg for forgiveness for the way he cast me out like a bucket of piss from the window?' Cypher cried, standing steady as the lightning and thunder surrounded the streets of blood.

Zaif's body shook with a single laugh as the corner of his lips twitched. 'Not quite. He's a proud man, but he's not too proud to admit he made a mistake. He wants you back. You can lead the interrogation of the plague doctors and the magi; a free reign.'

'A free reign?' Cypher repeated, nodding his head and rubbing his chin thoughtfully. 'And how do you feel about it all? Is there an apology in that soulless husk of yours?'

'Apology? You trained me. What do you think?' Zaif's eyebrows raised mockingly at the comment.

'Just as I'd thought. Taught you well.' Cypher grinned.

'So, what do you say? Ready to come back into the fold and leave these stinking peasants to the smoke and ruin?'

Cypher rubbed his gloved hands together and breathed slowly out from his nose. He watched the flames continue their journey through the city as panicked men and women ran for their lives across the street, some dragging or carrying coughing children whose screams ripped through the thick air. Through it all, he could hear the steady rhythmic sound of boots walking as one through the streets behind Zaif; the marching of men and women who had been trained by some of the greatest warriors in the land.

'How many have been sent?' he asked his old friend.

'Enough,' Zaif replied sharply. 'They'll cleanse the Lower City now that the Empire's soldiers have arrived to guard the palace and all the nobles in the realm. Always good to have friends in high places.'

'You don't say...' Cypher stuck a finger into his ear and pulled out a lump of wax, wiping it on his robe. The sound was clearer now. Close. He looked past Zaif and smiled at the slow marching of the Archanian troops, spears shining in the light of dancing flames. 'You seem to be making friends all of the time.'

'You've made a fair few yourself...' Zaif lifted his sword and pointed behind Cypher.

Cypher turned his head over his shoulder and grinned as a stream of black-masked warriors stomped up through the street, many with weapons drawn. A few had their faces visible, masks lost in the thrill of battle. 'What can I say? People love me.'

'This deal is a one-time thing, Cypher. It's now or never,' Zaif muttered, cautiously stepping back as The Doctors stopped suddenly behind Cypher.

'Archanians!' a voice called out amongst the soldiers gathered behind Zaif. 'What folly, to fight brother against brother, father against son. We are all of the same Kingdom, are we not?' Sir Dominic's armour was as flamboyant and over-the-top as usual. Even the horse he was mounted on behind the first ten rows of soldiers seemed annoyed with him. The armour had been finely made, as everything was for the knight, yet Cypher wondered what purpose the man had for a white feathered cape and sickeningly large rubies welded onto the fingers of his silver gauntlets. Unnecessary. That word could sum the man up at most times.

A stone the size of a fist flew past the knight's head, barely missing him. A comical groan sounded from the crowd behind Cypher, upset at the miss. Sir Dominic closed his mouth, a look of alarm now on his face as he pulled the reigns on his steed, heading further back amongst the rows of soldiers.

'People of Archania.' General Grey rode forward, elegant and militant where Sir Dominic had been relaxed and comical. 'Understand the seriousness of the situation before you. Many of you have cheered for the downfall of the monarchy, killed within this city, attacked the King's Guard and set fire to the very place you live in. The soldiers alongside me are some of the best fighters in the world, we have thousands more from the Empire in the East who are waiting for a signal in the Upper City. This is a fight you cannot win. Prince Asher, in his infinite mercy,' the general's impressive moustache twitched at the words, 'has allowed a moment of grace. Go back to your homes and put out the fires tearing them apart. Give up your leaders and they will face an open and honest trial. The rest of you will be spared if you do not take up arms against the monarchy again. Fair terms, I believe.'

Scattered muttering broke out behind Cypher as the crowd spread the message from General Grey. Cypher spotted a few of the angry looks change to ones of thoughtful contemplation. They didn't have the balls to go through with it until the end. Anyone could see that.

He looked at Zaif whose eyes flashed, reminding him of the deal waiting on the table. Now or never.

* * *

'Both the leaders of the magi and The Doctors are dead!' Aleister pushed through the crowd to stand between the two forces. 'Your battle has been won, General Grey. Spare these people. The last person you need for a trial stands here dressed in plague doctor garb, a mockery of all that they stand for. He is more plague than doctor, a sickness that must be cured.' He pointed at Cypher, noticing a flicker of annoyance on the bastard's face before the man's eyes turned to face a hulking figure Aleister didn't recognise; a man whose own eyes had never left Cypher.

'Mr. Zellin here was acting on the King's orders. A spy to break the corruption from the inside. Ain't that right Cypher?' the bulky figure asked, eyebrows lowering as he stared at the killer.

'It's true,' Cypher responded, spinning on his heel and backing away from the violent crowd, falling behind his friend. 'I am a true patriot of this great Kingdom, willing to die for my

King,' he said with a sorrowful look and a humble bow. Bastard should've been in the theatre and not on the battleground.

'He's right!' a voice called from the raging crowd. 'The leader's right here! The bastard wanted the King dead!'

Aleister dodged the blow at the last possible moment, feeling the rush of wind whip past him as a blade swung across his neck. He was rusty but his instincts had saved him once again. The wielder of the blade cursed behind his dark mask, stabbing again. This time Aleister was ready. He swatted the strike away with Soulsbane and smashed the hilt of his blade against the black mask, cracking it in one blow. A piece of the mask flew off as the attacker fell to the floor with a grunt.

The crowd surged forward, most eager to get their hands on Cypher, who rushed off to the welcoming arms of the soldiers behind him. General Grey cursed and led his horse to the rear of the soldiers, ready to direct his troops. More makeshift soldiers rushed through the side streets at the sounds of the crowd, swelling the mass of men and women looking for their vengeance.

Aleister stared down at his attacker who glared back with a golden eye, the other obscured by the half-broken mask.

'You don't even know who I am, do you?' the man spat with remarkable fury.

'Have we met?' Aleister asked, searching his memories for any recollection of the pale man at his feet. He had many enemies in the world, was he expected to remember everyone?

'You've met my wife.' Matthias.

The heat Aleister felt had nothing to do with the flames threatening to engulf the city now. 'Matthias... I...' Matthias stood back up, sword aimed at Aleister's throat.

'I don't want your excuses. We were happy before you arrived. I knew she loved you, but you had gone. A distant memory, a shadow to be left in the past. Why did you have to come back and ruin everything?' Matthias screamed, swinging his sword wildly.

Aleister jumped back, dodging the blow but not allowing himself to take the opening offered to him. He hesitated, waging a war in his mind over what needed to be done.

'Calm, Matthias. Ella is her own woman and she chose you as her husband.'

'You think that means anything?' Matthias roared back, missing wildly with his next attack as Aleister danced to the side, knocking into a soldier trading blows with a determined woman carrying a rusty sickle. 'It means nothing compared to the "Great Aleister Soulsbane", the leader of the Red Sons. She's lost to me, and she is all I have!'

'Matthias!' Aleister spun, recognising the voice. Ella ran towards them, horrified as she stared at the drawn blades between them.

'Ella,' he whispered, happy to see her, even amongst the blood and death. Her eyes and mouth widened as though in slow motion just before she reached him. He twisted just in time to parry the strike, glancing it wide. Relief at his escape turned to fear as the sound of steel meeting flesh found his ears. The world grew silent. He shut his eyes, praying to the Four that it would not be what he thought.

Matthias fell to the floor, rocking back and forth, weapon no longer in his hand, even though Aleister had not heard it clatter to the ground. He opened his eyes and looked down at the scarlet robed body at his feet, sword impaled through her chest. Those eyes, those beautiful love-affirming eyes no longer had their sparkle, their shine. They were lifeless and dull.

She was dead.

Rough hands grabbed him and pulled him away. His eyes stayed on her, staring at the love of his life. He wanted to fight back against the arms, to rush over to her and plant a kiss on her forehead and wake her up but he didn't have the energy. There was nothing he could do. He let the arms bundle him down a side street and away from the flames and battle.

'You can't help her now, Aleister,' came the booming voice of reason.

'He's right. We need to leave the city.' Another one

added gently. 'I'm sorry brother. I'm so sorry.'

Aleister felt hot tears burning his eyes. 'She's gone...'

A KNIFE IN THE BACK

Arden could sleep no longer. He blew a long breath out of his mouth and prised his eyes open. Not even a slither of light found its way into the room. It was not yet time to get up, but he knew that trying to force himself back to sleep would be a waste of time; a battle as one-sided as if he were to challenge Sly to a Battle of Bones. Pointless.

He stretched his arms into the darkness and fought against a strong yawn that rolled up from his throat. He wiped away the wetness from his eyes and stood up from his makeshift bed. His thoughts turned to Kiras and the situation he had left her in; the situation he had caused when he had let go. Socket had told him that it wouldn't be a problem: she fought as well as any other warrior in the Borderlands. Also, she had Herick and their tribe close by. She'd be fine. And yet, he couldn't help but feel as though he had left a sheep alone in a den of wolves. No word had got back to them from the Borderlands since the battle with the Barbarians. Anything could have happened, and it wasn't like Kiras to stay silent.

But Arden had his own issues. Korvas and Socket had told him about the power he was capable of wielding; a power thought lost. He was the first Guardian to be found in a generation. A nomadic warrior who had never fit in now had the ability to knock down thousands of warriors at once without even willing it. Someone who most warriors in the Borderlands just laughed at or, even worse, simply didn't even bother to pay any attention to. He'd never known his father and his mother had barely spoken of him. She had done her best to raise him; moving from village to village until she had died alone and cold. He was nothing special, like a raindrop falling into the ocean. If there had ever been Gods, then surely they were playing some sick, twisted joke on him.

He sighed and walked to the other side of his room where he knew his clothes were sat folded on the floor. He changed at his own pace and walked out of the room, eyes adjusting to the darkness.

'Can't sleep?'

Arden jumped nearly out of his boots, startled by the unexpected voice in the dark tunnel.

'Socket. Please, don't do that again,' he said as his heart struggled to regain its regular beat. 'How long have you been there?'

'Call it good timing. Let's go for a walk kid,' Socket said, scratching at the old scar by his eye.

'Korvus coming?'

'Nah. Probably asleep. Hood up, it's cold.'

Arden lifted the hood up from his shoulders and over his head; if Socket said it was cold then it was going to be fucking cold. A slight feeling of numbness attacked the tips of his toes reminding him to be thankful that he had thought to put on an extra pair of socks today, losing a toe was never fun. 'Korvus still angry with me?'

'He's pissed off,' Socket admitted, not shying away from the harsh truth. 'Welcomed you into his home and offered you help. You decided to release a prisoner. One who could cause problems.'

'One who was going to be killed,' Arden reminded him.

'Is it your role to decide who is killed and who lives?' Socket asked.

'No. But is it his?'

Socket only shrugged his shoulders. 'Maybe. Maybe not. Still don't change the fact he's pissed off...'

'Shall I grab my bow?' he asked as he followed Socket down the tunnel. What was the point in arguing? He felt like he had done the right thing. Too many sleepless nights hearing the thud of Ovar's head hitting the floor. He didn't want to add to that. Yet, he knew Korvus had a right to be annoyed with him. He'd take it, shoulder the anger, the blame. He deserved it. Now, he had to prove himself big enough to handle that weight.

'Nah. You won't need it. Won't be out long anyway,' Socket answered pulling his own hood up.

'So, you and Korvas – there's a story there,' Arden pried, using the time to find out the link between the two old men. They obviously went way back; two old warriors trying to keep up with the changing world. However, they didn't like to give too much away.

Socket turned to look at him with his good eye, but he kept on walking. 'Aye. There's a story.'

'Care to share?' Arden chanced, aware that pushing his luck too far would have consequences. Screw it. What was the worst that could happen?

'We have a similar goal. He can be as ruthless as anyone in these lands, but his intentions are good; that's more than I can say about most people,' Socket grunted. 'He uses his gift sparingly, knowing the damage it can cause. He helped me when I hit rock bottom and there's no one that I trust more than him.'

'Not even Reaver? You were close back in the day. That's how it sounds in the songs,' Arden replied. He'd grown up loving the tales of the two warriors who had brought true power to the Borderlands and united the tribes.

'I wouldn't trust everything you hear kid. Songs about the dead are rarely written to store history. They entertain. They inspire. They make money. That's it,' Socket spat bitterly. 'Bards earn their keep by pouring gravy on shit and calling it chicken.'

Arden lowered his head, brows narrowed. Socket didn't seem to be in a mood to expand any further on what he'd said, and Arden respected that. He knew his place.

Finally, they reached the end of the tunnel and walked out together into the open night. A picturesque, snowy mountain range loomed large and comforting to the West whilst a dense, dark forest covered the world to the East, wrapping itself like a shield around them. Arden's eyes didn't stay on the mountains or the forest for long; instead, they stared up into the display being cast on the night sky above him.

Green and purple lights embraced in the clear night sky and danced amongst the stars. A great green sheet of light seemed to ripple in the sky like a flag caught in a storm. Arden felt his jaw drop at the marvel before him. He had heard of the Lights of The Four but had always assumed the tales he had heard had been exaggerated, blown up out of proportion; drunken travellers with nothing else of interest to do but tell tall tales in the remote villages they passed by.

In this moment, he had to admit, the stories had undersold the spectacle he witnessed before him.

'Is this what you wanted me here for?' he asked.

Socket breathed in and out through his nose. 'I thought you needed to see it, while you're here.' A hint of sadness crept into his voice; soft but there, nonetheless.

'You've seen it before.'

Another nod.

The pair of them stood in silence, content with the show of nature they had to enjoy.

'I stabbed him in the back, you know,' Socket broke the silence.

'Who?'

'Reaver. He was a good man, a good friend. Always looked for the best in people.' Socket almost whispered it into the wind. A confession to the wilderness.

'Why?'

'He'd made a deal with Archania and its King. A Prince had been born. A Prince who would grow up to be the first guardian in a generation. Reaver and the King made a deal to get the Prince out of there and into the Borderlands, away from any danger,' Socket continued to stare up at the display above them.

Thoughts raced through Arden's head faster than lightning, 'Why did they do that? Don't they have guards who could protect me and keep me safe while I was growing up?'

'You're a Prince,' Socket stated simply. 'Things aren't so simple. Looking after a Prince is tough enough. Throw in the fact that you're a Guardian and the whole thing becomes bigger, becomes too much to handle. The sights of the world would be locked on you if anyone had found out; to keep you out and steer a Kingdom out of its darkest period in generations would be a task too much for any to handle. Your father made the correct choice, as difficult as it may be for you to handle.'

Arden stumbled back from Socket, boots crunching against the snow. Gods and their fucking jokes! A Prince and a Guardian. Twice the pressure. Twice the opportunity to fuck things up.

'It's true,' Arden turned to see Korvus walking towards them, grey cloak billowing in the wind. Emerald green eyes fixed upon him, boring into his soul. Arden could almost feel a heat emanating from them. He wanted to run away, to hide. Shield himself from the danger. But he didn't. He was frozen. Unable to move. 'You were too big of a risk in a kingdom like that. Best to be out in the wilderness, away from danger.'

'You think that was for the best? Ripping me away from my family? Making me grow up in the Borderlands? Seriously?' Arden snapped, feeling the anger rise inside him. 'Every day out there was a danger. I've seen people slain for looking at the wrong person at the wrong time. What is safe about that?'

'Reaver felt guilty. He even changed his mind at one point. Around the time a powerful preacher took hold of the United Cities of Archania. We couldn't allow it. We couldn't let Reaver's guilt destroy what we had worked for. Socket stabbed him in the back. It was for the best.' He said it easily, no hint of pain in his voice.

'The best for who?'

'This world and everyone on it,' Korvus said with steel

in his voice, commanding attention. 'You're a Guardian: things like family and monarchies pale in comparison to the work of a Guardian, now more than ever.'

Blood pumped around Arden's head, throbbing like mad. His eyes found Socket, pleading with him to say it was all a joke; a prank gone wrong. The old man just stood there, unable to even look him in the eyes, instead gazing up into the dancing lights.

'I trusted you. You said I could be a part of something, that I wouldn't have to be alone anymore. You knew all of this and you didn't even tell me. I have a family. A father and a brother. All that's happened since we left the Borderlands has been a pile of shit. I've been beaten up and stabbed. I shouldn't be alive. So much for keeping me safe.' He turned his back on the one-eyed warrior and stormed off towards the mountains. His head thumped with the pain of a thousand questions and ideas racing around inside him, crashing into each other like enemies in battle. 'I'm going back. I need to know if Kiras is safe. We left her there on her own, for *this*.'

'You can't leave, Arden.' He felt Korvus' hand press against his left shoulder. Arden lowered his hand to the dagger hanging at his hip, ready for any reason to explode, to have any outlet for the whirlwind inside of him.

'Are you going to stop me, Korvus?' he asked, tightly gripping the small, worn hilt of the dagger.

He looked into the mage's eyes and felt his shoulders drop as he stared into two, green pools of sadness and regret.

'No, Arden. I won't stop you.'

'Then get your hand—'

Arden felt a punching thud in his back, making him pause. He tried to breathe but he felt a wall rise within his chest, blocking any air from making its way through. A sudden, cold wind swept through his body as Korvus dropped a hand from his shoulder, shaking his head.

'Many people have been searching for you, wanting to use your gift for their own gains. A Guardian can choose to be a healer or a destroyer – choose the path of light, or of darkness.

It is a decision every single Guardian has made since the beginning of time. It's a decision that can only be made in one place: The Sky Plane. And there's only one way to get there...'

Arden circled slowly on the spot, still struggling with his breathing.

Socket just stared straight at him, bloodied dagger glinting red in the beautiful light from the dazzling night sky. He brushed the dagger against his cloak on either side and held it up in the light, searching for something with his good eye. Arden's vision blurred with tears as he looked back towards the old archer, pleading for answers.

'Why?' he choked out at last as he felt something warm dripping down his back. He looked at the dagger and then back at the man he had called a friend, unable to put the two together.

'Peace at all costs, kid. Most people thought it too dangerous to let you walk around, putting other lives at risk. You're a good lad, but in another world, we would have thrown you off the rocks when we were given you by your daddy. I like you. Shame it has to be like this, but it does. Always been this way.' Socket took a step forward and stabbed him as easily as cutting a piece of chicken. This time, it felt more than a punch; Arden could feel a jolt of pain as though being struck by lightning beneath his ribs. He fell to his knees and then dropped onto his side, unable to move. It felt colder than before, but he wasn't shivering; no need for that now. He kept his eyes open but couldn't turn his head away from the mountains that seemed to pierce the starry blanket of dancing lights above. 'I know you don't understand right now but you will. I've seen it.'

No pain now. Everything just felt... difficult. And confusing. His body knew how to do things, like breathe properly, but for some reason it just wasn't working out the way it should. Breathe. Breathe for fuck's sake. He felt annoyed. Frustrated. This wasn't his time to go. He had a family: an actual family. Even the Gods couldn't be so cruel.

A pool of blood snaked its way from his stomach across the white snow, painting a picture of his last moments in this hideous and beautiful world. Maybe it was the end. Maybe this is what it was like for everyone. Thinking that there was so much more to live for; questioning whether this was the right time for things to end. The fact is you don't choose your time to head to the black gate. You get chosen. He tried to laugh but his body fought against his command, preserving his energy. The fucking Gods. Biggest jokes of them all. He closed his eyes and forced another breath into his struggling lungs.

'Same day as his father. There is a certain poetry to it – like in the old plays. Tragic but beautiful.'

'The King's dead?' Socket asked.

'Along with all of his men. They made it as far the new temple – a few well-chosen men from the Empire were there to greet him and give them all a warm welcome,' Korvus answered clinically. 'The old fool was on his way out anyway. Wanted to see the boy, but such sentimentality can get in the way of the test.'

'How do you know this?' Socket asked, ignoring his dying friend in the pool of blood.

'I have my ways. This needs to be quick: The Borderlands...'

'What about them?' Socket growled. 'You said it would be fine.'

'You've seen what happened Socket, you don't need to ask questions.'

'I gave you my damned eyeball, if this doesn't work out...'

'Trust me, as you once did.'

Arden's eyes closed. He heard the crunch of snow beside him and felt breath hitting his face. 'I've given so much blood for this cause; it needs to work. He's a good kid.'

'That's why it will work,' Korvus answered, voice trailing away as his footsteps crunched against the snow. 'He has a week to make it back. After that, we must burn the body.'

Arden forced his eyes open. Dancing lights weaved around a dark shadow looming above him. The shadow knelt next to him, its silhouette almost blocking out the stars in the sky.

'You got this, kid. I know you do. Keep fighting.'

One of the stars danced its way down, falling next to the silhouette. Arden tried to catch it, but he didn't have the energy, only feeling his fingers twitch at the effort. The star faded along with all the others.

He kept his eyes open, staring up into the darkness.

FALLOUT

Asher sat on the marble throne: one knee raised up as his leg drooped lazily over the armrest, drumming his fingers on his forehead. Cypher knew what the Prince was thinking. He didn't need this tedious shit to be a part of his life. He was King now. He was in charge. If anyone disagreed with him... well, he had an unending supply of pikes that would so love to welcome their heads. People feared him. His people feared him. With fear, came power, and he wanted to be the most powerful King in all the history of these lands. 'How good it is to see you back in the Upper City, Cypher Zellin. All that business with The Doctors really was quite alarming.'

Cypher looked up past the stone steps at the young man on the throne and, not for the first time, he wondered why the fuck such assholes were born into powerful positions. If ever there was proof that the Gods didn't exist, it was the young bastard sitting all smug up there, staring down at the councillors in the room.

'Your Grace. Every now and then, peasants will believe they deserve more in life. Envy rears its ugly head.' Cypher sliced an empty hand through the air in front of him. 'Slice it off swiftly and without mercy; they need to remember this for the next generation to ensure it doesn't happen again.'

Asher bounced up with excitement, extravagant white fur cape waving around with the movement. 'Exactly!' he roared through gritted teeth, banging his fist against the arm of the seat and pointing at Cypher whilst looking over at Mason. The preacher looked almost bored as he sat next to the Prince, leaning against his hand as his elbow sat on the arm of his own elegant seat. 'This is what I was saying, Mason. A swift shot to the head. That's what was needed. We have the might of the Archanian army, the assistance of your sister in the East; we should have crushed them all! Now they have been able to cower in the Lower City, free and most likely laughing at me.'

'They are not free, Your Grace. Your men have created a perimeter around the Lower City. No one is getting in or out unless we decide so,' Mason answered.

'You have them right where you want them, my Prince. You can do as you wish, one of the perks of running a Kingdom,' Cypher added, scratching at an itch on the back of his neck.

'I do. I'm in control,' Asher muttered to himself, as though trying to convince himself. 'The rumours I've heard are disturbing,' he continued, louder this time, so that everyone could hear him. 'Some claim that Lord Tamir was actually the leader of The Doctors; his absence of late causes me to feel that there may be grains of truth to it. Did you come across Lord Tamir during your time with the peasants?'

'Perhaps,' Cypher rubbed at his chin. 'It was the fashion for everyone to wear those ghastly masks. Could have been speaking to my dear mum and I wouldn't've had a clue! Bastard things. Struggled to see anything properly.'

Asher's piercing gaze lingered on him for too long, his tongue pressing hard against his cheek. 'Of course. Masks... Yes. Well, it's good to have you back, as I said before. A man of your many talents is always needed in a Kingdom like ours. Zaif here will show you to your new quarters.'

'New quarters?' Cypher raised an eyebrow and turned to Zaif. The bastard just stood there smugly, staring up at the Prince. 'What's wrong with the old ones?'

'We're having a few friends move in from the East – ease the transition into the Empire. Your old home has been assigned to new guests. Not to worry, you'll find your new home just as welcoming.' Asher sat back in his seat and grinned wide, waving casually at the two guards waiting silently by the door. 'We're finished here.'

Cypher's smile dropped as he looked between the Prince and Mason, each grinning widely as the guards opened the door. Zaif slapped a hand on his shoulder and turned.

'Let's go, Cypher. The ship's docked and ready to leave.'

'The ship?' Cypher repeated, swallowing hard and staring around the room at the various looks of victory on the faces staring back. 'Why do we need a ship?'

'Seems a few folk in Norland aren't too happy with their lot. Time to go and put them down; teach them a thing or two about keeping their ungrateful mouths shut. Prince Asher thought you'd be the best man for the job.'

How fucking delightful...

'That's the last of the fires out. If those morons stop starting new ones, that should be it for now. No idea how we'll rebuild, but we will.'

Kane looked around the still smoking streets with a grim resilience. Tamir was right. They had no idea how they would do it, but it had to be done. 'Soldiers still circling the outer streets?'

'They've actually tightened the perimeter. A couple of scuffles broke out in the morning: a few disgruntled citizens too hungry to think rationally,' Tamir answered.

'What happened to them?'

'Dragged off to the Upper City. The Four only know what happened to them, though I think I could guess,' Tamir said bleakly. 'These people need supplies before another riot kicks off.'

'Any sign of Aleister and the others?' Kane asked, not expecting a positive answer.

Tamir shook his head and pursed his lips, as usual. 'Not since Ella... Ariel and Bathos would have taken him out of the city. It was the only chance they had.'

'And Matthias?' Kane asked bitterly, fighting back the

images of her young friend's lifeless body staring soullessly up at the night sky. 'Have you seen him?'

'Not yet, Kat. He'll turn up. They all will. Just need time. Such a tragedy...'

At first, the bodies had been buried in the graveyard just inside the city walls. Soldiers stood silently, watching like statues. Kane had found a spot for Ella under an oak tree, next to a bench where people would be able to sit and talk to her. Kane had loved to talk next to her husband's grave in the early years, finding time to keep him up-to-date with her life. Braego even joined her on what became an annual trip and conversation, offering her support when she most needed it.

Before too long, room was running out in the graveyard. Mass cremation was the only viable step to move forward. The smell of burnt flesh choked the air for miles, a reminder to the citizens of what they had lost during the ill-fated rebellion. Many citizens had resorted to roaming the streets with ripped pieces of cloth wrapped around the lower part of their face to lessen the effects of the hideous smell. Those fortunate enough to have houses that still stood ensured that the doors were closed tight to prevent the putrid smell being carried by the wind.

Kane had said the words of The Four over Ella's body, a few discreet magi had appeared, adding their own words and shedding tears as the soil fell onto her body. Ella's mother would most likely be unaware of her daughter's death; unable to move from her Upper City residence. She'd be worried sick, doing everything she could to find her daughter. As soon as the perimeter was lifted, Kane vowed to head straight to Ella's mother and tell her everything. It was the least she could do.

She smiled at a young girl racing past, following by five other children. Even with the horrors around them, they were able to maintain their innocence and continue as normal. Shame that the same couldn't be said of the adults. They were taking it in different ways. Some sat horror-struck on the streets, avoiding any eye contact as they rocked back and forth, replaying the battle over and over again. Others were fighting over the smallest of details, brawling over their place in the line by the well. Still, there were folk sitting in the square, tears falling silently as they stared up at the podium where they had witnessed what they thought would be the start of their new lives. In such a short space of time, their dreams had been destroyed, left in the smoke and ash of their city.

'Where does this end, Tamir?' Kane sighed as though the weariness of the past few weeks was rising up and forcing its way out of her, wanting the whole world to see it out in the open. 'What will happen to all of these people?'

'I wish I could tell you. Mikkael would have offered mercy, given support to rebuild the Lower City and make it better than ever. Now, with Mikkael away and unlikely to return, Asher will be in charge. I could tell you my thoughts on how that fool will handle the situation, but I'd hate to darken your mood.'

It was as she had feared. 'Asher will slice his own arm off just to prove that he is in charge and must be feared. These people will suffer more if we don't do something.'

'What do you suggest?'

'I don't know.' Tamir shook his head, snapping a twig in his hands and discarding the pieces on the ground beside what looked like a broken plague doctor mask. 'Asher and Mason will rule this Kingdom together. They must be dealt with but alone, we don't have the power. I truly believed the magi would tip the scales in our favour; all they did was burn everything in their path.'

'Many died for the cause, Tamir, remember that. Not all of them set flames to this city,' Kane warned, uncomfortable with the councillor's words.

'You're right. It just didn't work out how I had planned.'

'Things rarely do lately. That's life, sadly. The Gods don't seem to be on our side anymore.'

'Were they ever?' Tamir scoffed. 'Maybe it's time to stop asking the Gods for favours; stop asking Archania for favours; stop asking anyone else for favours. From now on, if I need something done, I'll do it myself.'

The sound of a trumpet interrupted their conversation. Two long rows of elegantly-dressed soldiers marched into the square, flanking a great horse. Sat on the horse was an extremely pompous-looking young man, chin raised so high that he may have been searching for the first signs of rain. His tabard was a sky blue, emblazoned with a singular gold crown. A herald of the King.

The crowd's interest was piqued, rarely would a herald make their way down to the Lower City. Their curious faces followed the pompous Kingsman as he reigned his horse back, pulling out an oversized piece of parchment and clearing his throat rather dramatically.

'Citizens of Archania,' he began in a clear but unexpectedly high-pitched voice, 'it is with great sadness that I bear the news of the death of King Mikkael, second of his name, King of the United Cities of Archania, ruler of the Northern Kingdoms.' Urgent mutterings broke out through the crowd at these words, shocked glances shared between the already troubled citizens. Tamir stared at the herald, waiting for him to continue, to finish the unwanted news. 'King Mikkael served this Kingdom with honour and respect, his son Prince Asher, first of his name, will strive to continue his legacy whilst building a new, promising future for *all* of its citizens. King Asher wants his people to know that he will be worthy of this exalted position and that he will prove that by demonstrating his mercy.

'King Asher decrees that if the citizens of the Lower City hand over any leaders of the rebellion that are left by sundown this evening, he will grant a royal pardon to all others involved in the devastating acts that were witnessed over the past couple of days. Fail to comply and he will be forced to send his army further into the city... He invites all Archanians to join him in leading the Kingdom into a future that is full of light! There will be the usual three days of mourning for the King with all formal events and activities suspended within the Kingdom. The three days will only begin once this matter has been settled. Think about the King and his family. Think about what is best for this Kingdom.' The herald rolled up the parchment and clicked his heels against the horse, spinning away, followed by the other soldiers.

'What are we going to do, Tamir? This city can't handle any more suffering,' Kane lamented, looking around at the fearful faces in the square. A few were looking over at Tamir – grim and angry. Their thoughts were painted clearly on their faces. There was no need for words.

'There is only one thing that I can do...' Tamir muttered, a crease forming between his eyebrows. 'Meet me at the perimeter by the Upper City at sundown. You'll see.'

The sun fell below the horizon but the mood in the city didn't change. Day or night, the Lower City was in pain, grieving for its loss. Children fell asleep in makeshift beds around the streets, cosied up under any shelter they could find, lest the storm returned. For now, the city was dry. The smoke and reek of burning and death still permeated the air as the few citizens with any energy left ambled through the streets with their mouths and noses covered.

Kane waited patiently, leaning against a closed butcher's shop and keeping an eye on the row of soldiers blocking the path to the Upper City. They stood motionless in their silver armour and white cloaks, proudly displaying the White Sun of the Empire on their breastplate. Tall, deadly spears aimed up at the sky and their eyes peered out through the gaps in their helmets, looking for any sign of disruption. No chance of that. Not now. These people had spent their remaining coin on the last shot. They had nothing left to give. Now they were just waiting for a decision to be made for them; to be put out of their misery. The energy and will for change had gone out with the flames, leaving not even the slightest hint of an ember left to build from.

Moments later, Kane spotted Tamir walking through the streets, ignoring the pointed glances that were aimed at him from the exhausted men and women he passed. They muttered to one another as he made his way to the rows of soldiers in silence, head bowed, taking once slow step at a time.

Kane lurched towards him, puzzled. Tamir spotted her and turned on his path. By the time he reached her with a small, sad smile on his lips, there was a crowd watching him with bated breath.

'It has been an absolute pleasure working beside you and getting to know you.' His dark eyes brimmed with tears that didn't quite fall past the purple bags sat beneath them. 'I've cut a deal: friends in high places... the council have agreed to offer you a pardon for your crimes against the Kingdom on two conditions: I give myself up for the trial, and you are exiled, never to return to the Kingdom. You will have three days before you are forced to go.'

'Lord Tamir...' Kane whispered, squeezing his shoulder gently, ignoring the hordes of onlookers. 'You didn't have to do that.'

'It was the only way, Kat. I have loved this Kingdom, my home. It offered my grandparents refuge during the most difficult time in their lives. I hope that one day it will find its way back, though I doubt it will be soon. Wherever your life takes you, know that you have my gratitude and I have prayed to The Four that you will be safe and happy.' They embraced, both understanding the gravity of Tamir's decision. 'Will you walk with me? One final time.'

'It would be an honour, Lord Tamir.'

Kane walked beside him as they headed to the line of soldiers leading to the Upper City. Both of them held their heads high, defiant and proud, true citizens of Archania. The line of soldiers broke in the middle, revealing a large man dressed in military clothing and a familiar outrageous moustache perched upon his upper lip. General Grey's eyes glistened with tears as they found Tamir's. The General stepped forward, away from the line of soldiers and towards the pair of them, meeting them in the middle.

For a moment, all three of them stood there in silence, still as statues.

General Grey swallowed hard, eyes never moving from Tamir who looked up into the broad man's face with resignation.

'I warned you not to go through with this,' Grey snapped, keeping his voice down so only they could hear him. 'I told you that there was only one way for this to end...'

'You did. But if I had stood there and done nothing, I wouldn't have been able to live with myself,' Tamir answered sadly. 'I don't regret it, Dustin, I don't regret any of it. We stood up against prejudice and hatred. We failed, but we have opened the eyes of many. The embers of a revolution still burn softly, ready to ignite one day and improve this world for the better.'

'Why couldn't you have just stayed in the Upper City?' Grey said bitterly, pinching the bridge of his nose with a finger and thumb as he closed his eyes.

'That's not the man you fell in love with,' Tamir answered, rested a hand on a chest heavily decorated with medals of honour and valour. Kane's jaw dropped as her brain struggled to process the words she heard. Tamir chuckled lightly as he looked at her. 'You're not the only one with secrets, Katerina Kane.'

Grey opened his bloodshot eyes and stared at Tamir as though trying to etch his face into his memory for life. He raised his voice now, so that all could hear. 'Lord Everard Tamir, it is my duty to escort you to the Hall of Justice. You have been arrested on suspicion of treason against the monarchy of the United Cities of Archania.' He swallowed hard once more and lowered his voice. 'Why did you ask for *me* to do this?'

'I wouldn't have it any other way, old friend.' Tamir started walking to the Upper City, 'One last chance to enjoy the glorious sunshine and the fresh air alongside you. Kane will ensure neither of us change our mind and attempt a daring escape.'

Kane and Grey turned to each other, sharing their grief and sadness with a slight nod, each aware of their duty. One to a Kingdom, another to a friend.

The soldiers broke to allow the trio through, like the sun shining through the breaking clouds. Behind her, Kane heard a soft clapping sound. Slowly, the sound increased in both speed and volume. Curious, the three of them turned; Tamir standing either side of his friends as the citizens of the Lower City stood together as one, their applause growing to a crescendo with a smattering of whistles and cheering to go with the fists raised high in the air.

One of the citizens broke from the crowd, bruised face grim and determined as he stared at the three of them. He raised his fist and shouted as loud as he could so all could hear him. 'For Archania!'

'For Archania!'

'For Archania!' The crowd repeated the words, chanting and raising their fists in defiance, tears rolling with ease down many of their bruised and battered faces; people not just from the city, but from all the corners of the world.

Kane nodded and glanced over at Lord Tamir. The councillor smiled and slowly raised a fist, tears of his own now streaming freely down his face. 'For Archania!' He echoed to great cheers. He turned, striding off to the Upper City with his head held high and a spring in his step. Grey followed, his hand brushing against Tamir's for one brief moment as his eyes dropped to the ground to hide his own tears.

Kane took one last look at the united crowd and whispered under her breath. 'For Archania.'

GREETING CHAOS

Arden propped himself up onto his elbows and opened his eyes. Bad idea. He closed them again, shielding them from the harsh, stinging light. He peeled one eye open, peering through his lid at the white light that surrounded him. He cautiously opened his other eye and blinked a few times as his eyes adjusted. The light faded slightly, allowing him a chance to look out at where he was.

Snow reached out, blanketed the entire landscape around him. There were no hills, mountains or rivers. He spun around, staring at the deserted landscape. Looking down at himself, he saw that he was wearing a black shirt and trousers but nothing on his feet. The snow wasn't cold, or at least, he couldn't feel its touch against his bare feet. He should have found it odd, but everything just felt so... right. He picked a foot up and pushed it back against the white snow. No footprint. He turned his neck, taking in everything. Or nothing. He couldn't work out which it was. He shut his eyes, trying to remember what had happened to him.

He scrunched up his nose and closed his eyes ever tighter, as though, through sheer force of will, he would be able to remember. He opened them back up and jumped back, shocked.

Lying on the snow beneath him was a still body, blood still pouring from a hidden wound. The blood seeped into the snow around him, destroying the purity and turning the snow into a comical pinky hue. The body's hair was messy, falling over the pale face and covering one of the once golden eyes that had now turned black and emptied of all life. A light shadow brushed against his jaw and around his mouth and neck: a mockery of a beard. Arden tried to call for help but he knew it was too late. There was no helping the body on the ground. He kept glancing back at the face, struggling to remind him of who this person was, but each time he was close, the spark of thought flared out and died, as though getting close was the problem.

He swore and turned away from the corpse. He began to walk and suddenly, everything shifted.

Arden felt his body jerk, as though a great wind blew against him. He raised a hand, blocking the force from hitting his face as he turned to the side. A moment later, it stopped. He lurched forward and fell to his knees. His breathing was ragged and uneven like when he had run through the forests too far and too fast as a young boy, laughing and screaming as his mother chased him.

His hands fell to the ground and he stared at what was beneath him. He squinted, looking down at the battleground. Some clarity returned to his thoughts, like a fog clearing away and bringing back some sense and vision. The Mournful Giant knelt below him, watching over the snowy ground littered with the lifeless bodies of both Borderland and Barbarian warriors, many of whom were there due to Arden's lack of control.

He remembered the battle – the pain, the thunder, the red mist.

He sighed with regret as his body was dragged closer, giving him a closer sight of the battleground. There was no storm here, not now. No rainfall, no thunder. Arden wondered how many he had killed. Did they have loved ones who had waited anxiously for their return? Loved ones whose world would be destroyed upon hearing the news that they would never return home again.

All because of him.

He wept, choking with emotion as he stared out at the makeshift graveyard and the Mournful Giant as dark shadows crept towards the corpses. Arden wanted to cry out for some assistance but there was no sound. The shadows sat above the bodies, hovering over them like dark flames. Arden leaned forward, eyes wide and staring as the shadows rose, lifting the corpses to their feet.

The world shifted again, slamming Arden onto his back. When the world was still again, he sat back up.

This time he was inside a long room with wooden beams and a roaring fire. Hundreds of Borderland warriors filled the room, eyes all facing their leader looking down at them.

Arden shook his head and tried to force his way to the front, knowing what was about to happen, remembering the horrific scene that had played through his mind time and time again. Each time he tried to move; his body rocked him back. He tried to close his eyes but no matter what, he could still see Ovar kneeling beside Saul, giving that sad, knowing stare; the one that had been burned into Arden's mind ever since. Calling out did nothing at all: there was no sound. It was like staring at a moving painting as Saul lapped up the adoration from his audience. Arden felt the hot tears running down his face and looked away.

Sly and Kiras were watching, each with a look of grim resignation. Sly ran a hand through his wild hair and looked away, muttering a silent curse to which Kiras nodded her shaved head. The others in the room snarled or spat as they ate up every single word snaking its way from Saul's mouth. The leader of the Borderlands drew his sword and Arden spun away, staring at the dancing flames in the centre of the room.

Once again, he couldn't escape the thud as Ovar's head hit the ground.

Arden fell to the floor, slamming his fists against the floorboards time and time again, wanting to feel anything else but this pain.

Nothing. He felt nothing else.

He breathed slowly and stood back up. The room was the same, but time had passed. The flames had diminished, only a few flickers danced on top of the embers.

Arden looked around him and felt his brow drop in confusion. The faces were different from Ovar's execution. Barbarians were littered amongst the group, smirking and sharing stories whilst swigging from their horns or jugs. More women were in the room than Arden had previously seen. Dangerous, violent-looking women with various weapons slung across their backs or hanging on belts tied around their waist.

Herick's tribe.

Panicked, he moved through the crowd, looking for any sign of Kiras, praying that he would find her. This made no sense. Barbarians standing next to warriors from Herick's tribe, smiling and somehow not breaking into bloody fights was unheard of. It was some kind of dream; a nightmare that he had to wake up from. He searched for his friend, gliding through the crowd without drawing the gaze of any of the warriors he pushed out of his way.

Reaching the front of the room, he froze; mouth wide open, eyes focused on the confusing scene before him.

The throne was exactly the same as when Saul had sat on it. The main difference was, there was another warrior perched smugly on it now; slender frame, pale skin, scratching at the white scar beneath his lip, grinning wildly at the men and women before him.

Herick the Late.

An onyx crown encased with pure white pearl stones sat on his shaven head – the King of the Borderlands. To his right sat a familiar, skinny frame and haggard face, happier than when Arden had last seen him. Rejgar leant casually against the arm on his chair and clicked his fingers. On cue, a Barbarian passed him a jug overflowing with ale. Some of the liquid dripped onto his clean, navy shirt but he only laughed, ignoring the mishap and throwing his head back, downing much of the drink to a multitude of raised fists in the room.

On Herick's left sat another Barbarian; he was older but had the same eyes as Rejgar, a few more wrinkles lined his face and a long, thin red scar ran across his jaw, breaking up the blonde beard that grew wildly but with a smattering of white streaks. Arden had never seen him before, but he knew who this must be – Rejgar's father, the leader of the Barbarians, Ragnar.

Arden raced through the crowd, his head a whirlwind of dark thoughts. He needed to get as far away from the three of them as possible. He needed to find Kiras. He'd left her alone with these bastards. If she was hurt, it would be another weight for him to bear.

The door to the frozen Borderlands swung open and Arden almost fell over in his haste to leave the room. There were no houses, no other buildings where there should be flanking the Great Hall. It was a wasteland, deserted and empty. Empty but for two pikes sticking up out from the snow.

Arden felt a familiar, acidic taste build inside his mouth as he looked at the first pike. The point of the pike speared through a boulder-like head, blonde hair flowing down, stained with dry blood. Even without his body, Saul looked fearsome.

It was the other pike that made Arden retch. He struggled for breath, bent over and trying his best to look away from the eyes of head in front of him, eyes that were so like his own but for the lack of gold. The slight bend in the nose, the wavy hair – silver – little pieces that Arden recognised from his own reflection. There was only one person this could be. His father – the King of Archania. Dried blood had pooled at the edges of his mouth and there was swelling above his right eye. His death had been painful. He'd died on his way to meet his son, to meet Arden. Another death on his conscience.

'It hurts, doesn't it?' Arden twisted his head. The Great Hall was no longer there. In its place stood a being, neither man nor woman. At least eight-feet tall and dressed all in midnight black, they towered over Arden. Long flowing robes fell to the ground and trailed off into the distance, further than Arden could see. The cloak had no sleeves. He could see long, pale, skeletal arms patterned with cuts criss-crossing over one another from shoulder to wrist. Long, straight, thick hair framed either side of a moon-white face, falling low down to their waist. It was their eyes that Arden struggled with. Both were black, sprinkled with white like the stars. Under their eyes flowed a black stream like tears dripping down to the corner of their purple lips. 'Dying doesn't. Well, perhaps it does but only for a moment. It is the death of loved ones that truly causes pain.' Their voice was soft and echoed as though two people were speaking at once.

'I just want to know what happened to my friend. She helped me when I needed her and then I left her here all alone,' Arden croaked, finally able to hear his own voice.

'Being alone; being forgotten. That can be worse than the void of death.'

Arden squinted, puzzled. 'Who are you?'

'You know me. We've spoken from time to time, though you may not have known it was me.' They leant down, bringing their face to within an inch of Arden's. He could faintly smell ash and smoke. 'You want to save your friend. You want revenge on those who you trusted and betrayed you.' Arden stayed silent, unable to deny anything being said. He felt pissed off, enraged. Socket and Korvus had said they were helping him and all he'd got was a dagger in the back, and in the front for that matter. Rejgar sat comfortably alongside his dad in the Borderlands whilst Arden's father had his head on a pike before they even met. Through it all, he had left Kiras alone and defenceless. Yeah, he wanted revenge. 'I can give it to you. Everything.' They slid forward, twisting their head to the side and smiled, displaying a wide array of sharpened teeth, like daggers. 'I can give you exactly what you want...'

'And what might that be?'

'Chaos...Pure, unbridled *chaos*.' The being whispered with glee.

'And what do you want in return?' Arden asked, mind already made up.

'Just a dash of blood. Nothing more.'

Arden peered down at his hand and realised that he

was holding a dagger. A simple blade, iron hilt with dark leather wrapped crudely around it. He ran the blade across his hand, wincing at the rush of pain as the skin separated, drawing a slow stream of blood. He pulled his fingers into his palm tightly and held it out to the being. 'What do I call you?' The being took his hand tightly and licked his dark lips.

They smiled.

A NEW AGE

Rain battered the windows in the Hall of Justice. Candles provided the only light entering the room as black clouds obscured the light of the sun. An ill omen. Though, in fairness, Kane had lost all signs of hope. Though a storm raged on outside, the room felt stuffy, too warm.

The elite of society gathered, filling every nook and crevice available, crying out for justice and condemning the man sat unmoving on the middle of the stage. Kane always saw it as a stage; the performances she had witnessed there over the years had rivalled any she had seen in the theatres across the city. They were fortunate to be graced with the Kingdom's finest actor this evening too – Mason D'Argio.

The preacher stalked the stage like a wild animal, switching between riling up the crowd and glaring at Tamir who took it all in his stride, fully aware of what happened next. General Grey had been excused. Tamir had asked him to promise not to watch, that knowing he was there would sap the last bit of strength he had. Grey had begrudgingly agreed, shedding a tear before heading away from the hall. Asher sat on the seat dedicated for the King. Though he had not officially been coronated, no one here would argue with the smug bastard. To her dismay, Kane's eyes fell on Prince Drayke. He sat next to his brother, staring absently at the marble floor as though wanting the thing to open and swallow him up.

'Never would have had him down as a traitor.' Kane groaned, recognising the voice of Sir Dominic. 'A good man, I thought. It's not often I'm wrong but there is an exception to every rule!' The knight sat down next to Kane, his perfume choking her. She coughed into a balled fist and turned away. 'I wonder how they will do it... burning is a favourite of Mason's, though it does leave a bad smell and the screaming, my Gods, the screaming! I prefer hanging, personally. Less messy and usually faster. No smell either, that's if you get the corpse out quick enough. Glad that your little mess was resolved as well. Never thought for a moment that you were a part of the deplorable events.'

'I heard you fought in the battle at the People's Square, Sir Dominic,' Kane said, wanting any excuse to change the subject away from thoughts of her friend's death.

'You heard?' Dominic's voice went up a key before he cleared his throat. 'Yes, well front line. Always doing my duty. Gave courage to those who followed behind me, as always.'

'Oh, I heard you ran to the back of the line after a few stones were thrown.'

Dominic pulled at his collar nervously, face turning an awkward shade of pink. 'They were great, bloody rocks I tell you!' he roared before composing himself. 'Grey thought it best if I headed to the back as the battle spilled through the city. A man of my experience is most useful when directing those who need assistance in battle.'

'Of course, a man of your experience. Let's hope you are near in case anything else happens to erupt in the city,' Kane said, not having energy to give even a wry smile.

'Yes, indeed. I believe I see Lady Marissa. Good day, Katerina.' The knight raised a hand in greeting to a heavily powdered woman on the far side of the room and shuffled away without a backward glance.

'Ladies and gentlemen of the United Cities of Archania,

the past few days have been some of the most difficult for you to endure since the days of the plague, and the loss of our dear Queen.' Mason looked with pity at the King-in-waiting who dutifully bowed his head at the mention of his late mother. Drayke continued to stare a hole into the floor, unmoving. The room fell silent, focusing on every single word. 'Riots have broken out, innocents have died, and *traitors* have been unearthed...' Mason glared at Tamir who offered nothing back in response, his hands tied behind his back. The crowd roared their disapproval at their former councillor, hate and vile language thrown from all four corners of the room. Even some of the soldiers guarding the perimeter of the room went against protocol and yelled in the poor man's direction. 'Everard Tamir, you have been charged with the crimes of treason and inciting rebellion against the crown. How do you plead?'

Tamir raised his head and looked out at the crowd of rage-filled Archanian citizens. 'Guilty.'

The audience screamed and spat, purple faces frothing at the mouths as the elite of Archania shook their fists in the air and called for Tamir's head. No subtlety. It was clear what they wanted. Kane slumped against the bench and sighed.

Mason's lips twitched with the shadow of a smile. 'Citizens of Archania, we have heard your cry. Everard Tamir, we find you guilty of these crimes. Do you have any last words?'

'Everything I did, I did it for one reason only. For my home. For my people. For Archania.' More cries and abuse from the bloodthirsty audience, all eager to see the punishment handed out.

'You will bathe in the light of The One,' Mason cried, arms aloft to the Sky Plane. The flames took hold quickly. Tamir didn't scream. He just let the fire dance and lick at his body in silence. He twisted and shuffled in his seat, unable to free himself. But till, there were no screams.

Drayke rushed from his seat and exited the room, pushing past two silent guards as Mason and Asher stared daggers into his back.

Kane watched the flames burn as tears streaked down

her face. Another friend lost to this madness. Another friend dead before his time.

All others watching fumed at the way in which Tamir endured his punishment, furious that the man didn't have the decency to pander to their will and scream for them as they had so desperately expected and wanted.

Mason's eyes narrowed with a silent fury as he watched Tamir struggle valiantly. He turned back to the King-in-waiting. Asher gave the barest of nods, his face a mask of disappointment and hatred. The preacher spun on the spot and clicked his fingers. From out of the shadows at the side of the room, T'Chai marched forward across the stage, drawing his scimitar with ease and sliding the blade across Tamir's neck.

His head slumped against his chest as the flames continued their feast.

Kane cursed and stood to leave, unable to bear the sight of her friend. She had two more days to leave the Kingdom. Two more seconds would be agony.

'Let this be a warning to any who wish to stand against the might of the Empire of Light, the might of *King* Asher of the United Cities of Archania!' Mason screeched, golden pupils reflecting the still dancing flames. 'This is a—'

A loud rumbling interrupted the preacher and silenced the violent crowd. Kane was thrown off her feet and back onto the bench as the room shook. Panicked cries and screams broke out amongst the crowd as a third shake hit the room, throwing the Hall of Justice into darkness.

The rumbling halted for a moment. A blanket of darkness shrouded all as Kane sat back up. Urgent muttering broke out in the crowd as citizens checked on friends and loved ones. Calls for the lights to be relit were answered and the darkness slowly fell back. Kane stared up at the stage, mouth wide open.

Smoke rose up from Tamir's charred body, a gruesome, horrific sight. No one else looked at the councillor's corpse. No one else noticed that the flames had stopped when the shake had hit the room. Even more interesting was the look of fear on

Mason's face as he stood on the stage, a heavily jewelled hand pressed against his chest. Something had changed.

Something had gone wrong.

Katerina Kane grinned as she stared into the preacher's panicked eyes.

They were golden no more.

ACKNOWLEDGEMENTS

This section could end up being longer than the entire book if I had to name drop everyone that has helped me on this journey so I'll try to keep it brief and my apologies to anyone that I will surely miss out. You can be in the next one...

Firstly, to my parents for always encouraging me to read and for introducing me to world of fantasy literature.

To my sisters for putting up with a nerdy, little brother who spent far too much time with his head in books.

To anyone who has read my work and given me any kind of feedback: Luke, Pete, Jon, Dave, Dom, Nicky, Matthew, John, Sam, Jesse, Bobbi, Nick and many more.

To Adnan for his unflinching assessment of earlier drafts of this work.

And to Sarah, for allowing me the time I needed to shut myself in a corner and type away in my own little world. Words can't do you justice.

Extra thanks go to Rachel Rowlands for her early assessment which made me tearfully tear up what started as Blood of the Heretic whilst I was still at university and turned into Flames of Rebellion eight years later. The path of a writer is paved with the blood of early manuscripts.

To Jon Oliver for his excellent work editing the novel for me and picking up on the thousand errors I had missed.

To Mars Dorian for the incredible cover design. He made my work look good!

And to the many authors who have inspired me over

the years – from Tolkien to Abercrombie and Dostoevsky to Gareth L. Powell. I'm always learning from outstanding writers and I can't wait for you all to read more from me. To anyone who I have spoken with on Twitter and Reddit, thank you so much for your support and help – the writing community is incredible and I'll continue to be a part of it. Until then – leave a review on Amazon or Goodreads (or both) and ***Embrace the Chaos…***

'In the darkness they are waiting, biding their time. When the last light goes out – all will be Chaos…'

Printed in Great Britain
by Amazon